CALL WAITING

CALL WAITING

Dianne Blacklock

THOMAS DUNNE BOOKS
ST. MARTIN'S PRESS
NEW YORK

THOMAS DUNNE BOOKS.
An imprint of St. Martin's Press.

CALL WAITING. Copyright © 2002 by Dianne Blacklock. All rights
reserved. Printed in the United States of America. No part of this book
may be used or reproduced in any manner whatsoever without written
permission except in the case of brief quotations embodied in critical
articles or reviews. For information, address St. Martin's Press, 175
Fifth Avenue, New York, N.Y. 10010.

www.stmartins.com

LIBRARY OF CONGRESS CATALOGING-IN-PUBLICATION DATA

Blacklock, Dianne.
    Call waiting / Dianne Blacklock.—1st ed.
        p.   cm.
    ISBN 0-312-30348-3
    1. Women teachers—Fiction.   2. Female friendship—Fiction.
3. Grandfathers—Death—Fiction.   4. Australia—Fiction.
I. Title.
PR9619.4.B56 C35   2003
823'.92—dc21

                                                    2002014574

First published in Australia by Pan Macmillan Australia

First U.S. Edition: April 2003

10   9   8   7   6   5   4   3   2   1

To Diane Stubbings Murray

Acknowledgments

First thanks must go to Diane Stubbings, because I doubt I'd even be a writer without the influence she has had on my life. We started school together, went to university together and served our "apprenticeship" as writers together. Her encouragement and generosity toward me has been awesome. I am forever indebted to her.

Thank you to my first readers, Dane, Sharon, Robyn, Lynda, Jenny, Desley, Ros, Anne and Dori. Do you know how hard it was for me to show my work to anyone? And do you have any idea how much your unreserved support meant to me? It was the only way I could ever bring myself to contact Pan Macmillan, where I am so grateful that Roxarne Burns found me in the slush pile and passed my submission on to Cate Paterson.

Thank you to Cate for her generous mentorship and her brilliant editing. I feel very lucky indeed that for some reason she decided to give me a go. Thank you to everyone at Pan Macmillan and thanks to Julia Stiles for her painstaking copyediting.

Also, heartfelt thanks to my American publisher, St. Martin's Press, particularly to Tom Dunne for giving me this opportunity and to Carolyn Chu for looking after the details.

Thank you, Mum and Dad, Deb, Bob, Brett, Brad and Ros, their spouses and children, for being a warm, funny and wonderful family.

Thanks, Frances, for being you, and Danny, for being my number one fan.

And most of all, thank you to my boys, Paul, Joel, Dane, Patrick and Zachary. How could I have done this without you?

CALL
WAITING

PROLOGUE

"Are you listening to me, Ally?"

She sighed, "Yes, Bryce."

"Okay, let me go through this one more time."

Terrific. Ally took the mobile phone from her ear and held it in front of her, still keeping one eye on the road. She could almost see the words flying out of the earpiece as Bryce's voice became more histrionic. The word opportunity was getting quite a workout.

"Opportunity of a lifetime . . . never have this opportunity again . . . throwing away a golden opportunity."

Ally sighed again. She had always hated the way Bryce lectured. She didn't have to listen to this. In fact, she realized, breaking into a satisfied smile, she really didn't have to listen to this anymore. Ever again.

She glanced out the window. She was on the open freeway now and the atmosphere was quiet, almost surreal. Midafternoon on a weekday and she couldn't see another car in her field of vision. She looked at the phone. She had always wanted to do it, imagined doing it. But she couldn't. It was so impulsive, reckless. So wasteful.

She wound down the window, still holding the phone. They were so light and small, these modern mobiles. Almost disposable, she thought with a grin. She was approaching a bridge that spanned a deep ravine, and she slowed the car down to a crawl. Ally considered the phone for another moment. She could still hear Bryce's voice rabbiting on as she stuck her arm out the window and hurled the phone across the railing, watching as it sailed down and disappeared out of view.

December, the previous year

Ally closed her eyes, rubbing her forehead. She was tired. It couldn't be much longer till bell time, she thought hopefully, glancing at her wrist where once again she had forgotten to place her watch.

"When you're finished, please stack your work carefully on the drying racks."

A primary school teacher had given her this idea, painting Aboriginal designs onto didgeridoos, and Ally thought it might work with her Year 8s.

The results were, however, less than encouraging. And the constant tuneless foghorn she'd had to endure as twenty-three boys all tried out their instrument was driving her insane. It was the last week of the last term of the year. No one wanted to be here anymore, least of all Ally.

In fact, most of these boys never wanted to be here. They loved the unit on photography, and sculpture, despite the god-awful glazed lumps they ended up with. But painting and its abstract theories were beyond them. The overwhelming majority had no interest in art, but they had to do one double period a week, and Ally had to fill in the time, one way or another. So the didgeridoo exercise had seemed a good way to cover pointillism and primitive art.

One mention to Mark, the head teacher, and that was it. It was so exquisitely politically correct and would score big time with the parents. Mark had, unbelievably, located a didgeridoo supplier, of all things, and a load was duly delivered to the school. If she'd still been at Fairfield West, they would have been lucky to scrounge some discarded cardboard tubes from the paper factory up the road.

"Damien, why is your didgeridoo painted plain brown?" Ally asked as she noticed him sneaking it onto the drying rack.

"Well, Ms. Tasker, I'm ideologically opposed to copying Aboriginal artworks," he explained importantly.

Ally looked squarely at him, willing herself not to laugh. Ideologically opposed to *any* work, more like it.

"Justin Mellor!" Ally exclaimed in her best teacher's voice. "Stop this instant or you're off to the Principal!"

Justin froze, his didgeridoo just short of connecting with Cameron's head.

"Put it down!" He did so. She turned back to Damien. "What exactly are you ideologically opposed to?"

"Stealing Aboriginal artworks, Ms. Tasker. People have been going into the Northern Territory over the last decade or so, since Aboriginal art became fashionable, and buying artwork for as little as a bottle of rum, then taking it overseas and selling it for a fortune."

Nice little speech, he must have seen it on *Behind The News* in history class.

"And what has this got to do with painting Aboriginal designs on a factory manufactured didgeridoo in a high school art class, which I assure you no one will pay a fortune for?"

Damien looked momentarily disarmed. At fourteen, it was obvious he was going to be a heartbreaker, when the braces came off and he grew another foot taller. He would be an excellent barrister one day—he could argue the leg off an iron pot, if he couldn't charm it off first.

The bell saved him. Ally called out instructions to collect up the paintbrushes and pots of paint and leave them in the sink, and after the boys scrambled out of the room, she saw that they had done this, in a fashion. She started rinsing out the pots and stacking them to drain. One advantage of working in a private school was that, strictly, Ally didn't have to do this at all, it could be left to the cleaner. But she didn't mind. The brushes had to be soaked at least, or else half of them would end up congealing and have to be thrown out. The rate they went through resources in this place alarmed Ally as it was, and she wasn't about to add to it.

Her last period was free on Thursdays, so she had plenty of time to clean up and still leave school early. Intent on trying to wash off the paint that always settled stubbornly in the crevices around her fingernails, Ally surveyed the state of her hands. She remembered an ad on the telly years ago, comparing a woman's hands to a dried-up autumn leaf that could be restored to a new green leaf with the particular brand of cream they were touting. Ally's hands were like the autumn leaf—dry, red and cracked. Bryce was always nagging her about them, pointedly giving her gift vouchers for manicures. But she thought it was a waste of time and money when the next day they would be covered in clay or paint or charcoal. Still, she must remember to bring a pump pack of sorbolene in to work. She had been telling herself that every second day, and now the term was all but over. Oh well, next year.

Next year. The idea filled Ally with dull despair. Working at St. Ambrose was a breeze compared to some of the places she'd worked in in the past. She supposed she shouldn't complain. But sometimes she wondered what on earth she was doing here.

At art college no one wanted to be a teacher, or if they did they certainly didn't admit to it. It was so *establishment*. And it was as good as compulsory to despise the establishment. They worked hard at not conforming to society, and just as hard at conforming to each other's notions of nonconformity.

You would only become a teacher if you couldn't succeed as an artist, and of course they were all going to succeed as artists. There was barely a handful of successful artists in Australia's two hundred year history, what were the odds?

Ally had always felt a bit of an imposter anyway. She hadn't particularly wanted to be an artist; truth was, she hadn't known what she wanted to be. She'd only known she wanted to get away from home. Fifteen years ago, it wasn't so competitive to get into art college, and as it was literally the first offer that had arrived after her HSC, it was as good a place to escape to as any.

She sometimes wondered how many had made it. David Blakely won the Archibald a couple of years ago, and she'd occasionally seen his exhibitions advertised. The rest she'd never heard of again.

So eventually, with a diploma under her belt, and after a brief stint in the public service as a clerk, Ally had decided teaching might be a better option, at least for a while. And here she was, ten years later, having progressed no further than out of the public system and into the private.

Ally heaved the cardboard box of Year 7's lino block prints into the back seat of her battered little Laser, along with her briefcase. She hadn't recorded the marks onto the assessment sheets yet; she planned to do it tonight while Bryce was at racquetball. Thursday was his regular night, and Ally's regular visit to Meg's on the way home, for a Harrison fix.

Meg and Ally had met at college. A few years older than Ally, Meg had worked first after she left school, to save money so that she could devote herself entirely to her studies.

That was so Meg.

She planned everything. She had studied her options and learned that computer graphics were going to be the next big thing. So she took night classes, learned computer skills and landed an amazing job in advertising. Of course, the rest of the class claimed she was just falling for the capitalist ethos, and went and applied for the dole.

"Make yourself indispensable," she'd told an uninterested Ally more than once. Meg had made herself indispensable. So after Harrison was born, she had the choice to work from home, reduce her hours, whatever she wanted. *Imagine!* would do anything to keep her. So she did work from home for a while, until she realized that one of the pay-offs for a working mother was to actually get a break from the child and the house. So she went back to the office two days a week, and after Harrison's first birthday, three days. She had a delightful mother-in-law who adored her only grandson and couldn't wait to be asked to care for him.

So all in all, Meg had the perfect life. And no surprise. Of course Meg was a success: she planned, she set goals, she made lists. Ally never made lists. Occasionally she made lists, when Meg gave her a pep talk about getting her act together. She would write a list that started with the jobs she had already done. And then she would cross those items out straight-away. Meg said that was not really the idea. But Ally maintained there was nothing so satisfying as drawing a thick black line through a task, even if you had done it yesterday, or the day before. Very satisfying.

Somehow they stayed friends. Meg, driven and ambitious, and Ally, drifting from one thing to another, with little idea of what to do next. Yet something held them together, perhaps their very differences.

Before they'd married, Meg and Chris had literally stalked Watsons Bay for two years in the hope of scoring one of the old fisherman's cottages, just below the HMAS *Watson* reserve. And they had finally succeeded. It was an idyllic spot, in a tiny leafy lane, with glimpses of Camp Cove from the back deck. The only drawback was parking. Ally usually had to park at least a block away, and today was no exception.

Knocking on Meg's front door, Ally could hear Harrison crying from inside the house. Meg opened the door looking harassed and fed up.

"Thank God," she declared at the sight of Ally on her doorstep. "Harrison! Look who's here, Ya-Yee!"

There was no break to the screaming.

"Come on, he's so wound up he's not even listening. He'll only stop when he actually sees you."

"Is he alright?" Ally asked, following Meg down the hall to the kitchen.

"He just got up on the wrong side of the cot after his nap. It happens."

Harrison was sitting in the middle of the kitchen floor, red-faced, tears streaming down his cheeks, clenching his chunky little fists tight.

"Harrison!" Ally cooed, but loud enough to be heard over the din.

His shoulders jumped at the sound of her voice, and he twisted around to look at her. His face broke into a broad grin.

"Ya-Yee!" he squealed, scrambling to his feet and toddling a little un-steadily over to her outstretched arms.

Ally stood up, hoisting him into her arms. Harrison leaned his head on her shoulder and let out one of those shuddering half-sigh, half-sobs that signaled an end to the tears.

"I don't know what magic you possess," said Meg, pulling a chair out for Ally.

"I'm the fairy godmother, while you are just the regular mother. Not nearly as diverting."

"I don't care what it is or why, but move in with us."

"Oh, I'm sure Chris would just love that," Ally grinned dubiously.

"He'd put up with it if I wanted it."

True enough. Chris Lynch would do anything for Meg. They had met while they both studied for their MBAs, and had fallen hard and fast and completely. He was a great big bear of a man, with a crooked nose and a crooked smile, and sandy brown hair that always sat skewiff. But he had the kindest eyes Ally had ever seen on a man, and he was constantly in awe of the fact that a woman like Meg had consented to be his wife. Ally envied their relationship.

"Glass of wine?"

"I've got work to do tonight."

"Oh, have at least half a glass," Meg persisted, already pouring the wine. "Then I won't have to tick the box in the *Cleo* quiz that will push me over into the 'you have a drinking problem' category. As long as I don't drink alone, I'm still in the 'you could develop a drinking problem' category."

Ally shook her head. "You still read that crap? It's so . . . last century!"

Meg rolled her eyes.

"In this brave new millennium women have far more important concerns than whether eyeliner is in or out, or how to have multiple orgasms."

"You think there's something more important than that?" Meg winked, handing her a glass.

Ally laughed. She had a point. Meg plonked herself down opposite Ally and swung her long legs onto another chair. She was tall and lean, with flawless skin and glossy dark hair cut into a perfect bob. Meg was one of those people who always looked elegant, even in shorts and a singlet top. Ally was not one of those people. She was, she felt, quite ordinary. Her mop of unruly curls ensured that she would never be called elegant. Of an indeterminate color, her hair could most favorably be described as "amber" or "honey" but was, in all honesty, just mousy.

"Haven't you read that copy of *The Beauty Myth* I loaned you yet?" Ally continued. "It'll open your eyes to all that nonsense."

"Ally, you need a *brain* to read that stuff, and I only have half one now, since Harrison was born."

Ally kissed his soft, blond head. "How can you say that?"

"It's true. Women lose half their brain to each child. So after your first, you're about even with the baby. But of course their brain develops. Yours is past that. If you have anymore children, you go into serious intellectual depletion."

"That's garbage."

"Not at all. I figure I can have one more baby, tops. After that I'll have the mental capacity of a head of lettuce."

"So how do you explain women with three or four children?"

"I rest my case!" Meg raised her glass toward Ally in a kind of a toast.

Ally shook her head. "Well, if I had a baby as beautiful as Harrison, I'd want a dozen more."

"So I keep hearing. And yet, strangely, it never happens!" Meg said with mock disbelief.

"You know why I haven't had a baby yet."

"No actually, I don't know why that man has not seen fit to give you your dearest wish, or to make an honest woman out of you."

Meg often referred to Bryce as "that man," despite the fact that she'd known him now for five years, as long as Ally had.

"He's not ready for fatherhood yet. At least he takes the idea seriously; I'm not going to push him."

"Oh, for crying out loud, Ally, he's thirty-eight years old. At this rate he'll be a grandfather before he's ready to be a father."

Ally pondered the logistics of that for a moment before retorting, "Well, lucky I'm patient."

"No, not patient, immobilized. You're just stuck in a dead-end relationship which you can't leave because that would involve making a decision." She took a good mouthful of wine and looked defiantly back at Ally.

Meg's bluntness was one of her least attractive qualities, Ally thought, mostly because she usually struck a particularly raw nerve.

"So," Ally started, breaking the uncomfortable silence. Well, Meg didn't look uncomfortable at all, but Ally was. ". . . what was on Oprah today— 'Women who love too much,' or 'All men are bastards?' "

Meg grinned. "No, I believe it was 'Women who can't bear hearing the truth from their best friends.' Top-up?" she said lightly, jumping up from her chair.

Ally hadn't touched her drink yet, but Meg had drained hers.

"Sure, if it'll make you feel better. Actually, I think our boy might need a change."

"Oh here, give him to me."

"No, I'll do it," Ally insisted. She walked up the hall to Harrison's room. She loved this room. She had spent an entire July vacation sanding and painting and sponging it. It was her gift to Meg and Chris when they were expecting Harrison.

The walls and ceiling were painted like a blue sky covered in tufts of white cloud, and she'd hidden those stick-on, glow-in-the-dark stars in all the white bits so that with the lights out it looked like a country night sky. The light fitting was a cheap rice-paper ball, made over into a hot-air balloon for teddy bears. She'd painted an old wardrobe, some bookshelves, and the pine cot in Caterpillar, Divinity and Custard, while musing about the type of person who sat in an office somewhere thinking up these names. They probably had workshops with the people who made up names for nail polish colors. For the finishing touches, Ally had stencilled train tracks running around the edge of the wall, and a hopscotch pattern in the middle of the floor. And finally she'd made a Roman blind out of candy-striped fabric and matching bedding for the cot. The effect was gorgeous.

"You have to go into business!" Meg had enthused.

But Ally balked at the idea. It was not the first time Meg had suggested this, of course. Back in the days when they'd shared a rundown semi after college, Ally had achieved miracles with white paint, cheap bamboo blinds and meters of calico. But despite Meg's grand ideas, for Ally it remained merely a hobby. She didn't know the first thing about setting up a business. It sounded like a lot of stress, and a good way to spoil one of the only pastimes she enjoyed.

She picked Harrison up from the change table and held him in front of her.

"Kiss for Ally?"

He puckered up determinedly and pressed his plump lips against hers. "Kith Ya-Yee!" he repeated delightedly, throwing his arms around her neck.

Ally adored her little godson, but the time she spent with him was always bittersweet. She desperately wanted a baby of her own but had given up campaigning for one. Bryce had too much he wanted to "achieve" first. Meg was right as usual. And it made Ally feel hollow.

Bryce had his own ideas about Ally's future. She was wasting her time as a teacher, he believed, and she couldn't really argue with him there. But he wanted her to go into real estate, with him. She supposed it was a sweet notion, his and hers matching careers, but the thought of it turned her stomach. She didn't tell Bryce that of course, it might hurt his feelings. So he persisted with the idea, arranging relief work for her at the office every school holiday so that she could learn the ropes. She hated it. Despised it in fact.

The only part she did enjoy was having the chance to look inside other people's houses. That intrigued her. She always came out brimming with ideas. She could see the potential in the most desolate eyesore. Bryce appreciated this, and had let her show clients some of their worst properties, places even he would have trouble selling. But Ally wasn't trying to sell anything, she just let her imagination go, and her enthusiasm was infectious. Clients had, more often than not, been swept away by her imagination and signed before they realized what a dump they'd bought.

Bryce was adamant, she should get out of teaching and into real estate. So Ally's only recourse was to make herself unavailable every school holiday. Doing up Harrison's room had therefore served two purposes. Which reminded her. She wandered down the hallway back to the kitchen.

"Meg, are we going to do the family room in January?"

"Ally, you've renovated virtually every room in this house. I can't keep letting you do this."

"You know I love it, and it will get me out of real estate duty."

"Why don't you just tell him to bugger off?" Meg said with disgust. "You should be lying on a beach somewhere in your holidays."

"What, by myself?"

"Why not? Just because that man won't take a holiday, doesn't mean you shouldn't. Book yourself into a resort somewhere, you might even find yourself some gorgeous hunk!"

Ally was about to protest that she already had a gorgeous hunk, but she knew Meg would never let her get away with such a wet comment. Especially as it would sound a bit forced.

"What the hell is that?" Meg frowned at the electronic tune coming from Ally's handbag. "Your bag's playing the Lone Ranger theme."

"It's the William Tell Overture," Ally corrected, passing Harrison over to her. "Bryce programmed it into my mobile phone, he thought it would sound more insistent so I'd answer it more quickly."

Meg sniggered, "It's a bit kitsch."

Ally was rummaging around in her oversized, overstuffed handbag. "The problem is not the ring, it's the bloody size of the thing. They're microscopic, I don't see why they have to make them so small," she muttered.

"I thought you didn't want a mobile?"

"Bryce bought it for me—an early Christmas present."

"How thoughtful," Meg countered. "Why didn't he just get you a ball and chain?"

The phone stopped ringing before Ally found it. "Damn! Oh I hate the stupid thing. Sometimes I feel like chucking it out the window," she muttered, finally retrieving the slim black phone from the bottom of her bag.

Meg considered her for a moment, before popping Harrison down on the floor. She stood up and put an arm around her friend.

"There was an Ally I knew at college who would definitely have thrown it out the window. I wonder what happened to her? I miss her."

She gave her a peck on the cheek and followed Harrison into the family room. Ally missed that part of herself too, she was almost forgetting that it had existed. Coming to college in the city had made her a bit reckless and spontaneous. After an isolated childhood, it was like Pandora's box opening before her eyes. All those exuberant young adults, their first taste at freedom, all wearing black and feeling terribly bohemian. She used to have fun. Lucky she had Meg to remind her now and then.

She pressed a series of buttons on the phone and frowned at the number that appeared on the display.

"What is it?" Meg asked, coming back into the kitchen.

"Well, it's not my grandfather's number, but it's the same area code," she said slowly. Ally had an uncomfortable feeling. "Can I use your house phone?"

"Of course, go into my bedroom, Harrison won't disturb you there."

Ally hung up the receiver a few minutes later, but remained sitting on the edge of the bed, staring out the window. As soon as she went back out to Meg, she'd have to collect her thoughts, make plans, get her act together. She knew she was stalling, but she needed just a moment longer.

Meg frowned at Ally as she came down the hall. "Who was it?"

Ally took a breath. "Um, it was Lillian."

"Oh yes, I remember you talking about her. She's an old family friend, isn't she?"

Ally nodded. "She tried to ring me at work, they gave her my mobile number." She looked at Meg. "She was calling to let me know that my grandfather passed away this morning."

"Oh, Al. I'm so sorry."

Ally picked up her bag. "I have to go. I'll need to pack tonight, call in to work tomorrow, before I leave." Her thoughts raced ahead. "I guess I'll miss most of next week at school. Lucky it's pupil free. I'll need to have my marking up to date, though."

"Don't worry about all that," Meg insisted. "When is the funeral?"

"Monday or Tuesday."

"I'd like to come . . ."

"Don't be silly," Ally shook her head. "It's nearly two hours away. You've got work, and Harrison. I don't expect you to spend a day coming back and forward in the car."

"I don't mind. I'll do it, if you want me to," Meg said plainly.

Ally leaned forward and hugged her. She could feel Meg holding tight. Meg loved her like a sister. She had two brothers, but she said she'd always wanted a sister. And Ally, well, she had no one, especially now.

"I'll call, let you know what's going on."

She crouched down and called to Harrison, who toddled eagerly over to her arms. She hugged him close.

"Why don't you stay for dinner?" Meg suggested. "You'll be all alone at home. Bryce is out tonight, isn't he?"

That was the first time she'd used his name all afternoon.

"I'll be fine. I have to get myself organized, and you know how long that could take!" She smiled weakly.

Leaving Meg's earlier than usual meant Ally didn't hit the peak-hour traffic, and the drive to Edgecliff took only fifteen minutes. When she pulled up at the apartment block, she decided to leave the students' prints in the car. That was a job easily handled by someone else, so she would take them back to school tomorrow. Upstairs, she sorted through her clothes, realizing she was going to have to call in to the laundromat before work and leave a load. It would still be a little cooler in the evenings down in the Southern Highlands this time of year, she'd need to take a couple of warmer things with her.

Bryce would have to pack for himself. She knew he wouldn't be able to make it down tomorrow. That didn't bother Ally; he'd have to stay until Saturday. Saturdays were sacrosanct for a realtor, and fair enough. He'd probably come down Sunday, plenty of time before the funeral.

Barely half an hour after arriving home, Ally's suitcase was half packed and a bag of laundry ready to drop off. She could be organized when she needed to be. She didn't procrastinate when there was something to do. Like every time she'd moved into another rental property over the years.

While everyone else was still thinking about it, Ally had the walls half painted and had started on the window coverings. That was what attracted Bryce to her in the first place.

He had still been a mere property manager when she and Meg had decided to look for a place together. Not having much in the way of funds, they had asked to be shown the cheapest places listed. They'd settled on a dilapidated little semi in Alexandria, long before the gentrification of the area. It was a dump, it probably should have been condemned. In fact, it was as soon as they moved out. But in the meantime, Ally transformed it, whitewashing just about everything and covering anything else with swags of cheap fabric or potted plants or any other interesting bits and pieces she could lay her hands on.

Bryce was clearly intrigued, and he started to show up on the pretext of collecting rent, which he didn't have to do. They were supposed to pay at the office, but he said he'd save them the trip. At first Ally wondered if he was just nosy. But he arranged to have her reimbursed for the paint, and had repairs done as soon as she so much as mentioned them. It wasn't long before Meg started to make goggle eyes at Ally when his back was turned.

But Meg was around less and less. She'd met Chris by then, and she was only sleeping one, maybe two nights midweek at their place. She didn't even have to come home to do the washing because, unlike them, Chris actually had a washing machine, and a dryer, in his very own laundry. He was a catch. Ally knew they were serious, and that she wouldn't have a housemate for much longer.

Bryce seemed kind, and he was attractive. He didn't excite her, she was not infatuated like she had been with the series of men she'd dated through college. She had lost her virginity, and a fair slab of common sense along with it. She seemed to have no discernment when it came to the opposite sex. Anyone would do, the flakier, the better. And art college certainly attracted some flakes.

No, her heart didn't race when Bryce appeared at the door. But she felt comfortable around him.

So when she mentioned that Meg would probably leave when the lease was up, and she'd have to look for somewhere else to live, Bryce said, out of the blue, "Move in with me." And Ally, just as unexpectedly, said, "Okay."

They became lovers, through convenience. They were like two orthodox Greek teenagers who found themselves in an arranged marriage and decided to make the most of it. She'd grown to love him, but she didn't know that she had ever been *in* love with him. Ally had pretty much convinced herself there was no such thing anyway. It was an invention of Hollywood, she decided.

Ally looked around the apartment. There was nothing else she could do this evening. She started to feel restless. She checked the time. Bryce would be another hour or so. She went to the fridge and took out the bottle of wine she had opened last night.

Bryce only drank socially. It amused her how he could frown at her having one or two glasses with dinner, then quaff down straight tequila if the situation demanded. The situation being drinks with a client.

Bryce was a chameleon: all things to all men, or women, or whoever, as long as there was a sale in it. He didn't like football, but he never missed a State of Origin match. He didn't follow the stockmarket, but he knew his Dow Jones from his All Ordinaries. He hardly had the time for television, but through the juniors in the office he kept up with the storylines of the most popular shows. He knew more jokes from *Seinfeld* than Ally did, and she was a fan. At least he seemed genuine about keeping fit. She supposed so, it was a bit hard to know what Bryce really felt about anything.

He'd been a member of a fitness club for as long as she had known him, and he worked out religiously. Every now and then he'd motivate Ally to join him. Well, the motivation was usually that morning's despair at not being able to do the zipper up on a favorite skirt. Ally had never really struggled with her weight, but she couldn't resist a Tim Tam, and she yo-yoed like most of the women she knew. So about every six months she would become very determined and start going to the gym with Bryce. She'd trim down, feel energized and make all sorts of vows about exercising more, eating healthy food and using cleanser every night. But then it would turn cold, or worse, rain, and she wouldn't feel like going to the gym one night. Or she'd get her period. Or there'd be a Brad Pitt movie on Foxtel. Or she'd buy a packet of Tim Tams.

Ally searched through the cupboards, pushing aside Bryce's vitamin supplements, his protein powder and something in a jar labeled "macrobiotic" that looked scary. At home he was puritanical, claiming he had to make up for all the unhealthy lunches he was obliged to eat with clients. So Ally kept her stash of junk food hidden. She knew she should tell him to bugger off, to borrow Meg's expression, but it was easier to hide it than put up with a lecture.

She found a bag of Twisties and a Crunchie. Perfect, covering at least four of the main food groups—chocolate, cheese, sugar and salt. She could feel particularly guilt-free because the sugar in the Crunchie was technically derived from honey, not that she checked that too closely on the label. She poured herself a glass of wine and looked at the TV guide. She had to keep her mind occupied. She didn't want to think about what lay ahead of her over the next few days.

Bryce arrived home about half past nine, just as *ER* was finishing. Ally had tossed her wrappers and made herself a cup of tea after her two glasses of wine. She was glad to see him.

"Hi," he called absently, putting his gear away in the hall cupboard. Ally didn't expect him to run in and embrace her. They were well past that phase of the relationship. In fact, they'd skipped that phase altogether. But she needed to feel close to him tonight.

She switched off the TV and stood expectantly as Bryce came into the room. He pecked her on the cheek, but she put her arms around his neck, hugging him. It caught him by surprise.

"Hey, what's going on?" he said, though not unkindly, loosening her grip.

"I had some bad news today. My grandfather died."

He looked a little bemused. "You're upset? I thought you weren't very close?"

"Still, he virtually raised me," Ally reminded him. "And he was, you know, my only relative."

Bryce had moved away from her and was looking in the fridge. "Mm. But your mother's still alive?"

Ally shrugged. "Who knows?" she paused, watching him pour himself a glass of water. She walked over behind him and leaned her head on his shoulder. "I just feel strange, you know? I've been waiting for you to come home."

He looked at her. "Just let me have a quick shower, and I'm all yours, okay?"

She nodded. She followed him into the bedroom and sat on the bed watching him. He started talking about the game, then some new client at work, but Ally wasn't listening. She knew Bryce wasn't good at dealing with anything too intimate, he never had been. Not that it bothered her most of the time.

He pulled his T-shirt over his head. He had a nice body. Not overly pumped, he was careful to avoid that. And he didn't want to get too thin either—that made you look gay, he'd told Ally once, quite seriously. That was okay when he was selling real estate in Darlinghurst, but not now.

He had an average build. Firm and fit, but average. He was average height. His hair was light brown and he had it cut carefully and often into a simple, generic style. Meg said that he was bland, but Ally thought he was good-looking. Though she sometimes wondered how she would describe him to the authorities, should she ever need to. He didn't have any distinguishing features. And that's precisely the way Bryce wanted it. Part of his everyman appeal, he said. Not so good-looking as to make husbands jealous, but enough not to turn women off. Pleasant, not threatening. Okay, maybe a little bland.

Ally was getting restless. She forgot that Bryce never had a quick shower. She changed into a nightie, washed her face and unravelled the loose plait that kept her unruly mane in place. Bryce had never liked her hair. Early on he'd talked her into getting it cut like Meg Ryan. Ally had been dubious. The only person who looked good with Meg Ryan hair was Meg Ryan. On anybody else it was just a bad haircut. On Ally it was a disaster. Short tufts of hair stuck out at right angles from her head, and stray curly tendrils pointed every which way. Even Bryce had agreed she had to grow it out again.

She stared at her reflection in the mirror; there was a kind of melancholy in her eyes. Ally had green eyes, like Nan's, and her mother's apparently. A little too big for her face, she sometimes suspected. Anyway, they were nothing like her grandfather's. James Tasker's eyes were brown, almost black. They made him look forbidding. Ally shivered, wandering back out to the bedroom. She heard the shower stop as she pulled down the covers on the bed and propped up some pillows. She sat hugging her knees.

Bryce finally appeared, shaved and exfoliated and moisturized to within an inch of his life. He glowed. Ally knew she was probably being terribly sexist, but there was something odd about a man having a more elaborate skincare regime than she did.

He sat on the edge of the bed, facing her. "So how's my girl?"

She shrugged. "Sad, I suppose."

He leaned forward and kissed her lightly on the lips.

"When's the funeral?"

"Probably Tuesday."

"Are you going?"

Ally frowned, "Of course! I'm his only next of kin." She hesitated. "You'll come with me, won't you?"

"What?" he seemed taken aback. "I didn't even know your grandfather. I won't know anyone there."

"You'll know me!" Ally insisted. "I don't want to go on my own. I was counting on you, Bryce."

"Oh babe," he chided. Ally cringed, she hated it when he called her that. "You know how flat out we are at the moment. I'm assuming the funeral will be held in the Highlands?"

She nodded.

He pulled her into his arms, stroking her hair. "If it was in Sydney, I'd come, you know I would. But I need more notice to get off work for a couple of days."

"Sorry, I'll tell my relatives to consult your diary before they cark it next time," she spat sarcastically, pulling away from him. "What am I saying 'next time?' That's right, I don't *have* any more relatives. You're off the hook!"

Bryce looked at her, nonplussed. "I think you're being a bit unfair, Ally."

There was an uncomfortable silence, as she struggled with the impulse to say, "Yes Bryce, sorry Bryce." She didn't feel like it this time. They were always so *polite* to each other. Sometimes Ally wanted to scream. But she never did. She'd become a cardboard cutout of her previous self, like that singer, the artist formerly known as . . .

"Ally," Bryce was stroking her arm. She looked up at him. He shifted closer. "Let's not fight."

That was a fight?

His head was close to hers. "Ally?"

"Mm," she grunted.

"Don't shut me out."

She lifted her head and his lips were on hers, and three seconds later his tongue slid into her mouth. Then the hand crept up to her breast, like clockwork.

Ally pushed him off. "No, Bryce."

"What? What's wrong? I thought you said you wanted it tonight."

"No, I wanted *you* tonight."

"So, here I am, babe."

Ally shuddered inside. "Bryce, I just feel like being close to you."

"Well, you can't get much closer." His hand reached up under her nightie.

"Bryce!"

"I thought it would make you feel better."

"No, it will make *you* feel better!" she glared at him. "You know you can actually be close to a person without having to screw them!"

He stood up and marched around the bed angrily.

"Christ, Ally, I don't need this crap. I was just trying to be nice."

He flung back the covers petulantly and got into bed, turning away from her. Ally reached up and switched off the bedside lamp. She lay there in the dark, tears stinging behind her eyes. She blinked them back determinedly. She didn't want to start crying, she was afraid she might not be able to stop.

Ally stared at Bryce's back. She craved some physical contact with another human being. She'd have to take what was on offer. Beggars can't be choosers.

She moved over closer to him and nestled into his back. He stiffened.

"Sorry Bryce," she said quickly to placate him.

He turned over, hesitating. "Are you okay now?"

She murmured assent and he pulled her hard against him, kissing her. She didn't feel okay. She felt empty and hollow.

They made love on automatic pilot, according to the scheduled flight plan. Ally moaned accordingly and he came right on time. Afterward she cuddled into him, into the warmth of his body, trying not to feel so alone. But after a few moments he disentangled himself and rolled over. They never slept in each other's arms. Bryce complained he couldn't get to sleep that way.

She lay in the dark again, more alone than before. Ally wondered if Bryce felt empty too. He seemed content. Sex was always the same but he never stopped wanting it. He'd have it every night, but she'd worn it down to three or four times a week. If they went longer than four days without it he'd get cranky, and Ally would make sure they had sex that night. That had been the pattern since about six months into their relationship.

She'd hoped that love would feel stronger than this, more uplifting. That maybe it would fill the gap deep inside her. Then she wondered if having a child would fill it. But that would have to wait. It was okay, she'd told herself a hundred times. Bryce was a decent man, and for some reason he stayed. Even her mother hadn't done that. It was enough. Anything more was fantasy.

But the gap inside was getting bigger, threatening to swamp her. Her eyes filled, and she felt a single tear trickling down each cheek. One for James Tasker. And one for herself.

The next day

Meg steered her car into the staff carpark. She was not impressed coming in to work on a Friday and she was going to give Simon a piece of her mind, not least for phoning at six-thirty on one of the rare occasions Harrison had decided to sleep in.

Simon Ridgeway was Meg's boss, one of them at least. He was the creative director at *Imagine!* and, as such, the only person Meg felt vaguely answerable to. Simon kept trying to remind her that she also needed to maintain a relationship with the accounts manager, not to mention the managing director. But as head of the digital graphics department, Meg felt that as long as Simon approved of what she was doing, then he could handle the others.

But Simon had big ideas for Meg. He was the one who'd argued for a computer graphics specialist more than ten years ago, and he'd also been the one who'd pushed for Meg when everyone else had wanted to hire from a pool of more experienced men. The way Simon had looked at it, a woman who had become any kind of IT specialist was a rare and special breed. And his instincts had been right.

"You should become a director," he had announced over lunch one day.

"And just whose role would I take on, Simon?" Meg returned. She was never one to get too excited about anything until she had thoroughly sussed it out from every angle. "I'm only qualified to be Creative Director, and in case it's slipped your mind, that's your job."

"I think there's room for a new position. Well, more of an upgrade," he explained. "The digital graphics section is vital to this firm. These days there's rarely a campaign you're not involved in. And that's aside from all the outside contracts you've brought in."

Meg had built the department into one of the most highly regarded in Sydney. Smaller firms, without the technology and expertise, were now outsourcing work to *Imagine!*.

"You shouldn't be answerable to me," Simon continued. "And in reality, we both know you're not."

That was true. Simon was Meg's kind of boss. She told him what she was doing and left it up to him to find the budget, staff, whatever. He rarely second-guessed her. He trusted her intuition, and she had never disappointed him.

"So what are you suggesting?"

"That your current position be upgraded to director."

"What, I'd be 'Digital Director?' " She grimaced. "I don't like the sound of that."

"We'd have to come up with a better title," Simon dismissed. "But don't you see, this way you would have equal standing. You'd get to manage every aspect of your own projects and argue for resources on the same level as the rest of us."

Meg thought for a moment. "You just don't want to do my dirty work anymore!"

Simon grinned sheepishly. "Well, there had to be something in it for me. But it's a good idea, Meg. You must see the sense of it. And you'd finally get to put that MBA to use."

She did like the idea of running her own show. Meg had never been overly fond of the hierarchy of business and had often thought of working for herself. But she'd never got around to it because Simon was such an easygoing boss.

Not so much these days, she thought, as she parked the car. He was constantly dragging her in for client meetings, or planning sessions, or something else. Today it was a pitch to take on the campaign for the release of a new ice cream. Not exactly earth-shattering stuff, but Simon insisted she had to lift her profile, be seen as director material. Before Harrison was born, Meg could have thought of nothing more exciting. A challenge, a chance to have a greater degree of control, to manage her very own section. But these days she wasn't so sure.

It was not as though she wanted to be at home with Harrison full-time. She didn't have the constitution for that, she'd discovered. Harrison was a relatively easy baby, but Meg had obsessed about his routine, and when she had got that under control, she'd moved on to the housework. She drew up a detailed roster, setting herself daily, weekly and monthly goals.

The day she found herself spread-eagled on the floor with her cheek flattened against the shiny timber, intent on polishing the kickboards underneath the kitchen cupboards, was the day she knew she had to go back to work.

But she wasn't sure anymore that she wanted to climb to the top of this particular ladder. The shiny, hard edge of her career had dulled, merged into the same gray bilge as everything else. Lately Meg didn't know what she wanted. Even choosing something from a takeaway menu felt overwhelming. She was sick of making decisions and being responsible. She'd had enough.

Today was a glorious early summer day, Meg noted on her way into the building. The most taxing thing she had planned for the morning was to remember to reapply Harrison's sunscreen while they paddled on the shoreline down at the cove. She wanted to hold that thought until she was face to face with Simon.

She climbed the stairs up to his office, her heels clattering on the black metal. *Imagine!* was one of the most upmarket agencies in Sydney, so their premises had to live up to the hype. They'd fitted out a derelict warehouse in Surry Hills, leaving the rough brick walls with their patches of paint and faded signage. The ground floor remained one huge open space, segmented with partition walls to create the various work spaces. Above, seemingly suspended in midair, were the directors' offices and a boardroom, connected by perforated steel gangplanks. It had taken Meg a while to get used to all this, and it still gave her vertigo crossing the open space from one office to another.

Now of course, black metal and exposed bricks were becoming a little passé. The directors had lately interviewed a couple of avant-garde designers and were getting excited about beech veneers, louvred glass panels and bagged brickwork. That would keep them cutting edge until the next trend came round.

"Meg!" Simon greeted her expansively as she appeared at the door to his office. "You made it!"

"Like I had a choice," she muttered, throwing herself onto the leather two-seater. "I'm supposed to be at the beach."

"Don't get comfortable there," Simon said walking around his desk, ignoring her dark look. "We're expecting the clients any minute."

He put his hand out to her. Meg looked up at him and smiled despite herself. She couldn't really get mad at him, not for long anyway. Simon Ridgeway was gorgeous. He was impossibly good-looking and always immaculately dressed. He wore a beautiful silk tie over a crisp white shirt every day of the year, turning the sleeves back in summer in precise, even folds. Simon was conservative but classy.

But the thing Meg liked most about him was that he was so earnest. She had rarely known anyone as decent and genuine as Simon. It set him apart from all the go-getters that littered the industry. She had consequently developed the biggest crush on him when she'd first started working there. Finding out he was gay had been only a temporary setback. She'd decided she would be the woman to turn him around. Lucky for both of them, Chris came along and swept her off her feet, and out of Simon's hair.

"Is there coffee?" Meg affected a scowl.

He nodded. "And friands. I got them specially because I know they're your favorite."

She put her hand in his and stood up.

"Lead the way."

Meg sat on Simon's desk, picked up the phone and dialed Chris's direct number at work.

"Chris Lynch," he answered automatically.

"Hi, it's me."

"Hello honey," Chris replied warmly. "Your meeting's over?"

"Yes."

"How did it go?"

"They're launching a new ice cream in competition with Magnum and all the other ones that are supposed to be like an orgasm on a stick. Hey, that's what they could call it!" Meg threw at Simon who was staring intently at his computer screen, answering e-mails. "Orgasm!"

He frowned at her before returning his attention to the monitor.

"Anyway," Meg continued, "I was thinking, seeing as your mother's got Harrison, and this was supposed to be my day off, why don't we do lunch?"

"Umm . . ."

"In fact, we could even take off for the whole afternoon."

"What?"

"It's Friday, Chris. Let's start the weekend now. We could—"

"Honey, you know I can't just take off like that. I was going to say that I can't even spare the time for lunch today."

"You know the world's not going to stop because you take a lunch break." Meg didn't mean to sound curt, but she knew she probably did.

"I just can't," Chris said, the regret evident in his voice.

Meg bit her tongue, hoping her silence was uncomfortable for him.

"It's beano night tonight," he said in an attempt to placate her.

She sighed. When Chris was a kid, Friday night was "beano" night, not that anyone remembered how the term had come about. His dad brought home lollies for the kids, and a bottle of Porphyry Pearl for his mother. They stayed up late and watched *Gunsmoke* on the telly.

Chris adapted this when Harrison came along and their social life was somewhat curbed. Every Friday night he brought home a nice bottle of champagne, and oysters or prawns, Balmain bugs, whatever looked good at the fish markets. They watched a video and curled up on the lounge together.

These days they tended to curl up on separate lounges and fall asleep before the end of the video. Meg had started to get a little bored with beano night. She'd started to get a little bored with everything.

"Do you want to choose the video?" Chris was asking.

"No," she sighed. "You get it."

"Any preference?"

None at all. "No, whatever you think."

"Okay then, I'll see you around six. Six-thirty tops, I promise."

Meg hung up the receiver and slumped dramatically across the top of the computer monitor.

"What's the matter?" Simon murmured, his eyes not leaving the screen.

"I've got no one to play with!" she pouted.

"Chris is too busy to get away?"

"He's always too busy. You don't want to come and have lunch with me?"

Simon shook his head regretfully. "Can't, love, client lunch." Then he looked up at her brightly. "You could join us, you know."

That brought Meg to her feet. "No thanks." She picked up her bag and walked to the door.

Simon leaned back in his chair. "You could still make it to the beach."

Meg shrugged. "Maybe."

"Come on," he cajoled. "It's a beautiful day out there. The sun is shining on the harbor. You're in the best city in the world. Life is full of possibilities."

"City of Sydney tourism campaign, circa . . ." Meg thought for a moment. "1996?"

Simon grinned. " '97 actually. See you Monday?"

"Yeah, yeah, with bells on."

She clattered down the stairs and out into the bright sunshine. So, life was full of possibilities, was it? Funny it didn't feel that way.

Bowral

Ally pulled in through the gates of Birchgrove just after two in the afternoon. The morning had been trying. She'd made it to school early, to get through as much work as she could before classes started for the day. When Mark arrived, Ally went to see him about arranging leave. As soon as he heard about her grandfather, he insisted she finish up and go, he would handle anything still needing to be done. But Ally didn't want to put anyone out. She never accepted favors easily, it made her uncomfortable. She hated the thought that anyone felt obliged toward her.

So she'd stayed on, wading through the rest of her marking, organizing her paperwork so that at most, there were only marks to be recorded on the aggregate sheets. Finally Mark had almost pushed her out the door.

The sight of the colonial mansion, set among Lillian's beloved gardens, was an immediate comfort to Ally. The Ellyards' home had been a haven to her when she was growing up. To her childish eyes, it was like a palace. The rooms were enormous, filled with ornate polished furniture, overstuffed chairs and beautiful paintings and ornaments. It was so different from their ramshackle house and secondhand, mismatched furniture.

The tires made that wonderful crunching sound on the gravel as Ally steered the car slowly through the avenue of silver birches to the circular carriageway in front of the house. She pulled up into the guest parking, turning off the engine. As she stepped out of the car she heard the front door open, and turned to see Lillian on the verandah.

Roger and Lillian Ellyard had bought Birchgrove after their children had moved on. At first Roger still commuted to the city, and they toyed with the idea of turning it into a bed and breakfast. But Roger died suddenly from a massive heart attack, just five months before he was due to retire.

Lillian did not need the money so much—Roger had provided well for her—but she did need something to keep her occupied. She completed some minor alterations and opened the doors to paying guests. It proved so popular that a few years after that she embarked on some fairly major renovations, and Birchgrove became a fully fledged guesthouse and restaurant.

Ally was glad to see that Lillian hadn't changed. Her white hair was still cut into a short, sculpted bob, her tall figure clad elegantly as always, in tailored slacks and a plain linen blouse. It was hard to believe she was in her late seventies. She certainly didn't look it.

She started down the front steps as Ally approached her.

"Hello Lillian."

Ally stepped gratefully into her outstretched arms and felt instantly relieved. The slender thread that tied them to each other through her grandparents was still intact. She had worried she would feel estranged.

Lillian drew back and took hold of both of Ally's hands.

"I'd rather it wasn't in these sad circumstances, but I am so pleased to see you, Ally."

"I'm sorry I haven't been back to visit for a while—"

"None of that," Lillian interrupted her. "Young people have so much on these days, I wonder you have time to breathe."

She tucked Ally's hand into the crook of her arm and they turned back up the steps.

"And your grandfather knew that too," she added quietly.

Ally sighed as the guilt surfaced again. She had been too busy to contemplate it much in the last twenty-four hours, but every time she paused, it was there. GUILT, in great big capital letters.

Of course she tried to explain it away. They had never been close, she and her grandfather, she told herself. Her visits over the last decade had been excruciating affairs, made bearable only by the fact that they spent most of the time in Lillian's company. Her presence masked the great wall that had built up between them since Nan died and he found himself with a teenage girl to bring up on his own.

James Tasker was a Renaissance man who had upped and moved his family to a remote property in Kangaroo Valley. He had big plans about the house he would build and the self-sufficient lifestyle they would lead. There was a hundred year old barn on the property, which they would occupy while he built their house. He put down a floor and made it barely livable. It was only supposed to be temporary, but they'd never moved out of it.

Ally's mother had tired of it all and left. By all accounts Jennifer Tasker was a rebellious teenager, and she wasn't about to waste her youth in a drafty old barn. She made her escape. But five years later she returned with Ally, barely three at the time. Jennifer stayed for a while, until apparently she couldn't take it anymore. Ally never really knew the whole story. Nan used to say she'd tell her when she was older. But then Nan died when Ally was only twelve. Her mother appeared out of nowhere for the funeral, and disappeared just as enigmatically. Ally was left alone with her grandfather, living out her teenage years in lonely isolation. Until she too, made her escape.

At least she had visited, maintained some contact, however meager. But each time she went away, it was longer until her next visit.

And so the guilt remained, refusing to budge.

Lillian had set afternoon tea out for them in the conservatory. This was Ally's favorite room. It was flooded with sun in the winter, and she would curl up on one of the wicker settees, her head on Nan's lap, listening to the women talk.

"I always loved it out here."

"I remember," Lillian smiled, indicating a chair.

They both sat down, and Lillian started to pour the tea. Ally looked out across the grounds. She used to get lost in these gardens. In summer the grass was soft under her feet as she ran barefooted around the maze of trees and flowerbeds. In autumn she almost had to wade through the thick layer of leaves that blanketed the ground, fallen from the birches that gave the property its name. It was the only place she could remember feeling happy in during her childhood.

"The gardens look wonderful, Lillian," she remarked.

"Yes, not that I do much myself anymore. Everything seems to be contracted out these days."

Ally took the cup of tea and sipped. "I'm amazed you're still running the place at all, Lillian. It's quite an operation."

"Don't you start. Richard's forever at me. He and Carolyn want me to move in with them."

"What, sell Birchgrove?"

"No, they know I'd never agree to that while I'm still alive. But they talk about hiring in a manager, moving me down to Melbourne." Lillian rolled her eyes. "Heaven forbid, I'd have to be in a box first."

Ally smiled. Lillian's son Richard had followed his father into the law, and was a successful barrister in Melbourne. She recalled him being quite devoted to his mother, if a little stuffy at times.

"If I so much as sniffle during a phone call, then he's on to his sister, and next thing I have Phillipa on the phone from Cambridge, having a fit." Lillian paused. "I say to them, if I interfered in their lives as much as they do in mine, they'd call me a nosy old woman."

"They're just worried about you."

"I know, but honestly, I hardly lift a finger around here anymore. I have a wonderful woman who comes in the mornings. She does all the rooms and helps me with breakfast. Though to tell the truth, it's Evelyn doing the breakfast and me helping," she winked. "Then Nicola starts in the afternoon. She sets up in the dining room and turns down the beds. She's on a working visa from the UK. And then of course, there's Robert, the chef."

"I don't think he was here last time?"

"No. I've only had him for about eighteen months."

God, it's been that long, Ally cringed inwardly.

"But I doubt he'll stay much longer."

"Oh?"

"Yes, he's very talented. Came down from one of the big hotels in Sydney. Why he chose to work in our little dining room is beyond me." Lillian paused, taking a sip of her tea. "But he claimed he wanted a change of pace, and a bit of freedom to experiment. Well, he's become a real drawcard, we're booked out for months ahead. We even made it into one of those good food guides. He could choose wherever he wanted to work now. The only thing keeping him here at the moment is Nicola—not that Robert would ever admit to it."

Ally smiled.

"You won't meet either of them this weekend, though. Nicola is leaving for London on Sunday, to spend Christmas with her family, and coincidentally," she winked, "Robert asked for a couple of days off."

Ally loved listening to Lillian. She felt like Nan could be sitting here, joining in.

"But that's enough about me, Ally. What about you? You're still seeing that young man? What was his name?"

"Bryce, Bryce Horton. Yes, we're still together."

"How long is that now?"

"Five years."

Lillian was thoughtful for a moment. "Well, I'm sure you have everyone telling you that it's time you did something permanent and had a baby besides. So I won't say anything at all."

Ally grinned. Funny how she had managed to say quite a lot without saying anything at all.

"And where are you teaching now?"

"St. Ambrose's."

"Oh, yes, I remember."

Ally realized she had nothing much to tell. Same old, same old. Lillian's life was far more interesting than Ally's.

"Well, we can't avoid it any longer, dear. I'd best tell you what arrangements we've made for James."

"I didn't expect you to handle all this."

"Nonsense. I've made a couple of calls, that's all. Someone had to contact the funeral director straightaway. And then, well, you know your grandfather. He wouldn't step inside a church while he was alive, and I was quite sure he wouldn't want to be seen dead in one either."

That made Ally smile. Her grandfather's favorite pastime was churchbashing, though he claimed he was merely debating theology. He was usually on a first name basis with the various ministers, pastors and priests that served the region, simply because he was always baling them up in the street, in the pub, anywhere, to argue with them.

"Keith O'Halloran has kindly offered to lead a service at the cemetery," Lillian continued. "He said he'd be as true to James as he could without breaking the rules. After the burial, everyone is welcome back here for the wake."

"Are you sure? I don't want to put you out."

She looked thoughtfully at Ally. "Your grandfather and I were very good friends. Best friends I'd say, since we both lost our partners. I'd be doing this for him regardless. But if there's anything you'd like to change . . ."

"No, really. It sounds ideal."

Monday afternoon

Lillian and Ally sat quietly in the back seat of the funeral car. Lillian was an intuitive soul. She knew when to leave Ally alone, when to let the silences remain uninterrupted.

Ally had enjoyed a serene couple of days at Birchgrove. The garden was exquisite in the summer, and she lost time walking around the grounds, sitting under the cool shade of the trees. On Sunday afternoon she ventured out for a drive around the area, noticing the changes since she'd been here last. There were more houses, more cafés and restaurants, more people.

Back at Birchgrove, Lillian asked her if she'd been down to the property. Ally said she'd go on her way home on Tuesday. She knew she was putting it off, and so did Lillian, but she didn't push the point.

Ally didn't want to discuss how the thought of traveling down that road into Kangaroo Valley and seeing the house sent shivers right through her. When she visited her grandfather she never stayed overnight. Just being there flooded her with an aching but all too familiar sense of loneliness. It was no place for a teenage girl, cooped up with a bitter and resentful old man. Ally wished she didn't have to deal with it, but she didn't have much choice. She would stop in tomorrow, and hopefully not have to lay eyes on it again.

As they turned in through the gates of the cemetery, Ally remarked on the stream of people making their way along the pathways.

"There must be another funeral today," she wondered aloud.

Lillian looked at her, a little bemused. "No dear, they're here for your grandfather."

Ally frowned at her, then stared back out the window. The car had come to a stop. A considerable crowd was gathering at the graveside. She didn't realize her grandfather had even known this many people.

Ally and Lillian took their places to one side of the coffin. The minister came over and shook hands with Lillian and she introduced him to Ally.

"It's a great pleasure to meet you, Ally. Your grandfather spoke of you with such warmth and affection," he said, clasping her hand. "You were the greatest source of pride in his life."

Ally hoped her face wasn't giving away the bafflement she was feeling. The minister stepped back into position and waited for the attention of the assembly.

"Friends, we're here today to celebrate the life of James Tasker. We're not in a church because, as all of you would be well aware, that's not where Jim belonged, and it wouldn't be a fit place to send him off.

"Jim maintained that he didn't believe in God, but I do. And so I believe he's up there right now, and he's found the Almighty and he has him cornered.

" 'Okay, I realize I have to accept you exist,' he's probably saying. 'But explain AIDS, and while you're at it, third world poverty. What's the idea, letting all that go on?' "

Ally lifted her eyes and surveyed the faces in the crowd, most smiling knowingly, fondly. Who were all these people?

"You see, I don't really think Jim had a problem with the notion of a higher power as such. It was intolerance and injustice in the world that he couldn't abide. And the ineffectiveness he saw at times, in the way organized religion dealt with those issues.

"Who can argue with any of that? I know I speak for all the ministers in the area when I say he certainly kept us on our toes . . ."

Ally tuned out. This was surreal. She could feel the eyes of everyone there on her. What were they expecting? Were they waiting for her to break down? To say something? God forbid.

The limousine took them back to Birchgrove, ahead of a stream of cars tailing them. Ally felt like running away and hiding, but Lillian gently guided her to stand at the door and receive people.

For the next half-hour a sea of faces passed by, some she recognized, others not at all. But without exception they all pressed their hands into hers, murmuring, "He was so proud of you," "We've heard so much about you," "How you'll miss him" . . .

Eventually, the people stopped pouring in. Ally wandered among them, feeling like a total stranger. If she hadn't been here at Birchgrove, with Lillian, she would have believed there had been a terrible mistake and she was at the wrong funeral.

"Ally!"

She turned around to see her high-school art teacher approaching. They shook hands.

"Hello Mr. Finneran. It was good of you to come," she said, for what must have been the fiftieth time that day.

"Not at all, had to pay my respects. Your grandfather was very well regarded in this community."

"So it seems."

"And you're quite the career woman, according to Jim."

"I don't know about that."

"Don't be modest. Jim told me you were almost running the art department up there at St. Ambrose."

"I think that may have been a little wishful thinking."

Mr. Finneran smiled. "The fond grandfather talking? You must thank your lucky stars every day for the start in life that man gave you."

Ally couldn't take it anymore. "Will you excuse me, Mr. Finneran?"

She headed for the kitchen door, not making eye contact with anyone so that she didn't have to hear another tribute to James Tasker.

Lillian followed her.

"Are you alright, dear? You were dashing through the crowd like a mad thing."

"Sorry, Lillian, it's just I'm feeling a bit overwhelmed."

"Perhaps you should sit a while in the quiet. Have you had something to eat?"

"No, thank you. But you know, I've got the worst headache." Ally hesitated. "Would it seem very rude if I went upstairs and lay down?"

"Not for a second. You go on up, you don't need to be worried about entertaining people," Lillian reassured her. "Let me get you some headache tablets first, though."

Ally closed the door to her room and leaned against it, sighing with relief. She could feel tears welling, they had been threatening all day, but she didn't want to cry in front of all those people. Her tears would be mistaken for grief, when they were really tears of frustration, hurt and anger. Though maybe she was grieving, for the grandfather she never had.

The distant man who hardly spoke to her, rarely asked her how she was, and never, ever, put his arms around her.

She drew the curtains and shed her clothes. Climbing into bed, Ally wrapped the covers around her. She pressed her eyes closed to try and stop the stem of tears, but it was no use.

How could he be such a wonderful friend to so many people, yet so unattainable to her? Ally remembered the desolation after she lost her grandmother, and then her mother for the second time in her young life. It was almost more than she could bear. She was only twelve. She needed someone to comfort her. But James was just not there for her. Oh, he cooked her meals, washed her clothes, got her to school. He kept it up for five years. Then he must have been glad to see the back of her.

Tomorrow she would leave all of this behind. Being here only reminded her of her essential loneliness and the pain deep in her heart that she kept buried in case it overwhelmed her. It served no purpose to dredge it all up. It was better tucked away, hidden, suppressed. That was the only way Ally could get on with her life.

The next morning

Ally had been awake for a while when she heard the soft tap on the door. "Come in," she called.

Lillian opened the door, carrying a small tray.

"Oh Lillian, you shouldn't be waiting on me."

"Nonsense, I like to."

Ally sat up in the bed, curling her feet up to give Lillian room.

"How are you feeling this morning?"

"Much better now, thank you."

"Did your headache clear?"

Ally nodded. "I think I was just overwhelmed, Lillian. I didn't realize he knew so many people."

"Yes, he certainly got around," Lillian smiled. "You'll be pleased to know he was leading a very active social life right to the end."

Ally thought for a moment. "I don't understand it, Lillian. He lived like a hermit when I was growing up. I know I shouldn't speak ill of the dead, but my memories are of a crusty old man who didn't seem to enjoy much of anything at all."

"You have to remember, Ally, he did take a while to get over the grief of losing your grandmother."

Ally took a bite of toast, staring down at the pattern on the bedcover.

Lillian watched her. "Ally, I don't think he knew what to do with you. You were a teenage girl. I think he may even have been a little frightened of you."

"Frightened? I don't think so." She couldn't even begin to imagine how James Tasker could have been frightened of her. "I think he resented being stuck with me."

"No, Ally, you must never think that. He would have lost heart entirely after Margaret died, if you hadn't been there. You gave him a reason to keep going. He was so proud of you."

Ally blinked back tears that had unexpectedly sprung into her eyes. She sighed, "Then why didn't he ever tell me that?"

"Maybe he didn't know how," Lillian paused. "I don't know that you were the easiest person to get through to, Ally."

Ally stared at her, taken aback. She supposed she was a serious young thing. It wasn't as though there was anything to be very light-hearted about.

"What am I saying?" Lillian interrupted her thoughts. "You were only a child, you had enough to deal with, what with your mother and all. But you should realize that both your grandparents loved you very much. That's the memory you should try to hold onto."

Ally packed up her overnight bag and carried it to the car. She walked back up onto the verandah where Lillian waited.

"Thank you for everything," she said, clasping both Lillian's hands. "I couldn't have got through all this without you."

"It was my pleasure, Ally," she assured her. "You're going to call in to Circle's End, then?"

Ally nodded.

"You'll find everything in order. Evelyn and I went down after the undertakers had been. We emptied the fridge, took his laundry, stripped the bed, that sort of thing."

Ally hadn't even considered any of that. "Thank you."

Lillian looked at her for a moment. "Ally, you don't have to keep thanking me. We're family, you know that, don't you?"

Ally nodded vaguely, looking out across the gardens.

"I mean that, Ally, I want you to treat this as your second home. You're always welcome here."

"I might have to take you up on that—I still have the property to settle. I'll have to do something about it sooner or later."

"Let's hope sooner. And you'll come and stay here with me."

After she hugged Lillian and drove away, Ally felt a monumental emptiness well up inside her. She knew what had remained unspoken between them. Ally had no family of her own now. Although she'd hardly visited her grandfather, she'd known he was there. It grounded her, gave her some sense of where she came from, however meager.

Now, driving down toward Kangaroo Valley, Ally felt her stomach churning. This was the same route they had taken every day, up and down the mountain, to Bowral High School. Her grandfather would never allow her to take the bus, and his ute was always parked outside the school in the afternoon, waiting for her. It was so embarrassing. She had no extra activities outside of school, and she certainly never went anywhere. She didn't know whether he would have let her have friends home, because she never asked.

Ally glanced out the window to the valley below. It was a pretty place she supposed; lush, green fields draped across the hills like a patchwork quilt. She pulled up at the enormous stone pylons at Hampden Bridge and waited for the oncoming car to cross. It had always amused her that they had built such huge pylons for a one-lane bridge. As she followed the road on toward the township, she noticed more houses had been built along the way, and Ally was sure there were a few more cafés in the village. Even Kangaroo Valley was becoming trendy.

She turned down the road that followed the Kangaroo River. Circle's End was at the lowest possible point of the valley. A creek ran through it, and rainfall being what it was in the Highlands, they were regularly cut off for days after heavy rain. It never bothered her grandfather, but it drove Ally mad. She was glad it was dry this time of the year, or she would not have been able to cross even today.

She arrived at the gates of Circle's End and climbed out of the car to open them. It was a laborious procedure for one person, getting in and out of the car, driving through, stopping again to close the gate. She continued along the dirt track until the house came into view. Ally tried to decide if it seemed different, empty, abandoned. No, she sighed, it had always looked like that.

When she stepped through the front door, though, it did feel strange. Ally realized she'd probably never been here without her grandfather, so it almost felt like she was trespassing. She wandered around the rooms in the gloomy half-light. The house used to be even darker than this, till finally Nan insisted they needed more windows. James fitted a couple of sets of secondhand sliding glass doors across the wall of the dining area. It made a huge difference. They faced north, and so it was the only place that was warm on clear winter days, and Ally would sit at the table reading, her back to the window, the sun streaming in.

They could go for days, she and James, hardly saying a word to each other, beyond what was absolutely necessary. Lillian said he was grieving. Ally tried to recall, was it sadness on his face? He always seemed so grim, his jaw set firmly, excluding conversation. Had she made it hard for him, as Lillian had hinted? She couldn't imagine he was frightened of a teenage girl, what could have frightened him?

Ally looked out through the windows now, across the expanse of the property, the escarpment rising in the distance. She remembered when Nan died, he'd wanted to bury her here, on her "beloved" property, he said. He railed against the "bastard" bureaucrats that "wouldn't let a man scratch himself without a permit."

But although she was only young, Ally had realized that Nan did not love the land as much as she loved her husband. She followed him there, and Ally sensed at times she'd wearied of their makeshift home and life. Just by little things that were said during those long afternoons out in the conservatory at Birchgrove. Ally remembered she had resolved never to follow a man anywhere, never to live his dream.

Just as well he hadn't been allowed to bury Nan here, Ally could never have sold the property then, it wouldn't have felt right. Looking around the place now, she realized that it was going to be hard to sell regardless. Bryce had told her that Kangaroo Valley was becoming very popular for weekend retreats, especially to those wanting a more "rustic" experience. She wasn't sure they wanted quite this rustic. She would have to get some work done, but she didn't know where to start. There were dozens of half-finished projects around the place. Her grandfather seemed busy all the time, but he never finished anything before the next idea would take off and he'd get absorbed by that.

She had hardly spoken to Bryce all weekend, he was so flat out at work. Ally knew he was working today, but she needed some advice. She picked up the phone and called his mobile.

"Bryce Horton speaking."

"Hi, it's me, Ally."

"Hi, hun." He was on the speaker phone in the car. "I thought you'd be on your way home by now?"

"Well, I am, kind of," she explained. "I've just dropped in to the property first."

"So, how does it look?"

"Not great."

"It must be bad for you to say that."

"It's going to need a lot of work to sell."

"You never know, you have to get to know the market. There's a lot of people out there dreaming of a sylvan experience."

Ally looked around her. "You'd have to be pretty loose with the term 'sylvan.' Should I see an agent while I'm down here? I think there was at least one in the town center. Or I could go to Nowra."

"You're breaking up a little, Ally. I'll probably lose you soon, I'm heading into the Harbor Tunnel. Did you say you're going to see an agent?"

"Should I?"

"No, don't do anything until I've had a chance to talk to some people, put the feelers out, okay?"

"Okay."

"I'll see you at home later. We've got that cocktail party tonight, don't forget."

"Oh, no Bryce, I don't think I'll be up to a party tonight."

"What did you say?" His voice was breaking up.

"I don't really want to go . . ." But it was no use. The line had dropped out.

Ally tried Bryce on his mobile as soon as she was back in the metropolitan area, but he must have switched it off. That meant he was showing a house. He never took calls when he was showing a house. It was rude, he insisted. However, he frequently interrupted Ally to take calls. Then it was rude *not* to answer the phone.

She decided to call past his office on the way home. He had been considerate about the property on the phone. Even though he didn't come to the funeral, she knew she could count on him to help her with that. Maybe she did have her place in the world and it was not as she was feeling, that she was adrift, and in fact terribly alone.

Ally spotted Bryce's car as soon as she pulled into the small carpark at the back of the office. She realized he was still sitting inside, with a couple of clients. Ally knew not to interrupt, so she sat watching. They seemed to be listening to music, their heads bobbing around like those novelty dogs that sit in the back windows of cars. Bryce would have preselected the right CD to play for these particular clients. The ideal CD, in fact.

He had a gift. Ally almost admired it, she certainly marveled at it. Bryce could sum up a person in terms of the music they liked, the brands they bought, their tastes, everything, with uncanny accuracy, and then show them just the type of property that would suit them. He had an electronic organizer and when he keyed in a name, up came his carefully collated profile.

The CD must have finished, because the car doors opened and a "man-child" appeared out of the passenger side. That was what Ally called this particular subspecies of the male gender. As far as she was concerned, there was nothing sadder than a graying, middle-aged man wearing a loud Mambo shirt, cargo shorts, reef sandals and a ponytail. Nothing sadder, of course, except his wife who climbed out of the back seat. On the very far side of forty—Ally guessed most of those years had been spent in the sun, as she now resembled one huge melanoma waiting to happen—in white clinging hipster pedal-pushers and a midriff top. Yes, a midriff top. And if Ally was not mistaken, a navel ring.

She knew the type. He was a typical baby boomer who had made a lot of money. And now, as a bored, middle-aged executive, he had rediscovered his youth, taken up surfing and decided to move back to Bondi, not that he had ever lived there in the first place.

Bryce walked around behind the car and Ally realized he was wearing what looked like a Mambo tie. She didn't know Mambo made ties. They probably didn't, Bryce had most likely picked it up at the Balmain or Paddo markets. It was the right look, anyhow. He undoubtedly had another tie in the office, suitable for his next client.

Ally wound down her window a little. The man-child was raving about the music. Ally guessed it was the Eagles, or maybe Richard Clapton. Bryce was promising to burn him a copy, and he would. It would be his next calling card.

"If that left-hander is still working on Sunday," Bryce was saying, "I might see you out at the point."

God, he'd even learned surfie-speak.

Bryce waved the couple off in their electric blue Rav 4. He crossed to Ally's car as she opened the door. He must have known she was there, but of course he would never acknowledge her while he was with clients.

"What was the CD?" Ally asked with a smirk.

"Hotel California."

The Eagles, Ally was right. That was scary.

"What brings you here?" Bryce asked, automatically kissing her on the cheek as she stepped out of the car.

"I wanted to catch you before tonight."

He waited expectantly for Ally to continue.

She sighed, he had that look about him. Ally estimated he had three minutes and forty-five seconds to deal with her before his next appointment. How could she explain to him everything she was feeling?

"I just wanted to let you know that I'm not up to the party tonight."

"Nonsense, Ally," he chided. "A party is the best antidote for a heavy heart."

He must have read that on his desk calendar.

"But—" she started to protest but he had her by the elbow and was leading her toward the office entrance. Three minutes, eight seconds.

"There is a particularly important client that will be there tonight."

"There is always some important client, Bryce," she insisted.

"I really have to be there," he said, pulling his Mambo-esque tie loose. Two minutes and fifty seconds. "And I want him to meet you too."

"But why, Bryce? I just don't feel up to it."

He considered her briefly. "I know what will make you feel better."

He reached into his pocket. If he pulled out his wallet, handed her money and suggested she get her hair and nails done, Ally was going to scream.

"Here," he said, pulling out his wallet and handing her a hundred dollar note. "Why don't you get your hair and nails done?"

Ally didn't scream.

"I don't think I'll get in anywhere this late. It's nearly three," she said meekly.

She noticed his lips twist, almost imperceptibly. Two minutes ten seconds.

"Leave that to me." He pulled out his mobile and pressed auto dial. "Elise!" he exclaimed brightly.

Ally groaned inwardly. Elise—celebrity hair stylist; inner city apartment; stainless steel, pale timber; white wine spritzers; Macy Gray.

Of course they could fit Ally in this afternoon, for *Bryce*. Ten, nine, eight . . .

"See you tonight, babe."

Three, two, one, and he was gone.

Seven p.m.

"So what's so special about this client?" Ally asked Bryce as he stepped out of the shower.

"You're wearing that?" he remarked, eyeing her dubiously.

Ally looked down at her plain sleeveless black dress. "What's wrong with it?"

"Nothing," he shrugged. "If you don't mind looking like just about every other woman there."

Of course she didn't mind. That was the whole point of fashion, wasn't it?

"I like you in that green Lisa Ho, brings out your eyes."

Bryce was the only man she had ever known who identified women's clothes by their designer labels. He had bought the sea-green silk sheath for her. Ally could never bring herself to buy designer labels. She didn't feel comfortable knowing that the price of the outfit she was wearing could feed a small village in Africa for a month. Bryce said it was an investment. No, a block of flats was an investment, Ally tried to tell him. And he was the one in real estate!

Besides, the Lisa Ho made her stomach stick out. Well, to be fair, the dress didn't exactly *make* her stomach stick out, it just *revealed* that her stomach stuck out.

And why green? Ally liked black. Three-quarters of her wardrobe was black. Black was safe, black was slimming. Everyone wore black. You had to be stunning to carry off a green dress at a formal function. You had to be tall and glamorous. You had to be someone. Ally wasn't anybody.

Nevertheless, she walked automatically over to the wardrobe to find the green dress. It was no use debating the issue. She knew the routine by now. Bryce would frown, and furrow his brow, and make several more pointed comments while they were getting ready: "Are they the right shoes for that dress?" "No, I like the shoes, *it's not the shoes*." And so on. It was easier just to get changed now.

"So, who's the client?"

"Well, I was going to surprise you," he said smiling. It was his salesman's smile. Ally was immediately suspicious.

"Brendan Metcalfe. Heard the name?"

She shook her head.

"He is responsible for what are arguably the most original apartment developments in the eastern suburbs over the last three years!" Bryce explained, his enthusiasm building. "You remember Sandridge Towers, down toward Tamarama? We inspected them last year."

Ally grimaced, pulling her dress up over her head. Her friends at work sometimes complained about their partners; the electrician who never changed a lightbulb, the accountant who never got around to doing their tax returns. Men who were happy to leave their work at work.

Not Bryce. Real Estate ran in his veins, pumping his heart, keeping him alive. He thought there was nothing better on a free Sunday than to drop in on open inspections and see how the other side were doing. Keeping his finger on the pulse, he called it, as though no one had ever said it before.

"Have you been down to Clovelly lately?" He didn't wait for her to respond. "There's a new development, right on Ocean Street. The front apartments have panoramic views off two generous enclosed balconies. All quality inclusions, gourmet kitchens with European appliances, expansive, open-plan living and dining areas with a superb northeasterly aspect."

Ally wished he didn't always have to sound like an ad in the property section of Saturday's *Herald*.

"And?" She dreaded what was coming.

"Come on, Ally, you know where this is leading. Metcalfe is keen to have selected apartments occupied throughout January and February. You know, the usual routine."

All too well. They had moved nine times in less than five years. When she first moved in with Bryce, he was living in a grand old Federation house in Randwick, meticulously restored and sumptuously furnished. Ally almost gasped out loud when she saw the place. She didn't know how he afforded it on a property manager's income, but it would have been rude to ask, she hardly knew him. She was just getting settled when he announced one day they had to get out in a week, the owners were coming back from overseas. Ally was stunned. He didn't own the house, he wasn't even renting it. And none of the furniture was his. Bryce was unperturbed, there was another house-minding contract starting in a fortnight, so they'd just have to stay with his mother in the meantime.

Ally had met Bryce's mother by then, and opted instead to stay with Meg.

She had rather liked the duplex in Bondi they minded after that. They stayed for eight months—their longest stretch anywhere. Since then there had been a series of apartments, often in new developments that were not quite finished yet. Apparently it helped sales to have a couple of apartments occupied. Once, they had even lived in the display unit of a rather trendy, overpriced block in Surry Hills. Sales had not been up to expectations; the units were tiny, and potential buyers were leaving unimpressed, their checkbooks firmly closed. So the developers brought in a whiz-kid interior designer to revamp one of the apartments for display, and he decided it would be a novel idea to have real people as props. Bryce volunteered of course. They stayed there rent-free, but had to pay to have most of their belongings stored. They were not allowed to ruin "the look" with stray pieces of personal paraphernalia. Ally hated it. It was like living in a goldfish bowl, not to mention the weirdos that knocked on the door at all hours. She refused ever to be a display dummy again.

"Bryce, you're not suggesting we 'occupy' one of these apartments?"

"Well it's such a great opportunity."

"I don't want to move again!"

"But I thought you didn't like it here?"

That was true, Ally had never liked this apartment. It brought new meaning to the term "minimalist." All the walls were ghostly white, but there wasn't any timber anywhere to warm it up. Not even floorboards. The floor was polished concrete, and there were thick granite slabs for benchtops. She felt like they were living in a morgue.

"I don't, but I've told you before, I want a backyard, and a dog."

"Well, you can't have a dog in these apartments . . ."

"Exactly!"

"I don't understand what the big deal is about getting a dog!" Bryce declared. "I thought you'd like the idea of living closer to the beach again."

"I'm sick of moving all the time. Can't we just stop somewhere for a while?"

"Right, we'll spend the summer at these apartments on the beach, and then we'll look for a house, I promise."

"No, Bryce! You said that five moves ago. Always 'the next time.' I want to live in a house with a yard, and a dog. And I want to have a baby!" she finished, plonking herself on the bed in her underwear, and folding her arms resolutely in front of her. The green dress remained on its hanger. "And I'm not going to any stupid party tonight."

Bryce sighed. He pulled the bedroom chair over and sat down in front of her.

"I see what this is all about now," he placated. "You're just upset because of your grandfather."

"That's right, Bryce! And you haven't even asked me how I'm feeling since I came back."

"I know how you feel," Bryce insisted. "I've done loss. You don't have the monopoly on that, Ally."

Bryce wore his father's early death like a badge of honor. He knew every cliché on grief, and Ally was about to be served a selection.

"Your anger is a normal part of the grieving process, so I won't take it personally."

Ally just glared at him.

"And the baby thing, well that's because you're feeling a sense of your own mortality."

"Bryce, I've been wanting a baby since I turned thirty!"

"Yes, well that's a whole other story then, isn't it?"

Ally shook her head, frustrated.

"Come to the party, meet Brendan . . ."

"I don't want to meet Brendan. I don't want to move! I mean it, Bryce."

He considered her for a moment. "Okay, let's drop the subject for now. But come with me. I have to go, I'm expected."

Of course.

"You'll feel worse staying here on your own, and you can tell me all about the funeral on the way."

Ally relented. She shouldn't waste an expensive hairdo and manicure. Besides, going with Bryce to the party was probably preferable to staying at home alone in the morgue.

But she was wrong. There were so many movers and shakers in the place, the walls rattled. As usual, Ally couldn't have a decent conversation with anyone. People postured, they didn't listen. Especially Bryce.

"Why did you tell that man that we would take the lease?" Ally started once they were in the car on the way home.

"His name is Brendan Metcalfe."

"Whatever! Why did you tell him we'd take the lease?"

"Well, I didn't want to miss out—"

"But I said I didn't want to move, and I meant it, Bryce."

"Look, I know we still have to discuss it—"

"There's nothing to discuss, I don't want to move to that new apartment, and I'm not going to."

They had pulled up at some lights.

"Oh, I see, and I have no say in this?" he said tautly. "If you would just let me finish one sentence without interrupting, I was going to explain that this is really too good an opportunity to pass up . . ."

Ally groaned inwardly. "Opportunity" was Bryce's personal mantra. Everything was an *opportunity*. But an opportunity for what? Where was it all leading to?

Bryce kept talking but Ally had stopped listening. She watched the headlights of passing cars, staring, her eyes not focused. She knew what he was saying. He would work away at her, little by little, day by day, and in the end they would move. She would go along with what he wanted. Just like coming to the party tonight, just like changing her dress.

But somewhere inside her there was that voice again, screaming. She was doing just what she swore she would never do. Following a man around, living his life, his dream. She couldn't do it this time. She really couldn't.

There she'd said it, if only to herself, and now she had to decide what she was going to do about it. That was the hard part.

It was not as though she'd never thought about leaving Bryce. She had, many times. And she was not afraid to be on her own. In fact, a lot of the time that's how she felt anyway. Alone. They were not exactly sweethearts, but they got along. Ally had hoped they might be able to make it work. If they could just settle in a house, have a baby, they'd be a family. That was something she'd never had before.

Now she realized that was probably never going to happen. Not with Bryce. She'd been hanging onto an idea all this time, but it was like trying to hold onto a puff of smoke.

They parked in the basement garage and took the lift up to their floor. Bryce busied himself checking messages on his mobile, ignoring the uneasy silence that had fallen between them.

Ally followed him into the apartment and through into the bedroom. She watched him take off his jacket, open the wardrobe, take out a hanger, hang the jacket carefully onto it, pick off a stray bit of fluff, and place it back into the wardrobe. She realized that she hated how he did that, so precise and finicky. She watched him, hating him. That was it.

"Bryce, I want to move out."

He walked over to her and cupped her face with his hands.

"You're a contrary little soul, aren't you?" he smiled indulgently. "But I'm glad you came around, I knew you would."

"No, Bryce," she said, removing his hands from her face. "I want to move out, on my own."

"I don't get it?" he frowned. "You want one of the apartments to yourself?"

She sighed. "This has nothing to do with the apartments, Bryce. I'm leaving you."

"Oh Ally," he held her by the shoulders. "You really are upset about your grandfather, aren't you? Perhaps I've been a bit insensitive throwing all of this at you right now."

Ally looked at him calmly. Being a salesman gave Bryce an incredibly thick skin. He didn't register rejection.

"Bryce, I am upset by everything that's happened in the past few days, and maybe it has brought all this to the surface. But that doesn't make it any less real."

His hands dropped to his sides, and he watched her, frowning.

"I just don't know what we're doing together anymore. I want a baby, I want to settle down somewhere. You don't, and I don't know how long it will be before you do. I can't waste any more time."

He sat dejectedly on the bed, pulling his tie loose. "Thanks," he said weakly.

"Sorry, I didn't mean that the way it came out."

"I thought we were good together? You were going to get into real estate . . ."

"That was your dream, not mine."

He paused, looking up at her. "Our sex life has been good, hasn't it?"

"We have sex a lot, quantity doesn't necessarily mean quality."

He looked crestfallen. "You didn't tell me there was anything wrong."

Whoops. Ally forgot—*male ego, fragile, handle with care.* She didn't want to hurt him, there was nothing to be gained by that. She sat down next to him on the bed.

"The sex was fine, Bryce, it was good. But it's not everything. Can you explain to me why we're together?"

"We love each other."

"You love me?"

"Of course I do!"

Ally looked at him squarely. "What do you mean by that?"

He shrugged, taken aback. "What does anybody mean by that?"

"No, Bryce. I don't want you to tell me what everybody else means, I don't want a slogan off a desk calendar. What's inside of you?"

He looked blankly at her.

Neither of them spoke for a moment.

"It's nearly Christmas," Bryce said eventually. "You can't leave at Christmas."

Ally thought about Christmas dinner with his insufferable mother and unbearable sister, and decided that it was the perfect time to leave.

Imagine! Studios

It was the last day of shooting for the year. They had to finish today or they would never make the client's deadline, with everything closed down over the break.

As usual Meg had already cleared her schedule, and as usual Simon was swamped. He'd asked her to keep an eye on the shoot this afternoon and, after making him beg, she'd said yes. She still got a kick out of watching a shoot, despite the fact they could be unbelievably boring affairs.

Today they were photographing a roadside poster ad for a male deodorant that was supposed to make women chase after men. Whose wish fulfillment was that?

The set was meant to resemble a jungle, with Tarzan swinging through the trees carrying Jane, presumably. The caption would read, *Some guys will go to any length to get the girl, others just wear Tusk.*

The set designers were still fussing over the positioning of a palm frond when the photographer called for Tarzan and Jane to come on set. A big-breasted brunette in a spray-on leopard-skin bikini sauntered in a minute later, and plopped herself on a stool, crossing her legs. She looked bored already.

"Where's Tarzan?" the photographer boomed as a man appeared through a side entrance. He had blond, shaggy hair and wore a torn T-shirt, cargo pants and designer stubble.

"Haven't you been in wardrobe and make-up yet?"

"Sure," the man said, lifting the T-shirt over his head. "I was just waiting around so I went outside for a smoke."

He dropped his trousers where he stood, revealing the ubiquitous leopard-skin loincloth. Usually models for semi-naked shots were part-time male strippers, all rippling six packs and bulging biceps. But he was leaner. He had a body like a swimmer, broad-shouldered and smooth. Meg watched him, intrigued. He didn't have that self-awareness that a lot of models did. He moved fluidly, almost catlike, extraordinarily comfortable in his own skin. She couldn't take her eyes off him.

The photographer began to instruct the pair on how and where to stand, but it was proving difficult. The plan was for Jane to have her back to Tarzan, with his arms around her from behind. However, Jane was tall, probably nearly six foot, and although Tarzan was taller, the proportions were all wrong. And her substantial bosom was getting in the way as well.

Sean, the photographer, was histrionic at the best of times. "Didn't any of you morons actually put these two together when they were cast?"

Everyone mumbled, shuffling their feet and avoiding eye contact with Sean.

"Christ, I work with imbeciles!" he sighed, raising his arms dramatically. "Where's Meg Lynch, I thought I saw her before."

"I'm right here, Sean," Meg said, stepping forward.

"What can you do about her tits?"

"No one's touching my tits!" the girl protested in a high-pitched voice.

"We're only talking 'touching up,' er, Jane," Meg tried to explain.

"No one's touching up my tits either!"

Meg sighed. Sometimes models really got on her goat. "I mean post-production, on the computer screen."

"Can you make them smaller?" Sean broke in, exasperated.

"Geez, Sean, you guys are never happy. Usually they're not big enough."

"Oh thanks, Meg," he said tightly. "We really need a bit of comic fucking relief at the moment!"

Meg suppressed a grin, shaking her head. "Calm down, Sean. Anyway, I don't know that giving her a breast reduction is going to help."

"Why not?"

"Well, we're not seeing enough of Tarzan." Meg stepped closer to the pair. She glanced up at Tarzan. "Do you mind . . . ?"

"Not at all," he smiled down at her. His eyes were unusually pale, like discs of glass, tinted blue. Meg felt a bit rattled, which was not at all like her. She was always cool, calm and professional. She focused on maneuvering his arm into place around Jane.

"See, Sean, it's all wrong. I can trim the boobs, but she's still blocking too much of his face. And we can hardly see his chest."

Sean was frowning. "What's the market? Who are we targeting?"

"Gay men, and housewives—they buy it for their teenage sons," Meg said dryly. "Tarzan has to be the focus."

"This is fucking great," Sean exclaimed. "If we have to recast, we can't shoot before Christmas."

"That's not an option, Sean. Settle down," said Meg. "We have to think laterally. Let's try a different position. Jane, turn around and face Tarzan."

She did so.

"Now lean back. See, Sean, her boobs look smaller already."

He was frowning. "Yeah, but her head's covered by that palm leaf. Would someone cut the fucking thing out of the way?"

"But it will leave a gap—" one of the assistants offered timidly.

"We can patch it digitally. Don't worry, get rid of it," said Meg. "Now Jane, you raise your leg and sort of hook it behind his calf."

"What?" she whined. "But I'll fall."

Meg sighed.

"Maybe you should show her how it's done," said Tarzan.

Meg's eyes flew up to meet his. "What?"

"Good idea," said Sean.

She looked back at Tarzan. He was smiling mischievously at her, he was obviously enjoying this. She felt flustered, again. She looked around at the crew. Everybody was watching her, waiting.

"Go ahead, Meg," said Sean impatiently.

"Um, sure, right."

Jane moved out of the way, and Meg took her position. "See Sean, if Jane inclines back, then her height's not a problem. They can both hold the rope with the other hand—"

"Nah," Sean shook his head. "Let him hold the rope, bring your arm up under his shoulder."

Meg swallowed as Tarzan leaned in closer and she tucked her arm around him. She knew he was staring at her, but she avoided making eye contact.

"Okay, now what were you saying about the leg?" asked Sean.

"Um," she faltered. "Well, if she raises her leg, and he holds her here . . ."

"No, grab her on the backside," said Sean, his arms folded, watching them closely.

"And we haven't even been introduced," Tarzan murmured, grinning down at her as he slid his hand along her thigh. Meg felt a shiver.

"Now angle your chest toward me, Tarzan," said Sean, looking through the viewfinder on the camera. "That's it!" he clapped his hands together. "Mind you, I'll be buggered how anyone could actually swing through the trees like that. But it works for the shot. Thanks, Meg, you're a lifesaver. Okay, Jane, into position. Everybody, look alive!"

Meg looked up at Tarzan. "You can let go of me now."

"Do I have to?" he grinned.

"I'm not really dressed for the part," Meg said, trying to sound unaffected.

"Mm, pity about that," he murmured, releasing her slowly.

Meg walked back to the corner of the studio and leaned against the wall. She felt a little flushed. She stood there, watching the shoot, shifting restlessly from one foot to the other. From time to time Tarzan looked around and caught her eye, smiling at her, a sexy, knowing smile as if they were both in on the same joke.

After nearly two hours Sean was as close to satisfied as he was going to get. "That's a wrap, everybody."

Meg should have left that minute. There was nothing keeping her there. But she lingered.

She watched Tarzan as he signed a clipboard an assistant handed him. Then he looked directly across at her, meeting her gaze. Meg turned away, embarrassed. When she looked back again he was gone. She glanced around the studio, wondering where he went, berating herself for feeling disappointed. She picked up her handbag and wandered toward the exit.

"Hi," a voice said behind her.

Meg swung around. It was Tarzan, fully clothed. "Hi."

"I thought I should introduce myself, since I fondled your bum and all."

Meg was sure her face had reddened, even though she never blushed, it wasn't her style.

"Jamie Carroll," he said, offering his hand. She put her hand in his and he squeezed it gently.

"Meg Lynch."

"Can I buy you a drink, Meg Lynch?"

She started to protest, but he talked over the top of her. "It's the least I can do, after you saved the shoot. I needed this job." He still had hold of her hand, and he was looking directly into her eyes.

"They wouldn't have replaced you," Meg assured him. "Betty Buxom was more likely to go."

"Well, I'd still like to thank you," he said. "You know, for letting me cop a feel without slapping me."

Meg smiled, despite herself. He was awfully good-looking, in an untamed sort of way, with his two-day growth and his couldn't-care-less hairstyle. But it was his eyes that really drew her in, startlingly pale against his tawny complexion, crinkling at the corners when he smiled.

"Come on, I won't bite," he was saying.

She breathed out heavily. There was nothing wrong with an innocent drink with someone she met at work. I mean, she could even mention it to Chris. Not that she would.

"Okay."

They walked down the street to the pub where everybody went after work. Though it wasn't called a pub anymore. It had been done over in chocolate brown and chrome, and now it was a "bar."

They carried their drinks to a booth in the corner of the room. Meg watched him take a sip of his beer. Then he looked straight at her.

"So, what's the Meg Lynch story? You seemed to have a bit of authority in there."

"I'm the head of the computer graphics department," she explained.

He shook his head slowly. "So that makes you beautiful *and* clever?"

And that line makes you a flirt *and* a charmer, Meg thought to herself. He was staring at her again, and she found it unnerving. His eyes were so . . . penetrating, she thought, wishing that wasn't the first word that came to mind.

"So how long have you been modeling, Jamie?" she asked, shifting the focus off herself.

"On and off, maybe ten years."

How old would that make him? She supposed it depended when he started. Meg knew she had to be older than him, and that was flattering, to a degree. Beyond that it was just pathetic.

"On and off?"

"Well, I don't do it full-time."

"What else do you do?"

He shrugged. "I travel a lot."

Meg was intrigued. "You must be pretty successful to have such a jet-setting lifestyle?"

Jamie grinned. "It's not exactly jetsetting, lugging a backpack around on foot most of the time. And you should see some of the places I've stayed in. They're not what you'd call five star."

"So what do you do? Just travel around, sightseeing?"

"I pick up work where I can."

"Modeling?"

"Sometimes. In Japan they like blonds. But I'd rather do something different. I've worked on a few documentary crews. That's always fun."

Meg was fascinated. With her urging, Jamie told her about his travels: trekking along the silk route through China, working on sailing ships in the Mediterranean, bartending at night in Aspen and skiing through the day. He only stayed in Australia long enough to earn his next ticket overseas, with a little pocket money. Then he would pick a place on the globe and go.

"Just like that?"

"Just like that," he nodded.

"I always wished I'd traveled when I finished school, taken off with a backpack," Meg said wistfully.

"Why didn't you?"

She didn't want to explain to Jamie that at nineteen, she was working three jobs supporting the family. Only when her brothers had started university, and she'd covered their first year's fees, did she feel she could leave them to fend for themselves. She left Brisbane for Sydney and art college. There was no time for travel, no time to be young and irresponsible.

She shrugged. "Oh, you know, you go to college, start work, there never seems to be the right time."

"So what's stopping you now?"

"A very demanding male."

He lifted an eyebrow. "Oh?"

"Mm. He's two feet tall, and still in nappies."

"I'm guessing you're talking about a baby, not some sick fetish?"

Meg laughed. "I have an eighteen month old son."

"And he's part of a matching husband-father ensemble?"

"The lot."

"So," Jamie paused, considering her, "shouldn't you be getting home?"

Meg knew what he was inferring. "Soon enough."

He leaned forward. "Would you like another drink?"

She smiled slowly. "Sure, why not?"

Eleven p.m.

"Are you awake?" Meg couldn't sleep, and she wouldn't sleep until she got this off her chest.

Chris didn't respond. She turned on the bedside lamp and leaned right over the top of him.

"Chris, are you awake?" she said loudly.

He blinked and frowned up at her. "I guess I am, now."

"Good." She propped up some pillows and sat back against them.

He watched her, squinting. "What's up?"

"I was thinking . . ."

"Uh oh," he yawned.

Meg nudged him. "Why don't we go to London for Christmas?"

"What?" That seemed to wake him up.

"Let's go to London. It's snowing, and we could give Harrison a white Christmas. It'd be fun, and romantic, and well," she drew her knees up, hugging them, "a bit of an adventure."

"Meg," he sighed, rubbing his eyes and turning around fully to face her, "what are you talking about?"

"I just feel like taking off!" she exclaimed. "Doing something on a whim."

"But we've made plans. You know Mum and Dad are really looking forward to Christmas this year, now that Harrison's a bit older."

"I'm sure they could survive one Christmas without us."

"What about everything else? We're booked up from now until Christmas Eve. There's my work party, and yours—"

"I could miss that," she insisted.

"And isn't Ally coming to stay tomorrow? You can't leave your best friend with a broken heart at Christmas."

"I don't think it's broken exactly. Just a little bruised," she said glumly.

Chris leaned over and nuzzled into her shoulder. "What's the matter? What brought all this up?"

Meg shrugged. "I just thought it would be fun to do something spontaneous, like we used to."

"Did we?"

"Didn't we?"

"Not that I recall."

"We must have."

"I don't think we ever just took off before, not without making plans."

Meg had a sinking feeling he was right. They didn't do anything on a whim. That's what had drawn her to Chris in the first place. He was solid and dependable. He was nothing like her father.

Chris leaned across her and switched off the lamp. "We can talk about this in the morning, you should try and get some sleep."

She slipped down under the covers and turned on her side. Chris snuggled up behind her.

"Oh, by the way, Neil called," he murmured.

Meg twisted around. "He's in Sydney?"

"Apparently."

"What did he want this time?"

"Well, mostly he wanted to talk to you."

He must need money. Her brother only contacted her when he needed money.

"What did you tell him?"

"I invited him for Christmas."

"Chris! Why did you do that?"

"Because it's exactly what you would have done."

Meg sighed deeply. He was right, of course. Good old reliable Meg. She always said yes.

What would happen if for once she didn't? What would happen if she did just take off? Even the idea was ludicrous. People with babies and mortgages didn't do whatever they felt like doing. And if they did, then they were just like her father.

Meg closed her eyes and backed up closer to Chris. Even though she was tall, he still managed to enfold her completely in his arms. It felt safe, if a little stifling tonight.

Two days before Christmas

Chris walked into the room and threw himself into an armchair.

"All's quiet on the Western front."

"He's asleep finally?"

He nodded. "What is it with babies? The more tired they are, the more they seem to resist sleep."

Meg and Ally were sprawled out on the two sofas. They had opened a bottle of wine and were steadily making their way through it.

This was the first night since she had landed on their doorstep that they'd all been at home. Meg and Chris had been to one Christmas party after another, but at least it had given Ally lots of time with Harrison. They insisted they didn't expect her to babysit just because she was staying there. But Ally enjoyed it.

Meg heaved herself up off the sofa and picked up the wine bottle, holding it up to the light.

"Here," she said, leaning over to refill Ally's glass and draining the bottle. "I'll have to open another one."

"Not just for me," Ally protested. "Aren't you drinking, Chris?"

He shook his head. "Not after last night. Never, ever again."

"Ha, until tomorrow night!" scoffed Meg. "I was the designated driver last night, Ally, so I'm going to enjoy myself tonight. I'll get us another bottle."

She walked out into the kitchen.

"So when do you head off?" Chris asked.

Ally grinned. "Counting the hours, eh Chris?"

"You're kidding, aren't you? We've got a built-in babysitter. I'm in no hurry to see you leave."

"Well, thanks, but I told Lillian I'd be there Boxing Day."

"You don't have to rush off, though," said Meg coming back into the room. "She's not even going to be there."

"Yes, but she has a tradesman coming to do some work for her, so she's glad I'll be around to keep an eye out, you know."

"And the guesthouse is closed for the week?"

Ally nodded. "Lillian always closes it this time of the year, spends Christmas with her son down in Melbourne."

Meg uncorked the bottle and filled her glass. "So, Chris, hasn't the football started yet?" she asked him pointedly.

"You know as well as I do, darling, there's no football on this time of the year."

"Mm, basketball, golf . . . table tennis perhaps?"

"I have the distinct feeling that you're trying to get rid of me."

"No, not at all! We're just about to turn on the Chic's Flic Marathon on Foxtel," Meg said, consulting the guide. "You know, *Sleepless in Seattle*, *Terms of Endearment* . . . Oh look, *Pretty Woman*'s already started."

"Okay, okay, you've made your point, I'm out of here," said Chris, lifting himself out of his chair. He kissed Meg and walked to the doorway. "Night, ladies."

After he had left the room, Ally frowned at Meg. "We're not really watching *Pretty Woman*, are we?"

"Why, what's wrong with *Pretty Woman*? I love that movie." She picked up the remote control and aimed it at the television. "Oh look, here's the part where she goes shopping."

"Doesn't the premise of the story irk you, though?"

Meg didn't take her eyes off the screen. "Oh, don't get all politically correct on me, Ally."

"Come on, Meg, you have to admit, if you had a daughter, would you want her to believe that prostitution was the only way an attractive, intelligent woman could make a living? But that, not to worry, she would eventually be saved by Mr. Tall, Dark, Handsome and incredibly Rich?"

"Richard Gere's not dark."

Ally rolled her eyes. "The point remains, the story would be far more realistic if they showed her, I don't know, going to evening college, enrolling in a course, doing something to better herself."

Meg looked at her, dumbfounded.

"What?" said Ally defensively.

"Are you for real?" She held her hand to her chest and feigned a dramatic voice-over. " 'Julia Roberts is a girl with no future, until she picks up a copy of the university handbook.' They could call it 'Pretty Student.' I can see the queues forming now!"

Ally laughed, shaking her head. "You know, you've got a career woman's brain and fairy floss for a heart."

"I'm just a romantic."

"You actually believe in romance?"

"Of course I do! What kind of a world would it be if we didn't have some romance?" Or even just the idea of it. Meg considered Ally. "I assume you didn't just end one?"

Ally frowned. "Yeah, right."

"Why on earth did you stay with him for so long?"

"Because he stayed." She twirled the stem of her wine glass around between her fingers, staring at it. "He was kind to me, he took me in."

"You sound like a stray dog."

"Now there's an analogy!"

"Oh Ally," Meg chided. "What made you finally leave then?"

"I realized I was starting to hate him. I hated watching him getting dressed, grooming himself. I hated the way he was always brushing crumbs off everything, tables, the sofa, *me* . . . !"

"What?"

"Don't get me started! He was *so* anally retentive. And the way he ate! I couldn't even be in the same room when he was eating his stupid organic muesli. Hearing the crunching sounds, his jaw clicking." Ally shuddered, pausing. "I wasn't going to live like that, hating him. That would be unbearable."

Meg looked at her. "Have you spoken to him since you left?"

"No, actually. But he keeps leaving text messages on my mobile."

"Like what?"

"Oh, yesterday it was, 'What if I put together a proposal?' "

"Does he mean marriage?"

Ally shrugged, "Who knows? He only speaks in real estate jargon."

"He's such a weirdo. You're better rid of him."

Ally didn't answer her.

"Sorry, but you know I was never overly fond of him."

"No? Really?" Ally smiled wryly.

Meg looked directly at her. "Do you feel lonely?"

"No. I felt lonelier when I was with him."

Meg sighed, reaching for the wine bottle. "What you need is a nice, juicy love affair."

"Okay, get me one for Christmas? I'm sure they sell them in the Hollywood catalog of dreams and fantasies."

"Such a skeptic."

Ally cocked her head toward the TV screen. "You really believe that happens anywhere but in the movies?"

"Of course I do!" Meg insisted. "My knight in shining armor is lying in there, snoring as we speak."

"What does it feel like," Ally hugged her knees. ". . . being in love?"

"You just want to have a lend."

"No, really, I want to know."

"Are you telling me you've never been in love?"

"I don't think so. What made you fall in love with Chris?"

Meg paused, considering. This was not the best time to have to answer that question. Or maybe it was. If she could rekindle some of what she felt when they first met, maybe she wouldn't feel so restless now.

"I knew when I met him that this man would never let me down. I knew he'd stay by me forever." For better or worse, she sighed inwardly. Till death do us part.

Ally thought that if she had that kind of security she could face anything.

Meg thought if only there was a little passion, a little excitement. If only she didn't feel that everything was quite so safe.

"I don't know if that answers your question."

"Sure it does."

"It's not very romantic though," Meg said wistfully.

"I think it's very romantic. I wish I could find someone who could give me that."

They stared at the screen. Richard Gere had just spotted Julia Roberts in a stunning black dress sitting at the bar.

"Of course, it'd help if I looked like her."

"Who? Julia Roberts? Why would you want to look like Julia Roberts?"

"Why would I want to look like Julia Roberts?" Ally repeated, deadpan. "Oh, I can't imagine."

"It would be terrible to look like Julia Roberts."

"Yes, I imagine it would be a real burden."

"If you looked like Julia Roberts, you wouldn't get a moment's peace. Everywhere you'd go, even just walking down the street, people would stop you—'Has anybody ever told you, you look exactly like Julia Roberts?' "

Ally was laughing.

" 'But really!' " she continued. " 'You look exactly like her. Are you related or something?' "

"Enough!" Ally held her stomach.

"Seriously, Al," Meg poured herself another glass of wine, and handed the bottle to Ally, "your self-esteem is shot from living with that man! It will do you good to get away. I guarantee, a month in the Southern Highlands and you'll be swept off your feet by some gorgeous Man from Snowy River who'll carry you off on horseback to his mountain cabin . . ."

Ally laughed out loud. "Ugh, he'd have to catch me first, I'd be running a hundred miles in the opposite direction."

"Why?"

"Too much like my grandfather," she cringed. "Besides, I'm going to Bowral, not the wilds of Tasmania. It's très sophisticated these days. I think the entire population of the lower north shore migrate there every weekend. There's more cafés than in Darlinghurst."

"So, you'll get yourself a nice merchant banker."

"I'm sure they're all married with their families in tow!" Ally retorted. "Bowral is hardly a Mecca for single women looking for a man, and besides, I'm not looking. I'm going down there to settle my grandfather's property, and because I haven't exactly got anywhere to live at the moment."

"You can live here!"

"I think I'll have to, when I come back at the end of January. Just till I find a place, if that's alright?"

"Of course it is, that's if you come back."

"What makes you think I would want to stay down there?"

"Well, you're pushing thirty-five, you've been in the same job for ten years, and you've just left a long-term relationship. You're heading for a sea change."

"You watch too much television."

"It's a real term, not just a television show! It means a major change of direction."

"Well, it's not much of a 'sea change' to go back to where I started. I could think of nothing worse."

"Why? I haven't been down that way for years, but I remember it was lovely."

"It is, but it's just tainted for me. I wasn't happy there, and I can't change that."

"You should try to keep an open mind, Ally."

"I'm looking forward to the break. But I'll be back for the start of the school term."

"We'll see."

Boxing Day

Ally didn't expect the amount of traffic she hit heading out of the city. She should have realized that half the population of Sydney would start their holidays the day after Christmas. Anyway, it was no matter. She was not in any hurry. There was a certain luxury in only having to worry about herself. Just as well she could see something positive, she was going to have to get used to it.

Staying at Meg's over Christmas had stirred up all the emotions Ally had been trying to suppress. The scene as Harrison opened his presents surrounded by his loving family, belonged on a greeting card. Some people really did have that kind of a life. And she'd just wasted another five years of hers, moving farther and farther away from any chance of it for herself.

Meg had reminded Ally she would turn the dreaded thirty-five next year, surely the most desolate of all ages. She would suddenly be catapulted into the "over 35's" category on just about every form she had to fill in. And everybody—individuals and corporations—expected her to be married with at least one child. That was the demographic. And Ally didn't fit it. She felt like she was some strange unwelcome visitor on a planet that had never encountered her species.

She'd just pulled up at traffic lights when her mobile phone started ringing. She rummaged around in her bag to find it, as usual, too late.

Ally looked at the tiny screen. Bryce had left another text message.

Now that xmas is over, time to restart negotiations. What's your bottom line? Call me. B.

"No!" she said to the phone. "Leave me alone!"

She remembered what she had said to Meg, about tossing it out the window. But that was a waste. No, she would just switch it off, and put it away.

Once Ally joined the M5, the traffic moved more smoothly, and the rest of the drive took less than an hour and a half. This time when Ally pulled up at the gates of Birchgrove, they were closed. As soon as she had called to ask about staying, Lillian had forwarded Ally the keys by express mail. She'd asked Ally to phone her when she arrived, so that she would know she was safely inside and could give her any instructions.

"Merry Christmas, Lillian," Ally greeted her, after her grandson had called her to the phone.

"Thank you, Ally. Did you have a nice Christmas?"

"Lovely, thanks. How is the family?"

"Everyone is fine here. Stuffed to the eyeballs with food, naturally, but that's to be expected!" she added. "Did you have a good trip?"

"I hit a little traffic at first, but then once I was on the freeway I had a good run."

"Now, there is plenty of food in the fridge, Ally, and I don't want you to be shy, I left it for you. There's bread in the freezer. And there's wine, beer, whatever you fancy. You know where the cellar is."

"Thanks, Lillian."

"And you'll take a staff room upstairs. Nicola has the farthest room along the corridor, you take the first one. Will that be alright?"

"Of course, Lillian. Thanks for all this."

"Nonsense, Ally. I'm glad I'll be seeing you again so soon. And besides, you'll be there for Matthew."

"Of course. He starts tomorrow?"

"That's right," she confirmed. "I'll look forward to catching up when I get back."

"You'll call me, about the train you'll be on?"

"Yes, dear. I'll talk to you later in the week."

Ally carried her suitcase upstairs. She hadn't thought she'd be back here so soon after the last time. And homeless. It hadn't really hit her yet that she was "of no fixed address." Perhaps that's how she had felt with Bryce for all those years anyway.

She changed into something cooler and went back downstairs to make herself something to eat. She carried a tray out to the verandah and settled herself on a wicker chair looking out onto the garden. It would still be light for another hour or so, and the air was warm, though not as humid as in Sydney.

Ally sat sipping her wine, absorbing the peace, the extraordinary stillness. She felt an overwhelming sense of release. It was like she had woken up from a coma after living with Bryce for five years. That was the only way she could describe it now. Meg had said that her self-esteem was shot, but Ally had to wonder if she had any in the first place, to entirely subjugate her own dreams for so long.

But she was finally free. Though free to do what exactly, she wasn't sure. She was beginning to realize how much she needed this break. A chance to unwind, but also to step away, have some distance. She certainly wasn't going to stay here, but perhaps it was a good place to gain some perspective.

Ally didn't know how long she'd sat there on the verandah, but dusk had fallen, and she was suddenly feeling very tired. Upstairs, her suitcase still lay on the floor untouched. She was in no hurry to unpack, and it was almost indulgent to leave things lying around; she could never do that when she was with Bryce.

She slipped off her dress and threw it across a chair, climbing into bed in her underwear. The sheets were smooth and cool, and the bed felt huge. Ally stretched out, relishing the quiet. No traffic noise, no doors banging in adjacent flats. She fell asleep easily, with only the distant sound of an owl hooting.

The next morning

There it was again. A high-pitched grinding noise screaming through the window. She pulled the pillow tighter around her head. It seemed to have stopped. Ally lifted her head. She looked around the room, momentarily disorientated.

Suddenly a loud bang from the side of the house made Ally almost jump off the bed. She went to the window and stuck her head out. Down below she could see someone, with what appeared to be a window frame straddled across his back.

"Hey, what's going on?" she called.

The man settled the frame down on the ground and looked up. He was wearing a cap, she couldn't really see his face. Ally remembered she was in her underwear and pulled the curtain around herself.

"Hi there! I'm the carpenter. Lillian said she mentioned I was coming?"

Ally frowned, holding her hand to her forehead to shield the sun from her eyes. "Mm, not quite so early though."

"Well, it is nine o'clock . . ."

"Oh God, it's not, is it? Why didn't you knock?"

"I did . . ." He seemed to hesitate. "Listen, do you mind continuing the conversation down here? I'm getting a crick in my neck."

"Oh sure, sorry. Just give me a minute."

Ally threw on the shift she'd discarded last night and splashed some water on her face in the bathroom. She checked herself in the mirror. Her crinkly hair never behaved itself in the mornings, so dragging a brush through it now was having little effect. She gave up and hurried down the stairs barefoot, and out the back door to where the builder was working.

"Sorry about that," she greeted him.

He was leaning over the window frame, which he'd since hoisted onto two workhorses. He turned around to face her and pulled off his cap, smoothing back his hair. It was the first time Ally had seen his face clearly. It was a good-looking face.

"Hi," he smiled. "No, don't apologize. I'm sorry the noise woke you. Like I said, I tried knocking. When there was no answer, I waited around for a while, but eventually I really had to get started."

Ally felt herself redden. "I'm so sorry. Lillian was counting on me being here, you know, to let you in, whatever."

He grinned at her. He had these deep creases down his cheeks that formed furrows when he smiled. And really blue eyes.

"Is that what she told you?" he asked. "Well don't worry, I've got a key. I let myself in and out all the time."

Now Ally felt even more embarrassed. "So Lillian was obviously just being nice, about needing me to stay and everything."

"Of course she was being nice, you know Lillian! But I'm sure she wanted you to stay."

Ally smiled weakly at him. "Well, let me make you a cup of tea at least."

"It's okay, I brought a thermos."

"Don't be silly, let me make you a proper cup, from a pot. It's the least I can do."

Ally rushed back into the kitchen, filled the kettle and plugged it in. She searched through the cupboards until she found some generous, plain white mugs. She was sure—whatever his name was would drink from a mug. And he might be hungry, he'd already been here for a while. So she took out Lillian's Christmas cake and cut a couple of decent slabs.

She carried a tray out onto the back verandah and set it down on a wicker table. The sun was starting to feel quite hot, so she pulled the chairs into the shade. She walked back around to the side of the house to find him.

He was hunched over the window frame again, working with a chisel.

"Your tea's ready, it's up on the verandah."

He stood up, straightening his back and wiping the sweat off his brow with his forearm.

"It's going to be a hot one today," he remarked.

He followed her around to the verandah and sat down on one of the chairs. Ally poured the tea.

"Sorry, I didn't know whether you had milk or sugar."

He shook his head, "Just black thanks."

She handed him the mug. "I haven't introduced myself. I'm Ally, Ally Tasker."

He nodded. "You're Jim Tasker's granddaughter."

"That's right."

"I saw you at the funeral."

"You were at the funeral?"

"Sure, I couldn't come back to the wake, I was flat out finishing a couple of jobs before Christmas. But I was at the cemetery, to pay my respects. Jim was a terrific bloke. It must have been a great loss for you."

Ally nodded vaguely. Curiouser and curiouser. "Sorry, I think Lillian mentioned your name, but I've forgotten."

"Matt Serrano."

"Serrano? That's Italian?"

He nodded. "My grandparents were from Italy. My Dad was born here, and Mum's Australian. But I like to think I'm still part Italian."

That accounted for the dark hair and the olive skin. The blue eyes must have been from his mother.

"Is this Lillian's Christmas cake?" he was asking.

"Sorry, yes of course, please have some."

He reached for a piece. "You say 'sorry' a lot, you know. You don't have to keep apologizing for everything."

Ally reddened again, relieved he wasn't looking at her.

"Did you grow up here?" she asked, changing the subject.

"Where?" he frowned. "Here, in the Southern Highlands?" He shook his head. "My dad grew up in Griffith, that's where he met Mum. We lived around the Riverina District while I was growing up."

"So what brought you here?"

"I lived in Sydney for about ten years, until I couldn't stand it anymore. I wanted to get back to the country, but it's hard to make a living. This was a good compromise. Plenty of the kind of work I do, none of the traffic and stress."

Ally shuddered. Shades of her grandfather.

"What kind of work, carpentry?"

He nodded. "Restoration work mostly. You ask a lot of questions, Ally Tasker."

Ally knew she was blushing furiously this time. "Sorry..."

"You're apologizing again."

"Sorry, oh!" She hit her forehead with the palm of her hand. "Okay, no more questions."

"I'll ask one instead," he said. "What's Ally short for?"

"Who says it's short for anything?"

"It's not?" he frowned. "So it's just like that skinny American girl on the telly?"

"Did you have to bring her up?"

"Well is it?"

She shrugged. "Let's just say that it's the name on my driver's license."

"But not on your birth certificate?"

Ally glanced sideways at him and took a sip from her tea.

"For someone who asks a lot of questions, you're not very good at answering them," he said. "Why so secretive?"

"If you heard it, you'd understand."

He paused, considering her. "If I guess, will you tell me?"

She grinned. "You never will."

"Well it can't be something normal like Alison or Alexandra. It has to be embarrassing." He thought for a moment. "What about Alberta? Alfreda?"

She shook her head.

"I know! You were named after one of the Abba girls—what was she called—Agnetha or something?"

"Then I'd be Aggie wouldn't I?" Ally pointed out. "Besides, I was born well before Abba hit the charts, but thanks for thinking that was a possibility."

He narrowed his eyes, concentrating. "Alfonsia? ... Al-ger-non-ia?" he said slowly.

"You're making them up."

"But I can't think of anything else."

"Told you so, game over."

"Oh, come on, you have to give me credit for trying."

Ally looked at his plaintive expression and felt herself softening. But she never told anyone her real name.

"I won't tell anyone," he persisted, flashing her a rather disarming smile.

She sighed. If she didn't tell him, it would just become a greater challenge. "It's Alaska."

He paused, thinking about it. "Alaska Tasker. It rhymes!"

"Thanks for pointing that out," Ally said dryly.

"Is that why you don't like it?"

"That's the least of it. It's just embarrassing."

"Why, I think it's kind of exotic."

"Mm," she looked doubtful. "Alaska is cold and harsh and remote—Tahiti is exotic."

"What? You'd rather be called Tahiti?"

"No! I'd rather be called something normal, like . . . Elizabeth!"

"The suburb in Adelaide?"

Ally laughed. "No, I'd just like a normal name. Like yours. Matthew, that's a lovely name."

"But I don't think it would suit you."

She smiled. "You're determined to make a joke out of this, aren't you?"

"Well, I just don't think it's such a bad name. Do you know why your parents called you Alaska? They must have had a reason."

Ally sighed. "That's the worst part. My mother named me after where I was conceived."

"You were born in Alaska?"

"No, I said where I was *conceived*. She made that very clear. When I was a little too young to want to know."

"How old were you?"

Ally looked out into the distance. "Twelve. I hadn't seen her since she left me with my grandparents when I was three. I didn't even remember her. The only name I'd ever known for myself was Ally. Then, when Nan died, she showed up out of the blue and dumped it all on me. Then she left again."

Ally didn't know why she was telling him any of this. It wasn't as if she was in the habit of revealing much about her personal life to anyone, let alone a stranger.

"What about your father?"

Ally shrugged. "All I know is that he was someone living in Alaska at the time, my mother wasn't even sure of his name."

The cicadas had started to chirp on the lawn outside. The noise would crescendo by late afternoon in this heat.

"Well it could be worse, you know," Matt said eventually.

"Oh really?"

He nodded. "If my parents had called me after where I was conceived, you'd be talking to Wagga Wagga Serrano."

Ally burst into laughter.

"In fact, if my suspicions are true, maybe even Back Seat of a Holden Serrano!"

"Stop," said Ally holding up her hand, still laughing. "I take your point."

"Well, thanks for the cuppa," he said, standing up. "But I better get back to work. Do you want a hand with these?" He indicated the tray and cups.

"No, thanks. I'll take care of that. Now, does Lillian normally give you lunch?"

"I've got some with me."

"That's not what I asked," she persisted. "Does Lillian normally give you lunch?"

"When the kitchen's open and Rob is here, then yes, I normally get lunch. But as that isn't the case, I brought my own."

"So, tomorrow, I'll make you lunch—I have to earn my keep."

He turned and started down the verandah steps. "Okay, Alaska, if you insist."

"You promised not to tell anyone!"

"There's no one here," he protested. "Your secret's safe with me."

The next day

Ally heard Matt's truck pulling up in the driveway out front. This time she was up and dressed and had the kettle boiling. She had found an alarm clock and set it for seven, hoping that would give her at least half an hour before he arrived.

She opened the front door as Matt was unloading gear off the back of the truck.

"Morning!"

"Hi there. I didn't wake you?" he grinned.

"No, I was ready for you this time," she replied. "I was just making a pot of tea, would you like a cup?"

"Thanks."

"I'll bring it out."

Ally went back in through to the kitchen. She poured them both a mug, adding milk to hers. Yesterday, she had pottered around, unpacking and generally settling herself in. Around lunchtime, she had called to Matt to come inside out of the heat while he ate. And she made him a cup of coffee later in the afternoon, before he left.

But last night, she'd started to feel bored and restless. And rattling around alone in a huge empty house only exacerbated the feeling. It was a relief to have a bit of company.

She took his tea out to him.

"Thanks," he smiled, taking the mug from her.

"So what are you up to today?" she asked.

"Well, I still have another section of dry rot to cut out of the second window, and then I have to replace the piece, before assembling the window again," he explained. "Then I've got the third window to fix." He indicated the next one along the southern wall. "I wanted to have them all painted for Lillian, but if the heat keeps up, a storm will blow up tonight or to-morrow, and I bet it'll rain for a day at least, maybe two."

"I can paint!" Ally offered brightly.

He smiled at her. "Thanks, but they have to be sanded back, filled, undercoated. It's a big job."

"I know, I helped some friends do up their old place. Fourteen double-hung oregon windows we had to strip back of, like, a hundred years of paint. But they came up great in the end."

"So, you're a bit of an expert?" he nodded. "But you're on holidays, you don't want to spend it working."

"It's not work. It's how I spend most of my holidays anyway."

"What do you mean?"

"I'm a bit of a closet renovator."

"You renovate closets?"

Ally grinned. "No, I just like renovating, so I help friends when I've got nothing of my own to renovate. I'd love to help, really!"

He paused, looking her up and down. "Well, you're going to need covered-in shoes, I don't want to take off one of your toes if I drop a chisel.

"And you should wear a hat, too," he added, calling after her, because Ally had already disappeared inside to change.

Watsons Bay

"Neil, it's after eleven." Meg knocked on the door as she spoke.

"Righto," came the muffled reply. "What's happening?"

As if there had to be a special reason to get out of bed before midday.

"Just life passing you by," Meg returned.

"You can come in, I'm decent."

She opened the door and peered into the darkened room. Her brother's tall frame was sprawled diagonally across the double bed, a sheet draped across his middle. He stretched his arms out and cupped his hands behind his head.

"Where's Hazza?"

She wished he wouldn't call him that. "Chris took him down to the cove."

"Good! It'll give us a chance to talk."

That was the idea. They hadn't been alone since he arrived late on Christmas Eve, and Meg knew he was waiting for the chance to make his pitch. So she sent Chris out today with Harrison, to give Neil his opportunity. Then he would leave them alone.

It was his usual routine. Neil showed up probably twice a year, eating their food and drinking their alcohol, and charming everybody who met him. Ally thought he was funny, and Chris's mother said he was the nicest boy. Trouble was, he wasn't a boy. He had two marriages and three children behind him and he still hadn't grown up. Which was precisely why he had two marriages and three children behind him.

"I'm not talking to you in here, Mr. Horizontal," Meg informed him. "I'll meet you in the kitchen."

"Meggie," he called after her.

She popped her head back around the door.

"Put the kettle on?" he drew the words out plaintively. "Please, Meggie?"

She grunted. Of course she would.

A few minutes later she heard the toilet flush, and then he appeared in his boxer shorts, scratching his stomach. Neil had survived on charm all his life. He was boyishly handsome, more like their father than Meg cared to consider. But she'd always excused him for that, it wasn't his fault if it was in the genes. But enough already. He was nearly thirty-six and the years were showing. His dark hair had started to recede, and he was developing a paunch. Wife number three wouldn't be along in a hurry.

Meg poured boiling water into the teapot and sat it on a coaster in front of him. "Do you want some toast?"

"I'll get it," he offered half-heartedly, settling himself on a kitchen stool.

Meg turned away and popped some bread in the toaster. Then she took two cups out of the dishwasher and handed them to Neil. "Maybe you can pour the tea," she said abruptly.

He took the cups and peered across at her. "What's up?"

"Nothing."

"You got the shits with me?"

"No," she said briskly, opening the fridge door and peering inside. "What do you want with your toast? Butter, Vegemite, jam, a check?"

"What?"

Meg sighed, "Sorry."

"So you should be. I'm offended."

Meg looked at him. "Come on, Neil, you don't get offended that easily."

He smiled. "Lucky for me, eh?"

She smiled back at him, perching herself on a stool opposite.

"We both know why you're here, Neil. So why don't we just cut to the chase?"

"I came to visit my big sister for Christmas."

Meg considered him dubiously. "And you're not going to ask me for any money?"

"Jeez, what's wrong with you?" Neil shifted uneasily. "Are you and Chris having problems or something?"

Meg sighed loudly. "It's just that you do this every time, Neil, and I think we should be honest and stop playing games."

"Have you been talking to Glen?"

Not for a while, and not as often as she would have liked. Glen was the "good" twin. Meg wondered if two people born minutes apart had ever been so different. Unlike Neil, Glen had stayed at university after Meg left Queensland, working part-time to support himself through a mining engineering degree. After he graduated, he took a contract in South Africa for three years. Meg understood why he had to get away. Their family was parasitic. They'd almost sucked the life out of Meg, and they'd turned on Glen once she was out of reach.

"You two are so much alike," Neil complained. "Everything's always turned out for you."

"Oh sure, Neil. Hard work didn't have anything to do with it."

"You think I haven't worked hard? But you know how much bad luck I've had."

She used to believe all his stories, but they were wearing thin. And they sounded too much like their father's tales of woe. Mick Fitzgerald had taken his first gamble at sixteen, when he had unprotected sex on a beach with Cathy Morrow. It was the summer after they finished their school certificate, and they believed they could do anything without thought to the consequences. Well, Meg was the seven and a half pound consequence that arrived nine months later.

They moved into Cathy's parents' garage and played house. She was the Morrows' youngest child—their change of life baby—and as far as they were concerned she was still a baby. Cathy's parents indulged them, not wanting to do anything to drive them away. But when the twins came along fifteen months after Meg, they put Cathy on the pill and found Mick an apprenticeship as a mechanic.

If only they could have lived in that garage forever, they might have made it. But Meg's grandparents were elderly and passed away within a year of each other. Mick and Cathy inherited the house, but they had no one to look after them anymore. Until Meg was old enough, and by then it was too late. Her father had gambled away the house and anything of value the family owned.

"Look, I don't mind giving you money." Yes she did, why did she say that? "But I'd just like to see you do something a little less . . . speculative?"

Neil insisted he wasn't a gambler. He didn't bet on the horses, or throw his money away at casinos like his father. But he was forever falling for the latest get rich quick scheme, chasing the next big thing. He was a gambler by any other name.

"Well, this is bound to make you happy." Neil leaned forward eagerly. "Glen has offered me work."

"Glen?" Meg was stunned.

Glen had extended his contract in South Africa and married a pretty Afrikaans girl. For a while Meg believed he'd never come back. But when they were expecting their first baby, they moved to Western Australia. As far away as they could be while still living in the same country. She found it hard to believe he was actually inviting Neil to come to Western Australia.

"What work? Where?"

"In the mines, over in WA."

"There are plenty of mines in Queensland, and they're not so far away from your kids."

"Yeah, but I haven't got a brother in high places to get my foot in the door in Queensland." He looked at her curiously. "What's your problem, anyway? I thought you'd be happy Glen and I are reuniting, so to speak."

Meg sighed. "Of course I'm happy, as long as he's not doing it under duress."

"Jeez, Meg, you're making me out to be some kind of a con man or something, with my own brother," Neil declared, obviously miffed.

"I'm sorry, Neil. Here, your toast is ready."

She passed him a plate and he proceeded to slather butter all over his toast. Meg watched him uncomfortably. What that would do to his arteries, she didn't want to contemplate.

"So, tell me what Glen said."

"Okay, he said if I can get out there under my own steam, he'd get me a contract, six months minimum. It's good money, Meg, really good money. Anyway, I checked with the airlines, it costs a bloody fortune to get to Perth. But Glen wouldn't spot me the fare."

"He might have wanted you to work for it. Prove you're serious?"

"Well, it's a bit hard to work for it here when the job's over there!" Neil exclaimed, as though it was the most reasonable piece of logic. He'd failed to understand that Glen was probably hoping for evidence of some level of commitment from his brother.

"What about your kids?"

Neil avoided her eyes. "I don't see them much these days. They do alright without me."

"You shouldn't say that."

"Anyway, if I make as much money as Glen reckons I can, then I'll be sending them back plenty. I'll do the right thing by them, Meg."

She folded her arms and leaned back against the kitchen cupboards. "How much do you need?"

He looked at her warily. "Are you sure?"

Meg nodded. "It'll be cheaper than feeding you for much longer."

Neil laughed. "You're not wrong there." He paused. "This'll be okay with Chris?"

"Of course it will. You're family, he doesn't bat an eye."

"He's a good bloke, that man of yours. I hope you appreciate him."

"I do," she said, picking up the teapot. "Do you want a top-up?"

He picked up his cup and held it out for Meg to fill. "Mum and Dad said to tell you hello."

Meg put down the teapot and turned to the sink, busying herself.

"Don't you even want to know how they are?"

She glanced over her shoulder at him. "Are they well?"

"Yes—"

"Then fine, that's all I need to know." Meg didn't have any contact with her parents these days, save for Christmas and birthday cards. She found it easier that way.

"I'll go and have a shower," said Neil, changing the subject. "Then I'll phone the airline, if you're sure . . ."

"Forget about it, Neil. Just don't let Glen down."

Meg watched him leave the room. She hoped it would all work out. Glen had always been the giver in their relationship, since they were in utero. He was smallest born and had stood behind his brother from then on. Moving to the other side of the world was the only way he could get some independence.

Still, Meg couldn't let herself stress about their relationship now. If Glen had asked him over, then the two of them would just have to work it out. She wasn't responsible for them anymore. She should never have been responsible for them in the first place.

From about the age of eight or nine, Meg had known that her family was falling apart. It was like something had vacated inside Cathy when her parents died. Perhaps she looked around at her life and decided it was all too much for someone in her early twenties. She sat staring at the television most of the day. So Meg took charge, getting the boys off to school each morning, making sure their lunches were packed and their uniforms clean. She wrote her mother elaborate lists every day, so that she wouldn't forget what she had to do.

Cathy gladly handed the reins to her daughter. When she realized just how capable Meg was, she started leaving her in charge at night as well, giving her the chance to go out and join her husband, for the first time in years. She dressed up in skimpy clothes and heavy make-up and kissed the three of them on the forehead, leaving a smear of dark lipstick.

"Mind your sister, boys," she'd say on her way out. Every time. It was the one thing Meg could count on.

Sydney Airport

Chris and Meg stood waving to Neil as he disappeared down the passageway to the plane that would take him to Perth.

"Are you okay?" Chris said gently, watching her pensive expression.

"Sure, he'll be fine. Glen will look out for him, if he doesn't drive him batty first."

"They're big boys now, Meg, you're not responsible for them anymore."

"This from the man who just gladly paid for his plane ticket?"

Chris grinned sheepishly. "He's family, Meg."

"I know," she looped her arm through his and they strolled over to where Harrison stood glued to the window, watching the planes.

"What can you see, Harrison?" said Meg, crouching down to his level.

"Plane Mama!" he shrieked excitedly. "Plane go urrrm . . . wing . . ." and that was as much as Meg could make out. Harrison launched into an intense and comprehensive dissertation on the joys of aeronautics, with plenty of arm action and enthusiasm. But they couldn't make head or tail of what he was saying, save the odd word. Meg loved listening to him. He was so sure of himself: as far as he was concerned he was communicating just fine, and she supposed he was, just not in a language they could understand. Of course, they were recognizing more and more words, and pretty soon he'd be speaking English the same as everyone else. But Meg hoped it wouldn't happen too quickly.

"Do you want to go on a plane, Harry?" Chris asked.

"Plane, Dadda . . ." and off he went again, ten to the dozen.

Meg stood up and leaned back against the window, gazing around the airport. There were people lugging backpacks, or oversized suitcases, clutching wads of tickets and other papers, their excitement palpable.

"I think Mummy would like to go on a plane," Chris was saying.

Meg stirred, looking up at him. Harrison was now perched on his shoulders.

"I was thinking about what you said, before Christmas. We do need a holiday. We should start to plan something."

Meg nodded vaguely, "Sure." He'd missed the point entirely. She didn't want to plan something, she just wanted to do it.

"We should both put in for our holidays as soon as we can. And you pick the place Meg. Anywhere you want. Well, within reason. We have to consider Harry. But there are plenty of family-friendly places we could go. We'll see a travel agent, look at their packages, that way there are no surprises, everything's organized down to the last detail . . ."

Meg tuned out. They wandered slowly back out of the terminal to the carpark, Chris's enthusiasm building as they went. But he might as well have been Harrison babbling on in his own language for all that Meg was taking in.

Thursday

Ally had finished painting and now she was just waiting for the last window to dry. They had worked solidly for the last two days. All the windows were repaired and painted, ready for Matt to refit them today. The southerly change had held off, but not for much longer. The heat was so intense it was sure to break soon.

Ally dragged a chaise longue off the verandah and pulled it into the shade near where Matt was working.

"Are you quite comfortable there?" he said as she settled down with a cool drink.

"Yes, thanks for asking," she quipped.

"You're all finished?"

"Just waiting for the paint to dry now."

"You've done surprisingly well, if you don't mind me saying, Ms. Tasker."

"Why 'surprisingly?' " Ally asked. "Because I'm a woman?"

"I didn't say that."

"Yeah, well, not in so many words."

He glanced across at her. "It's not what I meant."

"Look Matt, I've been holding my tongue, not wanting to call you sexist, but—"

"I'm not sexist!"

"Well, then what's with all the 'oohing and aahing,' just because I can work a belt sander and I know what a mullion is?"

He straightened up, laughing. "When was I 'oohing and aahing?' "

"Constantly."

"You've got to admit, it's a bit unusual. Did your grandfather teach you all that?"

"Not likely."

"Well, you're good. I can't get a decent subbie down here, male or female, to do that sort of work."

"What's a subbie?" Ally frowned.

"A subcontractor. If I'm contracted to do a job and I need another tradesman sorry, *person*—I have to subcontract somebody."

"And you can't get a painter?"

"Oh sure, for entire houses, but not for little jobs, fiddly stuff like this."

"Mm, funny," Ally mused. "That's just what I like to do."

"Ever thought of a career change?"

"Only all the time."

He stopped to look at her for a moment. "You're a teacher in real life, aren't you?"

"How did you know that?"

"Jim mentioned it."

"Did you know my grandfather that well?"

Matt shrugged. "Well enough, I guess. But you know what he was like, a real talker. Used to talk about you all the time."

"So I keep hearing," Ally muttered. It was becoming quite obvious that she didn't know what James Tasker was like at all.

The heat was scorching. Matt pulled off his T-shirt, wiping his face with it before flinging it aside. Ally watched him, trying not to stare.

She could not deny finding him attractive. But she was wary. He'd told her that he lived up off Sheepwash Road, near Avoca, a blink-and-you-would-miss-it township on the way to Kangaroo Valley. He had been building his house for years, and it was still not finished. He wasn't wearing a wedding ring, and from the way he spoke, she was pretty sure he lived alone. His story had too many similarities to her grandfather's. A loner living on the edge of town in a half-finished house. She shivered.

"Could you come and hang onto this for a second?"

"Pardon?"

Matt had lifted the window upright and was watching her, waiting. She jumped up.

"Sorry!"

"If you could support this while I try the sashes. Just lean into its weight. It's not heavy that way."

Ally held the frame straight while Matt worked on the other side. She watched him through the glass. He was broad-shouldered, and his stomach was impressively flat. The muscles in his arms flexed as he slid the sashes up and down.

"How old are you?" she asked suddenly.

He looked at her through the glass, shaking his head. "You and your questions! What would you say if I asked you your age?"

"I'd tell you I was thirty-four."

He smiled. "Fair enough. I'm forty-two."

"You're in good shape for your age."

"See, when you add 'for your age,' it kind of undermines the compliment."

"Do you work out?"

He crouched down, adjusting the length of the sash cord. "Oh sure."

"How often?"

"Five or six days a week."

"Really? How long each day?"

He looked up at her, "Oh, probably seven hours a day."

"You're having me on!"

He stood up, grinning. "I don't need to go to a gym. I pick up heavy stuff all day, climb ladders, hammer. That's all the workout I need."

Ally thought about Bryce and all the money he spent on gym membership. "You don't do anything else, really?"

He shook his head. "Except ride a horse occasionally, if that counts."

Ally cringed. The Man from bloody Snowy River indeed. Meg would have a field day.

Matt was securing the last of the windows back in place while Ally collected up his gear and packed it into the truck. For the last hour a wall of dark cloud had been advancing from the south. The wind was building up, tossing the branches on the trees violently, cooling the heat from the ground. Ally felt the first large dollop of rain fall on her bare arms.

She let out a squeal. "It's starting to rain!"

"I'm done anyway," Matt announced, stepping down the ladder. He lifted it away from the wall and carried it to the truck.

The rain splatters came faster and faster until the sky opened and promptly fell on them. Ally squealed again, lowering her head as she went to run inside. She felt Matt's hand on her arm, holding her back.

"Where are you going?" He had to shout over the noise of the rain pelting on the tin roof of a nearby shed.

"Under cover."

"Why? It's been so hot, let the rain cool you off."

He still had hold of her arm. He was looking at her intently. Ally found it unnerving. She raised her face to the sky, closing her eyes. She could feel the rain soaking through her clothes, her hair. It did feel good, exhilarating even. When she opened her eyes, Matt was still watching her, smiling.

"My boots are getting wet," she declared, and dashed across to the verandah. Matt followed her and she handed him a towel from the laundry. They stood drying off, watching the rain fall. It was getting heavier by the minute.

"It's really set in now," said Matt. "It'll probably rain for the rest of the week."

Ally sighed. "Typical Southern Highlands. Wet one day, raining the next."

"It's not that bad."

"When I was growing up it felt like that. Every time it rained, the creek flooded and I had to stay home for days at a time. We couldn't get out."

"Most kids like any excuse to get out of school."

"Not when it's your only respite."

Matt paused. "I get the impression you didn't enjoy growing up here much."

"No, not much." Ally wanted to change the subject. "Can I get you a coffee, a beer maybe?"

"No, I'd better make tracks, get home before it's dark and check there's no water getting in anywhere."

Ally remembered her grandfather's drafty house, with gaps everywhere, and buckets placed haphazardly across the floor when it rained. "Leaks, huh?" she said knowingly.

He shook his head, "No, it's just that I've left windows open."

"Oh."

He handed her back the towel. "Well, thanks for all your help, Ally."

She shrugged. "It gave me something to do. It's a bit lonely wandering around here on my own."

"Sorry, I didn't think about that," said Matt. "Lillian will have my hide. I should have taken you up the road for a drink."

"That's okay." Ally suddenly felt a little shy of him.

"Do you want to get some dinner or something tonight?"

"No, please, don't worry about me. I think all I'll be good for tonight is a soak in a bath."

He nodded. "You're going to feel it in your muscles later."

"What do you mean later?" she grinned at him.

Matt smiled back. He seemed to be hesitating. "Well, I suppose I'll see you around."

Ally nodded. "Probably."

"Bye Alaska," he said, stepping off the verandah and back into the rain.

"Matt!" she scolded.
But he couldn't hear her over the rain.

Ally was aching from head to toe. She walked wearily up the stairs and turned the taps on in the bath, before peeling off her grimy clothes. As she leaned over the bath to test the water temperature, Ally caught sight of her naked body in the full-length mirror. She sighed, this was why she never kept a full-length mirror in the bathroom. It was always a shock to be confronted by her thirtysomething body. For some reason, Ally's mental picture of herself was as she was at seventeen. No wonder she was constantly disappointed.

She used to be so smug when she saw ads for cellulite treatments before she turned thirty. Then there was that particularly ugly evening, bingeing on fruit and nut chocolate and cooking sherry, after she'd seen the first hints of cottage cheese dimpling on her thighs. Meg complained that pregnancy had ruined her figure, but Ally insisted that it happened anyway. Everything went soft, and worse, headed south. She piled her hair into a loose bun on top of her head. There was another horror. Those loose bits under her arms. They were certainly not there when she was seventeen.

She stepped into the lukewarm bath, the weightlessness having an immediate soothing effect on her tired limbs. The effort involved in soaping her body proved too much. Ally sank lower into the deep bath and closed her eyes. She could feel herself drifting off. She'd heard that drowning was a very relaxing way to go, though how the ubiquitous "they" knew that, she had to wonder. Ally started to daydream, imagining Matt arriving at the house tomorrow, calling her name, then walking up the stairs to find her floating, blue and lifeless, like a baby whale in the bath.

Then she remembered he wouldn't be coming tomorrow. She sighed and dragged herself up out of the water.

The next day

Ally hadn't set the alarm clock, but she woke around seven anyway. She lay in bed looking out the window at the dull sky. The rain was still falling, but not as heavily as last night. It was depressing. It brought back too many memories of endless days trapped at the house, with nowhere to escape but into a book.

The air was cooler today Ally discovered as she stepped out onto the verandah with her morning cup of tea. She had automatically taken two cups out of the cupboard before she remembered she was alone. She went back inside, rinsed her cup and the plate she had used for toast and stacked them to drain. She put the milk back into the fridge. There, her chores were done for the day. Now what?

The phone rang, saving her from making that decision for the moment.

"Hello Ally?" a deep voice asked when she picked up the phone. "It's Matt."

How many men did he think she had ringing her? "Hi Matt."

"How are you feeling today?"

"I'm alright," she said tentatively.

"Your muscles aren't suffering too much?"

"Oh," she said, realizing what he meant. "Not yet, I rubbed a lot of that mentholated stuff in last night."

"At least you'll get to rest today."

"Mm," said Ally, hoping he didn't sense her despondency.

"Listen, I'll be coming up to town later on, so can I take you for that drink, or even for a meal?"

Ally held her breath. Why couldn't she speak?

"Ally?"

"Sorry Matt, I was just thinking. I have to wait for a phone call from Lillian."

"Gee, that's worse than saying you have to wash your hair."

"But it's true! She's calling to let me know what train she'll be on to-morrow. I have to pick her up from the station."

"When do you expect her to call?"

"I'm not sure."

There was a pause.

"I tell you what," said Matt, "why don't I give you my mobile number, and then, after she calls, you can phone me?"

"Okay, but I don't know what time it will be," Ally said, trying not to sound negative.

"That doesn't matter."

She jotted his number on the message pad as he dictated.

"So you'll call?"

"Sure, I'll talk to you later."

"Bye."

Ally hung up the phone and stared at the numbers she had just written on the pad. What the hell was wrong with her? Why couldn't she just accept a simple invitation to go out for a drink? She was over Bryce, wasn't she?

"You are over Bryce, aren't you, or aren't you?" Meg asked when Ally phoned her later.

"Yes!" Ally insisted. "It's not that, I don't think."

" 'Cause he's been ringing me, you know, driving me bananas."

"You're kidding, what does he want?"

"Oh, he keeps whining about you leaving your mobile off and that he can't get in touch with you."

Ally sighed. "I haven't had it on since I came down here. I didn't want him bothering me."

"Well, could you arrange to have him stop bothering me?"

"Sorry, Meg. I'll talk to him."

Beeps came onto the line. "That's your call waiting signal," said Meg.

"Is it? Don't worry, I usually ignore it. I think it's rude."

"Ally! This is a business line. Look, all you do is press—"

"There. It's stopped. And I wouldn't have answered it anyway."

"How can you stand it? It could be anybody on the other line."

"If it's important, they'll call back."

"But what if they don't? You might miss something that could change your life forever."

Ally frowned. "Yeah, like a pay TV salesman. Besides, you should stay with the original call," she explained. "It's common courtesy. I always feel second best when the person I'm talking to takes the other call, especially when they come back to you and say, 'Sorry, got to go.' I don't need that kind of rejection."

"Al, pull yourself together. It's only a phone call," said Meg dryly. "So tell me about this guy?"

"He's not a "guy!' Ally winced.

"What do you mean? What is he, a horse?"

"No, I mean, well, he's just a friend, a friend of Lillian's. And of mine, I guess. Well now he is, you know, a friend of mine. More than an acquaintance. Yes, I'd call him a friend."

"You're rambling."

"I'm not."

"What's he look like?"

"That's not the issue."

"Is he ugly?"

"No!"

"Is he thick?"

"I don't think so."

"Does he smell bad?"

"You're being ridiculous."

"I'm just trying to work out what's stopping you from going out with him."

Ally paused. "I just feel a bit uneasy around him."

"Why, do you think he might be an axe murderer?"

"No!"

"Then what is it?"

"I guess, it's just, well, he reminds me a bit of my grandfather."

"What, he looks like your grandfather?" Meg exclaimed.

"No, not at all."

"Then what is your problem?"

"He's like my grandfather in other ways. He lives out of town on a property, alone, in an unfinished house. It just feels like my childhood revisited."

"Ally, he's asked you out for a drink, not for your hand in marriage. He could live in a frigging treehouse. You can still have a drink with him."

"I guess you're right."

"And you might even get laid if you're lucky."

"Meg!"

"Oh, don't be such a prude. As if you never had sex with anyone before Bryce. God, you're so stitched up since you've been with him, you don't know how to relax and have a good time anymore."

Ally released an audible sigh.

"Now, will you ring him?"

"Okay."

"As soon as you get off the phone from me?"

She hesitated.

"Ally!"

"Okay, I'll ring him as soon as I get off the phone from you."

"You'd better, and I expect a full report next time we speak."

Meg put down the receiver as Simon appeared at the door of her office.

"Coming to the Carlton launch tonight?" he asked.

"Yes, I'm your date. We can't get a babysitter." She hadn't actually tried, and no doubt Chris's mother would have been willing, but she felt a night apart might do them some good. A product launch was hardly the most exciting prospect. But it was at the MCA. And they always served good champagne.

"Do you want me to pick you up?"

"It's okay, I can get a cab."

"I'll pick you up. Seven-thirty?"

"You're a sweetheart. But the launch doesn't start till eight."

"Yes, but by the time we drive in to town, park—"

"We'll be exactly on time!" Meg finished. "You're so *not* cool, Simon. You let your team down."

"My team?" he frowned, then rolled his eyes. "Oh, of course. The gay fraternity. Where everybody thinks and acts alike, and it's Mardi Gras every night of the year." He shook his head, turning to leave. "Don't forget it's black tie."

"But I don't have a black tie," Meg called after him as he walked off down the corridor.

Nine p.m.

"Why won't you dance with me?" Meg whined.

"Because you'll embarrass me."

"I promise I won't."

Simon considered her skeptically. "That's what you always say, and you start off fine, then as soon as the tempo picks up, you start jumping all over the place like an orangutan in heat."

Meg frowned. "That's not very flattering."

"My point exactly."

"You're not much of a date. Chris always dances with me."

"Then you should have brought him." He paused. "By the way, why didn't you? Is he finally getting sick of being dragged to your work functions?"

"No." Chris would go anywhere with Meg. He never complained like the other spouses did. "We couldn't get a sitter, I told you."

Meg sipped her champagne, avoiding eye contact with Simon. He could always see right through her, and he was using his X-ray vision on her now.

"You've never had any problem getting babysitters before. I thought Chris's mother was permanently on call?"

Meg shrugged absently, looking around the room. "Oh look, there's that actress who just had the boob job. I read it in *Who Weekly*."

"Is everything alright with you and Chris?"

"Omigod!" Meg breathed, looking wide-eyed over Simon's shoulder.

"What?" he said, turning around.

Meg yanked at the sleeve of his jacket. "No! Don't look now, he's watching. Did you know he was coming? Who would have invited him?"

"Who?" Simon went to turn around again, but Meg took hold of his arm firmly.

"Not now!"

"Meg, how can I tell you anything if you don't let me see who you're talking about?"

"Okay, but don't make it obvious."

Simon shook his head, clearly exasperated. He turned around slowly and scanned the room. Meg stood beside him. "He's over there, in the tux."

"You're not serious."

"What?"

"Meg, every man in the room is wearing a tux."

"Sorry. He's standing by the bar, blond hair." A smile played around Meg's lips. "He looks a bit like Brad Pitt, don't you reckon?"

Simon was squinting. "Oh, yes, I see what you mean. If the lights were dimmed, to a short-sighted person, he might bear a vague resemblance."

Meg dug him in the ribs. "Don't you think he's good-looking?"

"He's a bit scruffy. He needs a shave and a decent haircut if you ask me."

"Of course, but that's because your kind prefer 'thin and neat.' "

"Oh, here she goes again," Simon frowned. "What's with the blatant stereotyping lately, Meg?"

But Meg wasn't listening to him. "Shh! He's coming this way!" She swung around in front of Simon. "Just talk normally."

"What, pretend you're not a complete fruitcake?"

Meg affected a laugh. "Oh, is that right, Simon?" she said loudly, adding in a whisper, "Is he still coming?"

There was a twinkle in Simon's eyes. "He is! He's getting warmer. Warmer. Hot even! The excitement is building. I don't think I can stand it!"

"Stop it!" she said under her breath.

"Is that you, Meg?"

She froze, staring up at Simon. She could see the bafflement on his face. She took a calming breath and turned around slowly.

"Hi," she said demurely. "Jamie, wasn't it?"

"That's right. Good to see you again."

"And you."

Meg had almost forgotten how good-looking he was. The shaggy hair and the stubble on his chin made him seem free and unfettered. She found that incredibly appealing. And tonight, in a suit, he was positively edible.

Simon cleared his throat.

"Oh, Jamie, have you met Simon Ridgeway? He's the creative director at *Imagine!*."

They shook hands.

"Jamie Carroll," he added. "I met Meg at the Tusk shoot before Christmas."

Simon nodded. "Oh right. I must have seen your name on the schedule. You Tarzan?" he quipped.

Meg winced. Jamie smiled politely.

"What brings you here?" asked Meg, curious.

Jamie shrugged. "The agency sends us to these things. I don't mind. There's free food, and they provide the suit."

Mm, they ought to be congratulated.

"I just came over to ask if you wanted to dance? That's if I'm not interrupting anything?"

"Not at all," Meg assured him. "I was just complaining because Simon won't dance with me."

"Well, if it's okay . . ." Jamie glanced at Simon.

"Go right ahead. I've got schmoozing to do."

Meg realized the music had turned decidedly sultry. Good. If she was only getting a dance, she'd rather it was a slow one. And besides, she still had Simon's orangutan comment ringing in her ears.

Jamie took her in his arms, and they started to sway to the music.

"He's not your husband, Simon?"

Meg laughed. "No! He's my boss, and my friend. And he's gay."

"Oh," Jamie nodded. "Where's your husband then?"

"At home, on babysitting duty."

"He must be very easygoing."

"Why do you say that?"

"Well, if you were mine," he murmured, pulling her closer, "I wouldn't let you out of my sight, looking the way you do tonight."

"Oh, wouldn't you?" Meg said, arching an eyebrow. "You'd actually think you owned me?"

Jamie smiled slowly. "Bad choice of words. I wouldn't try to own you, Meg. I might even try to set you free."

He was gazing unblinking into her eyes, and Meg had to look away. Their bodies pressed against each other, moving to the rhythm of the music. She could feel his hand on her back through the thin fabric of her dress. Her skin prickled, and she felt hot all of a sudden. She stared at his lips, and then closed her eyes. She imagined what it would be like to kiss him. Whoa! She opened her eyes again, startled. Where did that come from?

"Penny for your thoughts," Jamie murmured.

Meg swallowed, avoiding his gaze. She had the feeling that he knew exactly what she'd been thinking.

The music stopped but Jamie didn't let go of her.

"Let's get a drink," Meg blurted, pulling away.

She walked a little unsteadily over to the bar and asked for a champagne, though she felt like something stronger. Jamie ordered a club soda.

"Are you driving?" Meg asked.

He shook his head. "I don't drink."

"You had a beer at the pub the other day."

"Oh, I have the odd drink," he said. "Let's just say that alcohol is not my drug of choice."

Meg almost snatched the glass from the waiter and took a few gulps. "Well, you don't know what you're missing."

He smiled at her. "I'd rather get my kicks in other ways."

"Such as?"

"Jumping off a cliff beats a stiff drink any day."

"Yeah right," Meg pulled a face. "Until you hit the bottom!"

"Well, maybe not jumping exactly. I meant rappelling, paragliding, bungee jumping . . ."

"You've been bungee jumping?"

"I have."

"You have to be crazy!" Meg declared, shaking her head.

"No you don't."

"Well what would possess a sane person to tie a rubber band around their ankles and leap off a tall structure?"

"I didn't leap off a tall structure."

She raised an eyebrow. "Okay, I'll bite. What did you leap off?"

"I jumped out of a helicopter."

"You did not!"

"I did!"

Meg considered him for a moment. "So, you're actually trying to kill yourself?"

"There's more chance of getting killed driving a car."

"Oh I get sick of hearing that argument," Meg groaned. "Here's the thing. You need a car in the society we live in, especially when you have a baby, just to get on with normal, day to day life. And yes, there's a risk, but you take every possible precaution—"

"Don't tell me, you drive a Volvo?"

"I do, as a matter of fact, and I've heard every single joke so you needn't bother repeating any," said Meg airily. "As I was saying, you need a car to get on with normal life. You don't need to fling yourself off mountains or out of airplanes."

"Except to have fun," Jamie suggested.

"I'd rather play Scrabble."

He laughed out loud. "Wow, that's living on the edge."

"I just don't need that kind of thrill."

"How do you know if you don't try?"

She looked at him. "I just know."

He leaned against the bar, scrutinising her.

"What?" Meg said.

"Well, you realize you've given me a challenge now."

"What do you mean?"

"I've got to get you over this irrational fear."

"It's not irrational!" Meg insisted. "It's sensible, life-preserving—"

"Fear."

She sipped her champagne. "Personally, I've always felt that fear is very underrated. If we didn't feel fear, early man would have jumped off cliffs willy-nilly, walked right up to woolly mammoths and done a lot of other foolhardy things. And we would have become extinct as a species. But we had fear," she went on, warming to her topic. "And we invented seat belts, and helmets and insurance policies and we survived! And thus we mastered the planet!"

Jamie looked momentarily startled, before bursting into laughter. "You're a funny chick," he said.

Meg hadn't been called a "chick" in a long time, and she decided she didn't mind at all.

"So, do you eat lunch?" Jamie asked.

"Pardon?"

"Is there time for busy advertising executives to eat lunch?"

Meg shrugged. "Usually."

"Will you have time next week?"

"Why, what are you suggesting?"

"Maybe we could have lunch one day."

She paused, trying to quell the urge to say yes immediately. "Have you forgotten I'm married?"

"Don't married people eat? Besides," he said, leaning toward her, "I thought nobody owned you?"

She considered him suspiciously. "They don't. But how do I know you're not going to whisk me away to some secret location and make me jump out of an airplane before you bring me back?"

He laughed. "I won't do that to you. Promise," he said, one hand on his heart. "So, how about it?"

Meg hesitated. This was dangerous, she knew it. She should say no. "What day did you have in mind?"

He shrugged. "This is next week we're talking about. I don't even know what I'm doing tomorrow."

Meg sighed. She knew what she was doing not just next week, but for the whole month. And most of next month.

"I'll call you, okay?" He was smiling at her. Those eyes. Penetrating. Just say no.

"Okay."

Saturday

The rain had cleared, thankfully, and Ally stood on the platform at Bowral Station under a cloudless sky, waiting for Lillian's train. She had woken with a start at ten last night, curled up on a settee in the conservatory. She'd tried to call Matt earlier, but he was out of range, probably holed up in his mountain shack, she'd decided grimly. She didn't call him again, and it was too late at ten o'clock. So that was the end of that.

Lillian looked tired when she stepped onto the platform. It was a long trip by rail, but apparently she couldn't be persuaded to take a plane, she hated flying. Ally rushed over to her when she saw her trying to lift her suitcase.

"I've got it, Lillian," she said, before heaving it onto the luggage trolley. "What on earth have you got in here?"

"Half my wardrobe, dear. Melbourne," she rolled her eyes, "has no regard for the seasons."

They started to walk back along the platform toward the exit.

"How was your trip?"

"Alright, it was alright," she replied. "Let me look at you."

Ally turned to face her.

"Have you lost some weight?"

"I'm not sure."

"You are eating properly, aren't you?"

"Of course. Thanks for leaving me all that food."

"I only hope you ate enough of it. You're not heartbroken, are you?"

"No," Ally frowned. "Why should I be?"

"Didn't you just break up with your long-time boyfriend?"

She reddened. "Yes, of course. Don't worry about me, Lillian, it was quite amicable and civilized, I'm fine."

Ally didn't like the way Lillian was looking. She was noticeably pale, and the walk to the car left her a little breathless. Ally pulled up in front of the house when they arrived home. She didn't want Lillian to have to walk any farther than was necessary.

"I'm getting the royal treatment today," Lillian remarked.

"It's only because I don't want to have to carry that thumping big bag of yours any farther than I have to!"

They went inside, and Ally watched Lillian gaze fondly around the place.

"If you don't mind, Ally, I might just rest in my room for a while," she said. "You know how no bed is quite like your own?"

Ally wandered thoughtfully back out to the car. She hoped Lillian was alright. She knew she wouldn't want to be fussed over, but Ally decided she'd keep a close eye on her over the next few days, to make sure she wasn't overdoing it. She was probably just tired from a long trip, it was nothing unusual.

Ally contemplated the suitcase wedged firmly into the compact boot of the Laser. She started to heave and pull and generally wrestle with it, until she had it balanced on the edge of the boot. Now how was she going to get it up the stairs and into the house?

She remembered Matt carrying things on his back, and thought that was probably the safest bet. She crouched down and backed up to where the bag rested, levering herself underneath it, and taking the weight of it as she straightened up again. Ally could feel every kilogram as she started to climb the steps. She thought she was going to have to settle it down some-where when suddenly it was lifted off her back. She turned abruptly.

"You looked as though you needed a hand."

She peered up, way up, at a very tall man with ruffled sandy hair and a serious expression.

"Oh, thanks," she said, flustered. "It was a bit heavier than I realized."

"Obviously." He set the bag down and looked at her calmly, but Ally detected a glint of curiosity in his eyes. Who was he anyway? And what was he doing here? The guesthouse was not opened for business until Wednesday.

"Can I help you?" she asked.

"I was just about to ask you the same thing."

Ally frowned. "My name is Ally Tasker. I'm a friend of the owner."

"Of course," he said, picking up the suitcase again. "I should have re-alized."

He started to walk up the stairs, past where Ally stood watching him, and toward the front door.

"Hold on," she cried. "And you are?"

"Rob," he said simply as he opened the door and walked through into the foyer. Ally ran up the stairs and followed him in, closing the door behind her.

"Rob . . . ?"

He turned around to look at her. "Rob Grady, I'm the chef. Where do you want this?"

"The chef!" Ally repeated, feeling stupid. "Oh, it's Lillian's suitcase."

"I'll put it in her room, then?"

"No, she's having a rest. I think it's best not to disturb her."

He didn't say anything, he just walked down the hall and left it beside the door to Lillian's rooms. He came back into the foyer.

"Can I help you with anything?" Ally said weakly.

She thought one eyebrow lifted slightly. "No, I'm fine, I know my way around."

He crossed to the reception desk and flicked over a few pages in the register, jotting notes on a pad. Ally wondered what he was doing, but he didn't seem the type for small talk.

"I'll be in the office if anyone is looking for me."

She nodded. Just then the phone started to ring. Ally dashed to answer it, not wanting Lillian to be disturbed. "I'll get it!"

She thought she saw his eyebrow lift again as he walked off in the direction of the office.

"Hello, Birchgrove. Can I help you?"

"Yes, it's Richard Ellyard here. Could I speak to Mrs. Ellyard please?"

"Oh hello, Richard. It's Ally."

"Sorry, Ally, I'm never sure who my mother has working there, I wasn't expecting you to answer the phone."

"That's okay."

"I was just ringing to see if she arrived home alright."

Ally was tempted to tell him of her concerns, but Lillian wouldn't appreciate her blabbing to Richard.

"She was fine, just a little tired. She's having a rest now."

"Oh? Are you sure she's alright?"

"Yes, of course. I could check to see if she's awake?"

"No, no, don't bother her. Just ask her to call me later."

Ally walked out into the kitchen to make a cup of coffee. She thought she could hear someone out in the pantry, and stuck her head around the door to investigate. It was Rob.

"Sorry," she mumbled, embarrassed. She turned around back into the kitchen.

A moment later he appeared at the doorway. "No need to apologize."

Ally looked at him and smiled awkwardly. Her eyes traveled to the notebook he was holding.

"I'm just doing the ordering," he explained. "The first of the guests arrive Wednesday."

Ally nodded. "I'm making coffee. Can I get you one?"

"No thanks."

He turned and stepped back into the pantry. So, that was the extent of his conversational skills. Ally sighed, pouring the water into the coffee plunger.

"Are you making coffee, Ally?"

"Lillian, you're up! That wasn't a very long rest."

"I only needed a short nap. I feel fine."

Ally thought that maybe she did look a little better, though she was still pale.

"Hello Lillian."

"Robert, I thought I could hear your voice," Lillian smiled at him as he came into the room. "Now sit and have a cup of coffee with us. You've met Ally, I take it?"

He nodded. "How are you, Lillian? How was your trip?"

Ally opened the cupboard to get extra cups. She noticed a slight smile on Rob's lips as he listened to Lillian, and what do you know? His face didn't even crack.

Ally sat next to Lillian, opposite Rob, and poured the coffee. She pushed a mug over toward him, and he nodded slightly, barely acknowledging her.

"How is Nicola, Robert?" Lillian was asking.

He shrugged. "Fine, last I heard."

"So she's not coming back any sooner?"

"Why would she do that?"

"I can't imagine," said Lillian, winking at Ally. "So, we'll have to get by without her for another three weeks?"

"Looks like it."

"Then I'll have to contact the agency. Gail is away for a couple of weeks as well, I believe. And besides, it's school holidays, she can't take on all of Nicola's shifts with the children home."

"I could help out," Ally offered.

Lillian glanced at her. "I wasn't saying any of this for your benefit, Ally. You are my guest."

"But I'd like to, really. I've been getting so bored. I'll go stir crazy if I don't have something to keep me busy."

"But you have to sort out about the property. That's why you're here, after all."

"That's nothing. I'll call the real estate agent later and make an appointment."

Lillian paused and considered her for a moment. "Ally, it's your holiday, you need to have a break."

"What do they say, 'a change is as good as a holiday?' " Ally insisted. "Please, Lillian, you'd be doing me a favor."

"Do you have any experience?" Rob interrupted.

Ally looked squarely at him. "No, I don't. But there are a few days yet. Lillian can show me the ropes."

"Still, you'll need someone experienced with you at first," he remarked, matter-of-factly. "Lillian, we could call Michelle."

"Good idea, Robert," she agreed. "That's if you're sure you don't mind, Ally?"

"Who's Michelle?"

"She's a local, a potter. She's always happy to earn a bit of extra cash. If she's available for a few nights, to get us over the weekend, I think you might manage after that, until Gail's back."

"I'd love the chance, Lillian. Really, I'd much rather keep busy."

Rob stood up and took his cup to the sink to rinse it. "I'll phone in the orders now, Lillian," he said. "See you on Tuesday, Ally."

Ally was slightly taken aback that he had addressed her directly. "Okay." She turned back to Lillian after he had left the room. "Is he quiet, or is it just that he doesn't like me?"

Lillian smiled. "Why, Ally, he doesn't even know you! You were always a little sensitive."

Ally frowned. She was sensitive?

"Oh, before I forget, Richard rang. He wanted you to call him once you were up."

"So that means he knows I was resting?" Lillian pulled a face. "I'd best go and face the inquisition." She stood up from the bench and picked up her cup.

"No," Ally said. "Let me get that."

"Starting already? Are you sure you don't mind helping out?"

"Of course not. I'll love it, really. I told you, you're doing me a favor."

Tuesday

Ally had called the real estate office on Saturday afternoon and arranged for an inspection of Circle's End. It turned out to be less than encouraging. The agent compiled a long list of the repairs he recommended, not so much to beautify the place but because prospective buyers would have trouble getting finance unless the minimum building regulations were met.

"Surely there must be a lot of properties around here that wouldn't pass council requirements?" Ally asked him.

"Of course. It's only if you want to sell that it becomes an issue," he agreed. "Do you know a builder? If not, I can arrange to have some quotes done for you."

Ally thought for a moment. "Only Matt Serrano. I met him at Lillian's."

"Oh, he wouldn't touch a job like this."

"No?"

"Matt's a specialist, he doesn't need to get his hands dirty on this kind of work. Besides, he doesn't come cheap, and you'd probably have to wait six months to get him."

"Really?"

He nodded. "Matt's out of your league. You want someone cheap and cheerful, who knows the building code. Do you want me to organize the quotes?"

Ally agreed, but she felt a little overwhelmed. She didn't have much in the way of savings, and her grandfather hadn't left her much either. She could probably scrape together a couple of thousand dollars, but she didn't think that would go far.

When she arrived back at Birchgrove, Ally saw Matt's truck parked out front and for some reason she felt nervous. She berated herself. He had obviously come to visit Lillian, and sure enough, she found them sitting together in the kitchen drinking tea. They both looked at her at the same time as she came through the doorway. She knew they must have been talking about her.

"We've just been talking about you," Lillian said.

Ally hoped she wasn't blushing.

"Oh?"

"Matthew was telling me about all the help you gave him with the windows. You didn't say a word about it, Ally."

"I'm sure he's making more of it than it was."

"Not at all. She's very capable," Matt remarked to Lillian. "I told her I'd subcontract her if she ever wanted to take it up seriously."

"I'm handy with a paintbrush," Ally dismissed. "It's going to take a lot more than a coat of paint to get Circle's End up to scratch."

"What did the agent say?" Lillian asked.

"Well apparently my grandfather ignored every building ordinance in existence, and then some," Ally sighed. "It's going to need a fair bit of work, just to make it, oh, what did he call it? You know, legal."

"Compliant?" Matt suggested.

She nodded. "Yes, that's it."

"I could go down and take a look if you like," he offered.

Ally thought about what the agent had told her. "No, that's okay."

"Let Matthew help, Ally," said Lillian. "He's the only carpenter I ever use."

"I'm sure Matt has enough to keep him busy, without wasting his considerable skills on an old shack," Ally insisted. "The agent is organizing some quotes, anyway."

Matt was looking at her, scrutinising her, Ally felt.

"Whatever you think," he said eventually. "I'll be away for a couple of weeks. I can look at it when I get back, if you want another opinion."

He was going away? Ally found herself wondering where, who with, why?

"Holiday or business?" she blurted, before realizing that she probably sounded nosy.

"Pardon?"

"You said you were going away."

"Oh," he smiled. "Holiday, up to Queensland."

Who with? She was dying to know. But instead she just said, "Lucky you."

"Will you still be here when I get back?" he asked.

"I'm locked in for January."

"Yes, I'm putting her to work," Lillian explained. "Not much of a holiday, I'm afraid."

"I told you I'd rather keep busy, Lillian."

"She usually renovates friends' houses in her holidays, she was telling me," Matt said. "I don't think she knows how to slow down."

"City living," Lillian remarked. "We'll see how she goes after a month in the Highlands."

Lillian and Ally stood on the verandah watching Matt's truck disappear up the drive.

"I wonder who he's going to Queensland with?" Ally said, she hoped nonchalantly. "Surely he wouldn't go so far alone?"

Lillian smiled. "Well, I suppose you should have asked Matthew that, while he was still here."

She turned and walked back into the house. Ally smiled, and followed her in.

Friday

Meg had not left the office for lunch all week. She had sat resolutely at her desk from twelve till two, until the hunger pains gnawed at her stomach and she'd dash up the road, grabbing something takeaway. As soon as she got back to the office she'd interrogate everyone to find out if there'd been any calls, any messages, anything.

She was getting a lot of strange looks.

When Jamie hadn't called by Wednesday, Meg went to Simon and offered to work the rest of the week, to make up for the public holidays over Christmas and New Year. Simon told her it was hardly necessary. It wasn't as though there was a lot of work on. Being the holiday season, there was never much happening in the way of new accounts, and they had met any urgent deadlines before Christmas.

"But I have staff on leave, so it's better if I'm here."

"Who's on leave?" Simon frowned.

"Um, whatsit, in animation, I think," she said vaguely.

He looked up at her, leaning back in his chair. He went to say something, but then must have thought better of it.

"Sure, Meg, do whatever you think."

She nodded and left his office without another word. She knew Simon was on the verge of having a talk with her. He'd been strangely quiet on the way home from the launch the other night, but she could see the concern in his eyes. He thought the world of Chris. He'd probably been mulling over what he should say, waiting, watching her, until he found the right time. Meg was going to avoid that for as long as she could.

She looked at her watch. Twelve-thirty. It was Friday. She was a fool. Some guy she hardly knows casually suggests lunch, and she changes her whole schedule around. She was like a teenager waiting by the phone in case "he" rang. Except she wasn't a teenager. She was closer to forty than thirty, and she was a wife and mother. What was wrong with her? Maybe she should go and throw herself in Simon's way after all, let him talk some sense into her.

"Is that you behind there, Meg?"

She jumped, startled. She was slumped in front of the computer, staring vacantly at the screen. And that was Jamie's voice.

"Hi," Meg said, peeking around the monitor.

"Hiya," Jamie smiled from the doorway. He was obviously fond of the torn T-shirt, oversized cargo pants look. "Is today a good day for lunch?"

"Well, it's the last chance this week. I thought you were going to call?" she tried to affect a casual-just-asking-no-inference-intended tone of voice. She didn't think she succeeded.

He shrugged. "I was in the area. So, are you free?"

Meg thought about saying no, for about one one-hundredth of a second. Jamie stood holding the top of the door frame, leaning forward. It made the muscles in his upper arms swell, and his shirt rode up, revealing a glimpse of tanned, taut stomach. Scruffy or not, Jamie Carroll was sex on legs. And Meg couldn't resist him.

"Sure."

A wall of heat hit them as they stepped out of the airconditioned building into the carpark.

"God, it's sweltering out here!" she exclaimed. "Are we going somewhere airconditioned?"

Jamie squinted up at the sky. He seemed to be thinking about something. "Is your car here?" he asked suddenly.

"My car? Sure, it's over there," Meg nodded, pointing across the carpark.

He grinned. "The Volvo."

"Take it or leave it."

"Okay, I know where we can go. Do you mind if I drive?"

Meg hesitated.

"It'll just be easier, I know the way."

"Um, sure," she started to fumble in her bag for the keys. She went to hand them to him, but stopped short.

"I have to ask, please don't be offended."

"What is it?"

"It's just the insurance." She took a breath. "You are over twenty-five?"

He laughed. "Of course I'm over twenty-five!" He walked around to the driver's side, shaking his head. Meg got in the passenger side. Right, now she knew he was over twenty-five. It would be nice to know by how much.

"Where are we going?" she asked as they took off out of the carpark.

"Surprise."

Meg frowned. "You're not taking me skydiving or anything?"

He grinned at her. "I told you I wouldn't do that, until you want to."

"Don't hold your breath."

They crossed the Harbor Bridge, and then continued on, past North Sydney, past St. Leonard's, past Chatswood. Where was he taking her? When they joined the Newcastle freeway Meg finally had to ask.

"It wouldn't be a surprise if I told you," he returned.

"Well, how long will it take?"

"Oh," he said, realizing. "You have to get back to work?"

"Well, that would be the expectation."

"Aren't you a boss or something?" he glanced at her.

"It doesn't mean I can just take off without telling anyone."

"Call in. Say you won't be back for the rest of the afternoon."

Meg looked at him warily.

"Go on," he said, casting her a sly smile. "I dare you."

She stared at the road ahead. Isn't this what she said she'd been missing?

Just being able to take off? But could she trust Jamie, she hardly knew him. If she was being brutally honest, she should really be asking if she could trust herself. Meg sighed loudly, she was a grown woman, for God's sake.

She took out her phone and pressed the auto dial number for work.

"Hi Donna? It's Meg. Look, I won't make it back to the office this afternoon. Okay? I don't think there was anything urgent. So, I'll see you Monday. Bye."

She snapped the phone shut. Jamie looked at her.

"Now, turn it off."

She bit her lip. "I don't know . . ."

"Live dangerously," he winked.

"I have to be back to pick up my little boy."

"What time?"

"Six—at the latest."

"Deal."

She switched off her phone and put it away.

Jamie turned off the freeway at Brooklyn and drove along a winding road until they reached a small village perched above the river.

"This is quaint," Meg remarked as Jamie pulled over and turned off the engine.

He smiled at her. "Don't use the Q word in front of John and Libby."

"Who are they?"

"Come on, I'll introduce you."

They got out of the car and walked across the street into a small café-cum-restaurant. There was no one seated at the tables, the place looked deserted.

"Just a minute," Jamie said, crossing to a staircase. "Libby, John?" he called.

"Is that—?" Meg heard a muffled cry from the floor above, and then footsteps. A woman appeared hurrying down the stairs and almost leaped from the last step, throwing her arms around Jamie.

He returned her embrace. "Hi Libby, it's good to see you."

She leaned back looking at him. "When did you get back?"

"Oh, a month or so ago."

"Shame on you! And it's taken you this long to come and see us?" She turned, noticing Meg for the first time. "Oh hello. I'm Libby."

"This is Meg," Jamie announced as Libby crossed the room, offering her hand to Meg. She was probably in her late forties, with long gray hair held in a loose plait. She wore dangling earrings, and strings of beads around her neck and wrists, a swirling tie-dyed skirt and a purple singlet with no bra. Her face was a bit weatherbeaten, but she had clear blue eyes and a warm smile. There was something about her that suggested calm.

"It's nice to meet you," she smiled warmly.

"Where's John?"

"Out on the boat. He probably won't be much longer. He'd die if he missed you. You'll stay and eat, won't you?"

"That's why we're here," said Jamie.

"What do you feel like?"

"Whatever you've got too much of."

"Okay, garbage guts, but what about your guest?" Libby admonished him. "What can I get you, Meg?"

She shook her head. "I'll eat anything that I don't have to cook."

Libby laughed. "Those are the words of a harassed housewife! Take Meg out onto the deck, Jamie. Would you like a glass of wine?"

"Not for me," said Jamie.

"I was asking Meg."

"If you're having one."

"Great!"

Libby disappeared into the kitchen and Jamie led Meg out onto the deck.

"This is beautiful!" she exclaimed. The deck appeared to jut out over the water, affording a view up the river until it curved out of sight. Angophoras edged the banks, their gray-green leaves reflected in the glassy water. The air was cooler here, the quiet only broken by the gentle lapping of the river against the pier.

"I thought you'd like it."

"It feels like we're a thousand miles away."

"That was the idea."

They sat on weathered timber chairs. Jamie pulled out a pouch of tobacco and proceeded to roll a cigarette.

"So, how do you know Libby and John?"

"Let's see, I met them . . . probably ten years ago, trekking in Nepal. Just after they dropped out."

"Dropped out?"

He nodded. "They used to be like you."

"Like me?"

Jamie shrugged. "You know, filo faxes and mobile phones and mortgages." He ran the cigarette paper along his tongue.

Is that what she was reduced to in his eyes? She watched him light his cigarette and draw back on it deeply. "So they dropped out."

"Just like that?"

"Just like that," he repeated slowly, holding her gaze.

Libby returned with a glass of wine and handed it to Meg.

"I was just telling Meg how you left it all behind for a better life."

"We did indeed."

"That was a brave step." Meg remarked.

"Not really, when you look at what we've gained," she said, gazing out over the river. "Ah, here comes John now. I'll get the food."

Jamie stood up and leaned over the railing, waving at the small tinnie making its way toward the jetty.

"Hey! Johnno!" he called.

The man looked up, shielding his eyes from the sun. "Is that you Jamie? I'll be buggered."

"How are you, old man?"

"Don't you 'old man' me! I bet I can still take you on!"

"Ah, you're all talk."

Libby carried out a huge platter of antipasto. "Jamie, there's a basket of bread and plates on the kitchen bench."

"This looks wonderful," said Meg.

"I thought you wouldn't want anything hot in this weather."

Jamie returned and set the plates down, passing the bread to Meg. John came through the doors from the restaurant.

"Jamie! Where have you been, you young bastard?"

The men shook hands and gave each other a hug, slapping each other on the back. John was a craggy-faced man with a big smile and twinkling eyes.

"Who's this beautiful woman?" he asked Jamie, looking at Meg.

"This is Meg, John."

He reached for her hand, enclosing it in his. "Well, you know Libby and I always say, any friend of Jamie's," he paused, "is someone who deserves all our sympathy."

Jamie slapped him on the back again.

Libby handed John a beer, "Sit down, let's eat."

"So what have you been up to, old son? How was India?" John asked, settling himself in a chair.

"Crowded."

John laughed. "So, it hasn't changed?"

Meg watched Jamie. His face lit up talking to the older man. John was probably old enough to be his father, and she got the distinct impression that was how Jamie considered him.

"So, Meg," said John eventually, "how do you two know each other?"

"I met her on a shoot, she works for an advertising agency."

"And the poor thing's a mute," John threw at Jamie. "You have to speak for her?"

He grinned. "Sorry. Go ahead, Meg."

Meg shrugged.

"What he said."

"So, you work in an advertising agency?"

She nodded.

"How long have you lasted there?"

"It'll be ten years in September."

John shook his head in disbelief. "That's perseverance."

"Oh enough, John!" Libby nudged him. "You were a stockbroker for twenty years before you gave it up."

"You were a stockbroker?" Meg remarked. "My husband is a futures trader."

As soon as the word "husband" passed her lips, Meg felt like she'd said the wrong thing. John and Libby exchanged a brief but meaningful glance. Jamie looked out over the water.

"So your husband's in futures. He's not burned out yet?"

Meg doubted that Chris would be the type to ever burn out. "Not so I've noticed."

"He's probably just growing a nice healthy ulcer on the quiet."

Meg leaned forward in her seat. "So tell me, Jamie said you up and left everything. How did you manage that?"

"We just did it," John shrugged.

"It wasn't quite as simple as that," Libby explained. "John had been ill. And every time he went back to work, he just got worse. We had to do something."

"When we looked at the amount we had saved," John continued, "and the equity in the house and whatnot, we realized we were sitting on a goldmine. Storing up all our wealth for some distant day when we'd retire. If I stayed alive that long!"

"So we sold up," said Libby. "It wasn't such a hard decision to make in the end." She looked at John fondly. "In fact it was the only decision we could have made."

"Is that when you bought this place?" Meg asked.

"Not right away," Libby said, refilling Meg's glass.

"We took off on an adventure first," said John, reaching for Libby's hand and grasping it firmly. "We traveled across Europe and Asia, staying in youth hostels—in our forties!" he laughed. "We had the time of our lives. We should have done it years before, but we were too busy building careers, slowly killing ourselves."

Meg sipped her wine thoughtfully.

"Have you done any traveling, Meg?"

She shook her head. "Only once overseas, just a short, organized tour."

Their honeymoon. Eighteen days. London–Paris plus a stopover in Bangkok for duty-free shopping on the way home. One of those "it's Tuesday today, this must be Notre Dame" trips. Most of it was spent on a plane.

"Make yourself a promise, Meg, that you'll get out and see the world while you're still young enough to enjoy it."

"Problem is, I've got a little boy now."

"How old is he, Meg?" Libby asked, interested.

"Not even two."

"Well, that shouldn't stop you," said John. "He's portable at this age. You can take him anywhere."

"I suppose so."

John looked at her. "But still she hesitates?"

"It's not just my little boy. There's the mortgage, the house, the job . . ."

"Think about it long enough Meg, and you'll come up with more excuses than you've got years left in your life. Get rid of the clutter, you'll breathe easier."

The afternoon passed in easy conversation. A cool breeze wafted up from the river, while the steep wall of the valley shaded them from the hot afternoon sun.

"Who would like coffee?" Libby asked after a while. She started to clear away the dishes and Meg jumped to her feet to help.

"Don't worry, Meg. Sit, take it easy."

"No, it's fine."

Meg followed Libby out to the kitchen. She started rinsing off plates while Libby made the coffee.

"I should apologize for my husband," Libby said.

"Why? He's terrific."

"Yes, but he has an almost religious fervor for our lifestyle."

"It's understandable though."

"Maybe, but he forgets sometimes that he didn't jump, he had to be pushed."

"Do you ever have regrets about not doing it sooner?"

Libby shook her head. "I try not to have regrets. Life takes you in many different directions, and you can learn from all of them."

Meg nodded wistfully.

"There's one thing I do regret, though, and the only thing I would change if I had my time over."

"What's that?"

"Not spending enough time with my children when they were little."

"How many did you have?"

"Just two. A son and a daughter. But I worked all through their childhood."

"I work three days a week."

"That's nothing," Libby dismissed. "I was putting in at least sixty hours every week, as well as bringing more work home on the weekends."

"What did you do?"

"I was a corporate lawyer." Libby laughed at the surprise on Meg's face. "I didn't dress like this then! It was another lifetime. We had a live-in nanny—she more or less raised the children. They seemed to grow up overnight. One minute you're tying shoelaces and the next they're asking for the keys to the car.

"I just wish I'd stopped and watched them more often." Libby paused. "I make sure I do that with my granddaughter now."

"You have grandchildren?"

"Just the one at the moment. Our son has a little girl, Sophie, she's nearly three. I can while away hours just watching her play. It's such a joy. Treasure it, Meg, it passes in a heartbeat."

"Don't be a stranger," Libby said as she hugged Jamie goodbye. She turned to Meg. "It was lovely meeting you, Meg, I hope we see you again."

John and Libby stood waving them off, their arms wrapped around each other.

"They seem happy," Meg commented as they drove away out of sight.

"That's because they are happy."

"Libby said John was ill. What was wrong with him?"

Jamie took a breath. "He had cancer. He probably still does. But he's been in remission for a long while."

He reached over and turned on the radio. Meg gathered he didn't feel like talking about it, and they drove on for a while in silence. There wasn't much traffic heading back into Sydney at this time of the afternoon, but northbound was a different matter. The other side of the freeway was clogged with commuters leaving the city behind them for the weekend. Possibly going to places like they'd just left. Meg felt as if she'd been away for a week. Which reminded her, she'd better check her messages.

Jamie glanced over as she pressed buttons on the phone.

"Sorry," said Meg. "I really should check in."

He shrugged. "It's your life."

A message came up on the screen from Chris.

Don't pick up Harry. Everything organized for tonight. See you at home.

Of course, it was Friday. Beano night. Meg sighed audibly.

"Everything alright?"

"Mm, I don't have to pick up Harrison after all."

"That's your boy?"

Meg nodded. "So, where do you need to be now?"

Jamie smiled. "Nowhere in particular."

"No, I mean to drop you off. Where are you living?"

"Bondi."

"Oh, we're just up the road, at Watsons Bay. How long have you lived in Bondi?"

"I'm just crashing at a friend's."

"How come?"

"I don't tend to take out leases, they tie me down."

Meg smiled. "I guess that's one way of looking at it."

When they drove into Bondi, Campbell Parade was clogged as usual. Jamie pulled the car over to the side of the road, double-parking.

"You right to jump across?"

Meg realized he was about to get out of the car. This was it. When would she see him again?

"You live here?"

"Up the road, but this'll do." A car honked its horn behind them. "I better go before you get hassled. See ya."

Meg sat shell-shocked for a moment, watching him disappear into the throng of people along the footpath. Then another honk made her jump. She climbed across into the driver's seat, and turned the key. It made that awful scraping sound, Jamie had obviously left the engine running. Meg released the handbrake and pulled out into the flow of traffic.

What was wrong with her? She was a married woman, for heaven's sake.

And she was feeling all wounded that he hadn't made another date with her.

So far she had done nothing wrong, and it was best to leave it that way. They were friends. It was no different to meeting a woman at work and getting to know her.

Who was she trying to kid?

Chris opened the front door as Meg was about to push her key into the lock.

"Hi, honey. I thought you'd be home sooner."

Meg swallowed guiltily as he bent to kiss her.

"Where's Harrison?" she asked, walking through into the hallway.

"He's at Mum's. Didn't you get my message?"

"Yes, I thought you were picking him up," she said vaguely.

"No, Mum's having him overnight. Don't you remember, we're going to the Tullys?"

Meg's face fell. "I forgot."

Frank Tully worked with Chris and was the most pretentious man Meg had ever encountered. He was only outdone by his wife, Andrea. If she was asked to pick the last people on earth she felt like seeing tonight, she would have chosen them.

"I thought you might have forgotten," Chris was saying. "I tried to ring you at work, and they said you wouldn't be back this afternoon, and then your mobile was off."

Meg held her breath. She looked up at Chris's face. Not a hint of suspicion. He wasn't even going to ask her where she'd been all afternoon. What a dear man. He was too good for her.

"What's the matter, Meg? You look winded."

She sighed. "I'm just tired."

"Why don't you go and have a bath?"

"But what time do we have to be there?"

He held her by the shoulders and turned her around in the direction of the bathroom. "You've got time to soak for ten minutes, it'll make you feel better."

Meg tested the water temperature and turned off the taps. It was still hot this evening so she kept the water barely lukewarm. She sank down to her shoulders and closed her eyes. There was a tap at the door and Chris appeared, drink in hand.

"I thought you could use this," he said, passing it to her.

Meg smiled up at him. "You're too good to me."

"Never too good."

She reached for his hand and pulled him down to kiss her.

"I love you," she said. "You know that, don't you?"

"I know," he smiled, settling himself on the side of the bath.

She considered him for a moment. "How was work?"

"Fine."

"No, really. How was work?"

"It was fine," he repeated. "Nothing out of the ordinary."

"Do you ever get tired, or stressed?"

"Why do you ask?"

She shrugged. "Well. It's just that you're in a very high-pressure environment. You should make sure you watch for signs of stress."

"Have you started a new campaign on workplace health and safety or something?" He grinned.

"No," she denied. "I just heard a story today about someone, a stockbroker, and anyway, he ended up with cancer—"

"Meg, I don't think a job can give you cancer."

"The thing is, he and his wife just sold up everything and took off around the world."

Chris looked blankly at her. "What's your point?"

She shrugged, staring at her glass. "I don't know."

"We're going to have to get on and plan that holiday, aren't we?" he said, leaning over to kiss her on the top of her head. He stood up. "Take your time. We've got half an hour before we have to leave," he said, walking out and closing the door behind him.

Meg complained of a headache and they left the Tullys before eleven, and not a moment too soon. The conversation had revolved around golf handicaps, new lamps for the living room, bathroom cleaner and interest rates. And they were the highlights. If someone had handed her a gun, Meg would happily have shot herself before she died of boredom.

She climbed into bed and snuggled back against Chris.

"Can we pick up Harrison early tomorrow?"

"You don't want to sleep in?"

"A little, but I miss him. I feel like I haven't seen him much this week."

"Okay, I'll call Mum in the morning. She'll have him ready."

Meg looked over her shoulder at him. "Maybe we could go somewhere all together then?"

"What did you have in mind?"

"Nothing special. Just the park, or the beach. Somewhere we can just watch him play."

Chris leaned forward and kissed her lightly on the lips. "Whatever makes you happy."

Late January

"Alaska!"

Ally turned around with a start. She was on the main road in the middle of Bowral, and she was sure she had just heard someone call Alaska. Maybe she was imagining it.

"Alaska!"

She looked across the road. Matt was waving frantically to attract her attention. She couldn't help smiling at him.

"You cannot be trusted, Matthew Serrano," Ally declared after he had crossed the road to join her.

"Why?"

"I told you my name in the strictest confidence and now you're blurting it out in public."

"Well, let me buy you a drink to make up for it."

Ally looked at her watch.

"Come on, you stood me up once already. My ego can't take another rejection."

Ally grinned. "Okay, maybe just one."

They started to walk up the street.

"I didn't stand you up, by the way," Ally said. "The truth is, I fell asleep that afternoon and didn't wake up till late."

"That's why you didn't hear me knocking?"

Ally eyed him curiously. "You came to the house?"

He nodded. "I realized my phone was out of range most of the day, so I came by, just in case you'd tried to call."

"I did try, earlier on."

"I'll just have to take your word for it," he winked.

He led her up to the Grand Brasserie and into the bar area.

"What would you like?"

"A glass of chardonnay, thanks."

Ally sat down at a table and watched Matt at the bar exchanging friendly chitchat with the barman. They obviously knew each other. Did he come here often? Was he usually on his own, or did he sometimes bring some-one? Maybe the someone he took to Queensland?

Okay, that was pathetic.

"When did you get back?" Ally asked when he brought their drinks to the table.

"Yesterday."

"How was it?"

"Good, thanks." He sipped his beer. "So, how do you like working at Birchgrove?"

Ally got the impression he didn't really want to talk about his holiday.

"I'm having a wonderful time."

"Is that right?"

She nodded. "I don't know if it's just the change of scenery. But it's so nice to deal with happy, relaxed adults all day, instead of smart alec, bored adolescents."

"So, what do you actually do?"

"Well, I was only supposed to be filling in for Nicola, in the restaurant. But I've been taking the morning shift as well, helping Evelyn with the breakfasts."

"That's a pretty full schedule, early morning into the night?"

Ally shrugged. "It's fine, really. I get afternoons to myself, and besides, I wanted to give Lillian a rest. She didn't recover all that well from the trip to Melbourne."

"Oh?"

She nodded. "She seems, I don't know, frail? I've never seen her like that before. She's always been so energetic, so capable."

"I guess it's harder to bounce back at her age."

"I'm trying to encourage her to sleep in for a while in the mornings, or at least not to get up and about so early."

"That's good of you."

"No, honestly, I'm enjoying myself," Ally insisted. "I didn't expect to. It'll make it all the harder to go back to teaching."

Matt was watching her intently. "So why don't you stay?"

Ally looked at him, startled. "I have a job back in Sydney."

"That you hate, as I recall."

"I don't exactly *hate* it."

"But you're not happy."

"Still, I have an obligation."

"To whom?"

"The school, of course."

"No offense, but I don't imagine they'd have a problem finding another teacher. And it is the start of the year, wouldn't that be the perfect time for a replacement to step in?"

Ally hesitated. She wasn't sure what to say. "You don't just get up and leave something on a whim."

"Why not?"

"Because you don't," Ally insisted. His attitude was annoying her. "Not if you're a responsible adult, at least."

He glared at her. "Oh, I see, so you're a responsible adult if you hate what you're doing but stick it out anyway?"

"I didn't say that."

"I've done that, I learned the hard way. Doing the 'right thing,' 'sticking it out,' because that's what's expected of you." He stared at his glass. "It doesn't get you anywhere in the end."

Ally wondered what he was talking about. There seemed to be a certain bitterness in his voice that she had never heard before. She decided not to push it.

"The thing is, I have no job here, nowhere to live."

"What about your grandfather's place? You could live there."

"Have you heard about hell freezing over any time soon?"

Matt grinned. She smiled back at him. The tension that had crept into the conversation had just excused itself for interrupting and crept quietly back out.

"So, where do you live in Sydney?" he asked.

"Um, well, I'm between places. I'll stay with friends when I go back, until I find something."

He looked at her curiously. Then he shook his head.

"What?"

"It doesn't seem like you're going back to much. You could rent just as easily down here."

"And how do I pay the rent?" Ally raised an eyebrow.

"Work at Birchgrove."

"I don't even know whether Lillian could afford to put me on."

"Then try another guesthouse, or a hotel. You said you like the work."

"But I don't have any qualifications, and barely any experience."

"Lillian would give you a recommendation. That would hold a lot of weight down here."

Ally sighed, staring at her glass.

"Or you could do relief teaching."

She pulled a face.

Matt smiled. "See, you really don't like it, do you? I can't imagine you wasting your life like that. Not when I've seen the way your eyes light up when you enjoy what you're doing."

Ally blushed. Her eyes lit up? He noticed?

"I could even give you some work."

"Doing what?" she frowned.

"Painting, I told you I can't get a good subbie down here. I reckon you could pick up quite a bit of work."

"Oh get real!"

"Why, what's wrong with that? Ally, you're young and single . . ."

"Not that young."

"Young enough that you can still make changes."

Ally sipped her wine slowly, thinking. This is what Meg had been on about. A total change of direction. But just quit teaching, and work as a waitress? Or a painter? That was ludicrous.

She sighed, looking across at Matt. He was smiling at her. Gosh he had a nice smile.

"Look, it's none of my business, Ally," he said abruptly. "I'm just playing the devil's advocate."

God, had he seen that dopey schoolgirl look in her eyes? She knew she was blushing. She seemed to blush all the time lately. Maybe there was an operation for that, some gland they could cut out or something.

Matt looked at his watch. "Are you working tonight?"

"Not till later on. Nicola arrived back a couple of days ago. Tonight's her first night on, so I won't have to start so early."

"Have you met her yet—Nic, I mean?"

Ally shook her head.

"She's good value, you'll like her," Matt grinned. "So, you've got time for another drink?"

"No, thanks. I had better be getting back."

"Are you sure?"

She nodded.

"I was on my way to visit Lillian anyway. I'll follow you."

His truck was parked over the other side of the shopping center, so Ally said she'd see him at Birchgrove. When she pulled up around the back of the guesthouse, the door flung open and a short, red-haired woman appeared, waving frantically.

Ally guessed it was Nicola. Was she just overenthusiastic, or was there something wrong? As Ally stepped out of the car, she rushed at her.

"Hi, it's you, isn't it? Ally?" she said in a distinctly English accent. "I've been waiting for you."

Ally hadn't imagined Nicola to be the nervy type. She ran the restaurant single-handedly many nights, according to Lillian. What was she so stressed about?

"There's been a bit of an accident."

"What do you mean?"

"It's Lil." She frowned, watching the color drain from Ally's face.

"What happened?"

"She's had a fall. Evidently she slipped on the tiles in the bathroom. I found her when I came in to set up today."

"What time was that?"

"Just after four."

She felt sick in the stomach. "Oh God, I left around three. She said she'd be fine."

"Well, of course she did! I'm sure she didn't expect this to happen," Nic exclaimed.

"I should have been here."

"You're not her nursemaid. Don't be blaming yourself for what was only an accident."

Ally took a breath. "I better go in and see how she is."

"She's not here, they've taken her to the hospital."

"What?" Ally almost shrieked.

"Calm down, you won't do anyone any good getting so worked up."

She was right. Ally took another deep breath, but she could feel herself trembling.

"Hi, Nic. How are you?" Matt appeared from around the corner of the house, walking toward them.

"Matt, I'm afraid we've had a bit of drama here," Nic explained.

He looked at Ally and frowned. "What's going on?"

"Lillian's in the hospital."

"What? Just now?"

"She had a fall, in the bathroom," Nic explained. "I had to call an ambulance, because she was in pain when we tried to move her."

"You don't think it's her back?"

Nic shook her head. "No, it was more likely her hip, maybe her leg. I hope she hasn't broken anything. They took her to the hospital for X-rays."

"I'll go," said Ally determinedly. "Hopefully she'll be allowed home later."

"Yes, you go. I can't leave here."

"Oh, what about the restaurant? You'll be on your own."

"It wouldn't be the first time. Besides, I can always call Gail or Michelle."

"Let me drive you," Matt offered. "You look a little shaken."

"Good idea," said Nic. "We don't need another accident in the household."

"I don't want to put you out," Ally said weakly.

Matt held her arm firmly at the elbow. "You're not putting me out." He walked her around to the passenger side of her car. "We'll take your car."

Ally was glad Matt was with her. She wouldn't have known her way around the hospital. She hadn't been here since Nan was ill, before she died.

She shivered. Nothing was going to happen to Lillian. It couldn't, not so soon after her grandfather. Ally felt a mixture of guilt and fear; guilt at staying away for so long, and fear that she was running out of time to make up for it.

"Are you okay?"

Matt must have been watching her biting her lip and frowning. They were sitting on a bench in a corridor of the hospital. Lillian was out of X-ray, and staff were settling her into a room.

Ally shrugged. "I'm just worried about her."

"She'll be okay, you know that. She's a tough old bird."

She smiled at him. "You wouldn't call her that to her face!"

The doctor came out of the room. Ally jumped up.

"How is she?"

"Fine," she smiled kindly. "Fortunately there were no fractures from the fall."

Ally breathed a sigh of relief.

"There is ligament damage, though. She's going to need physiotherapy."

"When will she be able to come home?"

"The nurse already explained to you that we're keeping her in overnight for observation?"

Ally nodded.

"Well, I'd like to run some tests tomorrow."

"What kind of tests?"

"She described feeling dizzy and disoriented just before her fall. Now, that's nothing unusual in an elderly person. But we'd like to check it out, just to make sure."

"Of course."

"Have there been any other episodes that you're aware of?"

Ally shook her head. "Nothing like this. She traveled to Melbourne by train for Christmas. She hasn't been quite herself since then."

"How do you mean?"

"Just more tired. She never really seemed to get over the trip."

"Well, it's best to give her a thorough checkup while she's here. Her records indicate she doesn't spend much time with her GP."

"That doesn't surprise me." Ally smiled. "Can I go in and see her now?"

"Sure, only for a minute though," she said. "She was experiencing quite a bit of pain, so we've had to give her something for that. She'll probably be a bit vague. Don't worry, it's only the medication."

Ally stepped quietly into the room. It was a shock to see Lillian lying there in a hospital bed. She looked old and frail, not unlike Nan the last time Ally had seen her. She swallowed hard. She couldn't let Lillian see she was upset.

She opened her eyes when Ally pulled a chair over next to the bed.

"Hello, Ally. What are you doing here? You should be helping Nicola tonight." Her voice was tired, and she spoke slowly, as though she had to think about each word.

"She's fine, Gail was coming in. I just wanted to make sure you were alright."

"I'm in a hospital, Ally, nothing much is going to happen to me here. Though I'm a bit dubious about that so-called 'doctor.' She looks about fifteen. I'm sure she's younger than Emily."

Ally smiled. She was certain the doctor she had just spoken to was older than Lillian's eighteen year old granddaughter.

"How are you feeling?"

"I have to admit, those drugs are not too bad. I feel warm inside, and the pain has stopped. It's like drinking red wine, only I hope I don't have a hangover in the morning."

Ally hesitated for a moment. "I was thinking I had better call . . ."

"No, don't do that." Lillian had closed her eyes again. Her speech was becoming a little slurred, but Ally could still understand her. "Don't ring Richard."

"But . . ."

"No buts." She opened her eyes and looked directly into Ally's. "Not for a day or two. Give me a chance to get my strength back before I have to deal with him."

"Lillian, I feel terrible, not letting him know."

She closed her eyes again. "Promise me, Ally."

"Okay," she sighed reluctantly. "I promise."

"She knows what she's doing, Ally, trust her," Matt tried to reassure her on the way home.

"Imagine when he finds out. He's going to hit the roof."

"Lillian will deal with him then, when she's feeling better."

"That's if she does get better. What if something happens, what if they find something when they run those tests?" A sob caught in Ally's throat. Damn, she didn't want to make a fool of herself and start crying in front of Matt. She pressed her fingers to her eyelids, forcing back the tears.

They had pulled into the guesthouse driveway, and Matt stopped the car along the row of birch trees.

"I'm alright, we should get back," Ally sniffed. "Nic might need some help."

"She would have called Gail by now," he said gently. "Just give yourself a minute. You don't want to walk in all upset. You'll set everybody off in a panic."

He was probably right. Ally breathed deeply, swallowing down the lump that sat stubbornly in her throat.

"I didn't realize you were so close to her," Matt said eventually.

"What?"

"I mean, it's just that I've known her for a few years and I've never met you before."

"What's that supposed to mean?"

"Nothing, Ally. It's just an observation."

Ally knew she hadn't been down here much. But she was close to Lillian, she could feel it. That's why she couldn't bear it if something happened to her now. She needed more time.

"I have visited her, often in fact, over the years. I'm sure she doesn't report all her comings and goings to you," Ally said curtly, trying to control the tremor in her voice.

"I didn't mean anything by it, Ally," Matt tried to reassure her. "Of course she means a lot to you. And on top of your grandfather dying, I'm sure this is all a bit much."

Oh God, now he was giving her pity. She couldn't stand it. Ally wasn't weepy anymore, just annoyed. "Can we go now, please?"

He didn't say anything as he drove the short distance down to the house, parking Ally's car out back. She jumped out as soon as it came to a stop.

"Ally!" he called as she started toward the house.

"What?" she turned around.

"Your keys," he said, holding them up.

She marched back toward him and snatched them out of his hand. "Thanks for the lift," she said brusquely, turning her back on him. "Pleasure," she heard him mutter as she walked into the house.

"Oh, here you are!" exclaimed Nic as Ally appeared in the kitchen door- way. "Is she alright? What's happening?"

Ally sighed. Rob turned around from the sink and looked at her expec- tantly. She'd have to go through it all again. She didn't feel like it now.

"Um, she's fine, no fractures, they're keeping her in for tests tomorrow," she said in a monotone.

Nic frowned at her. "Here, you could use a drink."

There was an open bottle of wine on the bench, and a half-empty glass. Nic grabbed another glass from the cupboard and poured one for Ally, then topped up her own.

"To Lillian's rapid recovery," said Nic, raising her glass. Ally could drink to that.

"What's been happening here?" she said, nodding toward the dining room. "Did you send everyone home?"

"No," Nic explained. "In all the panic, I'd forgotten it was a week night. We're only open for the guests, and there's barely anyone here. There's two couples in the dining room having port and coffee now, they'll be off upstairs soon."

"Well, that's a relief."

Nic looked at her closely. "Now that you've had a drink, tell me, is Lil alright?"

Ally nodded. She relayed the events to Nic in more detail while Rob hovered in the background.

Ally tried to put the two of them together in her mind. Rob was tall, very tall, and as somber as an undertaker. Nic was like a pocket-sized dy- namo. Surely she must only come up to Rob's waist? And she had so much energy, Ally got tired just listening to her. She had flaming red hair, an intentionally obvious dye job, and she wore it short, gelled to make it look like she had just got out of bed.

"I'll pop my head in and see if that last lot's finished," said Nic, after Ally had filled them in. "I'll give them a nudge if they're not!" she winked, disappearing through the door.

It was barely a second before she reappeared. "Yippee, they've gone! Girls' night! You go on upstairs, Ally, take your glass with you. I'll follow with the bottle in a minute."

Ally could already tell it was no use arguing with Nic. And she wasn't feeling all that tired anyway. She was worried about Lillian, and pissed off with Matt. Maybe a drink was just what she needed.

Ally kicked off her shoes once she got up to her room and looked around for a convenient place to rest her glass. She shrugged, draining it instead. She pulled out the scrunchie that held her hair back and rubbed her scalp with her fingers, freeing the curly locks till they stood out wildly from her head. Then she fell back on the bed and let out a deep sigh, staring up at the ceiling.

She shouldn't have snapped at Matt like that. But it was none of his business how long she'd known Lillian, or how often she'd visited. Ally was having enough trouble dealing with her own guilt, let alone having to explain herself to someone else.

Nic burst through the door with her arms laden. "Oh, you're not tired, are you? You can't go to bed now! I just got rid of Rob."

Ally grinned, sitting up. "I was only relaxing. How many bottles have you got there?"

"The rest of the one we were drinking, and some port!" she added wickedly. "Do you like port?"

"Is the Pope Polish?"

"My kind of drinking partner!" She started to unload her booty. "And I've got chocolate—real English Cadbury's, not that dead awful, waxy Australian stuff. But that's for later. I've got crisps for starters. Oh, I just remembered, you haven't had your dinner, have you? I'll run down and grab some leftovers."

"Take a breath, Nic!" Ally laughed. "These will do fine." She grabbed the bag of chips Nic had flung onto the bed and tore them open.

Nic refilled Ally's glass and one for herself and came over to the bed.

"Here, hold these while I climb up," she said to Ally, passing her the glasses. "They made these soddin' old beds bloody high, and people were shorter then!"

"Probably not shorter than you, Nic." Ally leaned over, giggling. She was already feeling the effect of the wine on an empty stomach.

Nic held up her glass again. "Let's drink to a good working relationship, even if it is only for another week."

"Mmm," Ally murmured, sipping her wine. St. Ambrose felt like it was a million miles away. "What's going to happen now, with Lillian out of action?"

Nic shrugged. "Haven't thought that far. Lucky we've got you here for the week. We'll have to organize someone in the meantime."

Ally swallowed a couple of mouthfuls of wine. "Or I could stay . . ."

"Could you?" Nic blinked at her. "But don't you teach or something? Won't you be expected back when school starts up?"

"I could probably organize some time off. I have long service leave owing."

"Really? That'd be brilliant. Lil would be so relieved."

"Do you think?"

"God yes. It would get her stuffy old son off her back," she exclaimed. "And she adores you. She was carrying on about you on the phone to me the other day. You're like a daughter to her."

Ally started to feel a bit weepy again. "Tell that to Matt!"

"What do you mean?"

"He couldn't understand why I was so upset tonight. He thought we hardly knew each other."

Nic shrugged. "What do men know?"

"Bugger all!" Ally declared, gulping down the remainder of her glass.

"I'll get the bottle," said Nic.

"No, I don't want you to fall!" Ally grinned, swinging her legs off the side of the bed. She walked across the room and picked up the bottle off the table, pouring herself another glass.

"So, what's going on with you and Matt?"

Ally swung around to look at her. "Nothing's going on. Why do you ask?"

Nic looked at her. "It seemed to me like there was something . . . going on."

"No thanks," Ally pulled a face.

"Why not?"

"He's not my type."

"Matt?" Nic frowned, holding out her glass for Ally to fill. "What's your problem? He's lush *as*!"

"You mean *luscious*?"

"No, you know, lush *as* . . ." she paused, considering. "I don't know, something or other that's luscious."

"Oh." Ally gulped down half of her glass. "There's only this little bit left in the bottle, you want it?"

Nic shook her head.

Ally drained the bottle into her glass. "Well, anyway, he's not."

"Not what?"

"Lush as, or luscious, or anything else."

"I think he's gorgeous."

Ally climbed languidly back onto the bed. "Oh, I guess, if you like that sort of handsome, rough-around-the-edges, macho type."

"And you don't? What would you rather? The ordinary, neat-as-a-pin wussy type?"

"You just described my last boyfriend exactly!"

They both burst into laughter. Ally hadn't had a drink or a real laugh since she was back in Sydney with Meg. Nic was good value, at least Matt had got that much right.

"So you and Rob are . . . ?" Ally asked tentatively.

"We are." Nic smiled.

"Has Rob said anything to you about me?"

Nic shook her head, frowning. "No, what do you mean?"

"I don't think he likes me."

"Why not?"

"Well, he doesn't say much . . ." Ally tried to explain.

"He's just shy," Nic dismissed. "Poor darling. He grew up in a family full of beefy, football-loving blokes, the youngest of four boys, and all he wanted to do was cook. You can imagine the ribbing he got. He learned pretty early to keep his head in. Once you get to know him, he's a teddy bear." She jumped up. "Time for the chocolate, I believe!"

Ally liked Nic unreservedly. And maybe Rob wasn't so bad after all. Perhaps she should stay on, help out for the next couple of months. It wasn't as though she actually had to resign. She could just take leave.

The morning after

"Here you go, love. Drink this up, it'll strip that woolly jumper off your tongue."

Ally opened her eyes, but the room was too bright. She squinted, focusing on the figure leaning above her. It was Nic, with a glass in her hand.

"Come on, sit up," she coaxed. "Now, drink this, it's only soda water."

Ally struggled to sit, but as soon as she was upright, her head started buzzing.

"Ohh," she groaned. "What did I drink last night? I thought there was only one bottle between us?"

"You're forgetting the port!"

"Ugh," she shuddered. She sipped from the glass Nic handed her. It was icy cold, and it did seem to penetrate through the furry coating on her tongue.

"You must think I'm a rotten drunk," she moaned.

"I was hoping so!" Nic exclaimed, a little too loudly for Ally's liking. "I've had nobody to go out with around here. They're all too sedate!"

"Well, you're going to have to at least *pretend* not to feel so well the next day, or I'll never drink with you again!"

"Darling, it was like this. You had the lion's share of the port last night. I hardly got to sniff the cork!"

Ally dropped her head onto her knees. But then she suddenly looked up, her eyes wide. "Shit, Evelyn and the breakfasts! What's the time?"

"Don't worry about any of that," Nic assured her. "Breakfast is well and truly over. I helped Evie this morning."

"Then I have to go and see Lillian."

"She's not expecting you till later. I've been in already."

"My God, what is the time?"

"It's half past eleven."

"I really have to get up!" Ally said, scrambling off the side of the bed. "I should visit Lillian, and there's so much to do today, with her not here."

"Ally, she was glad you were taking the morning off. She said you haven't had a morning free since you started."

Ally needed to sit down again as soon as she was upright.

"Are you alright?"

She nodded feebly.

"I think you're worn out. You're going to have to pace yourself, if you're staying on."

"Staying on?" Ally frowned.

"Yes," Nic looked warily at her. "Oh, don't tell me that was only the drink talking last night? Oh bollocks, and I've gone and told Lillian and all!"

"Calm down, don't worry," Ally sighed. "It's true, I was thinking about staying around. I guess I don't have to think about it anymore!" She smiled.

"Sorry."

"Don't apologize. Lillian needs me here now. I couldn't leave her anyway." Ally stood up again gingerly. "I'd like to go and see her."

"How are you feeling?"

She shrugged.

"Well, you go and have a shower, that will clear your head. And I'll get you some breakfast."

"Oh, I don't think I could eat."

"Nonsense, you have to eat. You've got the drunken hunger, you'll feel better with something in your stomach."

Ally arrived at the hospital feeling almost normal, if a little fragile. It was amazing the effect a shower, strong coffee and a plate of hot scrambled eggs could have on a hangover.

She had hoped Lillian would look better today, but she didn't. She looked like an old woman lying against the pillows. Her hair was lank and flat against her head, and her skin was pearly gray. Ally watched her stir. She fixed a smile on her face as Lillian opened her eyes and looked up at her.

"Oh hello, Ally! You shouldn't have rushed in."

"I've hardly rushed, Lillian. It'll be one o'clock soon."

"Nicola told me you stayed up late last night, getting to know each other."

"We did, and I slept in far too late as well."

"I'm glad. You haven't stopped since you got here, Ally. You'll be exhausted going back to Sydney."

Ally frowned. "Nic said she talked to you about me staying on for a while?"

"I couldn't ask you to do that." Her voice sounded like an old lady's voice. Ally had never noticed that before.

"But why not? I've been thinking about it anyway, Lillian."

"You're just saying that."

"You can ask Matt. We were talking about it only yesterday, before I even knew you were in hospital."

Lillian looked at her suspiciously. "You were?"

"Yes, I told him how much I've been enjoying the change here, and he was trying to talk me into staying."

Ally thought she saw Lillian's eyebrows lift slightly.

"Now, what about Richard?"

"What about him?"

Ally tried to sound firm. "Lillian, he's going to be absolutely furious when he finds out you've been in the hospital and he wasn't told. And I'll probably bear the brunt of it."

Lillian sighed. "Then I'll call him. I just wanted to have a little rest first."

"You've been so tired lately, Lillian. I've been worried about you."

"To be honest, Ally, I didn't really feel up to the trip to Melbourne this year. But if I'd said that to Richard he would have had me booked into specialists and God knows what. I just thought it was easier to go. I suppose it hasn't turned out that way."

Ally smiled reassuringly at her. "So what tests have they done so far, Lillian?"

"They've only taken blood. I'm to have an MRI this afternoon."

"That's like a CAT scan, isn't it?"

"Apparently so. They must want to see if my brain is still switched on."

"I'm sure they'll find that it is." Ally grinned.

Lillian reached out for her hand. "It's good to have you here, Ally. I want you to know that."

"It's good to be here."

"Are you sure about taking leave?"

"Absolutely. Honestly, I wasn't looking forward to going back, Lillian. This will give me a breather, time to think about my options."

"We're booked out solidly for another month at least, I'm not sure it's going to be much of a breather."

When Ally arrived back at Birchgrove, she found Nic stretched out on a settee in the conservatory.

"Hello, love!" she greeted Ally brightly. "Just putting my feet up before I get started for the night."

Ally smiled. "You don't have to make excuses to me."

"But you're the big boss lady now, aren't you?"

"No way, I'm not in charge."

"Well, someone has to be."

"We'll be in charge together."

"That'll never work."

"Then I'll be in charge if you tell me what I have to do."

Nic screwed up her face, thinking. "Right, then. Oh, by the way, your boyfriend brought these around." She indicated a large bunch of crimson roses, still in their cellophane, lying across one of the armchairs.

"Bryce was here?" Ally frowned.

"Who's Bryce?"

"Who brought these?"

"Matt, of course."

"*Matt?*"

Nic peered up at her. "Hey, your face has turned exactly the same color as the flowers."

Ally sat opposite her. "Mm, glandular problem," she murmured, staring at the roses. "Did he say anything?"

Nic swung her legs around and sat up. "Well, he wanted to speak to you, naturally. But I told him you were at the hospital. He thought about going there, only he didn't want to bother Lil, so I suggested he stay and wait for you, which he did, for a little while, but then I think he felt a bit naff, just sitting here waiting for you, holding a bunch of flowers."

Nic took a breath.

"Did he *say* anything?" Ally repeated, seriously wondering if he would have got a word in.

"He said that apparently he said something that upset you last night, and he didn't really know what it was, but he wanted to apologize anyway. I told him just as well, because you really had the shits with him."

"Nic!"

She looked at Ally innocently. "What's wrong? You did."

"But I didn't expect you to tell him!"

"And you said there was nothing going on," Nic scoffed.

"There isn't!"

"Then why did he bring you flowers?"

"I don't know. Because, um," she stammered, "to make up for what he said."

"To 'make up,' exactly. Sounds like something's going on to me." Nic folded her arms behind her head, grinning.

Ally stood, picking up the roses. "We are friends. That's all. I'm going to put these into some water."

Imagine! Boardroom

Meg sat staring across the room at the remnants of a sign from the building's factory days. She was playing a game of *Wheel of Fortune* with herself, trying to decipher the message. Some letters were missing, some were faded, some were just impossible to make out. For a while all she had was "lard tarts *something, something, something,* 11 limes." She had just realized it was "Hard hats must be worn at all times."

Another day, another meeting, another waste of time. Meg found her eyes drawn to Simon. He was staring at her, he'd obviously been trying to get her attention. He dropped his gaze pointedly to the pencil Meg was tapping on her notebook. She hadn't even realized she was doing that. She sat up straight in her chair and cleared her throat. She didn't want to disappoint Simon. He was the only person she was doing this for.

Meg looked back at the meeting agenda, trying to work out where they were up to. Then she saw the swirly letter "J" she'd been doodling all over the page. What? She started to scribble over them. She hadn't even heard from Jamie since they'd been to lunch that day. Though that hadn't stopped her from thinking about him, and dreaming about him. And fantasizing about him. She felt like a desperate, sad, middle-aged woman.

"You're not middle-aged," Chris had tried to reassure her last night as she squinted into the mirror counting her crow's feet.

"My grandparents died in their early seventies. I'm past the halfway mark, so that makes me middle-aged."

"Well, mine died in their nineties, so that means I'm not middle-aged, even though I'm older than you. So how do you figure that?"

Meg didn't try to, she just slapped on her new, sixty dollar a jar, wonder cream for eyes, not believing for a moment it would make a scrap of difference, but scared of not doing it. She seemed to be aging at an unsettling rate, despite the assortment of tubes and jars that lined her bathroom cabinet. But if she didn't apply them religiously, who knows how she might look now? It was like when she was a child and her mother used to tell her that if she swallowed watermelon seeds, a watermelon vine would grow inside her and they would have to take her to the hospital to have it cut out. Even after Meg learned about photosynthesis she still had a basic fear of swallowing seeds. Better safe . . .

"Finally to the last item," Barry, the MD, announced. "I think this will be of interest to you, Meg, and I'd really like to hear your thoughts on it."

Meg roused herself. Focus. "Sure, Barry."

She looked across at Simon. He lifted an eyebrow at her, as much as to say, "Here's your chance."

"I was watching *Gladiator* the other night," he began.

There was a Mexican wave of appreciative murmurs around the table. "Great movie." "Classic." "Epic." She knew it had won the Academy Award and all, but Meg had been disappointed. Not enough of Russell Crowe shirtless in her opinion. God, she was getting desperate.

"Did you know that the actor, what's his name, the drunk . . ."

"Oliver Reed."

"Yes, that's him, did you know he died during the making of the movie?"

Everyone did.

"And they still had scenes to shoot?"

"Yes, his image was computer-animated toward the end," said Meg.

Barry looked a little as though she'd stolen his thunder. "Well, it was very impressive, don't you think? I've never seen anything like it. Would you be able to do that, Meg?"

She frowned. "Well, with the right equipment . . ."

"It's just that I got to thinking," Barry went on. "There might be a whole new avenue of work for us in this. If they're going to do this in movies . . ."

"I'd imagine that Fox Studios would be pretty well set up for that kind of thing," said Meg.

"Okay, but I can see some interesting advertising opportunities."

"Using dead actors?" Meg winced.

"Famous actors who have passed on, yes. We're facing an increasingly aging demographic, everyone knows that. And old people like to reminisce, they think that everything was better in the good old days. Who better to appeal to them than the stars they idolised when they were young?"

"Cary Grant says 'suave,' " said Tim. He was Barry's PA and the biggest suck-up in the firm. "Jimmy Stewart says 'dependable,' John Wayne says 'tough.' "

"That's the way," Barry enthused. "Bring back a little class into advertising."

Class? Meg wanted to scream. It was the most tasteless idea she had ever heard. She tuned out of the buzz that started around the table, and started across at Simon. She knew what he'd think about it, and sure enough, he was staying quiet. He looked at her, shrugging with his eyebrows.

"So, Meg, any ideas?"

She looked up at Barry, then back across at Simon, his eyes almost pleading with her just to go along.

She cleared her throat. "James Dean, Grace Kelly," she began.

"Now you're talking!"

". . . Princess Diana."

A slight frown creased Barry's forehead. "Mm, not too sure about that one, might be a bit too close for comfort for some people . . ."

"All in the same campaign," Meg went on, cutting Barry off midsentence. "All talking straight to camera. All saying the same line—'If only I'd been driving a Volvo!' "

"Meg, that was the most crass, offensive . . ." Simon was ranting. He'd marched her back to his office when the meeting had finished, which it had pretty rapidly after Meg dropped her clanger.

"I just took his idea to its logical conclusion," she defended. "He was the one being tasteless."

"But he's the MD, Meg, you made a fool of him in front of everyone."

"He did that all by himself."

"Meg! You should have shown him a bit of respect."

"Simon, he's not the frigging Pope, he runs an advertising agency!" she cried. "He makes his living selling things nobody needs to people who don't want them, by convincing them that stuff will make them happy when it won't!"

"You've been in advertising for ten years and you've just figured that out?" Simon had raised his voice. He never raised his voice. "Christ, Meg! It happens to be your livelihood too! And mine."

She had never meant to insult Simon. "I'm sorry."

"It's not me you have to apologize to, it's Barry."

She screwed up her nose and collapsed back onto the sofa, sighing loudly. She looked up at Simon. He didn't seem angry anymore, just concerned.

"What's up with you? You haven't been yourself lately," he said, his voice back to its normal level.

Meg shrugged. "I don't know."

Simon walked over and sat on the coffee table facing her. He leaned forward. "Is everything alright at home?"

Meg didn't want to spoil his illusions. "Of course it is. It's always alright. You know that."

"Well then, what is it?"

She sighed. "Maybe I'm just not cut out to be a director, Simon. I'm sorry."

He got up and sat down beside her on the sofa. She looked sideways at him.

"Are you cross?"

"No, I knew it was coming." He smiled ruefully. "And I'm glad you said it before I had to."

"Oh, I've been that bad, huh?"

"Let's just say your heart wasn't in it."

"All the meetings, and the schmoozing. And I'd have to work every day, Simon. I'm not prepared to go back full-time while Harrison is so young. I don't want to miss him growing up."

They were quiet for a moment.

"Do you think you'll have another baby?"

Meg hit her head on the back of the sofa. "Why does everyone keep asking me that?"

"Well, it's inevitable."

"What, the question or the baby?"

Simon shrugged. "The question I guess, if not the baby."

"It's really no one's business. But everyone presumes if you've got one baby, you must automatically want another."

"You don't?"

"I don't know what I want, Simon."

He linked her arm through his, clasping her hand. "Maybe you should take a holiday."

"Maybe." She leaned her head on his shoulder. "So you forgive me?"

"Mm."

"And I'm off the hook now?" she said in a small voice.

"Not so fast. You still have to apologize to Barry."

She looked up at him, batting her eyes.

"Those puppy-dog eyes won't work on me. I'm immune."

"Is it really necessary to apologize to him?"

"Only if you value your job."

"*Well . . .*"

"Let me rephrase that, only if you value me!"

"Alright, alright. I'll do it," she relented. "Should I go and see him now?"

Simon shook his head. "Come up to the bar after work. He'll be more receptive after he's had a few drinks."

Meg didn't want to stay long. She had one drink, enough to give her a little Dutch courage, and then she walked directly up to Barry. He was leaning against the bar, surrounded by his little army of yes men.

"Meg," he nodded dubiously.

"Barry," she returned. "I'm sorry about what I said at the meeting today."

He watched her, waiting.

"I didn't mean to insult you. It was actually intended more to shock you. I just wanted to demonstrate the less tasteful side of what you were suggesting."

She took a breath, clenching her nails into the palms of her hands. "I'm sure we can work on your idea."

Barry studied her for a moment. "Don't worry about it. I told my wife at lunch today. She slapped me."

Meg walked back to the office. She wanted to phone Chris to let him know she was running late. The call was diverted to his mobile.

"Hi, it's me."

"Hi honey, you're still at work?"

"I had to see the boss about something. I was just about to leave."

"I'm on my way home, I'll pick up Harrison."

"Okay, thanks."

Call waiting beeps came onto the line.

"That's me, I'd better take it," said Meg.

"See you at home," Chris rang off.

She waited for the other call to connect. "Meg Lynch," she said wearily.

"Hello Meg Lynch."

She recognized the voice straightaway. It was Jamie. Her stomach lurched and she felt her heart racing. She was an idiot.

"Meg, are you there?"

She regained her voice. "Yes."

"It's me, Jamie."

"Hello."

"How've you been?"

"Fine," she said curtly.

He didn't say anything, but she could hear him breathing.

"Is there something you wanted, Jamie? Because I was just on my way home, my husband's expecting me," she said, as much to remind herself.

"I just wanted to let you know that I'm going away."

"Why would you bother calling to tell me that? I haven't heard from you in a month, you could have been on the moon for all I knew." She tried to keep a level voice, but she suspected she sounded like a fishwife.

"I'm going to New Zealand. Just for a week or so. Sea-kayaking."

She sighed, rubbing her forehead. "That's nice, Jamie. Why are you telling me this?"

"Do you want to come?"

"What?"

"I was wondering if you wanted to come along."

"What?" she repeated.

"I was calling to see if you wanted to come sea-kayaking with me in New Zealand," he said patiently. "It's not scary or dangerous, but it is heaps of fun."

Meg started to laugh. She leaned back against her desk. "Tell me, exactly what stratum of reality do you exist in?"

"The same one you do."

"I doubt it, or else you'd realize that it's impossible for me to come with you."

"Nothing's impossible, Meg."

"You know, some things are, when you've got a child and a husband and a job—"

"You've also got choices."

"No I don't."

"Of course you do."

"I've already made all my choices. And now the rest of my life is all mapped out."

"That's a cop-out. Of course you've got choices. And you keep making them every day."

Meg was silent, she didn't have a comeback.

"And that's okay, Meg, as long as you realize what you're doing. You're making choices every day, day in, day out. It's up to you if you want things to be different."

She sighed. "It's not as simple as you make out."

"It is that simple. That doesn't mean it's easy. It takes a lot of courage."

"And as we have already established, I don't possess any of that."

"Oh, I think maybe you do, it's just untapped."

For some reason, she felt a lump in her throat.

"So, I can't talk you into this trip?"

" 'Fraid not."

"Some other time, then?"

"Some other lifetime."

There was a pause. "See you, Meg."

"Bye."

March

Ally looked out the window of the kitchen. This was probably her favorite time of the year in the Highlands. The leaves on the trees were just turning, and the lawns were lush green now that the heat of February had eased. The days were still mild, the nights becoming just slightly cooler. Perhaps she could talk Lillian into taking a walk around the gardens today.

The guests had tapered off toward the end of February, though Ally had been taking a lot of bookings for March and April. Like herself, there was no shortage of people who preferred autumn.

The last month had gone by in a blur, Ally couldn't remember a busier time in her life. No wonder running the guesthouse was getting beyond Lillian, Ally was exhausted. There were so many details to remember. Nic was wonderful, she had energy to burn, and her sense of humor kept Ally going.

And Rob had thawed out, just as Nic had predicted. Once he'd come to know her better they had developed a solid rapport. Not that he was one to chat, but he wasn't curt either, as Ally had initially assumed. Rob just didn't need as many words as other people to express himself. It was hardly a character flaw. And besides, Nic talked enough for two people, at least.

She hardly had the time to work out whether she missed teaching. But she had missed Meg, and Harrison especially. She'd asked them to come down a number of times, but Meg kept giving excuses.

"It's not the easiest thing just to pack up a family and take off for the weekend, you know, Ally," she'd said crisply during one phone call.

"I realize that. I just thought you might like the break."

"You don't ever get a break when you've got a child."

It wasn't like Meg to play the martyr.

"Then you should come away just yourself."

"Chance would be a fine thing!" But then her voice softened. "Look, you're too busy to be entertaining me."

"If you came early in the week . . ."

"I can't get away from work at the moment. We'll see in a few weeks."

Ally wondered what was going on with her, and she kept meaning to phone her more often. But then another week passed, and another.

Lillian rarely seemed to come out of her room. The MRI had revealed what the doctors called a "shadow." That wasn't good enough for Richard, who was still reeling from the shock of the news of Lillian's accident. He flew up from Melbourne, spending the next week bringing in specialists from the city to give him an explanation. But no one could.

The shadow was a dense area in her brain that had probably expanded due to an atypical migraine, they told him. It would have disrupted oxygen flow, causing disorientation, dizziness, perhaps some loss of feeling in her hands or feet, all contributing to the fall. That was the consensus, anyway. No one could be really sure what caused it, or if it could happen again. Stress was the only contributing factor any of the doctors could pinpoint with certainty.

Ally prepared Lillian's lunch and carried the tray through to her apartment, setting it down as usual on the small dining table. She had brought a sandwich in for herself as well. This was usually the first chance she had to eat since a very early breakfast, so it was a good opportunity to have lunch and keep Lillian company.

She walked through the French doors into Lillian's bedroom. She was lying back on her bed, propped up with pillows.

"Lunch is ready, Lillian. Aren't you coming out?"

"You know, Ally, would it be a bother to bring it in to me?"

She frowned. "Are you alright?"

"Don't look like that, I'm fine. I felt a little dizzy before and so I did the right thing and stayed off my feet."

Ally didn't like her staying in bed like this. It made her seem more of an invalid. But she carried the tray in and set it down on the bedside table, handing Lillian her cup of tea.

"How did the morning go?"

"Quietly." Ally pulled a chair over and sat facing her. "The rush starts again at the weekend."

"So are you going to have a break this afternoon?"

"Yes. I was hoping that you and I could take a stroll in the gardens."

"If you could stand the excitement, dear," Lillian said dubiously. "Why don't you call Matthew? You could go for a real walk with him."

Ally smiled, shaking her head. Lillian liked to bring Matt's name up in conversation as often as possible. She had grand ideas about the two of them, and didn't seem to accept Ally's insistence that nothing was going on.

Ally had thanked Matt for the flowers the next time she'd seen him, and nothing had been said about the episode again. He called around for coffee now and then, and he had asked her out a couple of times, but she was so busy that she always had to turn him down. Truth be told, Ally was glad to have an excuse. She didn't want to start anything she wasn't going to be around to finish. She was only staying here temporarily, to help out Lillian.

"Matt's working, I expect, Lillian."

"Then why don't you go out for dinner or something? I'm sure they can do without you for a night."

"You know, Lillian, a night off is just that to me—a night where I don't have to do anything."

Lillian shook her head in disgust. "Young girl like you, attractive and single, and a young man like him, the same, and the two of you can't get your act together."

"Why are you so keen to matchmake?"

"Well, it just seems like such a waste."

Ally laughed.

"What I wonder is, why are you so reluctant?" Lillian continued. "I've had this conversation with Matthew, and he said that you keep turning him down."

Ally had turned red as a beetroot. "Why did you talk about this with Matt?"

"Because I was interested to know why nothing was happening."

"Lillian, just because we're two single people who know each other, doesn't automatically mean we belong together."

"Don't you like him, Ally?"

"It's not that," she sighed. Ally decided to be blunt, it might be the only way she would get Lillian off her back. "To be honest, Lillian, he reminds me a little too much of my grandfather."

"In what way?"

"Oh, living out of town, all alone, building a house . . ."

Lillian stared at her. "Yes, go on?"

Ally shrugged. "It just makes me feel uneasy."

Lillian studied her for a moment. "Why do you think your grandparents moved down to the property?"

Ally hesitated. What was she getting at? She may as well be honest. "My grandfather had his own selfish ideas about a lifestyle change and he dragged his family along with him, whether they liked it or not."

"So that's what you think?" Lillian paused, considering. "Did your Nan ever tell you anything about your mother?"

"Not much," Ally replied curiously. "She always said she would, when I got older. All I know is that she ran away. She must have hated growing up there. I did."

"You know it wasn't the first time she had run away."

Ally shrugged. "So, she tried more than once? That doesn't surprise me."

"She ran away before they ever left Sydney. I think she was barely fourteen the first time."

Ally frowned, waiting for Lillian to go on.

"Your mother was constantly in trouble, Ally. She played truant from school, she was caught shoplifting, there was always something.

"Your grandparents moved her to a very expensive private school, arranged counseling for her, but nothing seemed to work. In the end she was asked to leave the school in no uncertain terms. Back in the state system she just kept breaking all the rules, until they had no choice but to suspend her, which was just what she wanted. She was out of control."

"How did it get to that?" Ally was amazed that her stern, forbidding grandfather had not managed to pull his daughter into line.

Lillian shrugged. "She was in a 'bad crowd,' Margaret used to say, like every parent of a difficult child. Who knows? They decided the only thing they could do was to remove her from the environment altogether."

"Is that when they came down here?"

She nodded. "James resigned from his job."

"He was a solicitor, wasn't he?"

"Yes, that's how he and Roger knew each other. James heard that we'd brought a property down here and he asked Roger a lot of questions about the area. We invited James and Margaret down to stay, and they put a deposit on the Kangaroo Valley property the same weekend. Roger thought he was mad, but he did respect him. He had never known a man to give up so much for his family, especially in those days."

Ally stood up and walked to the window. She stared out to the garden, trying to absorb what Lillian had just told her. *He* gave up everything . . . for his family?

"It was unheard of for a man to leave a profession like law and try his hand at hobby farming. But he felt so strongly that he had to focus on Jennifer and not be preoccupied with a career. That's why they didn't spend a lot on the property—they didn't want to use up the funds from the sale of their house in Sydney. They both thought it was probably a good idea to live more simply anyway. Jennifer had been a spoilt only child, they realized, and she needed to learn a different way.

"But things were much harder than they expected. James didn't really know how much work was involved in looking after a property, and they realized that they had probably made a mistake. But it was too late, they wouldn't have been able to sell Circle's End anyway."

"Why not?"

"It was during one of the downturns in the market. So they had to live very frugally, and the long-planned-for house was never built."

Ally sank down on the window seat. She thought about Nan complaining quietly to Lillian. It wasn't about James, it was just about their predicament.

"Jennifer was resentful, she started to get herself into as much mischief as she could. In the end, I think it was a relief when she left."

Ally couldn't help feeling disorientated by all this new information. Surely there had to be more to it. "Well then, she was obviously not very welcome, when she came back with me."

Lillian shook her head. "No, they treated her like the prodigal daughter. And you, well, they adored you. They couldn't believe that something so wonderful could be salvaged from the whole mess." She watched Ally's expression. "You know, in those early days, you used to cling to your grandfather, you wouldn't let him out of your sight."

Ally stared at her. "I don't remember."

"I didn't think so. You were so little. Margaret was taken up looking after Jennifer, and so James devoted himself to you. He often used to tell me it was the happiest time of his life."

Ally blinked back tears. "Why did Nan have to look after my mother?"

"Oh, Ally," Lillian sighed. "You really know nothing about her, do you?"

She shook her head. "They didn't seem to want to talk about her. Not that they ever said anything bad."

"They were protecting you, of course." She hesitated. "Maybe I shouldn't be the one to tell you all of this."

"Then who else will?" Ally said plaintively. "There is no one else, Lillian."

She sighed. "Very well. Pour yourself a cup of tea, and come and sit here, closer. Some of what I have to tell you is not going to be easy to hear."

Two weeks later

Ally looked out the window of the kitchen. This used to be her favorite time of the year in the Highlands. Not anymore. The gold leaves looked pallid, lifeless. They only changed color because they had started to die. They were parched, not beautiful at all. Why hadn't she ever realized that before? Autumn was a dying season.

And now Lillian was dead too.

How could a *shadow* kill someone? Someone who was alive and talking one night, and lifeless the next morning when Ally went to wake her for breakfast.

Richard was relieved she had gone in her sleep. Relieved? He was more of a fool than Ally had realized. She had barely made it through the funeral, and now she had to deal with this noisy throng taking over Lillian's home, eating her food. She couldn't stand all the people smiling, pressing their hands into hers. Everyone saying it was a lovely service, Richard and Phillipa spoke beautifully, very moving. What were they talking about? There was nothing good in Lillian dying.

They were all in there now, celebrating Lillian's life, when all Ally wanted to do was mourn her death.

"Ally, could you carry this tray of canapés out?"

It was Rob. His voice was quiet, tentative. She turned away from the window and looked at him. She could see the pain in his eyes. Ally had tried to send him home the day Lillian died. But Rob dealt with his grief by working. He threw himself into preparing an elaborate spread for the wake. He'd hardly slept for the last two days, cooking as though it was the most important thing he had ever done. As though it was for Lillian.

Ally considered the tray. Canapés. What a fucking stupid name. She couldn't go back in there. Rob was watching her. He understood.

"Ally, get out of here," he said gently.

"No, I shouldn't . . ."

"Go, just go. It'll be okay."

He was right. She hurried out of the kitchen, through the laundry and onto the verandah.

Now she could breathe. The cold air hit her lungs and she gasped, sobbing. She ran down the stairs and past all the cars parked in rows along the grass. She ran through the windbreak of trees and into the depths of the garden.

"Ally!"

She turned around. It was Matt. She wiped her wet cheeks with the back of her hand.

"I thought no one would find me here," she said as he approached her.

"Do you want me to leave you alone?"

Ally hesitated. Part of her wanted to say yes, but Lillian would never be so impolite. So she just shrugged, and started walking slowly on through the trees. Matt walked a step behind her, keeping his distance, saying nothing.

They came to an enormous wisteria arbour that formed a protected circle underneath. Ally looked up at the knotted, twisted branches, devoid of their beautiful purple fronds, of leaves, of any signs of life. She started to pace around the circle. Matt leaned against a post, watching her.

"What do you expect me to say?" she said after a while.

"I don't expect you to say anything."

She sighed, still pacing. "I just couldn't take it anymore, in there. All those people, waiting to be fed, reciting all their stupid clichés, like human Hallmark greeting cards."

"What would you rather they did?"

"I don't know! How am I supposed to know? When Nan died, we just went home."

She sat down on a wooden bench, wiping more tears away with her hands.

"Have you got a cigarette?" she asked suddenly.

"No, I don't smoke."

"Never mind."

"I didn't realize you smoked?"

"I don't. It just seemed like the thing to do."

He caught her eye, and she smiled despite herself. He smiled back at her.

"Will this do instead?" said Matt, holding up a bottle of wine and two glasses. "When I saw you nicking off, I thought you might need a drink."

"Bloody good idea."

He handed her a glass and she held it out as he poured the wine. He sat at the other end of the bench and filled his own glass, then rested the bottle between them.

Ally sipped her wine. "I'm sorry, I'm not very good at this."

"What?"

"Bereavement." She sighed deeply. "I just can't believe she's gone. Every-one's gone now."

"It must feel like that, so soon after losing your grandfather."

"It's not just a feeling." Ally looked at him sideways. "There really is no one else. No distant relatives, third or fourth cousins, no benevolent uncle . . . no one. Zilch. I am completely without 'next of kin.' "

"What about your mother?"

"What about her?" Ally muttered dryly. "If she's still alive, she's probably so out of it that she'd be lucky to know her own name, let alone mine."

"What do you mean?"

"Well, according to Lillian, the last time anyone saw her she was a half-crazed junkie."

"When was that?"

"At Nan's funeral. I was twelve."

"Oh yes, you mentioned that."

Ally looked at him, frowning.

"When you told me your name," Matt explained, smiling faintly.

"Oh, right," she nodded. "But I didn't know any of this then. I didn't know anything." Ally felt tears rising again in the back of her throat, and she gulped down a few mouthfuls of wine.

Matt leaned over with the bottle to refill her glass.

"Thanks," she said lamely.

"Do you want to talk about it?"

"What, bore you to tears with the story of my life?"

"I've got nothing better to do."

She smiled weakly at him. "There's not that much to tell. Only that everything I ever believed about my family wasn't true."

Matt frowned. "What do you mean?"

"Well, apparently my grandfather was a wonderful man who gave up everything to try and save his wayward daughter. They lived in that hovel in the valley for all those years all because of her. And she ran out on them in the end anyway."

"When she left you?"

"No, she ruined their lives first, ran off, and then came back with me, I don't know, it must have been four or five years later."

"So then what happened?"

"She was hopelessly addicted to drugs, heroin apparently. They did everything they could to help her, yet again. Until they woke up one day and she was gone. She'd taken whatever cash she could find, and the only decent jewelery Nan owned. Anything of value." Ally knocked back the rest of her glass. "Of course, she left me behind."

Matt didn't say anything. She looked at him.

"Pretty appalling, eh?"

He shrugged. "Drugs make people do appalling things. It sounds like leaving you with your grandparents was the best thing she could have done for you."

"That's what Lillian said." Ally stood up and started to pace around the circle again, her feet crunching on the gravel. "And I know I'm supposed to feel grateful in some way, or relieved, something like that. I'm alive, I'm healthy, I have an education."

She paced some more. "But all I feel is . . . ripped off."

"Why's that?"

"It's bad enough to be abandoned by your own mother, but then to feel that he resented me, that I was in the way . . ."

"Are you talking about James?

Ally nodded.

"I always thought he loved you very much. That's what he made out."

"Oh, sure!" Ally exclaimed, stopping to look at Matt. "Everyone else knew, he told everyone but me."

He thought for a moment. "Maybe it was hard for him, a man of his generation, you know, to express his feelings."

"I don't care!" she cried. "I went through my teenage years with a sullen, distant man, feeling like I was a burden. He should have told me."

"He probably wished he had."

Ally felt the lump rising up in her chest again. "Well it's a bit late now."

She stood for a while at the edge of the arbour, looking out into the garden, now in darkness.

"We should go back, I suppose," she said eventually.

They started to walk slowly in the direction of the house.

"What are you going to do now?" Matt asked.

Ally shrugged. "Put on a false smile, until they all go home."

"No, I mean . . ." He seemed to be choosing his words. ". . . after all this."

"Oh," she nodded, realizing what he was getting at. "Richard asked me to stay until Birchgrove is sold. I'll have to extend my leave into second term, but that shouldn't be a problem."

"What if the buyer asks you to stay on, as manager?"

"I doubt they would, not once they see my credentials," she said wryly. "I don't think I could do it anyway. I wouldn't want to stay here under another owner. This has belonged to Lillian for as long as I've known her. It wouldn't feel right."

They walked along farther.

"So will you go back to Sydney?" Matt asked tentatively.

Ally glanced at him. "I really don't know." She sighed. "I don't know what I'm going to do."

Watsons Bay

"So has Ally made any plans yet?" Chris was asking.

Meg had been worried about her since the call came last week that Lillian had passed away. She offered to go down for the funeral, but of course Ally told her not to concern herself. She hated being fussed over. Meg was probably the closest friend Ally had, and she didn't even know what was going on inside her most of the time.

Meg shrugged. "I feel so sorry for her." Which she knew Ally would hate. "I mean, she has no one, no relatives."

"She has us."

Meg smiled at him. "That's what I told her. She'll probably have to end up coming back to Sydney. I said she was welcome to stay here, at least until she finds a place. That's okay with you, isn't it?"

"Of course it is." Chris drained his cup and walked into the kitchen. "What are your plans for the day?"

Meg gave him a wry smile. "Oh, it's a big one! I'm going up to the Junction. I need to go to the bank, pay a few bills, you know, exciting stuff like that."

"There'd be travel agents at Bondi Junction?"

"I imagine so. Why?"

"I've been meaning to pick up some brochures, so we can start planning our trip. It's a bit pointless putting in for holidays until we decide where we want to go, you know, to get the best time of the year. There's a lot to consider."

Meg sighed inwardly. Once upon a time, and not all that long ago, she would have taken to the task with relish. She'd have a specially labeled folder full of brochures, sorted alphabetically and marked throughout with yellow stick-it notes and highlighter pen. They would have narrowed it down to probably three options, and in another labeled folder Meg would have made lists of the pros and cons of each destination, using a rating system—so many points for facilities, costs and so on. They would have been close to making a decision, with just a little more research.

And all Jamie did was pick a spot on the globe and go. Just like that.

"Earth to Meg?" Chris was trying to get her attention.

"Sorry, daydreaming."

"Well, if you do see a travel agent, pick up some brochures so we can stop daydreaming and start planning." He kissed her on the top of the head. "I'll see you tonight."

She sat for a while after Chris left, staring into space. It was not until Harrison toddled in and tugged on her dressing gown that she roused herself. She'd been doing that a lot lately. Finding herself staring vacantly at the computer screen at work, wondering what it was she was supposed to be doing.

Meg decided to ignore the morning's chores, they'd still be there when she got home. She dressed Harrison and herself in whatever was at hand, and drove up to Bondi Junction, parking in the plaza station.

The bank and the post office were reasonably entertaining outings for Harrison, up to a point. There was usually a kiddies' corner, with blocks and a few scungy toys that amused him temporarily. After that, there were deposit slips to scribble on, as well as stamps on the hand from friendly tellers. Meg could count on an hour, tops, to get through anything essential before he'd start to get restless. After that it became an exercise in nego tiation.

"If you're a good boy while Mummy looks in this shop, I'll get you a treat."

Meg had given up shopping for clothes with Harry since he'd started to walk, particularly after the incident in David Jones when he wandered out of the dressing rooms. She had to run through the store in a backless evening dress, setting off the alarm when she dashed out though the entrance to reach him just before he stepped onto the escalator.

Today Harrison had already been bribed with a banana muffin. He'd half eaten, and half decimated the Vegemite sandwich Meg had packed for him, and he'd spilt juice down the front of himself. It was time to go. Meg was pushing the stroller back toward the plaza, when she passed a travel agent. She backed up, staring through the window.

"Go, Mama," came Harrison's voice from the front of the stroller. It would be pointless attempting to make any inquiries now.

"Just a minute," she said vaguely, gazing at the posters.

"Meg?"

She turned around, startled. Jamie was standing there, smiling broadly at her.

"Fancy meeting you here."

"Well, I only live up the road, I mean, you know, Watsons Bay," she stammered. There was a woman standing beside him. She couldn't have been twenty and she was stunning. Blond and leggy and young, *so* young! She was wearing a hipster skirt and a superior expression. Why had Meg dressed so suburban mumsy today?

"This is Taylor," Jamie explained, probably because Meg was staring at her. They nodded warily at each other. She had a surname for a first name. She really was young.

"So where are you off to?" Jamie asked.

"Sorry?"

He nodded at the travel agent's window.

"Oh, nowhere. Just thinking about it."

He smiled at her. "You've got to do it, Meg, not just think about it."

Easy for him to say.

"You want to get a coffee or something?"

No. She wanted him to go away with his twelve year old girlfriend and leave her to wallow in her middle-aged mediocrity.

Harrison craned his head around the side of the stroller. "Go, Mama!"

"Sorry, he's had enough today, I have to get going."

Jamie just looked at her.

"So, I'll see you," she said brightly. She took off like she was late for a train. Well, that was embarrassing. Imagine asking her for coffee! It would have looked like they were taking their favorite aunty out for a treat.

She made for the entrance to the plaza and navigated the stroller through the throng coming out. It was lunchtime and the volume of people had suddenly swelled.

"Hey, Meg! Hang on!"

She swung around. Jamie was weaving through the crowd toward her. Meg pulled the stroller out of the way and stood waiting for him.

"Are you on your way home?" he asked when he got to her.

She nodded.

"I couldn't bludge a lift, could I? Down to Bondi?"

She shrugged. "Sure. The car's in the parking station."

They started to walk through the mall, in the direction of the carpark.

"Where's your girlfriend?" Meg said eventually.

"Who?" Jamie frowned. "You mean Taylor? She's not my girlfriend." He grinned, shaking his head. "She's a bit young. She's just my mate's little sister."

"Oh," Meg swallowed. That was a relief. She wished she knew how old Jamie was. She really wanted to know whether she was totally pathetic, or just a little pathetic.

When they got to the car, Meg stopped the stroller and came around to lift Harrison out.

"Hi scupper," Jamie said to him.

Harrison frowned and buried his head into Meg's shoulder, peering out at Jamie uncertainly.

"Dat man, mama?" he asked, pointing at him.

"This is Jamie. Say hello." Harrison didn't respond. "Sorry, he's not usually this shy."

Jamie shrugged. "I don't have a lot to do with kids. I wouldn't know what was normal."

Meg strapped Harry into his car seat, collapsed the stroller and packed it in the boot. They got in, and she manoeuvred the car up the levels and out onto the street.

"I hate driving around here," Meg said, thinking aloud. "Between the bus drivers, who act like they own the road, and couriers whizzing all over the place, it's a nightmare."

"So I take it you didn't grow up around here?"

Meg shook her head. "No, I'm from Queensland."

"A banana bender?"

"Oh, that's original."

Jamie grinned. "So how long have you lived in Sydney?"

Meg thought for a moment. "It'd be sixteen, seventeen years now."

"So you were only a girl when you moved?"

"Flatterer."

"Seriously?"

"I came to Sydney to go to college."

"By yourself?"

Meg nodded.

"So you do have a bit of the adventurer in you?"

She shrugged. "I don't know how adventurous it was. Everything was all organized before I left. I had a place to stay, a part-time job."

"What? Your parents were worried?"

"Mm." Worried they'd have to fend for themselves. Meg remembered the shock on her mother's face the day she left, even though she'd told her repeatedly of her plans.

"But Megan, you know your father hasn't got a job at the moment. We count on your board to help with the rent."

"I've paid next month's rent for you in advance, Mum, and there are no other bills outstanding at the moment. Electricity is due on the twenty-second though. You have to pay attention to what comes in the mail from now on, Mum."

"I really think you should just postpone this trip, Megan, it's not the best time."

"It's not a trip, Mum, I'm going to college."

"But there are plenty of good colleges up here, why do you have to go away?"

"Because I have to, Mum."

"So, how was New Zealand?" Meg asked Jamie, changing the subject.

"It was great, you should have come."

Meg smiled, shaking her head. "Of course, I'm the woman with all the choices!" she declared. "Free as a bird." She pulled up at traffic lights as they turned orange. She glanced across at Jamie. He was looking at her curiously. "What?"

"Are you happy, Meg?"

She frowned at him. "That's a deep question."

"Well?" he persisted.

She shrugged. "Sure."

"I mean really happy?"

Meg breathed out heavily. "I don't know, Jamie. At times I'm really happy. I think it's probably more important to be content."

"So are you content?"

She'd walked right into that one. The lights changed, and Meg drove across the intersection. "Is there anywhere in particular you want me to drop you?"

He shook his head. "Just keep going right into Bondi." He shifted sideways in his seat, facing Meg. "What would you like to do if you could do anything?"

"What do you mean? For a job, or a holiday, what?"

"Anything, what's the first thing that comes to mind when I ask you what you'd like to be doing now?" Meg glanced at him. He was gazing at her with those glassy eyes like he really cared about her answer. She wasn't about to tell him the first thing that came into her mind.

She sighed, returning her attention to the road. "You don't think that way when you know you can't do anything about it."

"Why not?"

"It just reminds you of everything you're missing."

"Why do you have to miss anything? You should make a list of all the things you'd like to do."

She groaned.

"What?"

"I've made too many lists in my lifetime."

"I'm not talking about a shopping list! Call it a wish list."

"Wishful thinking list, you mean."

Jamie shook his head in frustration but he was smiling. "Meg, you'll be old before your time with that attitude."

They drove down into Bondi, which was a little quieter than usual in the middle of a weekday.

Meg slowed up. "Where to?"

"You could just pull up over there, thanks," said Jamie, indicating a spot somebody had just vacated.

Meg parked the car but left the engine running. Jamie looked a little hesitant.

"You sure you don't want to get a coffee? Or lunch?" he asked.

Meg eyed him dubiously. "You're game. Harrison's not really fit for adult company these days. Besides, he has to have his nap." She glanced into the back seat. Harrison's head was nodding precariously and he could barely keep his eyes open. "In fact, if I don't get him home soon, he'll fall asleep, and then he'll wake up when I try to carry him into the house."

"He can't miss a nap?"

"You really don't have much to do with kids, do you? If he misses his nap, I'll pay for it. He'll grizzle all afternoon, and then probably crash about four anyway. Which means he won't go back to sleep until maybe eleven tonight."

Jamie looked as though she'd given him more information than he cared to have.

"I'm glad I bumped into you today," he said. "I've been thinking about you, Meg."

"Oh?" she said, trying to act as though that had no effect on her at all.

"Would it be alright to call you again?"

Meg sighed. "Why?"

"I don't know. We could do something different. Get you out of your rut."

"Who said I was in a rut?"

"Aren't you?"

Meg felt flustered. Lucky Harrison was too young to be repeating any of this back to his father. She already felt conspicuous enough, parked here, talking to him. Anybody might see them.

"Why do you want to hang around with an old chook like me, Jamie?"

He laughed. "You're not an old chook!"

She looked at him, waiting for an answer.

"You're interesting, Meg." He paused. "And I like your face."

Flattery. Works every time.

"What did you have in mind?"

He shrugged. "Don't know that yet."

"When?"

"Don't know that either."

Of course, the man without a Filofax.

"Well, call me when you know. I'll give you an answer then."

"Fair enough." Jamie opened the car door. "Where should I call you? At work?"

Meg remembered her last pathetic effort, hanging by the phone at the office.

"No . . ." she said, reaching into her bag for her wallet. She took out a business card and handed it to him. "You can always catch me on my mobile. Or leave a message."

He smiled broadly. "I'll do that," he said, climbing out of the car and closing the door. He stood on the footpath watching her while she pretended to be waiting for a break in the traffic.

What was she doing, handing out her phone number to a younger man she barely knew because he said he liked her face? What was wrong with her?

She pulled out into the traffic, noticing Jamie wave out of the corner of her eye. It was okay, she'd just given her phone number to a friend.

Which did not account for the faint shiver that ran through her body when she felt his eyes following her as she drove away down the road.

April

"Please come with us!" Nic persisted. "We've packed enough food."

"But it looks like rain."

Ally didn't know how else to get out of this politely. Nic had invited her to join her and Rob for a picnic. They were only trying to be nice, she knew they were worried about her. Ever since the auction they had been constantly asking her what she was going to do, and she still couldn't answer them. Finally it had become obvious that all she really could do was go back to Sydney, where at least she had a job. But she was reluctant, and she couldn't work out why.

"There's shelter."

"What?"

"In case it rains," Nic explained. "Ally, you are coming, I'm not taking no for an answer."

She looked at Nic, all four feet something of her, standing defiantly, her arms crossed.

"Nic . . ." Ally drew the word out plaintively. "Three's a crowd."

"Oh bollocks."

She sat quietly in the back of Rob's car as he pulled out onto the highway, toward Moss Vale. They'd only been driving for a few minutes when he turned off the main road and into what appeared to be a private driveway. He stopped the car in front of the gates and Nic jumped out to open them.

"Where are we going?" Ally asked curiously.

"Just up here farther," Rob murmured, manoeuvring the car through the gates and stopping to wait for Nic.

She jumped in again and turned around to Ally. "Nice spot, eh? You know what they say, 'location, location, location!' "

"What are you talking about? Where are we going?"

"You'll see!" she grinned, turning back around in her seat.

Ally looked out the window. As they passed a windbreak of trees, a house came into view. It was a sprawling, early Californian bungalow, probably built before 1920. All the original detail appeared to be intact, though it was a bit shabby and worse for wear. Rob pulled the car up at the entrance and turned off the engine.

"Well, come on," Nic said impatiently. "What are you sitting there for?"

Ally wondered what this was all about, all the more as she watched Nic skip up the steps onto a covered portico and open the door with a key.

"What's going on, how did you get a key?"

Nic didn't answer as Ally followed her into a broad hallway that appeared to lead through to the center of the house. There were two doors off to either side.

"Is this for rent? Are you thinking of renting here?"

"No, it's not for rent," Nic said offhand as she flung open all the doors up and down the hall.

Ally walked into the first room on her right. It was huge, the ceilings must have been three meters high at least. There was a marble fireplace that had been boarded up, and a bay window facing the front of the house. There wasn't a stick of furniture, and the windows were bare, but there was carpet on the floors. Thin, threadbare, ugly carpet. Ally wondered what was underneath it. If the floorboards were in good order . . .

"Ally! What are you doing? Come on through!"

There were double doors joining this room to another, equal in size, also boasting a marble fireplace. The skirting boards were probably thirty centimeters deep, and the doors were heavy solid timber, cedar most likely, or maybe oregon. Everything was original, as far as Ally could make out, but it looked like nothing had been touched in years. Paint was peeling off the walls in thick jagged sheets, and the pressed metal ceilings were spotted with mildew. There was a strong, musty odor in the air. Ally wondered how long it had been since anyone lived here.

She came through another set of doors into a vast room, spanning the width of the house. This was where the entrance hallway led to, and it appeared another hall branched off to the left, perhaps to an entire wing. A series of doors on the opposite wall must have opened to the rear of the house, the kitchen and so on, Ally guessed.

Nic and Rob had spread a picnic blanket out on the middle of the floor and were laying out the food.

"So, are you going to explain to me what's going on?" Ally asked.

Nic was kneeling on the floor, pulling the cork out of a bottle of champagne. She filled three glasses and Rob handed one to Ally.

"We've been so excited, and we wanted to share it with someone," Nic blurted out. "Let's make a toast."

Ally dropped to the floor to clink glasses with them. "I don't understand. What are we toasting? Are you're buying this place?"

Nic nodded excitedly.

"To live in?"

"No, silly, we're going to open a restaurant!"

Ally looked at Nic's beaming face, and then Rob's. He was smiling too. In fact, he looked the happiest Ally had ever seen him.

"But how, when?"

"I know, it's amazing! I can hardly believe it myself!" Nic exclaimed.

"We've had an eye out for quite a while," Rob explained. "You know, well before Lillian . . ."

He was still not over Lillian's passing. None of them were. But it had brought them closer together, and maybe that was why Ally found it difficult to imagine leaving right now. Rob and Nic were Ally's only link to Lillian's memory, just as Lillian had been her only link to the memory of her grandfather.

"Anyway," Rob continued, "I was never going to leave Lillian in the lurch, but we were looking to the future."

He glanced at Nic as he said "we."

"Rob has always dreamed of having his own restaurant, we just had to find the right place." Nic's face was almost bursting with pride. "And we did! Don't you think?"

Ally nodded, still bewildered. "But don't you need licenses, and approval and that?"

"All done!" said Nic. "Seven hundred forms later," she added wryly.

"But how can you manage all this? I mean, I know it's rundown, but it must be worth a bomb."

"Oh, the bank's throwing money at us, what with Rob's reputation and everything. It's all very complicated, bridging loans and whatnot, and I doubt we'll make any profits for a year."

". . . or two," Rob added sagely.

"And we have to get a full commercial kitchen installed. You won't believe the shemozzle of rooms tacked onto the back out there." Nic rolled her eyes. "But we've got this huge overdraft to play with, quite daunting really."

"So we have to be careful not to waste it," Rob said seriously. "We've got to do up the rest of the place and start operating ASAP."

"Nothing like a challenge!" Nic grinned, taking a gulp of champagne.

"We've already booked the kitchen contractors, and we're getting Matt out to see about pulling down some of these walls."

"No, don't pull down any walls!" Ally jumped up and started circling the room.

"But we have to maximize our tables, we've got a big debt to work off."

"But how many tables could you fit in here alone, Rob? Maybe twenty?"

"Maybe, but only small tables," he said, looking around.

"So this could be your main working room, every night, taking the bookings for twos and fours."

"But what about big groups? We want to be able to cater for everyone."

"Not a problem. Look at the size of those rooms at the front, and they're adjoining." Ally dashed up the hall. "What about on the other side?" She poked her head in the first door. "Even better! They're separate. So you can have big groups, even small functions like a birthday party, over here," she said, indicating the double room, "and still fit a couple of large bookings in these individual rooms."

"She's right, you know," said Rob. They had followed Ally up the hallway. "Or if there were a lot of group bookings, like at Christmas, we could put them all out in the main room and give the couples somewhere quieter."

"That means we could close different sections on slower nights," Nic added. "So it doesn't look all half empty and pathetic."

"And not only that," Ally enthused, "but you could do each room up in a whole different style. Like in here," she enthused, bursting into the double room. She paused for a few seconds. "Deep Brunswick green on the walls, and all the woodwork white. Strip the floor and stain the boards really dark, but highly polished, and white cloths on the tables with padded velvet chairs."

Nic and Rob just stared at her.

"Then out here, in the main section," she went on, striding out to the other room, "you could even go all trendy bistro style. Have those little aluminium tables and chairs, polished floors again, and . . ." She thought for a moment, looking around. "White, all the walls white, but a wonderful warm white so it's not stark. And you could strip back all this timber, doors and all, and bleach it, or maybe lime it, that would work too."

Nic and Rob looked around the dingy, dilapidated room, imagining the bright open space Ally had described.

"And halogen trapeze lights, with these high ceilings. They're cheap, and you won't have to muck around up in the roof installing new wiring. Though I suspect you'll have to replace all the wiring anyway, given the age of the place."

"Have you done this before?" Nic asked, bemused.

"What?"

"Refurbished a restaurant?"

Ally laughed. "It's only ideas."

"But you're an artist, aren't you? I'd nearly forgotten."

"Hardly! A second-rate art teacher is all. The only things I'm good at painting are walls!"

Nic's eyes were shining. "Ally, you can't go back to Sydney!" she blurted out. "You have to stay and help us! Work with us, no, *for* us."

"Nic," Rob interrupted awkwardly. "You see, Ally, I don't know that we've got enough money to keep ourselves, let alone—"

"Oh, Rob, do you have to be so . . . practical all the time?" Nic said impatiently. "We have to do the place up, don't we? Why can't we pay Ally?"

"We have to use tradesmen for the building work, and the kitchen fit-out, and the exterior. I thought we'd be doing a lot of the painting inside ourselves."

"Come on, Rob, we can't do it all ourselves," Nic complained. "I'm sure along the way we'd be employing some painters."

"But that wouldn't be enough for Ally to live on."

"Unless," Ally interrupted. She had been listening to them, her mind ticking over. She couldn't believe what she was about to suggest. "How tight is your budget?"

"Think of a number that sounds enough, and then halve it," Rob said.

Nic dug him in the ribs. "You're being so negative. The bank's given us a huge overdraft."

"And it'll all be used in the kitchen. Nic, you've got no idea how much it costs to set up a commercial kitchen."

"He's right, Nic, you can't eat into that money or there'll be no restaurant." Ally hesitated. "But . . . how would you feel about someone investing in the business?"

Nic frowned. "What do you mean?"

"What if someone was to invest enough money to finance all the cosmetic work, and maybe that same someone could save by doing a lot of the work themselves, and they could even work in the business, when it first gets going, because they've got a little experience waitressing, and maybe . . ."

"Ally!"

She looked at Nic.

"What are you talking about? Are you the 'someone?' " Nic cried.

Ally smiled. "If you'll have me," she shrugged.

"Where would you get that kind of money?"

"My grandfather's property, I've been trying to sell it, remember?"

Nic frowned. "That's right, I'd almost forgotten."

"No one has been too interested in the place because it needs a bit of work. I've had one or two offers, but the agent said they were a joke."

"I don't understand," said Rob. "You're not going to take one of those offers? I wouldn't want you to do that, not to help us out, Ally."

"No, I think it's about time I actually just got the work done," said Ally firmly. "And I know this really good carpenter . . ."

The next day

"So what do you think?"

Ally looked expectantly at Matt's face, trying to decipher his expression. Amusement probably, she decided.

"I think," he said slowly, "that your grandfather had a pretty good sense of humor."

Ally winced. They were standing in the main room at Circle's End. It was seven in the morning. When she'd called Matt the night before, he'd seemed a little taken aback, probably because of her reluctance to let him anywhere near the place before.

But Ally felt they were friends now, she hoped they were. And the urgency of the situation made her put aside her phobia of asking for favors, at least for the moment. She had about three weeks left at Birchgrove until the new owners took over. Circle's End needed to be on the market by then, with the repairs well under way, to reassure any prospective buyer. After she'd blurted out the whole story to Matt, he'd agreed to meet her first thing, before he started for the day.

"Just tell me, is it doable?"

"Anything's doable," he grinned. "But it has a lot of character, don't you reckon? Just look at this staircase—people spend a lot of money to get an effect like that."

James had built the stairs to the loft out of rough-hewn logs and had used actual tree boughs and branches for the balustrade.

"No, people spend a lot of money to get someone professional to do it properly," Ally retorted. "It's not legal, is it?"

"Well, the police won't come around and raid the place," he laughed.

"Oh, you know what I mean!"

"They're 'non-compliant.' Treads are too close together, and the risers are too deep. If you want it done properly, it'll have to be ripped out and rebuilt."

Ally sighed. "What else?"

"I'll have to take a look around."

She led him into the kitchen. It was a haphazard collection of old cabinets and makeshift units her grandfather had put together to approximate a fitted kitchen.

"Just look at these benchtops, they're dreadful," said Ally.

"I don't know," Matt shrugged. "That's a solid piece of hardwood. He must have cut right through the middle of a tree trunk."

"Pity he couldn't cut straight," Ally sniggered. "You can't leave a plate or a cup near the edge, it just slides off."

Matt laughed, bending down to the height of one of the benches and closing an eye. "Mm, I see what you mean."

"And there's all these holes in the walls everywhere."

He nodded. "You can't avoid that with sawn-log construction. They used to fill in the gaps with mud, but it must have worn away a long time ago."

"Is there anything you can do about it?"

"I'll give it a go." He scratched his head, ruffling his hair. "Depends on how particular you are."

Ally sighed. "I'm not particular at all. I just want to make it legal . . . I mean *compliant*. But for as little cost as possible, in as short a time as possible."

She didn't have a lot of money to play with. She had just under three thousand dollars left after her grandfather's affairs had been settled. Lillian, and then Richard, had been generous with her wages, and because she'd had free room and board, she had not had to spend much money over the past few months. However, Ally realized she was going to need something to live on once she finished up at the guesthouse and until the property was sold. And then a large chunk of the proceeds from the sale would be sunk straight into the restaurant. She had hardly slept last night, realizing the tenuousness of her situation. But at the same time she was on an incredible high.

Matt eyed her. "What's the big hurry all of a sudden?"

"The whole schedule is really tight. I only have a few weeks left at Birchgrove, and of course Nic and Rob want to open as soon as it's feasibly possible."

Matt nodded. "Does this mean you're staying?"

Ally paused, looking at him. "I guess it does. For the meantime, anyway." She hadn't really stopped to think about that in the last twenty-four hours. She was going to have to apply for more leave from St Ambrose. Ally hoped that wouldn't stretch the relationship too far.

"Well, I'll tell you what I can do," Matt said, folding his arms in front of him and leaning back against the bench. "I'll reuse whatever I can, but the biggest expense will be the materials. You'll need to cover that, but I'll put it on my account, so you'll have some time before you have to cough up."

"Alright, Matt. But I have to pay you too, I'm not asking for any favors." She paused, frowning. "I mean, I guess I am, but within reason."

"You can pay me when the place is sold."

"I can't let you do that."

"Why not?"

Ally was feeling the familiar discomfort that always surfaced when someone wanted to do something for her. "It's too much, that's all. This is your livelihood, you can't go without payment for that long."

"Ally, I already have jobs lined up for months, I'm going to have to fit this in when I can," he explained. "I have a good cash flow, it's not a problem. You'll pay me when you can."

He straightened up, picking up his measuring tape and a notebook he'd left on the table. "I'd better take some measurements now, so I can start ordering."

Ally looked at him. "Matt, I don't know . . ."

"Stop worrying," he dismissed. "What else are you going to do?"

She watched him as he pulled out the tape and drew it out along the front of the cabinets. Then he jotted down some numbers on the notebook, replacing the pencil behind his ear.

"What's in it for you?" Ally said abruptly.

He swung around to look at her. "What?"

"Why are you doing this? You don't need the work, and you're not going to get paid for a while."

He shook his head, but he was grinning. "Such a suspicious mind. Maybe," he said, crossing to the door, "I'm just a nice guy."

That afternoon

"Meg, I only have another three weeks here. If you don't come now, I can't guarantee I'll be able to put you up after this. I don't know where I'll be staying. And I really want you to see Birchgrove, and the restaurant."

There was silence down the phone line.

"Meg?" Ally repeated.

Meg sighed. She would love to get away, alone, but Ally was probably hoping to see Harrison.

"It might be a bit difficult for us all to come down. What if it was just me?"

"Great! We'll have a girls' night."

"You don't mind?"

Ally sensed a certain relief in Meg's voice.

"Of course not. I haven't seen you in ages, I'm dying for a good yarn. It'll be a laugh."

"If you're sure then. When is the best time for you?"

"So, it's the last opportunity Ally has to show me the guesthouse," Meg was telling Chris that evening. "There's not really the space for us all to stay, unless we actually take our own room, but I assume it's probably booked out for the weekend, and I was thinking of staying on till Monday . . ." She took a breath.

"That's fine, Meg," Chris reassured her. "You go along, have a break. You've seemed tired lately, it'll do you good."

Meg wasn't tired. She was weary of facing the sameness every day. Of waiting for Jamie to call. It had been almost a month with no word from him. Just like last time. She was a fool, a sad, middle-aged fool.

A change of scenery would do her good, even if it was only for a weekend. Ally had sounded so excited about her plans. Meg just had to make sure she didn't come across as bitter.

Sunday

Ally felt a slight lump in her throat when she first caught sight of Meg stepping off the train onto the platform. Maybe she was not as alone in the world as she had imagined. Meg was the closest thing she had to family now, she mustn't let them drift away from each other.

"Now, I want to take you to the restaurant first," Ally told her as they walked to the car. "Then we can settle in for the night at Birchgrove."

When they pulled up in front of the house, Ally watched Meg's face for a reaction.

"Look, I know it's a little rundown, but it's got so much potential, don't you think?" Ally said, as they got out and walked toward the front portico. Meg was still looking a little dumbfounded.

"Well, say something!"

"I think it's wonderful."

Ally hugged her. "Do you? Do you really? I really wanted you to like it."

"Why does it matter what I think?"

"Because your opinion is important to me. And I know I have a tendency to take the next thing that comes along—you know, art college, teaching—"

"Bryce," Meg added.

"Exactly," Ally grinned. "I didn't know what I was going to do next, and this just sort of landed in my lap. I need a reality check that it's a good decision."

Meg smiled. "Come on then, show me inside."

Ally took her on a tour through the various rooms, bubbling over with all of her ideas.

"We pulled a little of the carpet up over here in the corner," she explained, standing in one of the front rooms. "The floorboards look like they may be alright. We don't want to pull it all up now, because the carpet will protect the boards while we're painting."

She prattled on, dragging Meg through every room in the place. In the last week she had scoured the local hardware for every color chart they had in stock. Then she had started collecting sample pots. Nic was worried she was wasting her money but Ally insisted. She needed to try out the colors in situ, see them at different times of the day and night. Now the various walls looked like giant artist's palettes, dabbed with splotches of paint, blended, streaked, sponged. Ally was having the time of her life.

"I always said you should go into business doing this," Meg remarked.

"I'm not going into business."

"Well, what else would you call it? You're investing your own money and renovating an entire restaurant."

"I'm not doing the whole thing, Meg. Only the pretty stuff."

"But you're so clever, Ally. You will have a business by the time this is all finished, when people see what you've done."

"I doubt it. Besides, I don't want to start up a business down here. I'm not staying."

"Oh, you're not still saying that, are you?" Meg frowned. "God, you came for a few weeks in January and now it's nearly May. It can't be all that bad."

"It's not, but that doesn't mean I want to settle here."

Meg considered her for a moment. "What are you doing about your job?"

"I can extend my leave, unpaid of course, till next year."

"So, you're still hedging your bets. Not quite ready to cut the apron strings?"

Ally shrugged. "Just keeping my options open. That's the attraction of doing this, it doesn't commit me indefinitely. But it does give me the chance to do something I love."

"Rob, are you there?" It was Matt's voice, coming from the front door.

"No, it's me, Ally," she called back. "Come on in."

"Oh, hi there," Matt said, walking into the room. "Rob's supposed to meet me here. I thought he might have borrowed your car when I saw it out the front."

"No, I'm just showing off the place. This is my friend, down from Sydney, Meg Lynch. Meg, this is Matt Serrano."

"Hi, *Matt*," Meg said, with a little too much emphasis.

"How are you?" Matt said, offering his hand. "Ally's told me a lot about you."

"Oh, she's told me a lot about you, too."

Ally sighed inwardly. She glanced at Matt, who was trying unsuccessfully to suppress a grin.

"So, what are you and Rob up to?" Ally asked, changing the subject.

"We're meeting with the kitchen contractor."

"Matt's supervising the renovation," Ally explained to Meg.

"So you'll be around a fair bit then?" Meg remarked.

"Here and there."

"Wait till you see what Ally does with the place. She's a genius."

"Meg!"

"It's true!"

"I'd believe it," Matt smiled. "I've seen her work."

"Well, you haven't seen anything yet."

"Okay, okay. Enough." Ally frowned. "We have to get going."

"Oh, do we? Already?" Meg countered.

"Yes," Ally said firmly. "I'll see you later, Matt."

"Sure. Nice to meet you, Meg."

"Bye, Matt, it was nice meeting you, too. Maybe we'll see you down at the guesthouse? I'm here for a couple of days." Meg's voice trailed off as Ally led her forcibly out of the room.

As they stepped out of the front door, Meg grabbed Ally's arm.

"That's *the* Matt?"

"Stop it!" Ally whispered. He can still hear us."

As soon as they closed the doors of the car, Meg turned to Ally. "I thought you said he looked like your grandfather?"

"No," Ally corrected her, as she started the engine and drove off. "He *reminds* me of my grandfather."

"So has anything happened?"

"No."

"Why not?"

"Because it hasn't."

"What, he never asked you out again?"

Ally sighed. "Oh, once or twice."

"And?"

"And nothing," she shrugged.

"What do you mean?"

"I mean nothing."

"Nothing happened?"

"No, I didn't go."

"You're a fool."

"I am not!"

"Well then, what is wrong with you?" Meg persisted, pretending to fan herself. "Ally, he is a seriously good-looking man!"

"So? Looks aren't everything you know," Ally said testily. "You can be so shallow sometimes, Meg."

They drove along for a while, not saying anything. Eventually Meg cleared her throat.

"He seems like a really nice guy as well," she said in a small voice. Ally smiled, glancing across at Meg. They started to laugh.

"He is," Ally said resignedly. "Oh, don't look at me like that."

"I don't understand you, Ally."

"You and me both," she admitted. "I don't know what it is. He is a nice guy, but I'm not sure. I don't really know him."

"You think too much. Just do it."

Ally shrugged. "And then what?"

"What do you mean?" Meg frowned. "You have a bit of fun together, enjoy each other's company, get some sex." She winked.

Ally rolled her eyes. "Meg, I just don't think I'm up to a relationship at the moment."

Meg sighed. "Who said anything about a relationship? I'm just talking about having some fun. A relationship is the quickest way to ruin the fun. I tell you what, Ally, if I was in your shoes . . ." She drifted off into a daydream, with Jamie in the lead role.

Ally glanced at her, frowning. "Don't tell me there's trouble in paradise?"

Meg folded her arms in front of her. "There can't be any trouble in paradise," she said grimly, "because paradise is too bloody perfect."

Ally looked at Meg, but she was staring at the road ahead. There was definitely something going on with her, but Ally decided to leave it until later, when they could talk properly.

"So tell me about Harrison, every word he can say, every cute thing he's done since I saw him. And I hope you've brought photos."

Ally offered Meg a room to herself, with the place empty, but she opted to share with Ally.

"We'll be sitting up half the night anyway, won't we?" said Meg. "Anyway how come there are no guests staying?"

"Sunday night is usually the quietest anyway, and even Monday and Tuesday, except during holiday periods. We had a full house right over Easter. But now with the new owners due, I'm just caretaking."

"When do they actually take over?"

"In about a fortnight, but now they've asked if I'll stay for another couple of weeks after that, to help them with the changeover."

Ally led Meg through to the kitchen. "Are you hungry?"

"Not really, but I think I'm ready for a drink."

"Sure, I'll open a bottle of wine."

"So," Meg said, taking a seat at the kitchen bench. "You'll be here for another month then?"

Ally nodded, twisting the corkscrew into the bottle. "At first I told them I couldn't do it."

"Why not?"

"I really have to get started on the restaurant. But they were great, they said they only needed me in the mornings, for check-ins, that kind of thing. They've run a restaurant before, but never the accommodation side."

She pulled out the cork and poured them both a glass.

"So it's worked out really well actually, because I haven't found anywhere to stay yet. Not that I've been looking, I've been too busy."

Meg held her glass up to Ally. "To new challenges."

"I'll drink to that." Ally looked at Meg. "So what's going on with you?"

Meg shrugged.

"You've been . . . kind of short every time I've spoken to you."

"Well that hasn't been often enough to make a judgment," Meg returned dryly.

"Is that what it is? You're cross with me?"

Meg sighed, putting her glass down. "No, envious, not cross."

"Envious of me?" Ally stared at her. "Why?"

"Look at your life at the moment. You've had one new thing after another. And now this restaurant, it's just so exciting."

Ally hadn't really looked at the past few months that way. It was still colored by the loss of Lillian. And of her grandfather. It was only gradually sinking in what a loss that was. She hadn't let herself dwell on the "what might have been" scenario. But it was there in the background, and sometimes it hurt.

"My life could only get more exciting after living in Blandsville for five years," Ally reminded her.

"Yeah, well just don't move to Perfectland, whatever you do," Meg smirked, draining her glass.

"That's the second time you've used the word perfect as though it was some kind of a disease."

"Mm, I hadn't thought of that. A disease," she pondered. "Yes, the disease of the middle class."

"What are you on about, Meg?"

"I'm just tired, and fed up. Tired and fed up, and *bored*. I'm bored to the back teeth."

"What with, your job?"

"You name it. My job, my house, my husband, my life. Even my hairstyle is boring."

"I think it suits you."

Meg grabbed the bottle and poured herself another glass. "Of course it suits me. It's *perfect*."

Ally narrowed her eyes, watching her almost skol the whole glass. She hadn't missed that Meg had thrown "husband" in with her list of gripes.

"I don't understand. I thought your life was exactly the way you wanted it. You've always been so disciplined, setting goals, making lists. Everything you've ever planned has worked out."

"Mm. Well, you know what they say, Al, don't wish too hard . . ."

Ally realized she was avoiding the issue. "Okay, Meg. What exactly is the problem? Has something happened between you and Chris?"

Meg wondered if she should tell her about Jamie. But then she realized there was nothing to tell. She looked squarely at Ally. "No, nothing. Nothing at all."

She frowned.

"Don't you see? That's the whole problem, there's nothing *wrong*, but it's not exciting anymore."

"I don't understand. You were calling him your 'knight in shining armor' only at Christmas. I've always thought that you two were living a fairy tale."

Meg paused, thinking. "Maybe you're right. Except now we're living the 'happy ever after' part. That's where the fairy tale always ends. The Handsome Prince snoring while Cinderella stares at the telly does not make for riveting storytelling."

"Maybe you have unrealistic expectations, Meg. You are a bit of a romantic."

"Look, I can't explain this, I don't know how to. I realize I have a great job, and a wonderful husband, a beautiful baby, a lovely home . . ." Meg sighed. "But it's like climbing to the top of a mountain, and then thinking, 'Oh, so that's all there is up here.'"

"But you're not even forty yet, there's so much more you could do with your life, if you want to."

"Like what?"

Ally thought for a moment. "Have another baby?"

"Oh, not you too!"

"What?"

"That's all anyone can say to me!" she said in a raised voice. 'Why don't you have another baby?' 'Isn't it time you gave Harrison a little sister?' And of course it would be a girl, because that's just so fucking perfect," she snapped viciously. "I can't stand it anymore!"

Ally just stared at her. She had never really seen Meg in full flight. She was always so level-headed, in control.

"Meg, I didn't realize you were unhappy. You seemed to have it all. I always wished I could have your life."

Meg looked up from her glass. "I bet you don't anymore," she said quietly.

Ally hesitated. At the moment she wouldn't give up the restaurant for anything, maybe not even a baby, she realized.

"I've got something to look forward to right now. But I'm still alone."

"You think because I'm married I'm not lonely?"

"Oh Meg . . ." Ally didn't know what else to say.

Watsons Bay

Blasted phone! Meg kept her eyes closed. She could hear Chris fumbling to reach it on the bedside table. It was still ringing.

"Hun, I think it might be your mobile."

Shit. Meg usually plugged her mobile phone in overnight to recharge. Bloody Simon, she was going to kill him if this was about some meeting. She didn't have to do this anymore.

"Hrrmph," she croaked into the phone.

"There's a southerly blowing."

"What?"

"There's a southerly blowing, a mild one, and it's a clear day. Do you want to come for a drive down the coast? I want to show you something."

It was Jamie. Meg opened her eyes. Now she was awake.

"Hold on."

She almost fell out of bed, and staggered to the door, closing it behind her.

"What are you doing ringing me here?" she whispered emphatically.

"I rang your mobile number, like you said. I didn't know where you'd be."

"Where else did you think I'd be at . . .'She crept down the hall to the kitchen and peered across at the oven clock. "5:58! Why are you ringing so early?"

"I told you, there's a southerly blowing and the conditions are perfect. Can you come down the coast with me today?"

"Where, when? Now?"

"We should leave soon, it'll take most of the day."

The fog was starting to lift from Meg's brain. "I work today."

There was a pause. "You never take a day off?"

"Not because there's a southerly blowing."

"Maybe it's time you did."

Meg thought she heard stirring in Harrison's room. "Just a minute," she whispered. She opened the door to the deck as quietly as she could and slipped outside. It was freezing. The sun was barely creeping over the horizon, not enough to take the chill out of the air yet.

"What about tomorrow? I don't work tomorrow."

"There's no guarantee that the wind will be up tomorrow," he explained. "Besides, the scupper can't come."

"Who?"

"Your little bloke. You can't bring him."

"Why not?"

"You'll see."

Meg was immediately suspicious. "Jamie, I've told you I'm not jumping off anything."

He laughed. "You don't have to jump off anything. I promise."

Meg hesitated. Why was she even considering this? She should have been cool with him. Stand-offish. After all, he hadn't called her for over a month. But this was the most exciting thing that had happened to her since, well, since the last time she'd seen him.

"Come on, you know you want to," Jamie coaxed. "You won't regret it."

She was not so sure. But that only made the prospect all the more appealing.

"Where will I meet you?"

Jamie made a whooping sound. "We have lift-off!"

"What do you mean by that?"

"Nothing, nothing. It's just an expression. Do you want me to come and pick you up?"

"No!" Meg exclaimed, glancing behind her nervously.

"Okay, we'll make a rendezvous," he suggested.

"Now you're making it sound sordid."

"I didn't mean to. How about," he paused, "the carpark at Bondi?"

Meg frowned. It might not be the best place to leave her car all day.

"Too conspicuous. Do you know the supercenter at Moore Park?" It had a huge carpark underneath. The car would be more anonymous there.

"Anywhere in particular?"

"The lower floor, outside Ikea."

"How soon can you get there?"

"Ummm . . ." She calculated driving time, getting ready, making an excuse to Chris. "I think I'll need an hour."

"I'll see you at seven then."

She swallowed. "Okay."

"Oh Meg, have you got leather pants by any chance?"

"What?"

"Never mind, just wear warm clothes, and covered-in shoes."

"Jamie!"

But he'd hung up. Leather pants? Where was he taking her? Why had she agreed?

"Another breakfast meeting?"

Meg jumped, turning around. Chris stood in the doorway holding Harrison.

"It's freezing out here," she shivered. She had to give herself a moment to think. "Hello darling," she held her arms out to Harrison. He reached for her, and they went inside, Chris closing the door behind them.

"So, that was Simon?"

Meg nodded. She didn't want to lie to Chris, but what else could she do? Jamie would be waiting for her, one hour from now, at the supercenter. She had no way to contact him to cancel, not that she wanted to. The kindest thing she could do for Chris was let him believe something else.

"He's asked me to go and scout locations today."

"Really?"

"Mm." she put Harrison down on the floor, and went to fill the kettle. "Down the coast. I'll have to leave soon, actually. Will you be right to drop Harrison off at your mum's?"

"Sure. Is Simon going with you?"

"No, one of the photographers, Simon's too busy. That's why he asked me."

Chris came up behind her and kissed her on the top of the head. "Should be a nice change. At least it gets you out of the office for the day."

"Mm."

. . .

Meg was still suspicious about the reference to leather pants, but she did as Jamie directed and dressed warmly. Chris hadn't suspected a thing, so Meg had almost convinced herself there was no harm in what she was doing. Now she had to convince Simon.

She pulled up at a set of traffic lights and dialed his home number.

"Hello."

"Hi Simon, it's Meg."

"Hey, what's happening? You sound like you're in the car?"

"I am. I'm not coming in today, Simon."

"Oh? What are you doing? You're not sick?"

"I'm scouting locations."

"What?" He started to laugh. "You don't do that!"

"Well, I am today."

"Who asked you to do that?"

Meg sighed. He wasn't getting it. "Look, I'm taking the day off. So if anyone asks, I'm scouting locations, okay?"

"You don't need an excuse, Meg. You can have a day off. No one's going to mind."

She took a deep breath. "I mean, if *anyone* calls for me."

"Who would be calling..." his voice trailed off. The penny had dropped. There was silence for a moment.

"Simon?"

"I don't feel comfortable about this, Meg."

"I doubt that Chris will call, he doesn't even expect me to be in the office."

"Meg..."

"Come on, Simon, you owe me."

"Why do I owe you?"

"Oh, okay, then I'll owe you."

"Yes, you'll owe me an explanation."

"One day."

"Are you going to tell me where you're going?"

"Down the coast to scout locations, that's as much as I told Chris. You don't need any more information than that."

"Yeah, or else I'll have to tell bigger lies," he said grimly. "Meg—"

"Simon, I have to go, the lights have changed."

"Then put me on speaker phone."

"Sorry, I can't." She hung up, switching off the phone so he couldn't ring back. He was going to be mad. Oh well, she wouldn't be back in the office till Monday, maybe he would have forgotten by then, or at least calmed down.

Meg drove into the carpark at the supercenter. It was almost empty, but she parked back a few rows anyway, tucked in close to a wall. She didn't want the car to be obvious. She locked it up and wandered slowly down toward the entrance to Ikea, checking her watch. It was nearly seven, he wasn't late yet. She heard an engine noise behind her and glanced over her shoulder. It was just a motorbike.

Meg stopped abruptly. A motorbike.

She turned around as Jamie brought the bike to a stop. She assumed it was Jamie underneath the helmet. He lifted the visor and a pair of glassy eyes smiled out at her. It was Jamie.

She watched him kick the stand out and turn off the engine. He lifted the helmet off his head. "Hiya Meg."

"What the hell is that?"

"Transportation."

"I don't think so." Meg turned on her heel and pranced off back toward her car. Jamie jumped off the bike and caught her by the arm.

"Don't just walk away, Meg!"

"You should have told me."

"Would you have come?"

"No!"

"That's why I didn't tell you."

"Well, what good did that do? I'm here, but I'm still not getting on that thing."

He breathed out heavily. "Just come over here for a minute. Check it out."

"It won't make any difference," she retorted.

"If you really don't want to go on the bike, we'll take your car."

She stood looking at him, her arms crossed. Jamie met her gaze, his eyes attempting to persuade her. He looked as sexy as all get out, dressed in leather from head to foot. She tried to imagine Chris in the same outfit. He could never pull it off. Meg sighed and walked back over to the bike.

"Is it yours?"

He shook his head. "No, it belongs to a friend. But I've got a license," he added quickly. "And it's insured."

She didn't say anything.

"Look, I brought you something." He opened a bag strapped to the packrack and drew out a black leather jacket. "See if it fits."

"Who does this belong to?"

"Just a friend."

Didn't he own anything?

Meg took off the coat she was wearing, and Jamie helped her on with the leather jacket. The friend must have been a woman, and it fitted fine.

"And," Jamie said, pulling a helmet out of the same bag, "you have to wear this."

Meg passively let him fit the helmet onto her head. "This is going to ruin my hair," she grumbled.

He laughed, standing back from her. "Well, look at you, Meg Lynch! You look like a real bikie chick."

Meg glanced nervously at the bike. "Look Jamie, they scare me. I realize that's not very cool, but that's the way it is."

"You'll be okay. I promise I'll take it easy."

"You're talking to a woman who drives a Volvo cautiously."

He smiled indulgently at her. "Just have a sit. See how it feels."

She looked doubtful, but she let him help her up to sit on the pillion seat. "How's that?"

Meg shrugged. "It's fine, it's not moving!"

"Why don't I take you for a spin around the carpark? Slowly," he added, noting the uncertainty in her eyes.

"Okay," she said in a small voice.

Jamie replaced his helmet and climbed onto the bike. "Now, the most important thing you have to remember is to lean with me, even if your natural reaction is to straighten, you have to go with me."

He turned the key and revved the engine. Meg's heart started to race. She inched closer to him.

"It's hard to hear anything once the engine's going," Jamie shouted over his shoulder. "Out in traffic it's impossible. Are you alright?"

She nodded.

"Okay, hold on."

He took off smoothly and crept at a snail's pace along the length of the carpark. Meg prepared herself for the corner. Jamie leaned to the right and she closed her eyes, leaning with him, sure they would topple over. But they didn't. Meg made herself relax and think about what she was feeling. It wasn't so bad. She knew it was a cliché, but there was something vaguely sexual about sitting astride a throbbing motor, especially with Jamie's back pressed up against her, her thighs straddling his.

They did a few laps of the parking lot, and Jamie eventually pulled up near the Volvo. He left the engine running.

"What do you want to do?"

Meg bit her lip. She was always such a coward. Neil used to tease her mercilessly when she was a girl. And even though she toughed it out, then as now, rationalizing her fear, there were times when she was secretly frustrated by her own timidity.

She took a deep breath. "If you get me killed, I'll never forgive you."

Jamie smiled. "I won't let anything happen to you, I promise."

Crossing over a lane of traffic as they left the carpark was enough to weaken Meg's resolve, but Jamie couldn't hear her protests. She closed her eyes and locked her arms around him. She was aware they had joined the expressway when they started to pick up speed. Oh God, why did she say yes to this? Meg kept her eyes closed most of the time, only peeking occasionally. They passed a golf course, then the airport. They finally stopped at traffic lights at Brighton beach.

Jamie twisted around, lifting the visor. "Could you loosen your hold a bit, Meg?" he shouted above the noise of the engine. "I'm having trouble breathing!"

"Sorry!" she said, letting go.

They took off again, and Meg tried to keep her eyes open and not crush Jamie. She took deep, calming breaths, but there was no way she could relax perched on the back of a bike traveling at eighty kilometers an hour. She squeezed her eyes shut and hung on for dear life.

After a while she felt the bike slow to a stop and the engine cut. Meg opened her eyes. They were in a McDonald's carpark, she didn't know where.

Jamie took off his helmet. "Do you want to get a coffee?"

She nodded. Her legs had cramped into position, so it was a relief to stretch them out. She followed Jamie inside and left him to order the coffees while she went to the ladies' room. She rejoined him at a table outside. He was rolling a cigarette.

"Your hair looks fine," he commented, glancing up at her.

She shrugged, sipping her coffee.

"How do you do that?"

"What?"

"You always look so . . ." He paused before striking a match.

"What?"

"I don't know. Neat?"

Meg frowned. "What's wrong with that?"

"Nothing, I just don't know how you do it." He lit his cigarette. "So how are you holding up?"

"Not wonderfully. I suppose we've got a while to go yet?"

"We're about halfway, but I wanted to give you a break before we hit the park."

"The park?"

He nodded. "The Royal National Park. We turn off soon. The road's a bit winding, and steep in parts. Do you think you'll be alright?"

"Is there an alternative?"

"We could keep on the highway. But you'd miss some pretty amazing scenery."

"I've had my eyes shut most of the time anyway."

Jamie grinned. "I think you might have broken one of my ribs, the way you've been hanging on."

"Sorry."

"You should try to relax. You might enjoy it."

"There's a concept—relax on the back of a motorbike. You realize there's nothing between us and the road, another car, a truck, anything we might hit."

"You've got a very negative way of thinking, haven't you?"

"I'd have called it realistic."

"The world's not such a scary place, you know, Meg. What's made you so afraid of it?"

Meg contemplated him. "Persuasive men dressed in black leather, riding motorbikes."

He laughed. "You're not frightened of me."

Just a little. But she kept that thought to herself.

The trip through the park was at once beautiful and terrifying. The scenery was superb, but Meg thought she would lose it as they snaked around steep hairpin bends, leaning so far over their knees almost touched the bitumen. From time to time Jamie would loosen her grip around his waist, patting her hand reassuringly.

When they made it to higher ground the road straightened out, and Meg looked out across the ocean toward the horizon. For a moment she understood the attraction of riding a motorbike. Until they hit the next series of bends.

After nearly an hour they came out of the cover of a grove of trees and the whole coastline opened up, stretching southward before them. Meg gasped. The escarpment stepped down to meet the ocean, undulating around secluded coves. It was breathtaking.

Jamie slowed right down, and for the first time Meg was not conscious of the bike. As they drew closer to the headland, she spotted a hang-glider up in the air, and then another and another. Their pastel colored wings were like so many butterflies dancing in the wind. She was enchanted.

They turned into the parking area right on the headland. It was filled with cars and people. There was an ice-cream van, and various other vehicles, all advertising paragliding and hang-gliding lessons, or tandem flights. They pulled into a parking spot and Jamie switched off the engine. Meg climbed off the bike and removed her helmet, shaking out her hair. She stretched and yawned, looking up to the sky.

"What do you think?"

"It's spectacular." Then Meg eyed him suspiciously. "You haven't got any more surprises up your sleeve, have you? Because you're dreaming if you think I'm going up on one of those."

Jamie laughed, shaking his head. "I told you I wouldn't make you jump off anything. So what about the bike?"

"What about it?"

"You made it all the way here. That's pretty good going. Was it as bad as you thought?"

"Worse," she returned flatly.

"Ah, come on."

"There were occasional moments of not bad."

They found a grassy spot to sit, out of the way of the take-off area. Meg watched, fascinated, as two men held a hang-glider steady, while a third harnessed himself in.

"Tempted?" Jamie said after a while.

"Not even vaguely," she returned. "Look, he's strapping himself to a kite made of tracksuit material, for godsake!"

"There's a little more to them than that, Meg."

She looked at him doubtfully. They watched as the man, obviously ready, nodded to the other two, and they tilted the glider slightly back so that the wind would pick it up. The man in the harness stepped forward, off the cliff. Meg held her breath as he dropped momentarily before the wind lifted him into the sky.

"Now that's the part I could never do."

"What?"

"Just walk off a cliff! How does anyone do that? I don't think I'd ever have the courage to take the first step."

"Maybe you have already."

She looked at him.

"You got on a motorbike today."

Meg grimaced. "Why did you have to remind me of that? I've got to get back on it eventually, haven't I?"

"It's a long walk otherwise," he smiled. "At least you can mark it off your list."

"It was never on my list, I assure you."

"Then maybe you can make another list—'things I thought I'd never do.' "

Yes, and she could add skipping work, lying to her husband and taking off for the day with a virtual stranger.

"Look how far he's going." Jamie was pointing south across the escarpment toward a stray glider that was rapidly becoming a mere dot in the sky.

He looked around at her. "You want to follow him?"

Meg winced. "Get back on the bike?"

"Don't think about it, Meg. You think too much." He jumped to his feet and put his hand out to help her up. "Just do it!"

She hesitated for a moment before putting her hand in his.

Meg realized she should have thought about it for longer, as they barrelled down the hill giving chase to the rogue hang-glider. They passed a couple of small townships before rounding a tight bend that jutted out over the ocean. The road ahead was all curves, hugging the cliff, the ocean dropping away to their left. Meg opened her eyes briefly to see waves crashing just below them as they veered around another sharp curve, all the while picking up speed. She could hear screaming, and then she realized it was her own voice. She hung onto to Jamie like a monkey clinging to his back. She didn't care if she did break a rib. It would serve him right.

The road straightened out and became wider, and Jamie slowed down, eventually stopping in front of an old pub perched on the side of the cliff overlooking the ocean.

Meg climbed off first, pulling off her helmet. "You could have warned me about that road!"

"Sorry," he said sheepishly. "But you made it."

She just glared at him. "Do we have to go back that way?"

"No, we can meet up with the freeway a little farther on," he reassured her. "Come on, I'll buy you a drink."

"And some lunch," she added, checking her watch. "I'm starving."

They sat out on an open deck that appeared to be suspended above the ocean. Meg sipped her wine gazing out at the expanse of blue to the horizon. At least Jamie had a knack for picking places that made her feel a long way from everything. Maybe even a little bit free.

"Where did you say you were going today?" he asked suddenly.

Meg grimaced. She wasn't free at all. "Scouting locations."

He nodded absently. Then he leaned forward, claiming her attention from the view. "What's your husband like?"

"Why do you want to know?"

"I'm just wondering if he's the arrogant type who puts you down, or the workaholic who ignores you, or the bastard that cheats on you."

Meg breathed out heavily. "No, he's the decent, trusting type, who would do anything for me."

Jamie looked at her. "So why do you keep coming out with me?"

"Why do you keep asking?"

"I told you, I like your face."

A waiter arrived with their lunch—huge open burgers, buried under a mound of chips. Meg tucked into hers hungrily, hoping Jamie would abandon this line of questioning.

"You haven't answered me," he said.

No such luck.

"I've forgotten—what did you ask?"

"I guess, under the circumstances," he said lifting an eyebrow, "I thought you'd be complaining about your husband, that he doesn't pay you enough attention or something. But you don't talk about him at all."

"I don't feel comfortable talking about him."

"Why not?"

"Because he's none of those things you said."

"So, I'll repeat the question, why did come out with me?"

"Maybe I like your face, too."

Jamie grinned. "Okay, so you don't want to talk about it."

"Let me ask you something instead," said Meg, taking the opportunity to change the subject. "How old are you?"

"Why do you need to know that?"

She groaned. "Don't make riddles. I'm interested, that's all."

"It shouldn't matter. People make judgments on irrelevancies like your age, or your star sign. It doesn't mean anything."

Meg crossed her arms. "Well, maybe it doesn't. But I reckon I've been a good sport coming all this way on the back of a motorbike, the least you can do is tell me a bit about yourself!"

Jamie leaned forward across the table. "Okay, if it'll make you happy, I was thirty-one on the eighteenth of December last year which, I'm told, makes me a Sagittarius."

"Thank you." Meg breathed a sigh of relief. He was in his thirties, barely. She was only a little pathetic. She bit into a chip.

"What about you?"

Meg looked across at him, frowning.

"How old are you?"

"I'm a Virgo. That's all you need to know."

Jamie started to laugh. "You're a funny chick."

"So you keep saying."

The wine obviously helped relax her. Meg realized she was probably a bit tipsy by the time she climbed onto the bike for the return trip. She found herself settling comfortably into Jamie's back, her arms tucked around him firmly, but not too tight now. She rested her head against his shoulder.

They stopped again for coffee about halfway, and that woke her up. The rest of the trip was slower, as they hit the afternoon traffic in the suburbs. They pulled into the supercenter at about five.

Meg climbed off the bike and handed Jamie the helmet. She took off the jacket, and Jamie fished hers out of the bag. Meg reached into the pocket for her car keys.

"Did you have a good day?" he asked.

"It was different."

"Is different good?"

She nodded. "I suppose so."

Unexpectedly, Jamie reached his hand over and stroked her cheek. "Your skin's all flushed. Must be the fresh air."

"Must be."

He was staring at her, Meg didn't know where to look. He took a step closer and before she realized what he was doing, his lips were on hers. It was a gentle kiss, but lingering. His hand was still on her cheek, but they stood apart, only joined at the lips. For a moment she forgot where she was, who she was.

Then he pulled away.

"Bye Meg," he said, replacing his helmet. He climbed onto the bike and started the engine. She stood, not moving, until he rode away, disappearing out through the exit with a brief wave.

Meg stirred, looking around to see if anyone was watching her. She unlocked the car and got in. Adjusting the rear-view mirror, she caught sight of her reflection. Her skin was flushed, like Jamie said. She touched her fingers to her lips for a moment before starting up the engine and driving away.

Birchgrove

"How's your friend Meg? Have you talked to her lately?"

Nic was packing her bags. She had finished her last shift at Birchgrove the night before. The restaurant was not opening again until next Friday, with the new owners in place. Rob and Nic had both found jobs at Milford Park, a huge tourist resort on the outskirts of Bowral. So Nic was moving into Rob's bed-sitter, the glorified shoebox, as she liked to refer to it. She claimed it was so tiny they were going to have to synchronize their breathing, one exhaling while the other inhaled, when they were both home at the same time.

"Meg's okay." Ally shrugged. She had made a point of phoning her more often, to keep in touch. "She seemed a bit brighter when I spoke to her yesterday."

Nic had joined them on the second night of Meg's stay. They had ordered pizza in and hit the wine heavily again. Meg went on and on about her terrible, perfect life. Ally was glad that someone else had been around as a buffer.

"So what's her husband like?" Nic asked. "Is he that bad?"

"He's not bad at all. I don't know what she's complaining about."

"Well, she didn't actually say he was bad, just boring."

Ally thought for a moment. "Chris is a really sweet, lovely guy. But . . ."

"But what?"

"He'd do anything for her. Really, *anything*." She paused. "But sometimes Meg can be, well, a bit demanding. I mean, she's so driven and efficient, she expects everyone to be the same."

"So what's your point?"

"Well, like I said, Chris is lovely . . . but sometimes I used to think, why don't you just say no?"

"To what?"

"Anything! Just say no, bugger off, I don't feel like it. I don't agree. Something other than yes Meg, three bags full Meg."

Nic paused, nodding sagely. "Mm, the SNAG dilemma."

"What's that?"

"Women dream of having a Sensitive New Age Guy until they get one, and then they fantasize about Mr. Chiseled Jaw from Mills and Boon land."

Ally screwed up her nose. "The arrogant, brooding type? No thanks." She fell onto the bed and stared up at the ceiling.

"I couldn't stand a man who was demanding or self-absorbed," she continued. "But that doesn't mean I'd prefer someone who'd just fall into line with everything I wanted either. You know, I whistle and he jumps." Ally shuddered. "No, I'd like someone who was strong and confident in himself, but sensitive to my needs."

"Oh, okay, Mr. *Perfect*," Nic quipped. "God, no wonder you're still single!"

Ally looked at her.

Nic covered her face with the shirt she was folding. "Sorry, I can't believe I said that."

She sighed. "Don't worry about it. You're probably right."

Nic peeked out from behind the shirt. "Oh?"

"Maybe I am aiming too high."

"Mm. Well, from my experience, people who set unrealistic goals usually don't want to achieve them."

The phone started ringing.

"Ah-hah! Saved by the bell!" Ally grinned as Nic reached to answer it.

"It's for you," she said a moment later, handing it to Ally.

She sat up. "Hello?"

"Ally, Bob Burton here." It was the real estate agent. "I may have some good news for you."

"Oh?"

"I have a very keen buyer. Your property is apparently exactly what he's been looking for."

"It is?" she said dubiously.

"Well, he hasn't seen it yet."

"What do you mean?"

"I sent him a flyer, with that rather flattering shot we took, remember? I told him it was about to come onto the market, that always piques their interest."

"That's good."

"Well, like I said, it's what he's been looking for. So how are the repairs going?"

"Oh God, I don't even know. I've been so busy I haven't been down there in weeks."

"Well, you'd best go check it out today. Sweep the floors, open a few windows to air the place out; fresh flowers help too."

Ally had a sinking feeling that wasn't going to be anywhere near enough.

"What's going on?" Nic asked when she hung up the phone.

"Someone's interested in looking at the property."

"Brilliant!"

"I don't know," Ally said doubtfully. "I haven't seen Matt for a while. I don't even know if he's had the chance to get any of the work done." She paused, her anxiety building. "Have you got his number?"

Nic fished around in her handbag and drew out a small address book. She read the number out as Ally dialed.

"That's his home phone number? Maybe I should call his mobile?"

"You can try that next," Nic said calmly. "Stop stressing."

His voice came onto the line. "Hello?"

"Matt? I'm glad I caught you," Ally said breathlessly.

"Is that you, Ally?"

"Yes, I just got a call from Bob, and he said someone is coming to look at the property—"

"Bob Burton?"

"Yes!" she said, her tone impatient. Who else did he think she meant? "He said someone is coming tomorrow who's really interested and that I should go down and make sure everything's in order."

"*Right* . . ." he stretched the word out slowly.

"So you'll meet me down there?"

"Pardon?"

He was acting incredibly vague, Ally thought, her irritation growing. "I'm leaving straightaway. I'll meet you there, okay?"

"You want me to come down to Circle's End?"

"Yes."

"Right now?"

"Well, yes!" What was so hard to follow? "We've only got the rest of the day, and into the night, I guess, if we need it."

"I can't come today."

"What, why not?"

She thought she heard a sigh. "Because I have plans, Ally."

"Well this is important!" Ally insisted. "You can't just leave me in the lurch like this!"

"Why do you think I'm leaving you in the lurch?"

"Well whatever you're doing is obviously more important than helping me out," she said shrilly. "And you were the one that offered to help me in the first place. I should have paid you, that's the problem, isn't it? I wanted to pay you, remember? But you wouldn't take it, and now that means you can just say no, you're under no obligation. But in the meantime, I'm screwed!"

"Ally, you haven't been near the place in weeks."

"I've been busy—"

"And I'm busy today. Goodbye, Ally."

"He hung up!" Ally said to Nic, mystified.

"I wonder why?"

"Shit! Now what am I going to do?"

"Well, take some lessons in tact and diplomacy for starters."

"Why, what did I do wrong?"

"You should have heard yourself!"

"Well you should have heard him," Ally said defensively. "He just said 'no.' Calm as you please."

"Sounds like your ideal man."

"What?"

"You know, the one who doesn't just jump because you whistle," Nic grinned.

Ally glared at her, "That's an entirely different thing. What am I going to do?"

"Calm down, Ally. It's not as if he could have done much in half a day anyway. Look, I'll come with you, we'll clean the place up, put lots of fresh flowers around . . ."

"That's what Bob said," Ally sighed gloomily.

"There you go! Everything will turn out alright, you'll see."

Half an hour later they were on the way to Kangaroo Valley, the car laden with vases and tablecloths, and about four tubs of flowers, after a frantic call to a friend of Nic's who ran the local florist. They headed out of Bowral along Sheepwash Road, toward Avoca.

"Doesn't Matt live along here somewhere?" Nic remarked idly.

Ally grunted.

"Do you know whereabouts?"

She shook her head. "I bet he'd drop everything for Miss Queensland. In fact, that's probably why he's busy today," she muttered, thinking aloud.

"What?"

"Never mind."

"Who's Miss Queensland?"

"I don't know."

"What are you talking about?"

"Nothing, never mind."

When they pulled up outside the barn, Nic let out a squeal.

"This is classic!"

"You reckon?" Ally frowned.

"Come on, let's unload the car."

"I'll go and open up."

Ally despondently turned the key in the lock and pushed the front door open. It usually shuddered, but today it swung back smoothly. She peered across the dim living room. It had a low ceiling, and heavy dark wooden beams to support the loft above.

"Something looks different," she murmured.

She walked through to the dining area, where the loft ended, and the room opened up to the roof. Ally stared at the stairs to the loft. She couldn't believe her eyes.

"Hey, this all looks new," said Nic, who had followed her in, carrying a tub of flowers.

Ally looked at her, then back at the staircase, all straight, wide and even. Not a tree branch in sight.

"Ally?" Nic said warily. "Did Matt do this?"

"I guess," she swallowed.

Nic's face broke into a broad grin. "You are in such deep shit!"

Ally groaned.

"Off to the kitchen with you, and start making some humble pie."

"The kitchen," Ally said weakly, walking to the doorway. She wasn't even surprised to see the bright new benchtops in place, completely revamping the whole room.

"Was I very rude?" Ally cringed.

"Rude? That's putting it mildly," said Nic, rolling her eyes. "Try obnoxious, offensive and insulting. Oh, and pushy, you were definitely pushy."

Ally collapsed on a nearby stool. "Well, he should have said something."

"You didn't give him much of a chance!"

"What am I going to do?" she moaned. "I have to go and apologize."

"Look, we've still got to tart up the place. Go and see him on the way home. He might have cooled down by then, and you never know, he may even forgive you!"

A few hours later Ally was doing a final check around while Nic closed all the windows.

"Well, there's nothing more we can do here. It's in the lap of the gods now," Ally remarked.

"I like the place," said Nic. "And what with that beautiful new staircase—"

"Oh, okay! You don't have to rub it in."

They had placed vases of flowers in every room, and covered the battered dining table with a damask cloth. A couple of the worst chairs were banished to the shed, along with anything else that was broken, stained, or otherwise just plain ugly. And they had scrubbed, cleaned and dusted the place to within an inch of its life.

"Thanks, Nic, I couldn't have done all this without you."

"Of course you could have, it just would have taken you twice as long. It's Matt you have to thank."

"I know, I know," she sighed. "Come on, we'd better get going before I chicken out."

Nic had brought her belongings with her so that Ally could drop her off at Rob's on the way back. She said she would have invited Ally in to see the place, but they might not all fit at the same time. Rob came out to the car to give Ally directions to Matt's, after Nic had taken great delight in relaying the story to him.

"Don't pay any attention to her, Ally." Rob smiled, leaning in the window of her car. "I try not to."

"I heard that, Robert Grady," Nic said from the footpath.

He placed a consoling hand on Ally's arm. "You'll be alright. Matt's a nice guy."

That only made her feel worse, Ally thought, as she drove off toward Avoca. All those years of hardly saying "boo" to Bryce, and here she was telling Matt off when he had been nothing but decent to her. She had saved a large bunch of flowers for him, as a kind of peace offering. She hoped it wouldn't look silly, but she couldn't think of anything else.

"Men have it so much easier in the 'apology' gift-giving department,"

Nic had said. "Which is just as well, they usually have to do it more often."

Ally found the entrance to Matt's property easily. Rob had given her good directions, but it wasn't as out of the way as Ally had imagined. After closing the gate behind her, she drove along an unsealed driveway edged with wattles. It dipped a little, crossing a tiny stream. She wondered if he ever got rained in here, and she had a sinking feeling. That comparison with her grandfather was never far from her mind, especially now as she neared the house. There was a small grove of trees ahead, and as she rounded them the house came into view.

Ally was surprised. Set on the crest of the hill was a neat timber cottage with a steep corrugated-iron roof and two dormer windows facing north. A deep verandah wrapped around three sides of the building. The front of the house seemed to be almost all windows, looking out to a valley that dropped away gently at first, then steeply down a ravine.

Ally could see someone moving around inside. Bugger, she'd forgotten about Miss Queensland. What if she was here? That would be just too embarrassing. But Ally couldn't do anything about it now. Her car was in plain view from the inside of the house. There was nothing to do but stay calm, give him her thanks and the flowers, and then get away as fast as she could.

The front door opened as Ally stepped onto the wide timber stairs leading to the verandah.

"Hello," said a female voice, a very young female voice, Ally realized. She took a breath and looked up. She hoped the shock wasn't registering on her face. The girl standing in the doorway was surely too young to be Miss Queensland. She looked just like Matt: dark hair, olive skin and big, blue eyes.

"Dad!" she sang out. Ally thought she was going to fall backward down the stairs. She reached gladly for the railing and steadied herself.

"I'm Rebecca," the girl said brightly.

Ally hoped her face was smiling back and not betraying her total bewilderment. "Hello, my name is Ally."

Matt appeared behind Rebecca. He just stared at Ally, a slightly bemused frown crossing his face. His eyes flickered to the flowers in her arms. She wished she could dive down into them and disappear, like Alice in Wonderland.

"I just came from the house, from Circle's End. I wanted to thank you. And say sorry, and give you these, you know, to say sorry," she blurted, looking at the flowers. "But I didn't mean to impose on you and your family. Sorry."

"It's just me and Beck." Matt's expression seemed to soften. "Three sorrys in one go. That must be a record," he smiled.

She smiled feebly back. Did he say it was just him and Beck?

"So, you've been to the house?"

"Yes," Ally roused herself. "I got such a shock, when I saw everything you'd done. I didn't expect it at all."

"So I gathered," he said, lifting an eyebrow.

Ally reddened, remembering her outburst. "Sorry. But I don't understand, when did you get the chance?"

"Easter. Beck was away, so I had some free time."

Ally looked at him, frowning. "It rained all over Easter."

He nodded.

"You didn't get rained in?"

He smiled. "Just one night."

Her eyes widened. "Oh no! I feel so bad about this."

Matt shrugged. "Don't worry about it, you didn't make it rain. And besides, it's probably why I got it all finished."

"I don't know how I'm going to repay you."

"Wait till you get my bill," he grinned.

"It's not just the money," Ally said seriously, taking a breath. "No one has ever put themselves out like that before, for me . . ."

They stood for a moment looking at each other, not saying anything. Beck glanced at her father, and then at Ally, and then back at her father.

"Why don't I put those in water?" she offered, taking the flowers from Ally. "Come inside, Ally."

"Oh, I don't think so. I should be going."

"Do you have to?" Rebecca stood beside her father and Ally thought she saw her elbow him.

"Come on in, Ally," he said.

She didn't want to be rude, again. "Just for a minute then."

Matt stepped back for Ally to pass. Her mind was working overtime. Did Rebecca live with him? Who was her mother? Were she and Matt ever married? Were they separated now, or divorced? Or maybe she'd died, in some awful tragedy . . .

"Dad! Don't you have any vases?" Rebecca called from the kitchen.

"I don't think I've ever needed one before."

"I didn't know what else to bring, sorry," Ally said meekly.

"Enough with the apologies, Ally."

"Well, I'll bring you down one from Mum's next time," Rebecca said, crouching under the cupboards. "You should have at least one vase, it'll probably be one of your old wedding presents anyway. A crappy one, that Mum would never touch."

"Language, Rebecca."

So he had been married, and Rebecca obviously didn't live with him full-time. Matt had crossed to the kitchen and was helping his daughter find something to put the flowers in.

His daughter. This was one for the books. Ally had to completely revise her Matt Serrano dossier. Not *single loner,* but *divorced* (she supposed) *father of one teenage girl* (or more?) . . . God, she was getting as bad as Bryce. Next she'd be trying to guess his favorite music.

She looked around the room. All three walls leading to the verandah were comprised largely of floor-to-ceiling windows and sliding glass doors. The aspect was superb, especially now, as dusk was falling. There was really just the one main room, and it opened right up to the pitched roof. There was a slow-combustion wood heater in one corner, and two huge rugs on the polished floorboards, marking out the lounge and dining areas. A free-standing bench divided the kitchen from the rest of the room.

The most prominent feature, apart from the view, was a striking timber staircase. It swept upward in a graceful arc to the loft above the kitchen.

Ally walked over to it and touched the curved rail. "Did you do this yourself?"

"Yes, isn't he clever?" Rebecca said proudly as she placed the flowers on the dining table. "This is the best we could do, I'm afraid. It's just an old coffee jar."

Ally smiled at Rebecca. She was delightful. Ally guessed she was probably around fourteen or fifteen, not any older. She was tall, but she had that slight self-conscious ungainliness that comes with a recent growth spurt.

Matt was standing in the kitchen, cooking apparently. This was too much—he couldn't cook as well, surely?

"Will you be staying for dinner, Ally?" Rebecca asked.

"Oh no. Really, I should go," Ally replied, embarrassed. She didn't want to intrude.

"I wish you would stay. Dad's cooking lasagne, and he can only do it in the one size—enough to feed, like, forty people!"

"It's my grandmother's recipe, and she always cooked in bulk. What can I do?"

"Have you ever thought of halving the ingredients, Dad?" Rebecca suggested, grinning. "You should see him cook spaghetti. He does that by the bucketload."

"Well, at least he can cook," Ally offered.

"Don't get too excited. Lasagne and spaghetti is about it."

"I can barbecue," Matt said, defending himself.

"Dad," Rebecca said, crossing back to the kitchen. "Anyone can barbecue. That's why it's always left to the men."

"You've been listening to your mother too much."

Rebecca grinned. "You know I love you, Dad, despite your shortcomings." She reached up and kissed him on the cheek. Then she looked at Ally. "So, will I set three places?"

"Um . . ." Ally glanced uncertainly at Matt.

"She's the boss," he shrugged. When Ally didn't say anything he looked at her directly. "Stay."

Rebecca started rummaging in the cutlery drawer.

"I won't be a minute," said Matt. "Then I'll get you a drink."

"I'm fine, don't worry about me." Ally smiled. "I love the house, Matt. You did it all yourself?"

He nodded. "In stages, whenever work was a bit slow. It's still not finished."

Obviously Matt's idea of "not finished" was light years away from James Tasker's.

"Apparently," Ally told him, "there's a Chinese proverb that says when you finish your house you die. My grandfather liked to quote that."

Matt grinned. "I'll keep that in mind."

"I suppose you get rained in here for days too?"

He looked nonplussed. "Never. What gave you that idea?"

"I crossed a stream back on the driveway . . ." Ally faltered.

"The water runs away down the valley. Didn't you notice we're on a hill here?"

"Of course, I wasn't thinking."

But she was. Her mind was racing. She was trying to absorb all of this new information. There was much more to Matt than she had realized. Much more than the narrow mold she had slotted him into.

She wandered around the room. At intervals around the walls there were slim columns of shelves, built in between the windows. They were filled with books.

"You read?"

"Mm, since about Year 1," he said wryly.

"Oh ha," she returned. She studied the titles of the books. Just about everything by John Grisham, Tom Clancy, Stephen King. And then there were classics. She pulled out a copy of *To Kill A Mockingbird*.

"I haven't read this since I was at school," she murmured. "Have you read it?"

Matt looked up. "No, I just keep it for show, makes me look intelligent."

Ally leaned against a doorjamb and folded her arms. "You know, you keep surprising me."

"I do?"

She nodded. "Just when I think I've got you figured out, I find out something new."

"That's where we're different."

She looked at him, waiting.

"I don't try to figure you out at all." He turned away and opened the oven door, sliding the tray of lasagne onto a rack and missing entirely the interesting shade of scarlet that flashed across Ally's face.

"I've finished setting the table," Rebecca announced. "Dad?" she said, leaning her head on his shoulder. "Can I go on the internet until dinner is ready?"

"Oh, I get it now." Matt shook his head. "Ally, I think you've been part of a ruse."

"Never!" Beck feigned innocence. "I'd love to sit here and talk. But I have to look up something for an assignment, for school. Really!"

"And I was born yesterday!" Matt said, but he was smiling indulgently at her. He kissed her on the forehead. "Go on, but excuse yourself to the guest you invited."

"Don't mind me," said Ally. She watched Beck skip off out of the room. "She's lovely."

"Mm. Has me wrapped around her little finger though."

"Well, it hasn't spoilt her."

He reached for a bottle from a rack above the kitchen cupboards. "Do you like red wine?" he asked.

"Sure." Ally watched him searching in a drawer for the corkscrew. "How often does she stay here?" she asked.

"Every couple of weekends. And at least some of the holidays. I took her to Queensland back in January."

Ally had figured that out by now.

"How old is she?"

"Just turned fifteen." Matt pulled out the cork and opened a cupboard for some glasses.

"Her mother doesn't get a look-in."

"Sorry?" He turned around.

"It's an expression. I mean she looks exactly like you."

"Oh, yeah. I think it pisses Sharyn off, actually."

"That's her mother?"

He nodded, pouring the wine. "Not that there's bad feeling between us. Not anymore anyway. We get on for Beck's sake."

He handed Ally a glass. "Why don't we go out onto the verandah? I'll introduce you to the dogs."

"You've got dogs!" Ally exclaimed.

"Yeah, they're supposed to be guard dogs," Matt explained as she followed him out through one of the sliding doors. "But they're usually too busy chasing rabbits down the back of the property to notice anyone coming."

He whistled a couple of times. Before long, two lanky Dobermans came running up from the valley and bounded up onto the deck.

"Settle!" Matt said sternly, but it didn't have much effect.

They jostled around Ally, licking her free hand. "Here, hold this," she said, handing Matt her glass. She bent down and patted the dogs warmly.

"What are their names?"

"That's Sam, and the other one's Dave."

"Sam and Dave?" Ally grinned, looking up at him.

"Beck named them when she was about six. Dave is after my brother, her favorite uncle. And Sam is after a little boy she had a crush on in kindergarten, though she'll deny that."

The dogs started to calm down, and Matt indicated a couple of chairs where they could sit. One of the dogs rested his head on Ally's lap.

"I think Dave likes you."

"It's mutual," she smiled. She sipped her wine, looking out to the view. "It's beautiful here."

Matt shrugged. "It's grown on me. I never intended to buy an acreage, but because the land was so steep, it was cheap at the time. It was all I could afford after the divorce settlement."

"Do Beck and her mother live in the area?"

He shook his head. "They live in Sydney, on the north shore."

"Is that where you met her?"

"No, Sharyn and I knew each other since we were kids. We went out together all through our teens, and married when we were barely out of them."

"And that's when you moved to Sydney?"

He nodded. "Sharyn didn't want to live in the country anymore."

"But I thought you hated the city?"

"I do."

"So why did you go?"

"A twenty year old girl has got a lot more savvy than a twenty year old guy," he smiled ruefully. "What did I know? Besides, I loved her. Or I thought I did. Who knows anything when they're only twenty?"

"Is that what went wrong? You were too young?"

Matt looked at her sideways, hesitating.

"Oh, I'm doing my twenty questions thing again, aren't I?" she said sheepishly. "Sorry, it's none of my business."

"It's not a state secret. Sharyn had big plans for us. She'd done a business diploma at tech, back home. She got a job, and she was powering along. Pretty soon it was embarrassing to have a tradesman for a husband, so she pushed me into a job as a salesman."

"You were a salesman?" Ally had met a lot of salesmen in her time, Bryce most notably. Matt didn't seem the salesman type at all.

"Oh, don't worry, I hated it. I was working for this firm that built project houses, and they were that shoddy. Cheap, flimsy houses that people bought by the square meter. The bigger the better, never mind the quality.

"I couldn't stand it. I wanted to quit, but we'd had Becky by then, and Sharyn kept at me that we needed the money. We were fighting all the time."

"So what happened?"

There was that hesitation again. Ally didn't want to pry, but she was intrigued.

He sighed, staring out across the valley. "One day I just walked out."

Ally stared blankly at him.

"I went north. I didn't care where I ended up, I just had to get away. I couldn't be around her anymore."

Ally felt a chill inside. Her throat went dry. "But what about Rebecca?"

"Well, she's the reason I went back. I mean, I was sending money, but that wasn't being a father." He paused. "I woke up one day and realized I was nearly thirty. I'd lost six months of my daughter's life. She probably wouldn't even know me. I had to grow up, make a go of it for her."

"What, you got back with Sharyn?"

"Oh no, that was never going to happen," he said tightly. "We had a pretty rocky time until we sorted out what we both wanted."

"That's when you came down here?"

"I had to get out of the city, but I didn't want to be too far away from Beck. Working for myself meant I could knock off early on Fridays and come to Sydney to pick her up."

"And Sharyn's okay with that?"

"Sure. Look, to her credit, she's always supported our relationship. Besides, she's not too bad, we just wanted different things. Though she's a bit pushy with Beck—you know, private school, after-school lessons in everything under the sun. I try to lay off her a bit when she's here. Just let her relax and be a kid."

"It must be working. She seems very well adjusted."

Matt shrugged. "I don't know how much longer she'll want to keep coming, though. That's why I got her the horse, something she can't have living in a townhouse in North Sydney."

"You got her a horse?"

He nodded.

"I always wanted a horse. But my grandfather wouldn't get me one, he said they were too expensive."

"Well, he's not wrong there. And they need a lot of looking after. I have to ride him at least once a week, especially when Beck hasn't been here for a while. And I'm not exactly the Man from Snowy River. The horse has it all over me."

Ally smiled self-consciously.

They sat quietly, watching dusk turn into twilight. The dogs sat at their feet, content. Ally mulled over everything that Matt had said. He'd just walked out? How bad could it have been? She wondered what Sharyn was like. She must be okay if she let him back into Beck's life, after what he'd done. Leaving his own daughter like that. She was only a baby. How could he just abandon her?

"The oven's beeping, Dad," Beck called from inside.

"I hope you're hungry," said Matt.

Monday

Meg walked resolutely up the stairs to Simon's office. She had avoided him all day, even ignoring a direct summons to his office this morning.

"I'm tied up with something, Simon. I promise I'll come and see you later on."

"Meg—"

"You have my word."

"Well, that's not worth as much as it once was," he'd returned, hanging up the phone.

She had bought him a bottle of red as a peace offering. The man in the bottle shop had recommended the wine, fortunately, because Meg wasn't a connoisseur. Not that she didn't enjoy good wine, but she happily drank wine from a cask, it didn't really bother her. Simon thought she was a peasant. Add to that the fact that she liked instant coffee, and it was lucky he even spoke to her.

She tapped on his door and opened it when she heard a muffled "Come in."

"Hi."

Simon looked up at her and frowned. He returned his attention to the papers on his desk. "What do you want?" he muttered.

He really was cross.

"I was wondering if you had time for a drink?"

"Not really," he replied without looking up. "I don't feel like going to the bar tonight."

She held up the bottle. "We don't have to!"

He still looked unimpressed. He sat back in his chair, folding his arms. Meg closed the door behind her.

"Look, Simon, I'm sorry I asked you to lie for me," she began. "But it was only a little lie."

"Meg, that's like being only a little bit pregnant. A lie is a lie."

"But you didn't have to lie at all. Chris didn't even ring here in the end," she added brightly.

Simon remained unmoved.

"You're right. Of course. I should never have asked you to lie in the first place." She put the bottle and two glasses down on the desk in front of him and took a corkscrew out of her pocket. She'd started to twist it into the stopper when he finally stood up.

"Here, give me that."

He opened the bottle and poured them both a glass, handing one to Meg.

"What should we drink to?" she said hopefully.

Simon seemed to be choosing his words. "Friendship. Honesty. Trust." He paused. "Loyalty, fidel—"

"Oh, okay, okay! If I wanted a sermon I would have gone to church." Meg plonked down on the sofa and put her feet on the coffee table.

"I still expect a confession."

"I have nothing to confess."

"Is that the truth, the whole truth this time?"

"Nothing but the truth," she said, holding her glass up to him.

"Then what's going on?"

Meg sighed. "I'm not doing anything wrong. I don't think."

Simon came and sat beside her on the sofa. "What does that mean?"

"Can I ask you something, hypothetically?"

He nodded.

"If I met a woman at work and went out with her a couple of times and had fun, would you think I was being unfaithful to Chris?"

"No. Not unless you've changed your stripes."

Meg ignored his inference. "Okay, so what if it was a man instead of a woman. Can't a married woman be friends with a man?"

"Are you attracted to him?"

"I'm speaking hypothetically."

"And I'm Fred Nile," he said wryly. "You can't be friends with a man, Meg, if you're sexually attracted to him."

"I'm friends with you, and I'm sexually attracted to you."

"You are not."

"Well, I used to be."

"That doesn't count, it was before you realized I was gay."

Meg turned sideways, leaning her head on the back of the sofa. "Why didn't I realize you were gay?"

He sighed. "Because I don't have it tattooed on my forehead."

"But usually I can tell, I think."

"How do you know?"

Meg frowned at him.

"How do you know how many men around you are gay?" he repeated.

"I've got as good a barometer as the next person."

He laughed, shaking his head. "Hets and their gaydars! I guarantee you, there are a lot more gays around than you realize."

"Really? Like who?" said Meg, jumping up to get the bottle.

"You'd be surprised."

She refilled their glasses. "Tell me."

Simon considered her. "No."

"Why not?"

"Because you're changing the subject."

"I didn't mean to," she said innocently.

"So back to what we were saying. Friendship between a single man and a married woman—you're asking for trouble."

"You and I are friends," Meg said, sitting back down again.

"I'm gay, Meg!" he reminded her. "I'm not exactly a threat."

"Mm," she murmured. "Is that why women and gay men always get along?"

Simon nodded. "Sex is out of the ratio. I think women get tired of fighting men off. You know, they look sideways and guys take it as an invitation. Women can get friendship and affection from a gay man without the pressure."

Meg sighed. "That's why Rupert Everett was more appealing than the other guy in *My Best Friend's Wedding*?"

"No. Rupert Everett *was* more appealing than the other guy."

She grinned. "Mm, I reckon. I was so disappointed to find out he was really gay."

"Why? Were you expecting a call?"

Meg laughed at herself. "Okay, so what you're saying is, I can't be friends with a single, straight man if I find him attractive. But when do you cross the line? When does it become adultery?"

" 'Whosoever looketh on a woman to lust after her hath committed adultery with her already in his heart,' " Simon recited.

Meg just stared at him.

"I'm sure it goes both ways, you know, a woman looking upon a man with lust, yada yada. And lust is 'an excessive desire for the sinful pleasures forbidden by the sixth commandment.' Which brings us back to adultery—"

"Slow down, altar boy!"

"I was an altar boy actually."

"What, on a Mardi Gras float?"

"Meg!" He shook his head. "How else do you think I'd know all that stuff?"

"I have no idea."

"Believe me, when Sister Annunciata is standing over you with a ruler, rapping you on the knuckles for every word you get wrong, you learn pretty fast." He smiled ruefully. "It's no wonder I've never looked upon a woman with lust in my heart."

"You're Catholic?"

Simon nodded. "Well, lapsed these days."

"I didn't know that."

"International man of mystery, they call me."

Meg grinned. "At least it explains why you're so conservative on the issue."

"I'm not conservative at all, Meg," Simon insisted, turning around to face her fully. "I know married men who sleep with women, when they're away on business, at a conference or whatever, and I wouldn't call them adulterers."

Meg looked dubious. "That's generous of you."

"They haven't betrayed the spirit of their marriage contract. They still love their wives, they were just getting their rocks off. It's only a physical release."

"It's nice for men how they can pretend their penis has a life of its own."

"On the other hand," Simon continued, ignoring her, "you could be committing adultery without laying a hand on another person, if your emotions are involved."

Meg took a long, slow mouthful of wine, staring off into the distance.

"So, I should just jump into bed with him," she said after a while. "Then I wouldn't have to feel guilty?"

"Jump into bed with whom, may I ask?"

Meg glanced sideways at Simon. "His name's Hypo Thetical."

"His name's Jamie Carroll."

She looked at him warily.

"I've seen him skulking around here once or twice since that night at the launch when I had to wipe up the trail of drool you left behind."

Meg sighed. "Nothing's happened."

"Then why did you want me to lie to your husband?"

She couldn't answer him.

"I don't get it, Meg," Simon said in a quiet voice. "I thought you and Chris were happy?"

She shrugged. "It's hard to explain . . ."

"Try me."

Meg looked at his eyes. They were so earnest, wanting to understand.

"The excitement's gone."

"That's normal, Meg. You can't be like newlyweds forever."

"Why not? It doesn't seem fair."

"But it happens to everyone. You can't maintain that first flush of love after you've been together for a long time. It's an oxymoron. You only feel that way because it is new."

"Well, then it's unfair. Are married people just not supposed to have any passion in their lives?"

Simon paused, reflecting. "I think you're supposed to work at it."

Meg pulled a face. "This from a serial monogamist. I haven't seen you stay in too many relationships past the use-by date."

"We're not talking about me."

"Then let's stop talking about me, too. It's boring."

He frowned at her, but his eyes still looked concerned. "I just don't know how you can risk losing everything you've got."

"I'm not risking anything, because I won't take it any further. We're just friends." She was trying to forget the kiss, but it was not an easy thing to forget.

"Meg, you know what you sound like? Those people who go into casinos, setting themselves a strict limit . . ."

She stared at him.

"Then, once they get a taste for it, they push it just a little more, and a little more, and before they know it they've lost the shirt off their back."

Meg was startled. "That's a stupid analogy!"

"No it isn't. It makes the point."

"Well, I'm not a gambler. I won't do anything to jeopardize my marriage." She swallowed. "Or hurt Harrison."

Simon touched her arm gently. "I believe you, Meg. Just be careful."

She breathed out heavily. "You know me, I'm always careful."

The following week

"What are you doing?"

Jamie had a habit of not announcing himself on the phone and launching into conversations from a point somewhere farther down the track.

"Working," Meg replied shortly, propping the receiver between her shoulder and chin and pretending to be occupied with whatever was on the computer screen. She didn't know why she was bothering with the charade, it wasn't as though he could see her.

"Have you had lunch yet?"

"Nope."

"Do you want to get some lunch?"

"I can't today."

"Why not?"

"I'm getting my hair cut."

"Oh? You need a haircut?"

She sighed. "I have a regular appointment every six weeks."

"You're kidding?"

"No I'm not. There's something wrong with that?" she said defensively.

"Okay, don't get touchy." He paused. "Do you want some company?"

Meg laughed.

"Are you bored?"

"No, I want to see you."

She stopped, taking hold of the receiver. "You don't really want to come and watch me get my hair cut, Jamie."

"Yes I do. What time's your appointment?"

Meg looked at her watch. "In about forty minutes."

"Then I'll meet you in the carpark in half an hour."

"I won't hold you to it."

"I'll be there, Meg."

She tried to focus back on her work, but she couldn't ignore the debate going on inside her head. Only a friend would come to the hairdressers with you, she told herself. In fact, only a *girlfriend* would do that. She'd show Simon. Of course she and Jamie could be friends. There was nothing wrong with him keeping her company at Fringes. Her heart started to race. Oh God, yes there was! Almost all the women from the office went to Fringes.

Meg picked up the phone and dialed. "Hi Karen? It's Meg Lynch. Look, I won't be able to make it today, we're flat out here. Can I call to reschedule? Great. Thanks Karen, talk to you soon."

Half an hour later Meg told Donna she was going for a long lunch if anyone asked, because she had some errands to run. She walked out of the building and spotted Jamie straightaway, leaning against her car.

"Hiya," he said languidly as she approached him.

Meg tried to suppress the haphazard flutter she felt inside. He was just a friend. You didn't get all giddy when you met a friend.

"Where to?" he asked.

"I canceled my appointment."

"Why did you do that?"

Meg shrugged. She may as well be honest. "You know what hairdressing salons are like. They do a sideline in gossip. I'd rather not be the latest hot topic."

He studied her for a moment. "Have I stuffed up your schedule?"

"No," she insisted. "I'm not as rigid as you think I am."

"You could still get your hair cut."

"No, it's alright."

"I know a place."

That you obviously haven't visited in a while, she could hear Simon saying.

"No, it's alright. I always go to the same woman."

He nodded. "And get the same haircut?"

"Well, yes." Meg touched her hair self-consciously. "You don't like it?"

"I didn't say that. Your hair always looks . . . perfect."

Meg stared into space. "Mm, it does, doesn't it?" she said vaguely. "Where did you say this place was?"

"Newtown."

"Oh right, and come out with dreadlocks?"

Jamie laughed. "You can get regular haircuts in Newtown, you know."

Meg took a breath. What the hell. "Okay," she said, tossing him the keys. "You drive, I suppose you know the way."

He looked surprised. "Yeah? You're really going to do this?"

"You were the one that told me not to think about things so much."

The salon was not too outrageous, and the Jamaican woman who cut her hair was delightful. They had to wait for more than half an hour, but just as well, it took Meg that long to decide on a style.

"You've got such gorgeous hair," the hairdresser remarked when Meg told her what she wanted. "You're sure you want to do this?"

What was it, did she have a big sign on her back that read *Caution— woman terrified of change?*

"I've had my hair in this style for at least ten years," Meg said dryly. "I'm over it."

"Nuff said," the hairdresser replied, picking up her scissors.

When Meg surveyed the end result in the mirror, she decided it wasn't half bad. It was cropped short at the nape with a jagged, tousled fringe. Meg couldn't decide if it made her look younger or older, but it was certainly different.

"You know, red highlights would look great."

"One thing at a time," Meg smiled.

She stood up and walked through to the waiting area, where Jamie sat stretched out in an armchair. His face broke into a broad grin when he saw her.

"Hey, look at you."

"Is it alright?"

"It's great. Suits you," he said, getting to his feet.

Meg paid the woman, and they stepped out onto the street.

"Are you hungry?"

"Starved," said Meg.

"Come on then."

They walked up to a doner kebab stand and bought two with the lot. Meg didn't want to sit and eat. She was in a different place, and she felt like a different person with her new hairstyle. She wanted to wander along, look at the shops and the people. It was unlikely that anyone she knew would see them.

However, eating a doner kebab and walking was not the easiest thing to do. The hoummos turned liquid and leaked out of the bag. It dripped up Meg's arms while she tried to eat, and left a trail of white dots down the front of her top. The flimsy paper napkin the vendor supplied was next to useless.

"Do you know if there are any toilets about?" she asked Jamie. "I can't go back to work looking like this. I have to clean up."

"I'll take you to my place," he offered.

"What, in Bondi? I may as well go home."

"No, I'm staying here now, just a block back that way."

"Another friend?" Meg asked, lifting an eyebrow.

He nodded. "I like to spread myself around, don't want to outstay my welcome anywhere."

They walked around the corner to a row of rundown terraces. Meg followed Jamie to the last one. The door was wide open, leading to a hall that ran through the center of the house. A pungent, musty odor hit Meg as soon as she stepped over the threshold.

"Thommo!" Jamie called. "Anyone home?"

"In here."

"The bathroom's at the end of the hall upstairs," Jamie told Meg.

She climbed the staircase, mindful of not actually touching anything. The walls were stained yellow, a mixture of damp and nicotine, she suspected, and the carpet was rotten, at least it smelled rotten. The place was like the worst student digs she'd ever laid eyes on when she was at college.

Meg walked gingerly down the hallway. She shuddered to think what the bathroom was like. The first door on her left was closed. The next one was open. There was a bed in the center she assumed, under a pile of clothes. More clothes and shoes were strewn over the floor, as well as empty bottles, an overflowing ashtray, and what she suspected was a bong.

She came to the door at the end of the hall. Opening it, Meg physically blanched. At least she had expected it to be filthy. There was no soap in the handbasin, though there was plenty of soap scum. Meg splashed water on her face, and washed the sticky residue off her hands and up her arms. She didn't dare touch either of the two towels hanging over the shower rail, and she averted her eyes from the toilet bowl as she reached for some toilet paper. She dried her hands and face, and then wet some more paper, dabbing at the white splotches on her top.

Meg came back down the stairs and followed the sounds of music playing on a stereo. She peered in through a doorway coming off the downstairs hall.

"Here she is," said Jamie. "Come in and meet everyone."

A man and two women were lounging around a low coffee table. There were no chairs in the room, just two mattresses covered in batik fabric, piles of tatty cushions and a purple corduroy beanbag. An old television sat in the corner, and a sound system stretched across one wall, with speakers that were taller than Harrison. Meg didn't recognize the music playing, but then she only tended to listen to the Wiggles these days.

"Everyone, this is Meg. Meg, this is Thommo, Annie and Kez."

"Hiya Meg," they chorused.

"Hi." She smiled feebly. She'd just noticed what was on the middle of the table, the reason for the gathering. There was an ashtray, various implements, including a bong, and a fat plastic bag full of shredded green leaves. Meg sighed, she was too old for this.

"Take a load off," said Jamie, whacking the mattress next to him.

She went to protest that she really ought to get going, but she didn't want Jamie to start preaching to her about loosening up. She'd join them for a while, and quietly leave once they were too stoned to notice.

Meg sat on the mattress next to Jamie and crossed her legs, glad she'd worn trousers today.

"How long's it been, Meg?" he asked.

"What?"

"Since you got stoned?"

"Who says I ever did?"

"Come on, you went to art college. Everybody's permanently stoned at art college."

"Or else how do you explain some of those paintings," added Thommo with a grin.

Meg didn't want to tell them that she actually took college seriously and rarely joined in any of the extracurricular activities, so to speak. The one time she shared a joint, it had little effect on her, and she couldn't understand what the big deal was. She'd rather have a drink.

Thommo was preparing the bong. Meg had seen people do this before, but had never paid much attention. He lit the end of the glass tube protruding at an angle from the side of the bottle. Then he passed it to Meg. "Visitors first."

"Oh no, that's okay."

"Come on, for old times' sake," said Jamie.

Meg felt stupid. She realized she wasn't quite sure what to do with it. "You go first, Jamie."

He took it from her and drew in the smoke from the neck of the bottle, then he passed it back to her.

"Just take it easy at first," he said quietly. He must have sensed her lack of experience. Meg inhaled a little smoke and drew it back into her lungs. So far so good. She passed it on to Annie. When she looked back at Jamie he was watching her, an odd look on his face. He rested his hand on her thigh and leaned over, kissing her lightly on the cheek.

"I like your hair," he said close to her ear, his breath tingling on her neck. Meg felt suddenly hot. She wondered how long it would take for the bong to come back around.

Meg opened her eyes slowly, blinking. There was a window just above her, and she stared through the dirty pane at the streetlight outside.

Her head was buzzing. She turned onto her back and peered around the gloomy room, taking in her surroundings. Yellowed, faded wallpaper, an old brown wardrobe in the corner: she could just make out a motorbike helmet sitting on top.

Shit! Meg sat bolt upright, and then had to wait for a moment until her brain caught up. She was somewhere in Newtown. The last thing she remembered was . . . Oh Christ!

She looked down at herself. She was a little crumpled but she was fully clothed, except for her shoes. Surely nothing had happened? She tried to check her watch, but she couldn't see the hands in the half-light. She stumbled out of the room into the hallway. The whole house seemed to be in darkness, except for light coming from the television in the room opposite. She stuck her head in the doorway. Jamie was sitting in the purple beanbag staring at the screen, clutching a huge bag of cornchips and giggling like a teenage girl.

"Jamie, do you know what the time is?"

"Oh, hiya Meg!"

She felt for the light switch on the doorjamb and turned it on.

"Jeez Meg!" he said, shielding his eyes. "What are you doing?"

Meg was staring at her watch. "Oh shit, it's after seven!"

"Yeah, *The Simpsons* has started," Jamie confirmed. "Now, turn the light off, would you?"

Meg ignored him, searching among the cushions for her handbag. She pulled out her mobile phone and pressed a series of digits. "Oh fuck!"

"What's up?" said Jamie through a mouthful of corn chips.

"Didn't you hear my phone ringing?"

"Yeah, maybe. I don't know how to work those things."

Moron, Meg thought to herself. He would have to be the only person in Sydney without a mobile phone. It appeared that both Simon and Chris had tried to ring her at least twice each. She found her shoes and slipped them on. Jamie was still giggling at the television. "That Homer. He cracks me up."

Meg picked up her bag and walked out, disgusted.

"Hey, aren't you going to say goodbye?" he called, but she was already out the door.

Oh no! Where was the car? Meg hurried up the street and turned at the first corner, coming to the main road. She spotted her car, sitting under a streetlight, a gold envelope under the windscreen wiper.

"Fuck, fuck, fuck! What else?" she said under her breath, snatching the parking ticket and shoving it into her bag. She unlocked the door and got in. She sat there, breathing heavily. She realized she was trembling.

Meg took out her phone and pressed auto dial, her heart in her mouth. "Hello?"

"Simon, is that you?"

She heard him sigh at the other end. "Meg, are you alright?"

"Yes, has Chris—?"

"Don't worry, I covered for you."

Meg breathed out, relieved. "I'm so sorry. I owe you for this."

"I'm just glad to hear you're okay. No one knew where on earth you were. Donna said you were taking a long lunch, and somebody else thought you had an appointment with the hairdresser, but when we checked, they said you canceled. I've been worried sick about you, Meg."

She felt like crying. "I'm sorry I put you through that, Simon."

"Are you going to tell me where you've been?"

"You won't believe this, I fell asleep . . ."

"Meg! I thought you weren't going to take it any further?"

"No, it wasn't like that. I swear, nothing happened." She hoped that was true. "I really did fall asleep at his place, he was too stupid to realize he should have woken me."

"I'll have to take your word for it."

"What did you tell Chris?"

"Well, the first time he rang—"

"There's been more than once?"

"Yes. Anyway, Donna just said you were out to lunch. But when he rang again later, that's when we started looking for you."

"So what did you tell him?"

"I said you were up at the studios, and that's why you weren't answering your mobile. I told him I'd get a message to you. When we still hadn't heard anything after another hour, I rang him and said you were working back."

Meg rested her head on the steering wheel, sighing heavily.

"So he said not to worry, he'd pick up Harrison and see you at home. And not to work too hard."

"I'm sorry, Simon."

"You've got to pull yourself together, Meg. You can't just go AWOL like that."

"I didn't mean for any of this to happen. Really. I'm so sorry."

"It's over now." His voice softened. "Are you alright?"

She felt tears rising in her throat.

"Meg?"

"I'm fine," she sniffed. "I'd better get home."

"Take it easy, okay?"

. . .

Meg unlocked the front door and stepped wearily into the hall. It was warm and dry inside, and she could smell dinner cooking. The tears stuck in her throat threatened to well again.

"Honey, is that you?"

Chris came into the hall from the kitchen, wiping his hands on a tea-towel. She was never so happy to see him.

"Hi," she said, stepping forward under the light.

"You've had your hair cut."

Meg had almost forgotten. "Oh, yes," she paused, looking at the expression on his face. "Don't worry, it'll grow back."

He smiled. "No, it's . . . nice, I just wasn't expecting it."

Meg walked into his arms, hugging him tight.

"Heavy day?"

"Mm," she murmured into his chest. "Is Harrison in bed already?"

"Well, I didn't know when you'd be home . . ."

"It's okay."

"Dinner's ready. Are you hungry?"

She pulled back from him, nodding. "What did I do to deserve you?" she said, her voice trembling.

"Hey," he stroked her cheek, his eyes concerned. "Meg, you look exhausted. Even your eyes are bloodshot. You're working too hard."

She swallowed. "I'm okay, really. Just glad to be home." She hugged him tightly again. "I love you, Chris."

"I love you too."

A week later

"Why aren't you taking my calls?"

Meg jumped, swiveling around in her chair. Jamie stood leaning against the doorway to her office.

"We've been flat out around here, Jamie."

He looked unconvinced. He stepped into the room, closing the door behind him.

"You've got the shits with me."

Meg shrugged, pretending to focus back on her work. She shuffled some papers around, avoiding his gaze.

Jamie walked around the desk, dragging a chair with him. He sat down and leaned across her, taking hold of the arms of her chair and swiveling it around so she had to face him.

"You can act like a spoilt teenager, or we can talk like adults. It's up to you." He looked directly into her eyes.

"I wasn't the one acting like a teenager," she retorted.

"Oh, I see," he said, leaning back in his chair. "Weren't we mature enough for you, Meg? It didn't seem to bother you at the time."

The color drained from her face. "That's the whole thing," she said in a small voice. "I don't even remember what happened."

He considered her for a moment, then leaned forward in his chair again. "Nothing happened, Meg. You were fine at first, and then you started to pass out. I put you in my room so you could sleep it off."

Meg sighed, relieved. "I've tried it before, it never had that effect."

"It was probably stronger than the stuff you've had. You have to get used to it."

"Well, I won't be doing that," she said flatly.

"Look, I'm not a pusher, Meg. You don't like it, we don't have to do it."

"Don't talk about 'we,' Jamie. There is no 'we.' "

His eyes narrowed, considering her.

"I can't see you anymore," said Meg. "It was a mistake from the start. I should never have said yes when you asked me out for a drink that day."

"So why did you?"

She breathed out heavily. "I was bored."

"Just filling in time, eh?"

"Look, I don't mean to offend you . . ."

"It's okay, Meg," he interrupted. He seemed to be thinking about what he wanted to say. "Look, I was never trying to steal you away from your husband. I just wanted to show you a good time."

"I wish it was as simple and innocent as that," she sighed. "But I don't want to skulk around, waking up in strange places, worrying my husband because he doesn't know where I am, and then lying to him."

"Okay, I should have woken you when you got a call. I just don't think like that."

"And that's fine for you, Jamie, you haven't got a care in the world. Good luck to you. But we're not the same, and I can't do this anymore."

He stared at her intently. Meg wasn't sure what was in his eyes. Disappointment maybe. Or was he just annoyed? Whatever, she couldn't meet his gaze any longer. Those eyes were almost her undoing.

"I have to get back to work," she said quietly.

He nodded, getting to his feet. "Can I at least have a kiss goodbye?"

He put his hand out to her. She considered it for a moment, before gingerly taking his hand and rising slowly out of her chair. They stood barely apart. Meg stared at her shoes, too nervous to look up at him. Then she felt his hands cupping her face, drawing her closer as he brought his lips down on hers. She was rocked by the force of it. This wasn't a gentle kiss goodbye, this was a kiss to say "see what you're missing." Meg felt her heart pounding hard, sending a bloodrush through her body.

He pulled back slowly. "Goodbye Meg."

She stood rooted to the spot. He must have left her office, she realized as she heard the sound of the door closing. She sank down into the chair, catching her breath.

Late in May

Circle's End had promptly sold to the first buyer, though he'd requested an extended settlement. Everybody assumed Ally would stay at the property in the meantime, after she'd finished up at the guesthouse, but she couldn't do it. She did try. She drove down the day she left Birchgrove, brought her bags in from the car, and then it started to rain. She was stricken with fear. What if she got rained in? For days? The walls seemed to close in around her, and Ally felt trapped again. She couldn't breathe. She had to get out.

So she packed up enough clothes for a few days and headed back up the mountain. Stopping at a camping supply place in Mittagong, she bought a sleeping bag and one of those thin foam mattresses. And she also bought a cooler and a heavy-duty torch.

Nic usually didn't arrive at the restaurant till at least nine in the morning, having late shifts at the hotel. And she had to leave again around four in the afternoon, to get ready for work each night. Rob was in and out at various times of the day, as was Matt, so they didn't suspect she had set up camp. Really, why would they? Why would anybody? One of the men working on the kitchen asked her one day if she ever went home, but he was only joking.

And she had taken to using her mobile phone again, after Nic commented she could never catch her at Circle's End.

"Call me on the mobile. I'm hardly ever there anyway."

Which was true. No one had asked her if she was actually sleeping down there, so she had never actually lied. They wouldn't understand, and she certainly didn't want to have to try to explain it. It was just too hard. If she had to stay at Circle's End, she couldn't stay here in the Highlands, it was as simple as that.

So Ally rolled up her sleeping bag and mattress each morning and packed them into the boot of her car, usually just as the tradesmen were arriving. She ate cereal for breakfast and had stocked up on packet snack-food to keep her going through the day. She tried to get out in the late afternoon to buy dinner, but it didn't always work out. Cup-a-soup had become her staple.

The worst part was showering. There was a functioning bathroom, but there was no hot water, and as she had to take showers when nobody was around, it was usually at the coldest part of the day, very early morning or at night. Her head was blocked up, and she was starting to feel weary, but adrenalin kept her going. This was only temporary, until she had time to look for somewhere to live.

"Preparation is the most important part of any painting job," Ally had insisted repeatedly to Nic.

"And the most boring," Nic had grumbled.

They'd hired a steamer to remove the wallpaper, and once Nic had got the hang of using it, she stuck to that. It was much easier than stripping the walls of paint, so that was largely left to Ally. She wore a mask most of the time, but the fine dust still got up her nose, through her hair and into just about every bodily crevice it could find. What with the brief cold showers she was forced to have, Ally hadn't felt really clean since she left Birchgrove.

She looked at her watch. Nic had left about a half an hour ago. Cup-a-soup did not appeal tonight. She could do with a proper meal, something hot and filling. She'd felt hungry for a week now, especially as the weather had turned wintry. And she was cold during the nights. She was thinking about treating herself to a hotel, just for one night, maybe two. The thought of slipping under warm blankets onto a soft mattress, after a hot shower, was becoming irresistible. She only worried that she might never come back.

She took off her mask and the elastic that held back her hair and shook it out, vigorously rubbing her scalp to release a shower of paint dust.

"Ally?"

She poked her head around the door. "Oh, hello."

It was Matt. Ally had been trying to keep their relationship strictly business since the evening at his place. Every time she saw him now, she could only think of Rebecca, and his wife, after he left them. Alone. Maybe wondering what they had done to make him leave like that. Ally could relate to them more than she cared to.

"How's it going?" Matt said, peering into the room. "Jeez, you're getting a lot done."

Ally shrugged, stifling a yawn.

"You look tired."

"Thanks."

"How much sleep are you getting?"

"Enough."

"Does it bother you, being down there on your own?"

"Not at all," Ally dismissed, hoping that wasn't a lie. "What are you doing here?"

"I've got a job for you."

She frowned.

"All the doors are getting picked up for stripping the day after tomorrow. So you and Nic are going to have to take them off their hinges."

Ally looked at him, dumbfounded.

"I'll leave you one of my drills." He noticed Ally's mystified expression. "What is it?"

"I don't know how to use a drill."

"You don't?"

"What made you think I would?"

"Well, I've seen you handle power tools."

"Only a belt sander."

"Okay, I'll show you then, you'll be right." He picked up the case he had brought in with him and laid it on the bench Ally had set up. He released the catches and opened the lid.

"Now, this is a standard cordless drill, but it's a tradesman's model, so you might find it a bit heavy. You'll mostly use a medium flat-blade screwdriver bit, but the screws might vary on different doors, you might need a Phillip's head. Anyway, it's a keyless chuck, so it's easy to change." He glanced over his shoulder at Ally, still standing in the doorway. "You'll see better from over here."

"Can't we get one of the builders to do this?"

Matt put down the drill and turned around to face her. "Well, Ally Tasker, I'm surprised. I thought you'd try anything."

She shrugged. "They make holes in walls! I don't want to end up with one through my hand or something."

Matt laughed out loud. "You won't put one through your hand! It hasn't got a mind of its own. It's like anything, if you use it safely."

Ally frowned dubiously.

"Come on, give it a go. I bet you'll enjoy it once you get started."

Matt showed Ally how to choose the right size screwdriver bit, and then how to fit it into the drill. He removed one hinge and then steadied the door while Ally tried the next. She held the drill in place, but when she pressed her finger down on the trigger, the force of the motor startled her, and she closed her eyes.

"Ally!"

She released the trigger, looking at Matt.

"It's a good idea to keep your eyes open."

She smiled sheepishly and started again. Ally could feel the screw releasing from the hinge, and she squealed.

"Are you alright?" Matt asked.

She nodded. "This is fun. Can I try another one?"

"Sure."

By the time they had removed all four doors from the two adjoining rooms, Ally felt like an old hand.

"So how do you make a hole?" she asked Matt.

"What?"

"You know, drill into something."

"Oh. Just take it off reverse."

"But how do you know where to drill?" Ally said, examining the wall.

"Well, these are double brick and plaster walls, so you have to use a masonry bit, and special screws, with a plug."

"Don't you have to tap the wall, to find the right spot? I've seen people do that."

"That's on a timber-framed wall. You have to find the stud behind the plaster board, so you have an anchor."

"And how do you do that?"

Matt checked his watch. "Ally, I'd love to go on with the lesson, but I have to get home. I've got two hungry dogs to feed."

"Sorry."

"Don't apologize." He paused. "Why don't you come for dinner? It's on your way home."

"No, that's alright, I want to keep going with this."

"You really should have someone to support the door, especially when you get to the last hinge. You'll have plenty of time to get through it tomorrow with Nic."

"Couldn't I just take off the middle hinge, and maybe one or two screws off the outer hinges?"

Matt frowned at her. "What time do you knock off usually?"

"Whenever," Ally said evasively.

"And you drive down the valley in the dark?"

"It's dark down there from about five anyway."

He looked puzzled. "You're mad you know. You'll make yourself sick working at this pace. You already sound like you're getting a cold."

"I'm fine," Ally dismissed. "Now, is it alright just to remove the middle hinge?"

Two days later

Ally thought that maybe it was lifting all those heavy doors that had made her aches and pains worse last night. But now as she lay shivering inside her sleeping bag, she realized it was probably more than that. She struggled to sit up, keeping the sleeping bag around her. The air in the room was biting cold, and as she leaned against the wall, she could feel the chill coming through the thick, padded layer of the sleeping bag, boring into her back. Her skin was sore. Ally felt tears spring into her eyes. Stop being a baby, she told herself.

She checked her watch. Four A.M. She had to be up at six. Gingerly she brought her arm up out of the sleeping bag and reached for her backpack, dragging it closer. She prayed that she still had some Panadol, she didn't remember finishing the packet. She found the box and pulled out the foil sheet. One left. She sighed, it wasn't enough, but it would have to do. She swallowed it down and slid back onto the mattress. Some time later, she drifted off.

"Ally! Ally!"

She opened one eye, but the light was too bright, and it stung. She closed it again, pulling the pillow over her head.

"Ally! What the hell are you doing here?"

That was Matt's voice. What was he doing here? Where was she anyway?

She sighed, rolling over onto her back. Every muscle and joint of her body was screaming with pain. She felt Matt's hand on her forehead. It was icy. She tried to pull it away.

"Stop it, Ally! You're burning up. Have you taken anything?"

He sounded annoyed. What was his problem?

"Leave me alone, I don't feel very well."

He stood up. "I think I've got some Panadol in the truck. I'll be back in a minute."

He'd left the room, Ally realized. She opened her eyes, squinting. Shit. She must have slept through the alarm. She wasn't even sure if she'd set it, she was so tired last night. She tried to sit up, but her arms hurt, everything hurt. She slumped against the wall and closed her eyes.

Matt strode back into the room. He kneeled down in front of her, and she felt him propping her up into a sitting position.

"Here, take these."

She tried to focus on his hand, but her eyes were still stinging.

"Open," he said gently, his thumb on her lips. She did as he said and he pushed one tablet into her mouth. Then she felt a glass against her lips.

"Take a sip, it's only water."

He did the same with a second tablet.

"I'll be fine now," Ally murmured. "I just have to get some sleep."

"No, Ally, don't lie down." Matt kept his arm around her, holding her upright. "This mattress is damp, the whole floor's damp. It'll be a bloody miracle if you don't end up with pneumonia."

She thought she sensed irritation in his voice again.

"I just want to sleep."

"Okay! Just let me spread this blanket out." A moment later, she felt him easing her down until her head rested on the soft blanket. He brought it back over her, wrapping it round her.

Matt said something else, about someone arriving, and that he'd be back in a little while. She wasn't sure. She felt his hand on her forehead, then smoothing back her hair. A moment later, she fell asleep.

Ally woke up with a start. She could hear building noises. She looked at her watch. *Nine-thirty!*

She sat bolt upright. What was going on? There were voices outside the room. She strained to listen to what they were saying.

"Surely she hasn't been sleeping here all along?"

That was Nic.

"Well, it didn't look like it was the first time. She's all set up with a mattress and a sleeping bag. I don't know if she's even been down to the valley at all."

Matt. She remembered now. He'd been here earlier, fussing and frowning at her. Great.

"And she's sick as a dog. I wondered if I shouldn't be taking her to casualty."

Oh, for crying out loud! She was feeling fine now. She stood up, a little unsteadily. Okay, maybe she wasn't a hundred percent, but she wasn't *sick*. She was just overdoing it, she needed to knock off a little earlier in the day, book into that hotel.

Ally decided to get dressed and look presentable before they came in to check on her. Trouble was, she had nothing very presentable to wear. She hadn't been to the laundromat all week, and her clothes were covered in paint, dust and grime. She picked up a sweater and shook it out. A cloud of dust billowed into the air, and before Ally could help it she let out a loud sneeze.

A moment later there was a tentative knock on the door.

"Are you awake, Ally?" It was Nic.

She glanced down at the old tracksuit she was wearing. She supposed it was no worse than her grotty work clothes.

"Come in."

Nic opened the door a little, and stuck her head in. "You're up!"

"Yes, hi. Sorry I overslept!" Ally tried to sound bright.

Nic pushed the door open and stepped into the room. Matt stood behind her in the doorway.

"How are you feeling, Ally?" he asked, frowning.

"Fine, right as rain."

Nic looked at her. "You don't look very well."

Ally touched her hand to her face. "I mean I'm tired. Naturally. Who wouldn't be?"

"Ally, where have you been staying?"

She glanced nervously at the sleeping bag. "I've stayed here a few times, when I've finished too late. You know, that road's dangerous in the dark, down to the valley."

She avoided looking at Matt.

"Ally, have you been down to Circle's End at all since you moved out of Birchgrove?" he asked bluntly.

"Of course I've been down there!"

"Have you stayed the night?"

Ally felt flustered. "You know, where I stay and what I do is really nobody's business but my own."

"Ally." Nic touched her arm gently. "You can't stay here. Look how damp everything is, and there's gaps under the doors. The place isn't sealed against the weather. You'll freeze, and you're not well."

"I'm fine," Ally insisted. "I might have been coming down with something during the night, but I feel great now."

"That's just the effect of the Panadol."

Oh shut up, Matt. She didn't like all this fuss. Why couldn't they just leave her alone?

"Look, if it will make everyone happy, I'll take the day off today. Okay?"

"I think you're going to need more than a day off, Ally," said Matt.

"And you can't stay here. We have to find you somewhere else. Why don't you go down to Circle's End?" Nic asked.

Ally looked at her. The pain was returning to the base of her neck, moving up the back of her head. She started to feel a bit woozy, and a hot flush broke out across her skin. She glanced quickly around the room. There was no chair, and she knew she was not going to be able to keep standing. There was nothing she could do but sink down to the floor.

"Ally!" Nic shrieked, dropping to her knees.

"I'm fine," Ally said calmly. "I just needed to sit down."

"You're sick. We have to get you to a doctor."

"No—"

"Do you have a doctor here in Bowral, Nic?" Matt asked.

She nodded.

"Okay, we'll take her there. Should we phone ahead?"

Nic looked at Ally. "Maybe you'd like to get changed first, have a shower? You look pretty wretched."

"I don't want to go to a doctor."

They ignored her.

"Where are all your clothes, Ally? Are they here, or in your car, where?" Matt sounded impatient.

Ally was starting to feel hot again. "Most of my stuff is down at Circle's End. But don't make me go there, Nic," she whimpered, grabbing her arm. "I really don't want to go there." A sob caught in her throat, and she felt tears stinging behind her eyes.

Nic patted her arm. "What's so bad about it? I think it's charming—"

"It's not fucking charming!" Ally almost screamed. "It's a fucking prison!

It's cold and drafty, and I can't get warm no matter how many clothes I put on! I'm not allowed to go anywhere, and no one comes to see us, ever, and he never talks to me, and—"

Her voice dried up. Matt and Nic were just staring at her. She covered her face with her hands. What did she just say? God, she must be having a breakdown.

Nic put her arm around Ally's shoulders. "It's okay, Ally, no one's going to make you go there."

She couldn't speak, she was too humiliated.

"I'll drive down and get her things," Matt was saying.

"She can have a shower at my place in the meantime," said Nic. "But where is she going to stay? There's no room in our little bedsit."

"Then she'll have to stay with me."

Ally tried to protest but they talked over the top of her.

"Have you got the room?"

"She can have Beck's room."

"Okay, well, what say we meet you back at my place? She'll need to change her clothes before she sees the doctor."

Ally sat quietly defeated in the front seat of Matt's truck. He was in the pharmacy having her prescription filled. The doctor diagnosed her with the flu and was concerned the infection had traveled to her lungs. Ally was sure it wasn't that bad. She felt much better since she'd had a shower and put on some fresh clothes. Though her temperature had started to spike again and the doctor did not hesitate to give her a stronger dose of paracetamol.

Ally hated all the fuss. But it was more than that. She was mortified about the way she'd behaved. She wished she could just slink away quietly down to Circle's End where no one would bother her. But that was the whole problem. She couldn't stay there, and now Nic and Matt knew it. No doubt they also thought she had a screw loose. There was something in their eyes when they looked at her now. She was pretty sure it was pity and she couldn't stand it.

Matt jumped back in the car and started the engine.

"You have to take one capsule, three times a day, before food," he said, pulling out into the traffic. "Don't worry, I'll remind you. And I bought some more Panadol. You have to keep that up four-hourly."

Ally didn't say anything. She didn't trust herself. She could feel Matt looking at her, but she just stared at the road ahead.

"What's wrong?"

"Nothing."

He sighed loudly. "Why do women always say that? Ally, let's not play games. What's the matter?"

She had to restore her dignity somehow. "I just don't appreciate people taking over my life and treating me like I'm a child."

"Well, when you act like one—"

"What?"

"It's true, Ally. What were you thinking? Staying up at that place on your own? It's a building site, for crying out loud!"

"So? I wasn't bothering anyone."

"That's not the point. It was dangerous. And you could have got a lot worse. What if I hadn't come in early this morning?"

"Well, I guess I would have got a lot more work done today!"

"What did you say?"

"You heard me."

"Fine." Matt pulled off the road and slammed on the brakes, dust and gravel flying up behind them.

"What are you doing?" Ally asked nervously.

"You want me to take you back?" he said through clenched teeth.

"I didn't say that—"

"Do you want me to take you back?" This time he was almost shouting.

Ally swallowed hard. She could feel tears welling again. She didn't want to go back there. "No."

Matt took a deep breath and relaxed his hold on the steering wheel. He flicked on the indicator and looked around for a break in the traffic. A moment later he pulled out smoothly and they drove on toward Avoca.

"You're a pain in the arse, Ally Tasker."

"What did you say?"

"You heard me."

They drove the rest of the way in silence.

The next day

Ally opened her eyes and looked around the room. There were posters of horses and pop stars lining the walls. She remembered staring at them as she fell asleep yesterday. It reminded Ally of her bedroom, when she was growing up. It was the only nice room in the house, thanks to her own efforts. Ally had painted the furniture and sewn curtains, and put posters over the gaps in the walls. She remembered her grandfather shaking his head, in disapproval she'd assumed, but he didn't stop her.

Matt had come in a couple of times during the night with her tablets, and Ally had a sudden, distinct recollection of her grandfather, doing the same thing. She must have been fourteen or fifteen. She remembered his face, frowning down at her. She thought he was annoyed, but she could see his expression again now, in her mind's eye. He looked concerned, maybe even anxious.

Ally wondered what the time was. The house seemed quiet. She hoped Matt had gone to work, she didn't feel like facing more of his self-righteous disapproval. She sat up and swung her legs off the bed. Alright so far. She still felt achey, but that was as much for being so long in bed.

She stood up and stretched, catching sight of herself in the mirror in her baggy, flannelette pajamas. She couldn't go out there looking like this if Matt was still here. Though as he'd pretty much seen her at her worse now, it hardly mattered. She stuck her head out the door.

"Matt, are you there? . . . Matt?"

No reply. Ally tiptoed up the hallway into the main room. She looked out across the valley. It was gray and overcast, and Ally felt cold in her bare feet. Matt would have scolded her if he was here. She wondered if there was a clock on the oven. She walked into the kitchen, but something caught her eye on the bench. There was a note sitting propped against her packets of pills.

> *Ally*
>
> *I hope you're feeling better this morning. I'm working in Berrima today, you can reach me on my mobile if you need anything.*
>
> *Don't forget to take your tablets as soon as you get up. And make sure you eat, there's plenty of food in the fridge. And keep warm, start the fire, or at least use the electric heater. I left it out for you.*

So this was what it was like to have a mother, Ally thought.

> *Meg called, she asked if you could give her a ring when you're feeling up to it.*
>
> *See you around 5.*
>
> > *Matt*

Ally glanced at the clock. It was after one already. She swallowed down her tablets and then took the telephone off its cradle on the wall. She really was feeling cold, so she picked up a throw rug off the sofa and wrapped it around herself. She sat down and dialed Meg's number.

"Hi Meg, it's Ally."

"Ally!" she exclaimed. "How are you?"

"I'm fine, really. I feel a lot better."

"Oh come on, you don't get over a serious lung infection that quickly."

"I don't have a serious lung infection! Who told you that?"

"Matt said that the doctor had you on antibiotics, and that the infection had probably gone to your lungs."

"That's a worst-case scenario," Ally dismissed. "Why did you call here anyway?"

"I rang your mobile, and Nic answered. Apparently you left it at the restaurant. She gave me Matt's number."

Ally was imagining the chain of fussing and clucking between the lot of them.

"You could have got really sick, Ally!" Meg continued. "I mean, it sounds like you are really sick."

"I've got the flu, and now that I've had a good night's sleep, and the antibiotics are kicking in, I'm feeling a lot better. Don't carry on about it."

"But why on earth were you sleeping on the floor at the restaurant? Ally, if you didn't have enough money to rent somewhere, you only had to ask."

"It's not that! I just haven't had the chance to look for a place." She sighed. "We've been so flat out trying to get everything finished, it was just the easiest solution. I realize now, I didn't really think it through."

"You know, you always make fun of me, but a little forward planning is not such a bad idea."

"Lesson learned."

"Well, I'm glad Matt's taking care of you."

"He's not taking care of me! I'm out of here as soon as I can find somewhere else."

"Not until you're all recovered, Ally. You shouldn't be on your own. I was nearly going to come down there myself to look after you . . ."

"Matt has made a lot more out of this than it is," Ally insisted. "I'm hardly on death's door."

"Just relax and let him take care of you if that's what he wants to do."

Ally didn't respond, she didn't want to encourage her.

"Are you sleeping in his bed?"

"Meg!"

"I realize he'd be on the couch or something. For the meantime," she added, her voice dropping suggestively.

"Meg, you are so full of romantic shit," said Ally, annoyed. "I'm sleeping in his daughter's room."

"What daughter?" Meg shrieked into the receiver.

Ally had forgotten she hadn't told Meg the latest. "He's divorced, and his daughter stays every second weekend."

"Ooh, a man with a past," Meg cooed. "Intriguing."

"Oh give me a break!" Ally rolled her eyes.

"So what's going on with you two?"

"Nothing!"

"I beg to differ," said Meg. "Remember what I said about you being swept off your feet by a rugged man and taken away to his mountain cabin?"

"And remember what I said about you being full of shit?"

"Well, I just think he genuinely cares about you."

Ally sighed. "Maybe, but as a friend. We're just friends."

"But isn't there some attraction between you?"

"I doubt it. Especially now that he's seen me in my daggiest tracksuit—"

"Not that horrible old faded maroon thing?"

"That's the one. With no make-up, a runny nose, and a fever rash. I think any attraction has been well and truly extinguished."

"Not necessarily . . ."

"And he said I was a pain in the arse."

"Oh," said Meg, the disappointment heavy in her voice.

"Ally."

She opened her eyes. The room was dim. "What time is it?"

"It's just after five," said Matt. "What are you doing sleeping out here? And without even a heater on?"

He had tossed another blanket over her and was tucking it in close around her body. "Your feet are like blocks of ice."

"I sat here to phone Meg after I woke up. I must have drifted off."

"Did you eat anything?"

"No . . ."

He sighed one of those exasperated, parental sighs, and walked over to the fire. He must have lit it as soon as he came in—it was already burning steadily. He opened the door and moved the logs around with a poker.

"Did you take your tablets?"

"Yes Dad."

He looked around at her, frowning. "Do you know what time that was?"

"Around one."

Matt checked his watch. "So you can take the next dose now." He walked across to the kitchen, flicking on the light switches on his way. "And Rob made you some soup. I'll heat it up for you."

"I'll do it," Ally said, struggling to sit up.

"Stay there, I've got it."

Ally sat up, rearranging the rug around her shoulders and the blanket across her knees. "What kind of soup is it?"

"Chicken," said Matt, ladling some into a bowl.

"Chicken soup. What a cliché."

Matt placed the bowl in the microwave and then slammed the door, turning around to glare at her. "Do you always have to make some kind of smart-arse remark?"

Ally just looked at him.

"A *cliché*? Fuck, Ally! What is it with you? Why can't you just say thanks if someone does something for you?"

Ally was stunned. She hadn't meant to hurt anyone's feelings. She was just not comfortable being fussed over. No one had ever made her chicken soup before. She didn't know what she was supposed to say.

"Sorry."

The microwave oven beeped and Matt took out the bowl of soup. He carried a tray over and set it down on the coffee table in front of her. Next to the bowl were her tablets and a glass of water.

"Thank you," she said quietly.

"I'm going to have a shower," he said, and walked off up the stairs to the loft.

The next evening

Ally was showered and dressed and had lit the fire when Matt arrived home. Nic had phoned earlier to say that she and Rob were coming over tonight. They both had the night off, and they wanted to see how she was. Matt had invited them to stay for dinner.

He'd hardly spoken to her the night before, and he was gone before she was up in the morning. Ally felt like she was in the way. It was almost worse than staying at Circle's End. Matt obviously didn't feel comfortable with her around. He probably didn't like sharing his space with anyone. This was the man, after all, who had walked out on his wife and child when it had all got too much for him.

Ally tried to ignore thoughts that kept coming into her head about her supposed ingratitude. She hadn't asked for help, and while she didn't mean to be rude, she didn't want anyone to feel responsible for her either. She could look after herself. She was feeling much better today, she'd only needed a short nap this afternoon. Tomorrow she was going to find somewhere to live.

Matt didn't ask her if she had taken her medication when he got home, in fact he barely acknowledged her.

"I spoke to Nic, you know they're coming over?" he asked disinterestedly, not making eye contact.

"Yes."

"I'm going to have a shower."

Nic and Rob arrived about twenty minutes later, just as Matt came down the stairs, his hair still damp.

Nic walked through the door and hugged Ally. "You're looking a lot better. Though you're still pale."

"Don't fuss. I'm feeling a hundred percent better."

Rob stooped to kiss her on the cheek. "You do look better, Ally," he said kindly.

"It must have been the soup. Thanks Rob, it was wonderful."

Matt offered them drinks and they sat down at the table. He stayed in the kitchen, preparing dinner.

"You know this changes things, at the restaurant," Nic started. "We either have to open later, or wind back on what we first planned."

"I think opening is the priority," said Rob. "It has to be."

Ally nodded. "I've stuffed everything, haven't I?"

"No!" they chorused.

"Ally, we wouldn't have come this far without all the work you've done," Rob insisted gently. "But we're not going to let you keep going at the same pace."

"It's out of the question," Nic agreed. "I mean, you're not even setting foot in there for at least another week."

"A week?" Ally protested. "But I'll be right in a couple of days—"

"No way, Ally!" Rob countered flatly.

"But I could just do a little . . ."

"We'll lock you out if we have to!" Nic said sternly. "What is it with you? Were you an overachiever as a child, or something?"

"Hardly," Ally denied. "What am I going to do in the meantime? It seems like such a waste of time."

"Well, we have to get you your own place, for starters," said Rob.

"I might have something." Matt walked out from behind the kitchen bench and leaned against the front of it. "I've done some work for a bloke up on Mount Gib in the past. I remembered he had a granny flat. He stopped renting it out because he had trouble with tenants. So I gave him a call today, to see if he'd reconsider. He said to come and look at the place. I'll take you up there tomorrow if you're up to it."

That was quick. Just as Ally suspected, Matt didn't want her around a minute longer than was absolutely necessary. And she certainly didn't want to stay where she wasn't wanted. She'd spent enough of her life doing that.

"Thank you," she said pointedly, to make sure he registered her gratitude. He just shrugged and walked back into the kitchen.

"So, that's solved," Ally mused. "What else am I going to do?"

"Here's the fun part." Nic jumped up from the table and went to her bag. She pulled out a bundle of what looked like magazines.

"What have you got there?" Ally asked, curious.

"Catalogues. Have you thought about everything we're going to have to buy for a restaurant?"

Of course she had. Ally had daydreamed about it often, letting her imagination run wildly over budget.

"Plates, and glasses—"

"Flatware and stemware if you want to sound professional," Rob corrected her.

"Linen, cutlery . . ."

"Candles, lamps, artworks, vases," Ally chimed in.

Nic grinned widely, her face about to burst. "We are going to have the biggest legitimate shopping spree ever!"

Friday

"This isn't fair, your place is bigger than ours, and there's only one of you."

Nic had come to help Ally move in. Not that Ally had much to move, and not that Nic was doing much to help.

Matt had dutifully brought Ally to meet Richard and Beverley Jones as promised. The granny flat turned out to be a charming former groundsman's cottage, with its own street access, set on a rather impressive estate.

The Joneses obviously had serious money and, fortunately, they were happy to rent out the furnished cottage at a rate Ally knew was more than reasonable, probably as some kind of favor to Matt.

"I'll put in a good word for you when I leave."

"When are you leaving?" Nic frowned.

"Oh, not for a while, don't worry."

Nic threw herself down on the bed.

"I was just about to put my suitcase there."

"Oh, sorry." She edged across to make room. "So what's your landlord like?"

"Nice enough. He's a bit . . ." Ally shrugged. "I don't know, a bit of a fuddy-duddy. He looks about the same age as Matt, but he seems older."

"What does he do? He must make a few quid."

Ally nodded. "He's a gynecologist and obstetrician."

"Oh, yuck!"

"What's the problem?"

"You know what he looks at all day!"

"He hasn't seen mine," said Ally. "It doesn't bother me."

"Well, I won't be shaking his hand if we're ever introduced." Nic shuddered at the thought.

"You're a twit."

Ally opened her suitcase and started sorting through her clothes, deciding what to put on hangers. It all had to be ironed anyway, everything had been crushed in her bag for so long. She needed to buy an iron, and an ironing board, unless there was one down at Circle's End. She liked this feeling, of settling in. It would actually be fun to go and shop for groceries, she hadn't done that for ages. She might even make a list.

"So anyway," Nic was saying. She had the habit of returning to previous conversations without warning. "I told Rob that we have to take the trip up to Sydney, there's no way we can order everything over the phone."

"Have we got the time though?" Ally said dubiously.

"We need the R & R, especially you, Ally."

"Well, I'll call Meg, we can stay at her place."

"The cost of a hotel would be counted as a business expense, you know."

"Yes, but you still have to pay for it, and I'd rather we spent the money on other stuff."

"But I need a girls' night out."

"We can still go out, Meg would love it."

"Into the city?"

"Sure, she lives right on Watsons Bay. We can catch the ferry across."

"Brilliant! I love the harbor. I love the whole city!" she swooned, her eyes shining.

"What, Sydney?"

"Mm. It's what I miss most about living down here."

"Then why are you living down here?"

"Why do you think?"

Ally raised an eyebrow.

"I love the city, but I love Rob more."

"Shouldn't you have compromised?"

"What's your point?"

Ally shrugged, taking a pile of underwear over to the chest of drawers. "I don't know, you seem too independent and feisty to be following a man around."

"I am independent!" she insisted. "And I'm not following Rob around, this was my choice. Besides, we're partners in the restaurant now."

"And whose idea was the restaurant?"

"Rob always wanted to open his own restaurant. That's why he came down here. He could never have afforded it in Sydney. Well, not for a long time anyway."

"So, it's his dream?"

"It's my dream now, too," she said defensively.

One week later

"To be honest," said Meg, "at this point I'd settle for any dream, I wouldn't care who had it first."

Ally sat straddled on the floor, playing with Harrison. Nic was at it again, insisting she was not living Rob's dream. She had started with Meg as soon as she'd downed her first glass of wine. She'd been like a dog with a bone all week, rehashing it with Ally at every opportunity. She wished now she'd kept her opinions to herself.

Harrison had taken a while to get used to Ally again. She hadn't expected that. But then she realized it had been six months since she'd last seen him. That was a long time to a two year old. That's how long Matt had been away from Beck, and she had probably been much the same age. Ally couldn't imagine what it must have felt like, to have your own child not know you.

"Aren't you going to have a drink, Ally?" Meg asked.

"Harrison's just getting used to me again, I don't want to ignore him now."

"Cluck, cluck," Nic taunted.

"Anyway, we have our big shopping excursion tomorrow, I can do without the hangover."

"One or two glasses of wine won't give you a headache, Al," Meg frowned. "Here Harry, want a bok?"

"Bok" was Harrison's word for iceblock, his favorite thing, even in the middle of winter. He looked wide-eyed at Ally and repeated "bok" happily, clapping his hands together. He scrambled to his feet.

"Kiss for Ally first?"

He stopped in his tracks, and with a shy smile he leaned forward, puckering his lips and pressing them against Ally's.

"There, he still loves you. Now come and have a drink."

Ally got up onto one knee and then stood up. "Ow, my bum's gone numb. I always feel like I'm a hundred years old after I've been sitting on the floor."

"At least you're not sleeping on the floor anymore," Nic threw at her.

"Don't bring that up again."

"Are you really over the illness now, Ally?" asked Meg.

"Completely."

The best thing for her had been to have her own place. She was going to bed early every night, often after a deep, hot bath. The whole cottage was surprisingly warm. There was a little cozy heater in the living room which Ally lit each afternoon. And she was eating well, enjoying the novelty of cooking again.

"You've lost heaps of weight," Meg observed.

"Have I?" said Ally, looking down at herself. "I haven't been dieting or anything."

"No, just working eighteen-hour days and living on cup-a-soup," Nic frowned.

"Funny, if I was trying to lose weight, I wouldn't be able to. Then when I don't think about it, it falls off."

"Haven't you noticed your clothes getting loose?" Meg asked.

"A little, but I've only been wearing baggy tracksuits and leggings. They're all the warm clothes I've had."

"Mm, she's quite the fashion plate," Nic observed wryly.

Ally pulled a face. "That's why I want to go through my boxes and take some stuff back with me. Now that I've got somewhere to put it all!" she added happily.

Meg was refilling their glasses, draining the bottle. "To Ally's new place," she declared, holding up her glass.

"And to a successful shopping trip tomorrow."

"And to a fabulous night out tomorrow night," Nic added.

"You're really looking forward to this, aren't you?"

She nodded eagerly. "I love a good girls' night out."

"God, it's been so long, I've almost forgotten what it's like," Meg said wistfully.

"We've had plenty of girls' nights!" Ally insisted.

"Yes, but they were girls' nights in. We haven't gone out in ages."

"It's not a real girls' night unless you go out," Nic insisted. "I just love the anticipation, getting dressed up, putting on makeup, doing each other's hair—"

"How old are you?" Ally interrupted.

"Oh don't be such an old fogey," Meg scoffed. "Go on, Nic."

"And then, when you're out, the guys notice you because you're, like, in a pack—"

"Okay, so now you don't realize how old *we* are!"

"Speak for yourself, Ally. And then, Nic?"

"There's all that flirting. The guys approach, they buy you drinks, they ask you to dance . . ."

"They stagger when they walk, they slur their speech," Ally sighed.

"What is wrong with you?" Meg frowned.

"Nothing," she insisted. "I just think the best thing about being in a relationship is that you don't have to put up with all that. It's not as exciting as she's making out."

Oh yes it is, Meg thought privately. "And remind me, just how long is it since you *were* in a relationship? It must be six months since you and Bryce split up?" she said.

Ally nodded, sipping her wine.

"Don't you miss the sex?" asked Nic.

Ally thought about it. She shrugged. "Not really."

"Yeah, but that's only because sex with Bryce was, well," Meg hesitated, "sex with Bryce!"

They all burst out laughing.

"To Bryce," Ally raised her glass. "Or should I say, *Bruce*."

"What do you mean?"

"Bruce. That was his real name."

"You're kidding?"

"Didn't I ever tell you that?"

"No!"

Ally grinned. "Mm, he went to one of those success gurus who follow the latest trend. Numerology, feng shui, you name it. Anyway, they told him he'd be more successful if he changed the 'u' to a 'y.' I could have told him that. That was in the days when Bruce was about the dorkiest name you could be saddled with. Anyway, one little extra stroke of the pen, Bruce became Bryce, and it changed his whole persona."

"You never told me."

"I think I was probably sworn to secrecy. Not that that ever stopped me before."

"Did he know your real name?"

"What's your real name?" blurted Nic.

Ally dropped her head in her hands.

"Haven't you told her?" said Meg. "It's not that bad, I don't know why you don't use it now. You used it at college."

"I could get away with it at art college."

"Will somebody tell me?" Nic exclaimed.

Ally sighed. "Okay, but don't laugh. It's Alaska."

"Oh, that's so cool!" exclaimed Nic. And then she giggled. "Pardon the pun."

Ally rolled her eyes.

"You know there's a song by someone," Nic mused. "About a girl they called Alaska."

"Mm, they used to sing it to me at college all the time," said Ally bluntly. "It's about a drug addict. Can we drop the subject?"

"Okay, what were we talking about before?" said Meg. "I know. Sex. So you haven't been getting any for six months?"

Ally shrugged. "I'll live. I've sown my wild oats."

"That doesn't sound right," Meg frowned. "I don't think women have wild oats."

"Maybe they scatter their free-range eggs?" Nic offered.

"That's disgusting."

"But 'losing your virginity' sounds like you've just been careless."

"And it's not as though you can find it again."

"This conversation is getting out of hand," Ally interrupted.

"So, back to where we started. Do you miss sex?"

"I think I must be in a slump at the moment. You know, low biorhythms or something. It just seems like too much of an effort."

"I don't think Matt would take much of an effort," Meg winked.

"Has Matt—?" Nic started.

"No, nothing has happened, it's all in Meg's fertile imagination."

"Well, I think you might have had a chance with Matt once," said Nic. "But you've pissed him off well and truly now."

Ally felt as though her heart plummeted into the pit of her stomach. She drained her glass. "Have you got another bottle, Meg, or should we go to the liquor shop?"

The following night

"I can't believe you're painting your toenails!" Ally shook her head.

"Well, technically, she's painting my toenails," Meg corrected her.

"Do you want me to do yours next?" said Nic.

"I haven't painted my toenails since I was at college!"

"All the more reason you should."

"I would rather rediscover my youth in a more meaningful way. Like, maybe you could ground me tonight, Meg?" Ally said hopefully.

"You're not welching on us, Ally, I'm not going to let you. We drank just as much as you did last night."

"Except that you didn't go on the shopping spree of the century today."

"I did!" Nic piped in.

"Yes, but you're under thirty. I could do it at your age too."

"You should hear yourself, Ally!" groaned Meg. "Next it'll be a lecture about how the kids today show no respect. Lighten up!"

Ally was nonplussed. "I'm just not sure how my stomach will stand up to the ferry ride . . ."

She shut up when both Meg and Nic stopped what they were doing and looked up at her, clearly disgusted.

"I'm going to have a shower."

Ally was dressed and ready to go, sitting on the lounge, reading Harrison his favorite Dr. Seuss. Nic and Meg were still doing each other's hair. The blow-drier was working overtime in the bathroom.

Chris strolled casually into the room and perched on the edge of an armchair, just as Ally finished *"One Fish, Two Fish."*

"More?" said Harrison, his eyes gleaming, looking up at Ally.

As if she could refuse him anything. "Okay, go find another one."

"You'll never get away," Chris smiled, watching Harrison scramble off the lounge and totter across to the bookshelf.

"Suits me."

"What, you're not keen on the big girls' night?"

Ally shrugged. "I must be getting old."

"Well, you're younger than Meg, and she can't wait to get out of here."

He was staring at his feet, frowning. He looked around in the direction of the hallway, and then back at Ally.

"I don't expect you to break any confidences, but has Meg said anything to you?"

"About what?"

He shrugged. "Anything that's bothering her? She seems to have something on her mind lately."

Harrison plopped a book on Ally's lap. *Green Eggs and Ham!* My favorite. 'I don't like them Sam-I-am!' " she chanted, tickling Harrison as he climbed up onto the lounge again.

She looked up at Chris. "I think you should be asking Meg about how she feels, not me."

"But whenever I ask her what's wrong, she always says 'nothing.' "

"And you let her get away with that?" Ally said, lifting an eyebrow. Harrison had settled himself beside her. She opened the first page of the book.

" 'I am Sam,' " she started to read.

Thankfully it was a calm night and the ferry ride was bearable, out on the deck, with the fresh breeze blowing on her face. Ally gazed across at the city skyline as they approached the Quay. She thought that she would miss it more. Still, it was good to be here tonight.

When the ferry docked, Nic made a beeline for her favorite nightclub in Darling Harbor. Just as well, because it had been a long time for Ally and Meg, and they both admitted they wouldn't have had a clue where to go.

They found a table easily. Apparently nine o'clock was ridiculously early, the place wouldn't really start filling for at least another hour. Good, it would give them time for a quiet chat, though Ally kept that thought to herself.

"Look at his bum! Couldn't you just bite it?"

"Nic! You're such a perve." Ally frowned.

"What's wrong? They do it to us."

"Exactly, and we don't like it!"

"Who says we don't like it!"

"Don't like what?" Meg asked, arriving back with their drinks. She'd taken first shout.

"Ally was saying that we don't like guys looking at us."

"I meant, we don't like being objectified. Isn't that right?"

Meg shrugged. "I don't mind them looking. And to be fair, I don't know a man that doesn't enjoy being perved at by a woman."

"I give up," said Ally, shaking her head.

"Mind you," Meg continued, "the prettiest ones are all looks, no substance. That goes for men and women. You should hear what comes out of the mouths of some of the models we get into the agency!"

"Who cares?" Nic scoffed. "It's not as if I want to discuss the global economy or anything."

"Doesn't it turn you off when a guy starts talking and he's got the intelligence of a screensaver?" said Ally.

"Who wants to talk? Haven't you noticed how quiet Rob is?"

"I often wonder about you two," Ally admitted.

"He's my ideal man," said Nic. "You know how tall he is?"

They nodded.

"And have you noticed his hands, his feet?"

"Huge," Ally agreed.

"Well, the rest of his . . ." Nic cleared her throat, " . . appendages follow suit."

Ally shrieked. "I'll never be able to look him in the eye again!"

"Oh sure you will," she grinned. "Or else where will you look?"

Ally and Meg burst out laughing.

"Would any of you ladies like to dance?"

They all looked up suddenly, like they'd been caught at something, which they had, sort of. A pleasant looking man, probably in his early thirties, stood smiling down at them, waiting for an answer.

Nic nudged Ally, but she ignored her. "Not at the moment, thanks," she smiled.

"What's wrong with you?" said Nic after he walked away.

"Nothing."

"Then why wouldn't you dance with him? He looked alright."

"I'm not interested in picking up anyone."

"But you're the only one out of the three of us who can."

"I'm not here to give you some kind of vicarious thrill." Ally frowned. "Besides, why couldn't you dance with someone? It's not exactly cheating."

Meg glanced nervously at Ally.

"Most guys can't dance anyway, I just like to flirt," said Nic.

"Chris can dance," Meg mused wistfully. "We used to dance all the time."

"So why don't you anymore?" asked Ally.

"Maybe we're playing the wrong tune."

"Oh, I think I'm going to throw up," said Nic, tossing back her drink.

Meg started to laugh. "Okay, I admit, that was pretty bad."

"You've been in advertising too long, if that's your best material."

"I've been in a lot of things too long," Meg sighed.

Nic stood up. "I'll get this round. Same again?"

She walked away, and Ally leaned back in her chair, considering Meg. "Have you talked to Chris about the way you've been feeling?"

"What would I say? It'd break his heart if I told him I was unhappy."

"You don't think he can tell something's going on?"

Meg looked at her warily. "What do you mean, something's going on. There's nothing going on." She was sure Chris didn't suspect a thing.

Ally frowned at her. "I mean, he can tell things aren't right."

"Oh," she said, realizing. "Do you reckon?"

"Of course."

"But if I talk to him, then it all becomes real, and out there . . ."

"And you have to do something about it, instead of just complaining."

"And you say that I'm blunt," Meg frowned.

"If you can dish it out . . ."

"I tell you what, I'll talk to Chris, if you give it a go with Matt."

Ally stared at her, wide-eyed. "Give *what* a go? You act as if he's there for the taking. Didn't you hear what Nic said last night, she thinks I've missed my chance."

"Do you?"

"What?"

"Think you've missed your chance?"

Ally sighed, exasperated. "I told you before, I'm not even sure about him in the first place."

"Why?"

She looked over toward the bar. Nic was still waiting to be served.

"I didn't want to say any of this in front of Nic," Ally began.

Meg leaned in. "What?" she whispered, her eyes gleaming.

"It's just about Matt, she knows him, it wouldn't be right to tell her."

"What is it?"

Ally paused for effect. "He walked out on his wife and child."

"What, recently?"

"No, I mean when his daughter was a baby."

"But I don't understand, isn't she a teenager?"

"Yes, now she is."

"So what are you saying? He walked out on his wife, like ten years ago? What's your point?"

"He walked out and left them, for six months. Just like that."

"I'm sure there must have been more to it," Meg said, dubiously.

"I suppose. But I still don't think I could trust someone who could leave that easily."

Meg frowned at her. "It was a long time ago. People change, you know."

"Not in my experience."

Nic returned, setting their drinks down on the table. "Why all the serious faces?"

"Nothing," Ally said lightly.

"Well, if we're not dancing with any men this evening, that doesn't mean we're not going to dance at all. I'm off to charm the DJ and see if he's got anything more your pace."

June

"Meg," Chris began tentatively, across the breakfast table. "I was thinking, what if I ask Mum to keep Harrison tonight? We could meet in the city after work, have dinner, spend some time, just the two of us?"

Meg sipped her coffee thoughtfully. Why couldn't he have just gone ahead and made the arrangements, and then told her—"Meet me at Pier One tonight." Something romantic like that, instead of painstakingly checking every detail with her.

"Okay," she smiled faintly. "That'd be lovely." She knew it was important that they spend some time together. Ally was right, they had to talk.

"Where do you want to go?"

"Surprise me." Please.

Chris frowned. "Oh? But what do you feel like? You know, if I book Indian, and you're not in the mood . . ."

"Just pick somewhere fabulous."

"Prodigy it is then."

Prodigy was their special occasion restaurant. For every special occasion. It was starting to lose its specialness.

"Now you've gone and spoilt the surprise."

Chris shook his head, grinning. "Since when did you like surprises?"

They were seated at a table near the window, taking in the view across the city to the harbor. Meg surveyed the menu and put it down, frustrated. Chris was studying his closely.

"I don't know whether to have the veal, the risotto or the lamb shanks," he mused.

"I'm sure they're all good," Meg replied, hoping she didn't sound snitty. Chris always did this. You'd think he was buying a car, the way he deliberated over a menu. She remembered she used to find it endearing.

Meg threw back the rest of her champagne. "Pour me another, will you?" she asked him, twirling her glass around by the stem.

"Thirsty tonight?" Chris remarked, filling her glass.

The waiter returned to the table. "Can I take your orders?"

"What does the chef recommend this evening?" Meg asked, ignoring Chris's raised eyebrow.

"The swordfish is very good, and the kangaroo fillets with artichoke and fennel are a specialty."

"Okay, I'll have that."

"I don't think you'd like it, Meg," said Chris in a low voice across the table.

"How do I know if I don't try it?"

"It's just, I think you'll find the fennel a bit strong . . ."

"I feel like trying something different, okay?"

Now she knew she sounded snitty. Chris gave his order to the waiter and he left them. Meg gazed out the window.

"Honey," he said, reclaiming her attention. "Are you happy?"

The last person who asked her that question was Jamie. "What do you mean? Of course I'm happy."

He looked at her steadily. "Are you? Are you really happy?"

Meg sighed. If they were going to get anywhere, she had to be honest. "Not really."

She couldn't stand the lost look on his face.

"It's a lot of things, Chris. I don't know where I'm headed at work, I don't know if I want another baby."

"What about us?" he asked quietly.

She looked at him squarely.

"You're the best man I've ever known, Chris. This is exactly where I want to be." She'd been reciting that to herself a lot lately. Most of the time she believed it.

Chris was watching her. "But it's gone a little stale, hasn't it?"

"Is that how you feel?"

He shook his head. "To be honest, Meg, no. Just being your husband, and Harrison's father, that's all I need."

Meg's heart rose into her mouth. "Chris . . ."

"It's okay, honey. I want you to be happy. I'll do anything."

"Chris," she said firmly. It was getting too close to the bone. "You and I, we'll be fine. Married people go through peaks and troughs. We are not the problem."

She couldn't stand to hurt him. They would get through this, and besides, if she sorted out some of the other issues, maybe everything would seem better anyway.

"But you know," she continued, taking another tack, "since I dropped the idea of becoming a director, I feel a bit aimless at work."

"Do you want to rethink that?"

She shook her head. "No, that's the thing, I've realized this career is not that important to me anymore."

"Well then, what would you like to do?"

"I don't know."

Chris leaned forward, refilling her glass. "You're a bright, talented woman, Meg. You could do anything you put your mind to."

She shrugged. "Like what?"

"I don't know. What interests you?"

She really couldn't think of anything.

"Or you could take some time off," Chris suggested.

"Have another baby?" she asked, lifting an eyebrow.

"Is that what you want?"

"I don't know. I mean, I don't want Harrison to be an only child, but sometimes I get annoyed that everyone seems to expect me to have another baby, like I don't have a choice in the matter."

"Of course it's your choice, Meg."

"How would you feel if we didn't have any more children?"

Chris thought for a moment. "I won't pretend I wouldn't be a little disappointed. But we have Harrison, and I want you to be happy, not tied down to a baby if that's not what you want."

She smiled faintly at him.

"You can take time off without being pregnant, Meg," he continued. "Have a think about it. You could change jobs, or do a course, go back to university. Whatever makes you happy."

The waiter arrived with their meals, and they started to eat. Meg bit into a piece of fennel, and it took her breath away. Chris looked up, noticing the worried expression on her face as she sat chewing slowly.

"How is it?"

Meg looked up at him sheepishly. She swallowed, washing it down with a gulp of champagne. "It's a bit strong," she said hoarsely.

Chris smiled at her, and they both started to laugh.

"Well, at least you can't say you didn't try it."

Friday

Meg dialed Ally's number. She knew she was probably busy, they were planning to open the restaurant next month. But Meg didn't care. She was feeling restless, and she couldn't bear to spend another day at home.

"Hello?" said Ally.

"Hi, it's me."

"Hi Meg!" she replied warmly. "How are you?"

"Okay, I was wondering if you felt like a visit from Harrison and me?"

"What, for the weekend?" Ally hoped she didn't sound negative, but she couldn't possibly spare the time to entertain Meg at the moment.

"No, I was thinking of driving down for the day."

"You want to come all this way just for the day?"

"I've got nothing better to do."

But Ally did.

Meg sensed her hesitation. "Look, I don't want to get in the way, I know you're busy."

"No, don't be silly. I'd love to see you. Really."

"Are you sure?"

The others were always telling Ally that she needed to take a break, and she liked to keep them off her back since her illness.

"Absolutely. Look it's cold, but the days are beautiful at the moment. We could take Harrison to a park, veg out for a while."

"That sounds great, Ally. I'll go down to Double Bay on the way and buy some goodies, pack up a picnic hamper."

Ally went to protest.

"I insist. Then we'll be all set for lunch, and it won't take you away from your work for too long."

"Okay Meg. Do you remember how to get here?"

"I'm pretty sure, I can always call you on the mobile if I get lost."

"Then I'll see you when you get here."

It was around noon when Ally heard Meg calling out from the front entrance.

"Hi Meg," she said, poking her head into the hall. "Come on in."

Meg stepped tentatively into the room, Harrison perched on her hip.

"Hi Harry!" Ally said warmly. He smiled at her more readily this time, having seen her only a few weeks ago. "Just let me get cleaned up and we can go."

Meg looked around the room. "Wow, it's . . ." she faltered.

"Very unfinished!" Ally wiped her hands on a rag. "We've got so much to do."

"When do you open?"

"Last weekend in July. We're having a special Yuletide dinner."

"Sounds great."

Ally nodded. "I just hope we're ready by then, but Nic had her heart set on it, and they do need to start operating, making some income. Come and I'll show you the main room."

They walked down the hall. "This looks better," said Meg.

They had stuck pretty much to Ally's original idea, and the room was now painted all white. It looked fresh and bright and airy, especially in comparison to the rest of the place.

"What are you going to do with the floors?" Meg asked, noticing the tacky carpet, splattered with paint.

"They'll be stripped, but that's the last thing, or else they'll get wrecked with all the tradesmen coming and going."

"Speaking of tradesmen, is Matt around?"

Ally folded her arms. "He was here earlier, for a while. But now he's off on another job."

"So . . . ?" Meg asked pointedly.

"What?" Ally didn't want to talk about Matt. He'd cooled off considerably since the flu episode. They had a solid working relationship now, and that's all there was to it. Though sometimes she caught him watching her with an odd expression on his face.

"To be honest, Meg, we're so busy that if Mel Gibson walked through that door and asked me for a date, I'd probably turn him down."

Meg sighed heavily. "You know, Al, you give singledom a bad name."

"Let's go to the park."

"He's getting too big, Meg, and too grown up," Ally complained, reclining back on the grass, watching Harrison play.

"And I'm devastated that he calls me Ally now, instead of Ya-Yee."

Meg smiled vaguely. Ally glanced across at her.

"So what's going on?"

"What do you mean?"

"What did you want to talk about? You didn't come all the way down here just for the scenery."

"Well, mostly I did. I've been going stir-crazy at home lately."

"You're still working three days?"

Meg nodded. "When I'm at the office, I don't want to be there. And when I'm at home, I don't know what to do with myself."

She wasn't going to admit that there were times when she sat literally staring at the phone, willing it to ring. Willing it to be Jamie. But he'd taken her at her word. There had been no phone calls, no surprise visits at work. And she had no way to contact him, which was just as well.

Meg had been toying with the idea of telling Ally about him, knowing she'd be absolutely horrified. It might help her to put Jamie Carroll out of her mind once and for all.

"Have you and Chris talked?"

"We have actually."

Ally looked at her expectantly. "And?"

"He was completely understanding, of course. He doesn't mind if we don't have another baby. We can travel, if I want. Um, what else?" Meg paused, thinking. "I could take time off work, study, whatever I want really."

"That's great," said Ally. "So what will you do?"

Meg lay back on the picnic blanket, tucking her arms behind her head. "It's funny, you know. I thought I didn't have any choices." That's what she'd told Jamie. "Now I feel like I've got too many choices. It's like bathroom tiles."

Ally was mystified. "I'm afraid I don't get the analogy."

Meg glanced across at her. "Remember when we did up the bathroom?"

Ally nodded.

"I wanted something different, a *change*. Remember?"

"I remember how we went to every frigging tile shop in the Sydney metropolitan area, and beyond."

"That's right. There were too many tiles to choose from. Too many colors, every size imaginable, and patterned, plain, glossy, matt—"

"I get the point," Ally interrupted. "But do you remember what you ended up with?"

"Whatever's on the walls now."

"Well, if I remember right, they were the first tiles you saw, at the first shop we walked into."

Meg frowned, thinking. "I'd forgotten that."

"So what does that tell you?"

"I should leave everything as it is?" She pulled a face.

"Not necessarily," Ally mused. "I just wonder if sometimes we go searching for something when what we really want has been right in front of us all the time."

Meg sat up, facing Ally. She took a deep breath. "I almost had an affair."

Ally's eyes widened. "What?"

"I almost had an affair."

"How do you 'almost' have an affair?"

Meg shrugged. "I was seeing someone, but I broke it off before things went too far."

Ally was gobsmacked. "When was that?"

"What—the breaking off?"

She nodded vaguely.

"About a month ago. I haven't seen him since."

Ally roused herself. "This is a real person you're talking about? You actually did this?"

"I didn't 'do' anything in the end."

"Then what happened? Who is he? How did you meet him?" Ally felt flustered. This was something she had never expected to hear from Meg. Rational, careful Meg.

"I met him at work, at a shoot. He asked me out for a drink. Then he called around work a few times, took me to lunch." Meg smiled wistfully, remembering. "He even took me riding on a motorbike down the South Coast one day."

"You, on a motorbike? I don't believe it."

Meg looked at Ally. "That was the thing, Jamie made me push my boundaries a bit."

"Jamie?" Ally frowned. "How old is he?"

"Why do you ask?"

"Well, grown men don't call themselves 'Jamie'!"

"This one does," Meg refuted.

Ally thought for a moment. "And you're saying nothing happened?"

"Well, it came close, so I told him I couldn't see him anymore. And I haven't."

"So, how are things between you and Chris?"

"He doesn't know anything about it, okay?"

Ally nodded.

"We're fine," she sighed. "It certainly made me appreciate what I have with him . . ."

"But?"

Meg looked at her.

"I could hear a 'but' coming," Ally explained.

Meg drew her knees up, hugging them. "I just wish there was more excitement, a little romance . . ."

"You expect too much, Meg. Life's not really like that."

She groaned. "Why can't it be?"

"I'm sure if you settled down and had a child and a mortgage with this Jamie character, the romance would wane soon enough."

Meg didn't want to explain that she couldn't imagine Jamie settling down in a pink fit. And that was the attraction.

"You should think about doing a course or something. Keep your mind occupied. Find an interest."

Meg nodded. "Maybe. I'll have to get a hold of one of those course guides."

Ally would have to remember to prod her a bit in that direction.

"What about you?" said Meg. "What are you going to do once the restaurant is finished?"

"Well, it won't be for a while yet. We're not even starting on two of the front rooms until after the opening. And I'm committed to working there till Rob and Nic get the business established."

"So you'll see the rest of the year out down here?"

"Probably."

"Maybe something else will come up?"

Ally shrugged, gazing across to where Harrison was playing. She had been feeling lately that her life was drifting off in a direction that was unlikely to lead to ever having a family of her own. She loved her work, she even loved having the little cottage all to herself, but there was something missing, and she was going to have to get used to it.

"What's wrong?"

Ally looked at Meg. "Nothing."

"Yes there is, you look all broody."

"I just miss that little boy," she said, smiling faintly, watching Harrison.

Meg studied her. "You'd still like to have one of your own, wouldn't you?"

"Sure, and I'd like to have a million dollars, and straight hair," Ally dismissed. "Doesn't mean it's going to happen."

"Of course not, if you keep pushing away prospective suitors."

"Yes, that big stick I keep by the door really does the trick. Keeps the hordes at bay."

Meg pulled a face at her. "Ally, you know who I'm talking about. I just don't want to mention his name because it always sets you off."

"Matt Serrano is not marriage or father material," Ally stated resolutely.

"Because of something that happened a decade ago?" Meg said with disbelief. "That's such a cop-out, Ally."

"No it isn't. Maybe it wouldn't bother you, but it bothers me, okay?" She sighed heavily. "It's better if I start getting used to the idea that it's just not going to happen for me."

Meg felt overwhelmingly sad for her friend. "It could happen if you let it. It's your choice."

"Maybe I don't have all the choices you have, Meg."

July

It was just two weeks until the opening of the restaurant. There still seemed an impossible amount to be done, but they were committed now. They had a full house for the Yuletide dinner.

Now in the middle of it all, they had to give up a day to clear out Circle's End. Ally had almost forgotten about it, until the agent called to confirm a date for settlement. She'd promptly gone into a spin, but Nic had taken control. She lined up Matt with his truck, and she and Rob were helping until their shifts started in the afternoon. Ally had resisted at first, not wanting to put anyone out.

"What else are you going to do?" Nic exclaimed. "Cart all the furniture out yourself and tie it to the roof of the Laser? Guys are good at lifting heavy stuff, that's what they do. And Matt's got a truck."

"But—"

"You can buy him a case of beer. Get over it."

They spent the morning deciding what furniture was worth saving and what had to be tossed. Ally favored tossing the lot.

"You know, distressed furniture is dead trendy, Ally," Nic mused. "You might be able to sell some of this."

"This stuff isn't just distressed, it's suffering post-traumatic stress disorder," Ally returned dryly. "It'll be kinder to put it out of its misery."

Rob and Matt had already been back and forward once to St. Vinnie's and twice to the tip, with the truck loaded up each time. Now Matt was dropping Nic and Rob home so they could get ready for work, then he was meeting Ally back here.

They'd left her with the hard stuff, but she was the only one who could do it. Under her grandfather's bed they had found half a dozen old archive boxes filled with papers, documents, photographs, God only knew what else. Ally carried them out two at a time and dumped them on the floor in front of the fireplace. Matt had lit the fire when they'd first arrived, to check the flue wasn't blocked, but mostly because it was freezing. Ally started sifting through a box of old tax records. She was sure none of this would need to be kept, but she probably should check with an accountant. There were another couple of boxes, with similar bits and pieces, guarantees, old dockets, rubbish probably.

Ally reached for the next box. She opened the lid, and sitting on top was a photo of Nan as a young woman. It gave Ally a start. She sat back on her haunches, examining the picture, touching Nan's face, remembering.

There were more photos. Another one of Nan, with Ally this time, she must have only been about ten. Then one of Ally by herself, as a fairly serious young teenager. Ally looked closely at it, but there wasn't much light in the room. She picked up the box and carried it out near the glass doors.

There was no furniture left, so she sat on the bottom steps of the staircase Matt built. She studied the photo. She didn't look like a very happy child. Her expression was sullen, even a bit hard. Ally sat mesmerized, sifting through the rest of the contents of the box. There were old report cards from school, Christmas cards, birthday cards, letters Ally had sent to her grandfather over the years. Not very many. Not nearly enough.

She came to a photo of her mother, Jennifer, at about fifteen. She compared it against her own photo at the same age. They didn't look anything alike. Ally didn't look like anyone in her family, except for her green eyes. She assumed she must have taken after her father, whoever he was.

There was an envelope at the very bottom of the box, and one last photo, of Ally, aged about three, perched up on James's shoulders. She looked closely at her face. She was laughing. Ally felt tears spring into her eyes, and brushed them away, picking up the envelope.

The paper was a good quality parchment. There was a crest on the top left-hand corner which Ally didn't recognize. It looked official. She slid the thick folded paper out.

The sliding doors opened suddenly and Matt walked into the room. She hadn't heard his truck pull up.

"What's wrong?" he said, looking at her.

"Nothing," she sniffed, wiping her eyes.

"What's the matter?" he repeated gently. "Something's upset you."

She shook her head. "It's nothing, it's just stupid."

Matt sat down next to her. She was still holding the letter, and she didn't resist as he took it out of her hand.

He started to read. "It's from the Peruvian embassy," he murmured. " 'Regret to inform . . . Jennifer Anne Tasker . . . reported deceased.' " Matt turned around to look at her. "Oh Ally, I'm sorry."

"There's nothing to be sorry about," she shrugged. "I hardly knew the woman."

"But she was your mother."

"So? I hardly knew her." A sob caught in her throat.

Matt put his hand over hers. "Ally, it's okay. There'd be something wrong with you if you didn't feel something."

She shrugged off his hand and stood up. "Well there must be something wrong with me because I don't feel anything. I don't care, now I don't have to wonder anymore. I just wish he'd told me sooner."

Matt examined the letter. "It's dated last October, Ally. He must have got this not long before he died. Maybe he was waiting until he saw you, face to face, to tell you."

Ally snatched the letter out of his hand and put it back in the box. "Look, I don't give a shit. It's over. In fact I don't need any of this crap anymore."

She carried the box to the fireplace.

"What are you doing?"

She was standing looking at the flames. Matt came up behind her. "Don't, Ally, you'll regret it."

He reached over her shoulder for the box, but she pushed his arm away. "No, it's all a fucking joke. I don't want any of it."

She went to empty it into the fire, but Matt grabbed hold of the box. She wouldn't release her grip. She started to scream at him. "Let it go! I don't care!"

Matt didn't say anything as he prized the box out of her hands. She closed her fists and started pounding on his chest. She could hear herself screaming, but she couldn't stop it, she was out of control.

Then she felt Matt's arms close around her like a vise. She couldn't thrash about anymore, but instead she felt a huge wave of grief rise up in her chest, and she started to sob violently. Her whole body was shaking with the force of it. Matt stood holding her close against him, she didn't know for how long. Eventually her sobbing subsided into quiet weeping, broken only by an occasional, tremulous sigh.

"I'm sorry," she said against his chest.

"There's nothing to be sorry for." He relaxed his hold on her.

"I want to show you something," said Ally, dropping down onto one knee. She started rummaging through the box. She found the photo of her mother, and handed it up to Matt.

He took it from her, sitting down on the floor next to her. "This is your mother?"

She nodded. "They never talked about her much. I think it made them sad, but I didn't know anything about her, or my father. I used to make up stories that they were spies, or movie stars away on location."

Ally breathed deeply. "Then, when Nan died, she just appeared out of nowhere. She seemed like a kind of vision, sort of . . . ethereal. She stayed for about a week. Then she had a terrible fight with my grandfather, and she left." She paused, staring into the fire. "I remember hating him for making her leave, and hating her for leaving me with him."

Matt didn't say anything, he just watched her, listening.

"Lillian told me what happened. She wanted money. That 'ethereal' look was the drugs apparently. She was in a really bad way. She threatened to sue James for custody of me if he didn't give her money. Lillian said she'd never seen him so sick with fear. He was petrified, of losing me, of what would happen to me if she took me. He gave her what he could, but she kept asking for more. He eventually called her bluff and ordered her out of the house. He didn't let me out of his sight after that. But he never told me why."

Ally felt the tears stinging behind her eyes again. "It freaks me out sometimes, when I think about everything she did. She's my mother. What if I'm like her? And I don't even know anything about my father. Just some low-life one-night stand. It scares me."

Matt shifted closer to her. "Ally, don't make it harder than it already is. Just because he had a one-night stand with your mother, doesn't mean he was a bad person. After all, look what he produced."

Ally looked at him.

"I reckon," Matt said slowly, choosing his words, "that he was probably creative. He might have been a painter too. That could be where you got it from."

She had never thought about that. No one had ever talked about her father like he was a real person.

"And maybe he loved your mother very much, but she took off, frightened of becoming attached, staying somewhere too long." His voice was quiet, and he looked at her tenderly. "Maybe he would have loved her forever if she'd given him the chance."

Ally's eyes filled with tears, one spilling over to trickle down her cheek. Matt brushed it away with his thumb, cupping her face with his hand. He was staring right into her eyes and she couldn't look away, she didn't want to. He drew her face gently toward his. She could feel his breath on her skin. He was leaning in closer. Ally closed her eyes.

When his lips touched hers, she felt a shiver right down through the center of her body. She loved the way he tasted, the slight graze of his chin against hers. She brought her hand up to touch his face as Matt eased her down onto the carpet, his lips caressing hers, his tongue moving tentatively into her mouth. Ally became aware of her body responding, the gradual, exquisite arousal. She gave over to it, she wanted to experience every sensation, feel every slight quiver, the blood tingling in her veins. She arched herself against him, frustrated by the thick layers of clothing between them. She wanted to get closer, she needed that closeness. She had no one else. His lips moved down her neck and she opened her eyes, looking up at the ceiling. The heavy, dark wooden beams. Her grandfather's room above. He was gone. Her mother was gone. She was alone. She clung tightly to Matt. Would he go too? She wanted to believe he wouldn't. That there was someone she could count on. But he'd left his wife . . .

"No, stop," she cried, unravelling herself from his arms. "I can't do this."

Ally scrambled to her feet and hurried out through the sliding doors. She stood there shaking, leaning against the wall, the cold air stinging her face. It was a nice idea that her father might have stayed with her mother, a fantasy that Ally had allowed herself to indulge in for a fleeting moment. But it was just that, a fantasy.

Matt appeared at the sliding doors. "Are you okay?" he said quietly.

She nodded.

"I'm sorry, Ally . . ."

"It's not your fault, Matt." She looked over at him. "I just can't . . . Not now, not here." Her mouth went dry.

He nodded. He thrust his hands into his pockets, staring down at his feet. "I have the worst timing," he muttered.

They stood for a while, not saying anything. Ally felt cold. She hugged herself, rubbing her hands along her arms to warm them.

"You're cold. We should go inside."

Ally nodded. She turned to face him. "Matt, you've been so good to me. You're such a good friend. I don't want to spoil that."

She thought he was going to say something, but then he stopped.

"I need you to be my friend, Matt." She could trust him as a friend.

She couldn't quite read the look in his eyes. "It's okay, Ally. I understand."

Two weeks later

"We can do without it, Ally. It won't make that much of a difference."

"It will!" Ally insisted. "This room was made for a Christmas tree, Nic. I've been planning it from the start. It will set the mood—you know, the twinkling lights, the smell of the pine . . ."

"But if it can't be done, it can't be done."

Matt poked his head through the doorway. "What can't be done?"

"You tell her, Matt," said Nic, her hands on her hips. "She's been ringing around everywhere trying to find a live Christmas tree, and she can't get one. So it's one less thing we have to worry about if you ask me. Then there's the decorations, and lights and the rest of the crap."

"I'll do it, I've already got all the decorations."

Tempers had been close to the surface for the past two weeks. Nic and Ally had regular head-to-head yelling matches, to the point where someone had to step in and attempt to be an impartial third party, namely Rob or

Matt. What they couldn't understand was, five minutes later, they were joking about something else and all was forgotten.

Everyone was under pressure. The women were just better at releasing it. Rob was wound up so tight he could hardly look at anyone. Nic said if he kept it up, she'd dress him up on the night of the opening and he could be Frosty the Snowman out on the front porch. It fitted with the theme after all.

"I know where you can get a tree," Matt said tentatively.

"Matt!" Nic frowned.

Ally smiled hopefully at him.

"I have a mate . . ."

"Fucking mates!" Nic muttered, storming out of the room.

Ally grinned. "Could you call your 'mate'?"

"Is this going to get me into trouble?"

"Not after it's all set up. She'll come around."

Matt's friend operated a wholesale Christmas tree farm, just outside Bowral, toward Robertson, about a half an hour away. He wouldn't be home for the rest of the day, so he told Matt they should just help themselves.

Matt switched on the radio in the truck after they had been driving along for about five minutes without talking. Ally realized it was the first time they had been alone together since the episode down at Circle's End.

They were getting on fine, but there was no escaping what had happened. Whenever they made eye contact, it was there. And much to Ally's frustration, it was also there every time she closed her eyes at night. She kept remembering the way he felt, the weight of his body on top of her, the taste of his lips. Maybe she shouldn't have stopped him. She often wished she hadn't, imagining he was there sometimes, lying beside her in bed at night. Her hands reaching out to touch him, feeling his hands on her . . .

Ally squirmed in her seat, glancing across at Matt. He was watching the road ahead. The girls had asked her if she missed sex, and she hadn't, then. Now it was all she could think about. It was like he'd opened some kind of Pandora's box. She had not breathed a word about it to Nic or Meg, though—she would never hear the end of it.

It was way more complicated than simply sleeping with him. Try as she might, she couldn't get past the fact that Matt had walked out on his family. Maybe there were good reasons, or maybe he had changed, as Meg argued.

But Ally couldn't afford the risk of finding out. If she dropped her guard, if she allowed herself to believe there was someone who would stay, someone who might really love her . . . And then if he didn't.

Ally shivered.

"Are you cold?" Matt asked. "I'll turn up the heater."

She watched his hand as he adjusted the controls. She remembered that hand stroking her cheek, cupping her face. She remembered his lips against hers, how it felt to have his arms around her, his body up close against her . . .

"So, let's do it."

"Pardon?" Ally said startled, looking at Matt.

Then she realized the truck was pulled over to the side of the road, near a field of small radiata pines. Christmas trees.

She fumbled with her seat belt. "Sure, of course." She turned to him before opening the door. "Thanks for this, Matt. I appreciate it."

He looked at her, shrugging. "What are friends for?"

Saturday night

The first guests were due to arrive shortly. The green rooms looked sensational. The walls were deep forest, and Ally had used a special finish so they had the appearance of suede or velvet. All the woodwork was white and the floors were polished, topped with heavily patterned rugs in green, russet and ocher. On their shopping trip, Nic and Ally had found a striking pair of gilt mirrors that were perfect above the restored fireplaces.

But the pièce de résistance tonight was undoubtedly the tree. At more than two meters high, it filled the bay window. Ally had covered it in twinkling fairy lights, hand-tied red ribbons and gold baubles, as well as what seemed like hundreds of gorgeous wooden and ceramic traditional decorations.

"Where did you find all these?" Nic gasped after she apologized profusely and took back everything she had said the day before.

"They're from my own collection."

"What?"

"I'm a bit of a Christmas junkie," Ally explained self-consciously. "I've got boxes of the stuff. I used to decorate my own place, and the staffroom at school, and one year I even decorated Bryce's office, when they were having a party."

"And then you got a life?"

Ally ignored her, looking around the room, satisfied. "Well, we did it."

"Not yet," said Nic, biting her lip. "Come on, one last check around."

It wasn't like Nic to be nervous, but Ally realized she and Rob had a lot at stake tonight, much more than Ally. They walked out to the main room. The hall had a timber-paneled dado wall that Matt had restored and extended out into the main room, to form the bar and reception desk. Because he had copied the detail exactly, it looked as though it had always been there. Ally applied the same liming treatment to the dado and the bar as she had to all the other timberwork. Working up close, she realized why Matt had such a strong reputation. She had rarely seen such workmanship.

"You know," said Nic, "it doesn't feel right that Matt's not here, after everything he's done."

Ally had to agree. But he'd begged off, insisting he couldn't wait tables, and his culinary skills were too limited to be of any use in the kitchen. Nic had suggested he just stand in a corner looking handsome, but Matt had declined, claiming he didn't want to take attention away from the food.

The room was configured to seat eighty tonight. The largest single group was ten, the rest was made up of tables of fours and sixes. Ally had made gorgeous centrepieces for every table, and at each place setting there was a tiny box wrapped in red or green, tied with a sheer gold bow, encasing a single Belgian chocolate.

There was the sound of cars pulling up outside and doors slamming. Then they heard voices at the front door.

"You're on," said Ally.

Nic took a deep breath and walked up the hallway.

The guests could choose from a fixed menu: traditional Christmas fare, with the kind of innovative touches people had come to expect from Rob Grady. The ham was baked with a mustard seed and apricot glaze, the turkey stuffing a mixture of fig, orange and ground macadamias, and the roast loin of pork was basted with mango chutney. The wines were pre-selected, because of the fixed price, but they were all top of the range. Rob would settle for nothing less. For dessert, handmade individual puddings were presented on a bed of cherry coulis and custard, with a pot of hard sauce on the side.

By the time coffee and liqueurs were served, they were exhausted but relieved, maybe even cautiously optimistic. Ally started clearing the tables as the last guests were being shown to the door. She pushed through the swing doors into the kitchen, her arms laden with dishes.

"Hi," said Matt. He was leaning against the kitchen bench, talking to Rob.

"Oh, hello, when did you get here?"

"Just a few minutes ago. I timed it so there'd be nothing left to do," he grinned.

"Where is everyone?" Ally frowned, realizing the staff had all disappeared.

"I let them go," said Rob. "Early mark for working so hard tonight."

"Oh well, Matt, looks like there's plenty left for you to do after all," she grinned. "There's tables to be cleared, dishes to be washed—"

"Beer to be drunk . . ."

Nic stood at the front door until she saw the lights of the last car disappear down the drive.

"Robbie!" she shrieked as she turned and ran down the hall.

They all came out of the kitchen.

"What's going on?"

"We did it, darling!"

She ran across the room and literally leaped into his arms, wrapping her legs around his waist. Then they started to kiss, and kiss, seemingly oblivious of Matt and Ally, who both tried to look anywhere else in the room, except at them, or each other.

"I think I need a drink," Ally announced eventually.

"A drink!" Nic exclaimed, finally coming up for air. That got her attention. "What a good idea."

"Hold on just a minute, I didn't come empty-handed," said Matt, ducking back into the kitchen.

Nic slithered down off Rob. "And I'm starving. Let's bring out the leftovers."

Matt reappeared with a magnum of champagne.

"Congratulations," he said, handing it to Nic. He also had a gift-wrapped box, but he slipped that onto one of the sideboards, out of the way.

"Oh, Matty! You shouldn't have!" she squealed. "But I'm glad you did. Give us a kiss," she said, offering him her cheek. He did as he was told. "Can we open it?"

"That's what I bought it for."

Ally collected glasses from the bar and some clean plates from the servery. Nic and Rob brought out platters of leftovers, while Matt opened the champagne. They sat around a table, picking at the food, and toasting everything that came to mind.

"To Rob's superb food."

"To Ally's exquisite rooms."

"And the beautiful tree."

"To Matt's exceptional carpentry."

"What about me?" Nic pouted. "I feel like the unskilled laborer."

Rob leaned forward and took her hand. "To my inspiration," he said, raising his glass and kissing her hand.

"To this ham. My God, it's amazing."

"Have you tried the stuffing? It's bloody fantastic. To the stuffing."

It didn't take them long to work their way down the bottle.

"To the guests!" Rob said, after refilling their glasses again.

"Speaking of guests, we had some celebrities here tonight, didn't we, Ally?" said Nic. "Who was that journalist woman? You know, the one on the ABC, dead clever type."

"Frances Callen," Ally replied. "I'm a huge fan, what was she like?"

"Really friendly, full of compliments about the food, and the whole place actually. But what about that guy?" Nic said excitedly. "You know, at table seven? I'm sure I've seen him on the telly."

"I know, he's definitely been in something," said Ally. "Do you know if he lives down here, Matt?"

"You'll have to give me a bit more information," he said, bemused.

"Um, he was in . . . What's it called?" Ally looked at Nic.

"That's right, he played thingame . . ."

"It was on Channel Nine, I think, or maybe it was Seven."

"It was some kind of a cop show, you know."

"Gee that narrows it down," said Matt dryly.

"Well, anyway, it was him," Nic said emphatically, folding her arms.

"Yes, I'm sure it was too," Ally agreed.

"You two are spending too much time together, you're even starting to sound alike," said Rob, smiling indulgently. "Neither of you make any sense."

Nic looked across the room. "Hey, Matt, what's in the box?"

"Oh, I nearly forgot." He got up from the table and walked over to pick it up.

"Someone's been to the gift-wrappers," Nic chanted.

"This is for you," he said, putting the box down in front of Ally. Rob and Nic looked at her. Ally went red.

Matt had returned to his seat. "A little bird told me it was your birthday yesterday."

"Why didn't you say?" Nic squealed, jumping up.

Ally dropped her head in her hands. "Did the little bird have a great big mouth and answer to the name of Meg?"

Matt grinned. "She was trying to contact you all day yesterday, you must have left your phone off. So she ended up ringing me last night, when she couldn't get you at home either."

"Happy Birthday Ally!" said Rob, raising his glass to her.

Nic threw her arms around Ally's neck, and kissed her on the cheek. "Tell you what, we'll give you the day off tomorrow!"

"But we're not opening tomorrow."

"Sorry, it's the best we can do at the moment! Now, open your present," she said, plonking herself on the chair next to Ally.

"You shouldn't have, Matt."

He shrugged. Nic nudged Ally. "Go on."

Everyone was watching her. She lifted the lid off the top of the box and moved aside the tissue paper. "Oh my God!" she squealed happily.

"Do you like it?"

Nic was frowning. "It looks like some kind of power tool."

It was a drill. Ally lifted it carefully out of the box. "Matt, you *really* shouldn't have."

"I'll second that," said Nic, turning up her lip.

"It's too much," Ally continued.

"I get a tradesman's discount," Matt shrugged.

"But . . ."

"Look, I'll write it off on my tax if it'll make you happy."

She didn't want to seem ungrateful. Besides, it gave her a bit of a thrill, owning her own power tool.

"It's cordless," Matt explained. "But it's lighter than mine, and easier to handle."

"Does it have a keyless chuck?"

He nodded. "And variable speed."

"I don't know what to say."

Matt looked directly at her. "Thank you would do."

She smiled sheepishly, standing up from the table. "Thank you, this is perfect."

Ally walked around to where he sat, and bent to kiss him on the cheek.

She could smell his aftershave. She could smell him. She should have had sex with him. Okay, that was enough champagne.

Nic stared at them, bemused. "See, Rob, it's like I was telling you, we really should think about a gift register, for people just like Matt here, who have *no* idea."

Ally frowned at her. "What did you just say?"

"We were discussing the other day, about whether to register. And Matt's little effort here has just convinced me it might be a good idea."

"Do you mean . . . ?" Ally's voice started to rise.

"What?" Matt frowned.

Nic was grinning. She jumped up and threw her arms out to Ally. "I do! We are!"

Ally squealed and they hugged each other, laughing.

"What's going on?" Matt repeated, looking more confused.

Rob stood up to top up Matt's glass. "Nic and I are getting married."

Two days later

"Two months to finish the renovations, organize a wedding and get your business up and running," Ally frowned. "What's the rush? Why don't you just put the wedding off for a few months?"

"I told you," Nic insisted. She was lying on her stomach across Ally's bed, watching her iron her clothes. "My father can't get away at any other time until well into next year. Chambers are closed, it's our only chance."

"I'm still finding it hard to believe that your father's a judge, and you come from this upper crust family."

"You'd better get used to it. They'll be descending on us before we know it." Nic rested her chin on the heels of her hands. "You are going to help me, aren't you?"

Ally smiled. "Of course I will. We'll get the rest of the place tarted up in no time."

"And what about being bridesmaid?" she said in a small voice.

Ally sighed, adjusting a blouse on a coathanger. Nic had asked her the other night, and Ally had been brushing it aside ever since, despite Nic's assertions she was serious.

"Oh Ally, you have to. Rob's got three brothers and I've only got the two sisters . . ."

"So I'm a gap filler?"

"No," she insisted. "I need you, as a buffer between me and my sisters. You don't know how mad they are!"

Ally could imagine.

"Deidre is a bitter old piece of work, with a failed marriage behind her and not a nice word to say about anyone. She is going to hate *everything*. And Sally, well, she's a sweetheart, but she makes me look like a rocket scientist."

Ally laughed. "You know I'll be there for you, just preferably not in a pastel dress carrying a bouquet."

"You have to do it, Ally!" Nic pleaded. "My parents think I'm crazy living out here in the 'antipodes.' I have to show them I'm established, I have friends . . ."

She smiled weakly. "Nic, it'll be three times a bridesmaid for me if I do it . . .'

"Oh, you're not superstitious? I don't believe it."

"What about dresses? Isn't it easier if your sisters just buy something over there? How will we find something the same?"

"I've already thought of that." Nic jumped up onto her knees. Ally could tell she was coming in for the kill. "I've sent them pictures of the style I like. They're going to look, and once they've checked with me, they can buy one in your size, send it out here, and we'll take it to a dressmaker for any alterations."

"What kind of style?" Ally said dubiously.

Nic jumped off the bed and rooted around in her bag. "I've got more pictures. Here," she said, passing a clipping to Ally.

She looked at it, relieved. It was a simple dress with a fitted bodice and an A-line skirt.

"It's strapless," she said, pulling a face.

"What's wrong with that?"

"Bare arms."

"But it will be spring, it won't be as cold as it is now, Ally."

"It's not the cold I'm worried about. It's the flab."

"You don't have flab!" Nic exclaimed.

"Wait till you see my bare arms!"

Nic thought for a moment. "If it bothers you, you could all wear those nice sheer wraps—you know, across the shoulders, and then looped around your arms. It would look brilliant."

"You've thought of everything, haven't you?"

Nic grinned, nodding. "You're going to do it, aren't you?"

Not waiting for an answer, she threw her arms around Ally and hugged her tight. "Oh, thank you. Everything will work out now. I know it."

August

Meg battled the Saturday morning traffic and joined the queue into the carpark at Bondi Junction Plaza. She'd left Harrison and Chris at home, making cubbyhouses in the family room. It was a miserable wintry Saturday morning, and Harrison had been sniffling all week, so Meg wanted to keep him out of the cold.

She wandered along the shops, staring vacantly in the windows. She probably should have taken the opportunity to try on some clothes, without Harrison in tow, but she wasn't in the mood. She paused outside a CD shop, wondering if there was something Chris's niece would like, it was her birthday in a couple of weeks. As she stood there, Meg noticed a young woman browsing through the bargain stand. She seemed vaguely familiar. Then she remembered. Jamie's mate's little sister. What was her name again? It was a surname. Taylor, Tyler, Tinker?

Meg approached her tentatively. "Hello, it's Taylor, isn't it?"

The girl looked blankly at her. Just walk away, Meg, this is ridiculous. "I'm Meg. We met up here one day. You were with Jamie Carroll?"

"Oh," she nodded. "Yeah, I remember."

Taylor continued to flick through the CDs. Don't do it, Meg. Say good-bye and walk away. *Walk away.*

"Look, you wouldn't know how I could get in touch with him, would you?"

Taylor gave her a curdling look, as well she should.

"It's just he's done some work for our agency before, and we were interested in using him again."

"He's been staying with my brother since he got back," she said.

So, he'd been away. That made Meg feel better about the fact that he hadn't called.

"He could probably use some work then, if he's been away?" Meg suggested.

Taylor shrugged. "I guess. I'll give him a message if you like."

Bugger. If he didn't call, would it be because he didn't get the message or because he didn't want to contact her? She had to be sure.

"It might be just easier if I got his number. Do you mind?" Meg said, reaching into her bag for a pen and her diary. Taylor dictated the number while Meg wrote it down, her hand shaking just slightly.

"Thanks for that," she said. "Have to fly." She felt like she'd stolen something and if she hung around for too long someone might find her out and take it back.

All the way home she tried to tell herself that just because she had his number, it didn't mean she was going to call him. And even if she did call him, it didn't mean she would see him. Hearing his voice would be enough.

Yeah, right.

Meg parked the car in the garage and walked up the back steps into the family room. It was in complete chaos. All the furniture had been rearranged and draped with blankets to create a series of hiding places. Chris was on the floor and Harrison had disappeared inside one of the "caves" as Meg walked through the door.

"Hi Mummy!" Chris said in an exaggerated tone. "Do you know where Harrison is?"

"No, I haven't seen him!" Meg said, playing along.

"He was here a minute ago."

"Harry, where are you?"

An excited shriek came from under one of the blankets. Meg and Chris smiled at each other.

"Where could he be?"

Suddenly Harrison jumped out, revealing himself. "I here, Mama!" he cried happily, his eyes gleaming.

"Ah, hah! Now I'm going to get you," said Chris, coming at him on all fours. Harrison squealed as Chris wrestled him to the ground. Meg watched them rolling around on the floor, Harrison giggling ecstatically.

She walked into the kitchen and lifted the grocery bags onto the bench. Then she took out her diary and opened to the page where she'd written Jamie's number. She hesitated for only a second before she tore out the page and screwed it up, tossing it into the kitchen bin.

She had screwed it up so tiny that it took her ages to find it later that night, after Chris had gone to bed. She eventually had to transfer the contents of the bin into a plastic bag, bit by bit, until she spotted the crumpled ball mixed in with the scrapings from dinner. She smoothed it out, wiping it with a tea towel. Then she folded it carefully and tucked it into the zippered pocket inside her handbag.

Wednesday

Meg sat at her desk staring at the wrinkled, gravy-stained piece of paper in her hand for the ninety-seventh time that week. She knew the number off by heart now, though she didn't trust herself to remember it. She had thrown the note out repeatedly, but searching for it later was becoming tedious.

She'd lost count of the times she had picked up the phone, and twice she had even dialed. But she always hung up when she heard the ring.

The moral debate that had raged in her head all week was getting too much for her. Meg had no one she could talk to about it. Simon and Ally had both made it clear which side they fell on, so what was the point in bringing it up with either of them? She would only get a lecture.

The thing was, if she called Jamie and, assuming he wanted to, they started seeing each other again, she was crossing the line. And she knew it.

Meg physically jumped as her phone started ringing. She reached for the receiver.

"Hello, Meg Lynch."

"Why haven't you called?"

She froze. Her heart leaped up into her throat and stuck there.

"Meg? It's Jamie."

"What makes you think I was going to call you?" She had recovered enough to squeeze the words out.

"Taylor told me."

"Oh."

"I thought I'd let you make the first move."

"So why are you ringing now?"

"I got impatient."

Meg felt giddy. Her heart was beating faster, she couldn't seem to catch her breath.

"Meg?" He paused. "This isn't about work, is it?"

"No," she said, her voice so small it hardly made it out of her throat.

"When can I see you?"

"Well, um, I don't know, when are you free?"

"Now."

Meg swallowed. She looked at her watch. "I could go to lunch in about an hour."

"Okay, I'll meet you in the carpark."

"No," she insisted. She didn't want anyone to know a thing this time.

They had to meet away from the office. Somewhere inconspicuous, where they wouldn't draw attention. "Can you get to Hyde Park?"

"Sure."

Chris worked down in George Street, past Martin Place. He would never come up that far, nor would any of his colleagues, she was fairly certain.

"I'll meet you behind the Anzac memorial," she said.

"In an hour?"

Meg checked her watch again. She didn't want to wait that long. "Let's say twelve-thirty."

"I'll be there."

She hung up the phone, breathing heavily. What was she doing? This was madness. But why did it feel so good? It was like she'd just had a surge of electricity through her body. She felt charged. She felt alive.

At ten past twelve Meg told Donna she had to go into the city so she'd be back from lunch a little late. It was one of those unseasonably warm August days that hinted spring was coming. Meg walked to Crown Street, and then caught a bus to Taylor Square. She felt like running the rest of the way, but she contained herself, barely.

When she caught sight of the memorial, her heart sank that Jamie wasn't there. She checked her watch, it was just twelve-thirty now. Don't panic. Meg crossed the road with the lights and walked briskly up to the monument. She shifted restlessly from one foot to the other, pretending to read the inscription.

"Didn't you say behind the memorial?"

Meg glanced around to see Jamie's hand jutting out from behind the wall. She smiled. As soon as she placed her hand in his, he drew her around and in one movement had her pressed up against the smooth stone, his body against hers. Meg felt a delicious jolt. She looked at his face, his beautiful, pale eyes.

"Hello," he said, smiling at her.

"Hi."

Then his lips were on hers, and they kissed, ravenous for each other. Meg was not going to play coy anymore. She had dreamed about this, she had lain in bed at night with a yearning that was almost painful. And now he was here for the taking.

"Did you miss me?" Jamie asked eventually, his mouth close to her ear, teasing the lobe with his teeth.

"What do you think?" she breathed.

His lips started moving down her neck. She had to stop him, or else her knees were going to give way. "I'm flattered, Jamie, but I don't understand something."

"What?" he said, lifting his head to look into her eyes.

"Why you're interested in an old married woman like me?"

He stepped back a little, an expression of amazement on his face. "Look at yourself, Meg. You're beautiful." He stroked her cheek with the back of his fingers. "Your skin. And those brown eyes." Then he leaned in close again. He ran his hands up the outside of her thighs. "And these long legs that go on forever . . ."

Meg fastened her arms around his neck and drew his mouth back onto hers. She could feel him hard against her, and she was conscious of a throbbing sensation rising up the center of her body.

"Is there somewhere we can go?" he said hoarsely, his lips barely leaving hers.

"I have to get back to work."

"Call in, make an excuse."

"No, really I can't." Meg roused herself, pulling back from him.

"Why not? You've done it before."

"It gets too . . . difficult. You remember last time."

He breathed out heavily, leaning his forehead against hers. "This is cruel."

She couldn't believe what she was about to say. "Maybe I could get away for a weekend."

He stared at her. "Are you serious?"

Meg nodded. She'd thought about this, fantasized about it, planned exactly how she would do it. "I have a friend who lives in the Southern Highlands. I could say I was going to visit her. I've done it before."

"Say when."

She smiled at him, and they kissed, sealing the deal. "When does it suit you?"

"As soon as possible," he grinned.

"It will probably take a couple of weeks to organize. I'll let you know."

"That'll be a long couple of weeks."

Meg couldn't concentrate the rest of the afternoon at work, and she ended up leaving early, stopping by the bottle shop on the way to collect Harrison.

At home she put on a Wiggles video and stuck Harrison in front of the television. She opened the bottle of champagne she had bought and drank one glass straight down, then poured herself another. You were never supposed to drink champagne on your own. According to the *Cleo* quiz, that was a real nono. Who made up these rules anyway? Meg needed the bubbles. They made the alcohol hit faster, and she needed that hit tonight. A couple of mouthfuls of the second glass and she felt the familiar warm rush calming her. She topped up her glass again and plonked down on the sofa. She couldn't get Jamie's face out of her mind. Every time she closed her eyes, she could feel his lips on hers, and her heart would start to beat faster, sending pulsations through her entire body. She was inconsolably horny. It was going to be a long couple of weeks alright.

Meg tried to work out if she felt guilty, but she didn't. This feeling was so exhilarating, why shouldn't she experience it? She wasn't going to hurt anyone. Jamie said he was never intending to steal her away from her husband. They could just have some fun, some passion. And no one need ever know.

At six o'clock, with the bottle more than half empty, Meg realized she didn't have a hope of cooking dinner. She called Chris and asked him to bring something home. She drank a couple of glasses of water to dilute the champagne, and put all her concentration into feeding Harry and getting him ready for bed.

When Chris arrived home, she swapped him Harrison for the takeaway. After he had put him off to bed, he joined her out in the kitchen. Meg had opened one of the containers and was intermittently fishing chilli prawns out with her fingers, while trying to open the wine that Chris had brought home.

"Do you want me to do that?" he asked, watching her struggle with the corkscrew.

She grinned at him. "Maybe you'd better!"

He took the bottle from her. "Had a few already?"

"Is there anything wrong with that?"

"No," he smiled. "Hard day at work?"

She shook her head. "Boring more like it."

Chris sat back on a stool at the kitchen bench and poured the wine. Meg sidled up to him and circled her arms around his neck.

"How was your day?"

She didn't wait for an answer before pulling him closer and kissing him long and hard, and obviously totally unexpectedly, given the look on his face when she drew back. She started to unravel his tie.

"What are you doing, Meg?"

"Well, Harrison's in bed . . ."

"But we haven't eaten yet."

"Here," she said reaching for a prawn and popping it seductively into his mouth.

She undid the first couple of buttons on his shirt and kissed him in the hollow under his Adam's apple, her tongue making circles on his skin. She started to push his jacket over his shoulders.

"Meg . . ."

"Mm?"

"I thought you were hungry?"

She stopped to look at him. "I am," she smiled suggestively, undoing more buttons lower down on his shirt.

"Maybe we should go into the bedroom?"

"Why? Harrison's asleep."

"You want to do it out here?" he whispered, almost anxiously.

Meg's eyes were gleaming. "Why not, it might be fun."

"It's a bit cold."

"So, we'll turn the heater on. If we need it," she added, before kissing him again.

She could feel Chris warming to the idea. It took him long enough. He was acting like a schoolgirl about to be deflowered.

"Where?" he said after a while.

Meg looked around the room. "I don't know, on the floor, on the table . . ."

He sighed wearily. "We've got a nice soft bed in there."

"But that's where we always do it!"

"There's a reason for that!"

She looked at him, unimpressed.

"It's warm and comfortable," he said, getting to his feet. "And private." He turned her around and started to propel her toward the hall.

"Okay," said Meg, pulling her top up over her head. At least they were going to do it. "Race you."

Meg knew it was Jamie she was thinking about the whole time they made love. She needed to relieve the craving that had not abated since she saw him. But Chris was a gentle, considerate lover, and Meg couldn't see Jamie being quite so patient. She imagined he'd be a little rough, and urgent, and it excited her. Meg found herself playing the aggressor. Chris didn't seem to mind, in fact, he seemed pleasantly surprised.

But when he cuddled into her afterward as usual, murmuring that he loved her, Meg suddenly felt despair. And guilt, for the first time today. For some reason she felt like she had betrayed him, even though she'd just made love to him. Hadn't she?

Thursday

"Nic!" Ally yelled from the front door of the restaurant.

"In here," she returned.

Ally stormed down the hall. "I've got a bone to pick with you!"

"What about?" Nic was sitting at a table in the main room, her feet up on another chair and a pile of napkins in front of her.

"Just what do you think you've been doing?"

"Folding napkins," said Nic, absently.

"I just got a call from Frances Callen."

Nic looked at her, waiting.

"Did you hear me? I said *Frances Callen*."

"I heard you." She picked up a napkin and started smoothing it out on the table.

"And why do you think she was calling me?"

"Because I gave her your number."

"Exactly!" Ally fumed, pacing back and forward in front of her.

"What's the problem?"

"What's the problem?" Ally almost shrieked.

Nic waited expectantly.

"The problem is that she thinks I'm some kind of frigging painted effects specialist! Where did she get that idea, eh?"

"Oh. Okay, I'll have a stab," said Nic, swinging her legs off the chair and turning around to look squarely at Ally. "Maybe she noticed the painted effects in the restaurant. And then she got some wild idea that the person who did them could possibly have some real talent. Maybe she thought that same person could do similar things on other walls." She paused. "God, you're right, there's something really weird about this. I wouldn't answer her calls if I was you."

Ally pulled a face. "Well it's too late for that, I've got an appointment to meet with her next week."

"That's terrible! You might get some work out of this, and worse, she might be really happy with what you do. How will you cope?"

"Smart arse," she grumbled, plonking herself down on a chair opposite Nic.

Matt wandered out from one of the front rooms. He had been refitting the skirtings and architraves so that Ally would be able to finish up next week.

"You two at it again?"

Ally just scowled.

"What have you done?" he asked Nic.

"I gave her number to Frances Callen, who rang especially to ask for it because she was so impressed on opening night and hasn't been able to get the place out of her mind. She wants some work done on her house and hoped that Ally was available."

"That's great!"

"Of course you'd say that," Ally dismissed crossly.

"What's the problem?" asked Matt.

"That's what I said," Nic muttered.

"The problem is," Ally faltered, "I don't know how to do this."

"What, paint?"

"No, I can do that. But it's just a hobby, it's not a business. I don't know how to start a business!"

"Looks like it's starting itself."

Ally groaned, dropping her head onto the table. "I don't know the first thing about doing this for real."

"You've got a mobile phone, you've got a business."

"Oh right," she said, lifting her head to look at Matt. "Typical male, it will all take care of itself, eh? No wonder you can never get a tradesman when you need one!"

"Well, I've had enough abuse," he said, turning back toward the hall.

"I don't know how much to charge, how long to say it will take . . ." Ally moaned.

"Not long at the rate you work, I'd say," said Nic.

"I don't even know what to wear," she continued.

Matt let out a loud guffaw from the other end of the hallway.

"You needn't laugh, Matthew Serrano."

He appeared back in the entrance to the hall. "Am I allowed to say 'typical female?' Or is it only okay to bag men?"

"It's important."

"What to wear while you're working? It doesn't seem to have bothered you much to date."

"Not work clothes! I mean when I go to meet her."

"What's the difference?"

"The difference is that I have to impress her, show her I'm professional."

"And in this profession you wear work clothes."

"You don't know what you're talking about, Matt."

He turned back up the hall. "Of course not, I've only run a business for ten years. But what would I know? I'm just a bloke after all."

A week later

"This suit doesn't look right," Ally grumbled, surveying her appearance in the mirror. "I think Meg was right, I might have lost some weight. It's hanging funny."

Nic observed her from her favorite vantage point on the bed. "Yeah, you're right."

Ally groaned, "Well you're no help."

"I'm with Matt. You should wear overalls. And put a pencil behind one ear, tradesmen always have a pencil behind one ear."

"I don't have any decent overalls. All my work gear is old, daggy stuff."

"So I've noticed," she muttered. "Then what about a nice pair of jeans, or trousers and a shirt? You look a bit naff, like you're going for a job interview or something."

"Well I am, in a way."

"No you're not. She's the one in awe of you, you should have heard the way she spoke about you on the phone. And she was that thrilled to find out you're a woman."

Ally took off the jacket and placed it carefully on a hanger. "If you're trying to make me feel better, it won't work. I don't know what on earth she expects from me."

"She expects you to paint her house for her."

"But she also expects me to know what I'm talking about, to be businesslike."

"So sound businesslike."

"How?"

"Ally, you know your stuff. Don't you remember how we hired you on the spot?"

She lifted an eyebrow. "I think, technically, I hired myself."

Nic ignored her. "You're very impressive when you get inspired. Just go with it. And throw in some of that power tool lingo too. I could hardly believe my ears the other day, you and Matt discussing variable chucks or something or other."

Ally looked at her dubiously.

"I know! I'll call you on the mobile a few times while you're with her!"

"Why?"

"So you sound like you're important, that you've got a lot of work on. You can say, 'Sorry, I really have to take this,' " Nic affected a deep, pompous voice.

"You are seriously skewed."

"Well, just have a little faith in yourself."

"But anyone can paint a room."

"Not the way you do it."

"They could if they tried."

"How do you know that?"

"I taught kids all those years. The ones who applied themselves always did better."

"But maybe they had more potential in the first place. You know, they actually liked what they were doing, that's why they were good at it?"

Ally frowned at her. "But it's just a hobby. I might spoil it if I do it for real."

"But you did the restaurant for real. Didn't you enjoy that?"

She nodded weakly.

"Ally, most people dream of making a living doing something they love. You have to give it a go."

"I know. That's why I'm wearing this suit and you are about to do my hair."

"Okay, let's get to it."

She jumped off the bed and followed her into the bathroom. Ally squeezed out a dollop of creamy goo from a tube and started to massage it into her damp hair.

"What's that?" asked Nic.

"Gel wax, I think it's called."

Nic picked up the tube and read the label. " 'The hold of a gel with the styling and definition of a wax.' What the bollocks does that mean?"

"It better mean, 'keeps wild hair in place so that owner of said hair can look elegant yet professional at the same time.' "

"Well why don't they just say that?" Nic winked. "Where are you going to sit?"

Ally perched on a small stool, leaving Nic just enough room to maneuver around her as she blow-dried her hair.

"Remember," Ally said after a while, "don't let it frizz, the idea is to blow dry it straighter."

"Oh it's not frizzing," Nic said in a strange voice. "Not at all."

"What's wrong?"

"Hand me that stuff you put through your hair."

Ally passed it to her. "What's the matter?" She touched the top of her head. "Oh no!"

"I think this might have been too heavy, Ally."

"But I only used a little bit." Ally stood up off the stool to inspect the damage in the mirror. She picked up a strand of hair, it was lank and greasy. "Oh no! What am I going to do?"

"Don't panic—"

"That's alright for you to say! Look at my hair!" She checked her watch. "Bugger! There's no time to wash it again either."

"It'll be alright, Ally," said Nic, pushing her back down onto the stool. "We'll just pull it back, sleek . . ."

"Slick, you mean."

"Don't worry, it'll look fine."

It didn't look fine, it looked ridiculous. But it just went with the rest of her. Ally stood at the front door of Frances Callen's house, in uncomfortable shoes, an ill-fitting suit and slicked-back hair pulled into a bulky ponytail. So far the whole exercise was turning into a disaster.

She rang the doorbell again and checked her watch. Why wasn't she answering? God, there was probably war declared in some Balkan country somewhere, and Frances had been called off to report on it. That would be just Ally's luck.

"Ms. Tasker?"

She looked around. Frances Callen stood in the driveway, wearing a loose old jumper, khaki pants and gumboots. Bugger.

"It is you, Ally?"

She roused herself. "Yes, it's me. And it's you! I mean, I knew it was you, because I've seen you before. Of course, everyone's seen you before so you don't need to introduce yourself really, do you? Whereas me, well, you wouldn't necessarily know me."

Shut up. Right now. Not another word.

Frances looked momentarily nonplussed, but she smiled broadly and walked toward Ally with her hand outstretched.

"Well, it's nice to meet you. Thanks so much for seeing me. I love your work."

Ally shook hands with her. "Likewise!"

Likewise? As if interviewing the US Secretary of State was the same as painting a frigging wall.

"Do you mind coming around the back? I don't like to go through the front in these boots."

"Sure," Ally said, following her around the corner of the house.

"Have I caught you on the hop?" Frances asked.

"Sorry?"

"You have an appointment after this?"

"No."

"Oh, it's just that you're all dressed up. I thought you'd be in overalls."

"Oh, you mean an *appointment?*" Ally exclaimed. "Yes, I have an appointment, with the accountant, you know. I thought you were asking if I had an appointment with another client. Which I don't, of course, because then I would be wearing overalls, naturally."

Oh, shut up Ally!

At the back of the house there was a vestibule area where Frances pulled off her boots, turning them upside down and propping them on a stand. Ally inspected her own shoes.

"Oh, you've got mud on your good shoes. I should have warned you."

"It's alright," said Ally, slipping them off, "if you don't mind my stockinged feet."

She followed Frances into a large eat-in kitchen area. It was standard country style, quite pleasant, if a little unimaginative.

"We're here most weekends, and at least part of the school holidays," Frances explained. "We've had the place for two years, and I've wanted to do something with it from the start. It's hard though, when you're not here all the time."

"And when everything is so safe?"

"Exactly."

It was a typical Federation era house which had been typically renovated, probably a few years ago. The kitchen and bathroom had been made over, the floors were all stripped and the walls painted cream, right throughout the house. There was nothing exactly wrong, in fact the rooms were elegantly proportioned and most of the original detail was still intact. It just all looked like a display home; there was no personality.

Frances showed her down a spacious hall into the children's room. There were twin beds, bedside tables and a built-in cupboard. Not very inspiring.

"We have two girls, nearly two years apart," Frances told her. "They have their own rooms at home of course, but we thought we'd get them to share down here. I think it came from some idea in a parenting book, but it also frees up another room for guests."

"Do they like fairies or pop stars?"

Frances grinned. "Would you believe they are total opposites? One refuses to wear a dress, the other won't get out of one."

"Sounds pretty normal to me."

"Well, this is your challenge, 'should you decide to accept it,'" she quipped. "I figured it doesn't take as much courage to be adventurous in a kids' room . . ."

"Oh, I don't mind being adventurous," Ally assured her.

"I realize that! It's me! After the girls' room, we can work through the guestrooms, our bedroom, and by then I'll be game enough to try anything in the living rooms."

Ally smiled. "So I shouldn't tell you any of my immediate ideas?"

"Ooh, tempting . . . Give me a hint."

"Well, I'm thinking a burnt orange feature wall in the living room . . ."

"Okay, stop," she laughed. "I'd better work up to that."

They walked back up the hall.

"I'd like to meet the girls, talk to them about what they'd like."

"They'll be at total odds with each other."

"There are ways of making that work," Ally assured her.

"If you can make them both happy, then you really are a genius."

They came into the kitchen. "So what's your schedule like?"

"Pardon?"

"How long before you can fit us in?"

"Um, well," Ally hesitated. "I'll have to look into that."

"I see, of course," Frances paused. "And I have something else I have to ask. This might affect when you can fit us in as well, but I don't care, I'm prepared to wait."

Ally wondered what she was talking about.

"I hope you don't think I'm being pushy, but how closely do you work with your team?"

"My team?"

"Well, Nicola told me you were very hands-on with the restaurant project, but I understand you wouldn't always have the time for much personal involvement. But I really want you. I don't mind paying for the privilege."

Ally stared at her dumbfounded.

"Have I put you on the spot?"

Ally released a sigh, and covered her face with her hands. "Oh, I can't do this!"

"What? What's the matter?"

"I'm a big fraud."

"What do you mean? You didn't do the restaurant?"

"Oh sure, I did that. But I can't do *this*."

"This house? I would have thought it was nothing compared to that whole restaurant."

"It's not that. I don't have a team, I don't have a schedule, I don't have a business. It's just me. And you. You're my business."

Frances looked at her, a smile slowly breaking on her lips.

"Would you like a cup of coffee, Ally?"

They sat nursing mugs on an overstuffed sofa in the family room. Ally had taken off her jacket and curled her legs up underneath her.

"So I was sitting there," Frances was saying, "in my neat little suit, with my dictaphone on the table and my notepad in my hand, interviewing the Attorney-General, and I didn't have a clue what he was talking about."

"But how did you interview him? You had to ask questions."

"Oh sure, I said things like, 'Very interesting, do you have anything further to add to that?' Or, 'And is that the official government stance on the issue?' He looked at me a little oddly at times. But I got through it."

"So what happened?"

"I just kept thinking, it's all being recorded, I can ask someone back at the office to explain it to me." She paused, shaking her head. "Of course, when I got back to the office, I realized there was nothing on the tape, I had forgotten to turn it on."

They both collapsed into laughter.

"Ally, the point is, we're all frauds," Frances said eventually. "I don't think we ever get over that feeling that someone is going to find us out one day."

"But you must eventually feel confident in your own ability? I mean, with all the success you've had, the awards?"

"Still, whenever I arrive at Parliament House, or I'm about to interview the PM, I think someone's going to stop me and say, 'What do you think you're doing here, Fran?' "

"But you had training, a degree. That makes you bona fide."

"It took me a long time of walking the walk and talking the talk before I believed I was actually a bona fide journalist. The piece of paper didn't do it for me," Frances confided. "Ally, there's no question about your ability, the evidence is physically there on the walls of that restaurant. You don't need a piece of paper to prove that."

Ally contemplated what she was saying.

"What it all comes down to in the end," Frances said, breaking into her reverie, "is whether you like what you're doing. Do you?"

"I do, I love it."

"Why?"

Ally thought for a moment. "I can walk into a really ugly room, or it might be rundown, or maybe just very ordinary . . ."

"Like this place," Fran nodded.

"But I see something else entirely. I wonder why no one else can see it. But they can't. So I set to work, and I get completely lost in it, for days. I lose all sense of time."

Frances was listening.

"Then when I'm finished, and people see it, they think it's beautiful, and it makes them happy. And I realize, I did that! That's what I like the best."

Frances smiled at her. "Then you don't even have to think twice."

Friday

Ally dialed Matt's number and waited. He should be home by now, she couldn't get him on his mobile. He usually switched it off when he was finished for the day.

"Hello?" said a young, female voice.

"Hello Beck? It's Ally here."

"Oh hi, Ally!" she said brightly.

"Staying with your father this weekend?"

"Yes, we've just been to see the restaurant. It looks fantastic."

"Your dad's a clever man."

"But the colors and everything, Ally—you're pretty clever as well. You and my dad make a great team."

Funny she should say that. "Thanks Beck. Actually, is he there? I was hoping to have a quick word with him."

"Sure, I'll put him on," she replied. "Maybe we'll see you this weekend?"

"Maybe."

Matt's voice came onto the line. "Hi Ally, what's up?"

"Well, you know how I was going to see Frances Callen yesterday?"

"Mm."

"It's an old house, 1890s probably, maybe a little later. Anyway, there's rot in some of the windows, double hung, a lot like the windows you fixed at Birchgrove."

"Mm . . ."

"So, she's getting me to do up a few of the rooms, and the windows really need to be repaired before I can paint them."

He didn't say anything.

"Are you still there, Matt?"

"I'm here."

"I told her that I know someone who does that kind of work and that I could arrange it."

"I see."

"Well, are you interested or not?" said Ally, frustrated.

"In what?"

"In the job?"

"Fixing the windows?"

"Yes!"

"You trust me?"

"Of course I do!"

"Gee, even though I don't know much about anything?"

So that's what all this was about. "Oh, okay Matt. You win. Why do you always have to score points with me?"

He laughed loudly. "Haven't you got that the wrong way around?"

Ally sighed. "Alright Matt, I'm sorry if I didn't listen to all your worldly advice. I have to make some decisions for myself sometimes, you know."

"Mmm, and so how did the outfit work out, and the hairstyle?"

"Nic's been talking to you."

"She gave us all a good laugh yesterday afternoon," he chuckled.

"Well, I'm glad you've been enjoying yourselves at my expense." Ally felt hurt. She knew she'd made a fool of herself, but didn't they realize how hard this had been for her? And now she needed to ask Matt for help. She couldn't do it if he was going to make it difficult. "I'm sorry I bothered you . . ."

"Ally, don't hang up. I didn't mean anything."

She was silent.

"Ally?"

"I thought I'd get a little support from my so-called friends."

"I'm sorry, Ally. I would love to sub for you."

"What?"

"Sub, subcontract. That's what you're asking me to do."

"Oh. You'd be my subbie?"

"And you could be mine, if you're really serious about all this?"

"I am, I really am."

"Righto then. It'll be a pleasure doing business with you."

Call waiting beeps came onto the line.

"Is that me or you?" Ally asked.

"It's you."

"Oh, I don't know how to do this!"

"Just hang up and your phone will start to ring," Matt explained calmly.

"Okay, bye. Thanks!" Ally pressed 'end' on her phone and it started ringing almost immediately.

"Hello?"

"Hi, Ally, it's Meg."

"Hi, how are you?"

"Um, okay. How are you?"

"Well, actually, I'm great."

"Oh?"

Ally started to recount her news, but after a while she sensed that Meg was distracted, not really taking it in. Normally she would have been much more excited for her.

"Anyway, that's enough about me. How's everything with you, Meg?"

"Good. Fine, really."

"Okay," Ally said slowly. Meg had a strange tone in her voice. Something was definitely up.

"I want to ask you a favor," she said nervously.

"Sure, anything."

Meg breathed out heavily. "I don't know if you'll feel that way once you hear what it is."

"Meg, come on, we're best friends. You can ask me anything."

That's what she was counting on. "I'm going away next weekend, and . . ." She hesitated.

"Go on," Ally urged.

"If Chris was to call, well, he thinks I'm going to be with you."

Ally was confused. "What are you talking about? I'm not following you."

Meg took another deep breath. "I'm going away next weekend, and I've told Chris that I'm visiting you."

Ally realized now. "But you're not, I presume."

"No."

"Can you tell me where you'll be?" She didn't have to ask who Meg would be with. What was his name again? For some reason, Junior was all that would come to mind.

"It's better if you don't know too many details," Meg was saying. "You'll be able to get in touch with me on my mobile."

"Why are you doing this?"

Meg sighed. "I have to get it out of my system, Ally. I think I ended things too quickly."

"But Meg—"

"Look, I don't expect you to understand. I'm just asking you to cover for me."

Ally paused. Meg was her friend, she had to support her, even if she thought she was making a mistake. "Okay, Meg. I just hope you know what you're doing."

"You'll have to trust me on that."

Imagine!

"Meg?"

She jumped. "Oh, Simon, you gave me a fright."

"Sorry." He was standing on the other side of her desk. "I knocked, but you were in la-la land."

She'd been there a lot lately. She alternated between vague and jittery. They were going away this weekend and Meg felt like a criminal on the run. She was sure someone was going to discover her.

"Sorry Simon, what can I do for you?"

He frowned down at her. "Are you okay?"

"Sure I'm okay. I'm fine, why wouldn't I be fine?"

"If you say so," he said, a quizzical expression on his face. "I just wanted to check when you scheduled that meeting."

"What meeting?"

"The progress meeting for the team working on the Belva campaign."

She stared blankly up at him.

"Remember, I asked you to let me know," he said slowly, watching the bafflement on her face, "so I could sit in on it? We talked about it on Monday, after the presentation."

Something clicked. "Oh shit, Simon!" Meg exclaimed, standing up. "I'm sorry. I mustn't have written it down." She flicked through her desk calendar. "Oh, there it is," she said, perplexed. "I did write it down."

"Are you sure you're okay?" Simon asked her, obviously concerned. "It's not like you to forget something."

She sighed. "I haven't been sleeping all that well lately."

"What's up?"

"Nothing," she said defensively. "It doesn't mean there has to be something wrong."

Simon was frowning at her.

"It's probably early menopause. I've heard you can suffer memory loss."

"You're too young for that!" he scoffed. "I think you need a break. Have you and Chris organized that holiday yet?"

"We've finally booked for October, that's if his boss doesn't put it back again."

"October—that's still a while off."

"Well don't worry, I'm going away this weekend."

"Oh great. Where are you off to?"

She dropped her gaze. She couldn't look at him while she lied. "I'm going to see Ally."

"On your own?"

She nodded.

"Well I don't see that being much of a rest. I know what you two are like when you get together. You'll be up till three in the morning drinking."

Meg smiled awkwardly. She didn't want to keep talking about it. "I'll go and schedule that meeting right away. I'm sorry about that, Simon."

"It's okay. You're allowed a slip up now and then."

Saturday

"Just here will be fine," Meg said to the driver. He pulled over and she paid the fare, picked up her bag and stepped out of the taxi.

She was meeting Jamie at Thommo's house in Newtown. She'd caught the train to visit Ally last time, so Meg thought it was best to keep to the same arrangement so as not to attract suspicion. Not that she would. Poor trusting Chris would never suspect anything in a million years. Jamie was a bit put out at first that she wouldn't have the car. But he said he'd organize something.

Meg had intended to catch a taxi from home, but Chris insisted on driving her to Central Station. She experienced a moment's dread when he suggested they come in and wave her off.

"Don't be silly!" she blurted. "You'll never get a park."

"I could try . . ."

"Chris, let's not make a big deal, it might upset Harrison, you never know."

He frowned.

"And I don't want him out in this wind, he still hasn't got over that head cold."

"Okay, if you say so."

Meg had skulked around all the entrances making sure Chris had definitely gone before she flew out and leaped into a waiting taxi. The subterfuge of the past weeks had worn her out. Some of her initial excitement had waned, replaced with guilt and self-loathing. It was not the best frame of mind to be in at the start of their tryst, and meeting here, at the house of ill repute, only made it worse.

"Hiya."

Meg looked up. Jamie was standing in Thommo's doorway, watching her approach. He tripped down the path and stopped in front of her, taking the bag out of her hand.

"Where's the car?" said Meg absently, looking up the street.

"Hey?" Jamie stared into her eyes, frowning. He brought his hand up to her face, lifting her chin, making her look at him. "Hello," he said softly, before drawing her closer and kissing her. He didn't stop until she relaxed against him. "That's better," he said.

She smiled faintly at him.

"I know this is a big deal, Meg." He had a strange expression on his face. Meg worried he was going to go all sensitive on her. She had the SNAG at home. She wanted something different from Jamie. "So I've got a surprise first, to help you loosen up."

"I told you, no illegal substances."

He laughed. "No, we're going to get a natural high." He took hold of her hand. "Car's this way."

"Where's your luggage?"

"We're only going overnight, Meg." He shook his head, grinning.

He stopped beside a battered, rusted old Holden which Meg thought must have been dumped there. Jamie opened the back door and tossed her bag in.

"You're not serious?" Meg said, staring incredulously at the car.

He looked at her. "What's wrong? I know it's a bit old, but it passed rego last month."

"How much was the bribe?"

Jamie grinned. "Well, it's either this or the bike."

Meg climbed reluctantly into the front. There was a bench seat, they didn't put them in the front of cars anymore.

"What are you doing all the way over there?" Jamie said, sliding in behind the steering wheel and patting the seat next to him. "It's safe. There's even a seat belt."

Meg frowned, "I'm not sixteen you know."

He laughed. "Suit yourself."

He started up the engine, and it coughed, spluttered and eventually roared into life. They drove through the back of Newtown and came out onto Parramatta Road.

Meg remembered something Jamie said earlier. "This natural high, it doesn't involve jumping out of an airplane, does it?"

He shook his head. "It's safe and legal, and quite tame. Even kids do it."

They drove on through the inner western suburbs till they joined the freeway at Concord.

"You're not going to tell me where we're going?"

"You'll find out soon enough."

Meg glanced out the window. "Taylor said you'd been away?"

"Yep. Just up to Bali and back. I've got friends there, did a bit of surfing. I was only gone a couple of weeks."

Meg nodded.

"I haven't been on a big trip for a while, and I'm getting itchy feet. I'll have to make some money first though."

When she didn't say anything, he looked across at her. "Did you ever get around to organizing your trip?"

"What trip?"

"The one you were thinking about when I bumped into you up at the Junction."

"Oh, that was nothing. Just a holiday."

"Where are you going?"

Meg was almost embarrassed to say. "We can't do anything that adventurous, you know, with Harrison . . ."

"Where are you going?" he repeated.

She sighed. "Club Med. Tahiti. Ten days."

"Ooh, swanky."

"Stop it."

He smiled. "Nice beaches in Tahiti."

They drove on for about ten minutes. At the tollgates Meg noticed the billboard for Australia's Wonderland. She looked suspiciously at Jamie, but he was concentrating on changing lanes.

"Is it much farther?"

"Nup. Just up the road."

A few minutes later he turned off the freeway at the Wonderland exit and made a right turn into the entrance.

"Tell me this is a joke," said Meg dryly.

"Come on, Meg, it'll be fun."

"I hate amusement parks. And I'm not using the word 'hate' lightly."

They drove around the carpark, looking for a spot. Meg watched the families unpacking their gear. There were very young children, tiny children, bursting with excitement.

"I was always the one who held the coats and bags, you know," she said glumly. "While everybody went on the rides."

Jamie pulled into a space and turned off the engine. He sidled over closer to Meg, his arm across the back of the seat. "If you don't like it, we'll leave. But at least give it a go first."

He leaned forward to kiss her. Meg felt her pulse start to quicken, remembering what this weekend was all about. It filled her with a mixture of excitement and dread. Maybe a rollercoaster ride was just what she needed. Like having someone step on your toes to help you forget you had headache.

"What will we start with?" Jamie said, once they were through the entrance.

Meg saw a sign for Hanna Barbera Land.

"Don't even think about it," Jamie laughed, watching her. "Come on, I can see you're going to need shock therapy."

They lined up for something called The Demon. Meg couldn't see the ride ahead, they were in a covered walkway, obstructing the view, which was just as well. She was trying to convince herself she could do this, just the once. It was true what she'd said to Jamie. She was always the one that held everyone's gear while they went on the rides. She'd stand alone and watch their faces as they whizzed by her. Sometimes there was sheer terror, but mostly there was a kind of exhilaration. Meg used to envy that.

It was a long queue and Jamie passed the time telling her about his trip to Bali. He was unashamedly affectionate toward her, not bothered at all about holding or kissing her in public. Meg couldn't help wondering what people were thinking. Did she look a lot older than him? Did they look like the odd couple? She in her Country Road weekend coordinates, Jamie in the ubiquitous cargo pants and whatever jumper he'd probably picked up off the floor that morning. It was a big chunky thing, fraying at the edge of the sleeves, but he still managed to look sexy. How was it that guys could drag on any old thing and look perfectly acceptable, while women felt self-conscious if they went to the corner shop without make-up?

They were at the end of the queue. There were only a couple of people ahead of them, so they would be on the next ride. Jamie was working harder than ever to distract her.

"I know what you're doing," she smiled at him.

"Making up for lost time," he murmured, kissing her again.

"And keeping my mind off what's coming?"

"That too."

Their carriage arrived and Jamie led her to the middle section. Meg figured that seats at the front or back would be for much braver souls. Jamie reached over and lowered the solid metal harness over her shoulders, before staff came along to lock it in place. Meg was surprised when the carriage jolted off in reverse. She couldn't turn around to see what was coming, the harness kept her in a fairly fixed position. But soon it became obvious, as the carriage climbed steeply backward, coming to a halt in a vertical position, high above the track. Meg realized there was only one way they could go now. Straight down.

"Shit!"

Jamie reached across and clasped her hand tight as the brakes released and they dropped. Meg hardly knew what was happening after that. The carriage almost flew above the track, whizzing through corners, jolting her head around mercilessly. When she dared to open her eyes she saw a loop-the-loop ahead, or maybe there were two, she wasn't sure if she was seeing right.

There were two, Meg realized with dread after they had just endured the first. For the second time they shot through the air in an arc, twisting somehow so that they were on the outside of the loop, then coiling back inside on the descent. They bolted along the track and rose straight up until the carriage hung vertically in the air, as they had at the start of the ride. But this time they were facing the sky. Meg's heart sank as she realized they had to do this all over again. Backward. The carriage dropped and off they went, the world blurring by until Meg finally became aware they were slowing down, and they weren't in a vertical position this time.

When the carriage pulled up and their harnesses were released, Jamie was quick to jump out, turning to help Meg up. Just as well, her legs were trembling and she felt winded. Her heart was still racing. Jamie kept his arm around her as they walked slowly down the path, stopping at a quiet alcove, out of the way of the passing throng. Meg leaned back against the garden wall.

"Are you okay?" he asked.

She nodded. She was okay, but she felt weird. Overwhelmed maybe? She could feel tears welling, she didn't know where they came from. Jamie closed his arms around her and she leaned against him while he stroked her hair.

"You were very brave," he said eventually. "That's the worst one by far. You could handle anything now."

She looked up at him, her eyes glassy. "Thanks for bringing me here."

The next couple of hours passed by in a blur for Meg as she was dropped, spun around, twirled upside down and generally disorientated. When she could bear to open her eyes, she saw the sky rising to meet the land, trees hanging from their trunks, a vertical lake. And when she was scared at the top of the ferris wheel, Jamie held her close and kissed her. She didn't know whether the lurch she felt in her stomach was from the kiss or the subsequent descent, but at least she didn't care for that moment.

"I'm done," Meg said finally, plonking herself down on a nearby bench. "And I'm starved."

She had not trusted herself to have anything but a cup of coffee till now, in case she threw up.

Jamie smiled broadly at her. "Righto. Let's eat."

They sat at an outdoor table and he bought them burgers and a Coke each. When she'd finished eating, Meg took out her phone.

"What are you doing?" Jamie frowned.

"I should check my messages . . ."

He leaned over and plucked the phone out of her hand, slipping it into his pants pocket.

"This is your time, Meg," he said when she went to protest. "The sun is going to set tonight and rise again tomorrow without you checking on it."

Meg paused. "If I don't call home sometime today, it's going to look odd."

"Well, you can't do it here, the background noise doesn't exactly sound like the Southern Highlands."

Meg gazed around, listening to the jumble of sounds: screams of hysteria, laughter, piped music, barkers.

"Don't let me forget later then."

"I won't. Do you want a coffee or something?"

After lunch they wandered around for a while, delaying the inevitable. When they left here, there was one thing they were going to do. Meg was trying to recapture some of the pure lust she felt two weeks ago, when she met Jamie at Hyde Park. But she couldn't. It was too heavily laced with guilt now.

"What do you want to do next?" said Jamie after they had walked a full circuit around the park. "See anything that interested you?"

Meg shook her head emphatically. "No, I've done my quota."

"Had enough for today?"

"For a lifetime."

He laughed. "Then we may as well head off."

Where to? Meg thought. She wondered if he'd made a booking somewhere. It was not likely, considering his usual travel arrangements.

In the car, he slid over to her side and caged her in his arms. "What do you want to do?"

Meg swallowed. She knew she was flushed. He brought his lips down on hers and kissed her urgently, for the first time today. It was more salacious, and Meg stirred inside, hearing herself moan faintly. Now the feeling was returning.

"Do you want to go to a hotel?" he murmured, nuzzling into her neck. Then he stuck his tongue inside her ear! Meg shivered. So that's what it felt like. She'd seen it in movies, and thought it was a bit odd, but now she understood. She could have had sex with him right now in the car, if only there weren't small children around.

"How far do we have to go?" she breathed.

He pulled back from her, staring into her eyes. His pupils were huge and black. "We'll stop at the first one we come to."

Jamie started up the engine, and this time Meg moved over next to him. He smiled at her, putting his arm around her across the back of the seat. As they drove on up the highway, Meg leaned her head on his shoulder, resting one hand on his thigh. She felt like she had a pulse throbbing down through her core, and she wanted to savor it, imagining what Jamie would do to her. She felt hot.

After they had been driving for about ten minutes they saw a sign advertising a motel. Jamie pulled into the carpark another five hundred meters farther.

"You've got a credit card?" he asked rhetorically.

She looked at him with a blank expression. "Well, yes. But I'm not going to use it."

"Why not?"

"I don't want a motel bill coming up on my statement. How do you think I'd explain that?"

They sat not saying anything for a minute.

"Haven't you got a credit card?" she asked.

"What would I be doing with a credit card?" Jamie sighed loudly. "Well, have you got any cash?"

Meg started to feel a bit affronted. "Not much," she said in a small voice. "You want me to pay?"

Jamie looked at her. "Don't get all offended. I've paid for everything so far today, Meg. I'm not made of money, you know."

"Sorry."

They sat not saying anything, until the shrill ring of her mobile broke the silence.

"Fuck!" Jamie reached into his pocket and pulled out the phone, dropping it on her lap. He opened the car door. "I'm having a smoke," he said, getting out and slamming the door.

Meg pressed a button to answer the call, her fingers trembling.

"Hello?" she said warily.

"Hi honey." It was Chris. "Where are you?"

"What do you mean 'where are you?' Where do you think I am?"

"It's just you said that you'd call when you got there. I thought maybe the train was delayed."

"No, sorry. We've been catching up. I forgot. Sorry."

"Don't worry. I just wanted to make sure you got there okay."

Meg's voice was strangled with guilt. "I'm fine."

"How's Ally?"

"She's fine too."

"Say hi, won't you?"

"Of course." Oh please let this stop. It was unbearable.

"So what are you two doing tonight?"

Meg had to end this. "Haven't decided," she said brusquely. "How's Harrison?"

"He'll be fine, don't worry about him."

"I'd better go."

"Sure honey. Have a good time."

"Thanks, bye."

Meg turned off the phone and sat staring at Jamie's back. He was leaning against the hood, smoking his cigarette. She got out of the car and walked around in front of him.

"Was that your husband?"

Meg nodded.

"I suppose you want to go home now?"

She folded her arms and looked at him. "You think this was a mistake?"

He shook his head. "Not for a minute."

Meg swallowed. "I'm sorry about the money. I didn't mean to imply you should pay for everything."

He shrugged, dropping the end of his cigarette on the ground and stubbing it out.

"If we can find an ATM, I'll get some money out."

Jamie considered her. "You don't want to go home?"

She couldn't deny that guilt had quashed the desire she was feeling earlier. But she couldn't go home now anyway. What would she say to Chris, suddenly appearing out of the blue? She had to stay somewhere tonight. And she had to see this through with Jamie.

"I know somewhere we can go that won't cost anything."

Meg looked at him expectantly.

"Aurora's. She's got a big old place up at Katoomba. There's, like, a hundred rooms, and she's got an open house policy. If she's not there, I know where she keeps the key."

Meg never ceased to be amazed by Jamie's network of free accommodation.

"How do you know this Aurora?"

"I've known her forever. Everyone knows Aurora."

They climbed back into the car. Meg's mobile sat flagrantly in the middle of the seat.

"Well, I've checked in now," said Meg, picking up the phone. "So I won't be needing this anymore," she finished, opening the glove box and tossing it in. She snapped it shut and slid across next to Jamie. She clicked the lap seat belt in place and turned to look at him. He was watching her curiously. He brought his hand up to cup her face, stroking her cheek with his thumb. Then he leaned forward and kissed her. Meg responded urgently. She was determined to see this through. All the stress and scheming of the past weeks had to be for something. Like she said to Ally, she had to get Jamie Carroll out of her system. No one would ever know, no one would get hurt.

It must have been after five by the time they drove through the township of Katoomba, and Jamie took a left turn off the main road. It was virtually dark and Meg was freezing. The heater didn't work, she was not surprised to discover.

Jamie took another left and then stopped the car. "Oh," he murmured under his breath.

"What is it?" Meg looked ahead. They were in a tiny cul-de-sac that appeared to be filled with parked cars. There was music coming from a large house on the right which was all lit up, with people spilling out of the doors and onto the verandah, despite the cold.

"This is Aurora's?" Meg guessed.

He nodded. "You know what I said about the open house policy? Well, it's either empty or like this. You never know until you get here." He paused. "Maybe we should go find an ATM after all?"

Meg decided she wouldn't mind being around people, at least for a while. She could have a drink, get into the mood.

"Why don't we go in?" she suggested.

"You want to?"

"Sure, it might be fun."

He smiled at her. "Okay."

Jamie parked the car around the corner. It didn't seem as cold out as it was inside the car, and when they stepped into the house, it actually felt warm, even with most of the doors open. The place was packed.

"Let's find Aurora," Jamie shouted over the music. He took her hand and led her through a series of rooms to the back of the house. There was a haze of fragrant smoke hanging in the air, and bottles, bongs and ashtrays littered every surface. The women were dressed in cheesecloth, batik or crushed velvet, or combinations of all three. There were a lot of funny little hats and embroidered vests. A higher than average proportion of the men were bearded, with long hair growing from a bald pate, a look that Meg had never understood. She felt like she was on the set of a seventies movie, a bad one at that.

They made it to the kitchen without finding Aurora, but an awful lot of people seemed to know Jamie. Every second person stopped him.

"Hey Jamie, how've you been? Does Aurora know you're here?"

"Jamie! Far out! Wait till Aurora lays eyes on you!"

"Did you tell Aurora you were coming? She's going to flip when she sees you, man."

Obviously Aurora had some kind of vested interest in Jamie.

"Do you want a drink?" he asked Meg, opening the door of the fridge.

"Is it alright?"

"Sure, Aurora won't mind."

He poured her a tumbler of red wine out of a cask and got himself a beer.

"I thought you didn't drink?"

He shrugged. "When in Rome . . ."

They spent the next hour working their way through the maze of rooms but never coming across Aurora. Meg tried to relax and enjoy herself. She joined in a few conversations, but everyone was either in a daze or so intense her head hurt listening to them. Jamie eventually went off to get another drink for Meg, leaving her to settle a debate on the relative merits of Bob Dylan over Bob Marley. Meg was starting to feel a bit dazed herself. She wondered if there was such a thing as passive dope smoking.

She drifted out to the largest room where there was a roaring open fire and stood staring at the flames. Meg loved open fires. There was a working fireplace in their house when they bought it, and Ally nearly had a conniption when Meg talked about boarding it up. But she'd done her homework. Open fires lost ninety percent of their heat up the chimney. Gas heating was the most efficient. Ally coped when they only sealed up the flue and set a gas heater into the alcove instead. Now Meg wondered why they didn't keep the fireplace open. She was too sensible for her own good sometimes.

She felt somebody behind her and she glanced around. It was Jamie. He put his arms around her shoulders, handing her the tumbler of wine. Meg leaned back against him.

"Having a good time?" he asked, his lips close to her ear.

She shrugged. "It's different."

"You always say that."

Meg glanced back at him. "Only when I'm with you."

He smiled, bringing his lips down onto hers briefly, tantalizingly. "Come with me. I want to show you something."

She had a feeling the invitation had a lot more to it. She skolled half her glass, and left it on the mantelpiece. Jamie took her hand and led her up the hall to a narrow staircase. He indicated for her to go ahead and he followed her up to an attic level. There was a door at the top of the stairs where Meg hesitated.

"Go on in," said Jamie.

She opened the door and stepped into the room. It was dominated by a vast brass bed covered with a gorgeous patchwork quilt made of squares of satin and velvet. Lamps draped with sheer pink scarves cast a warm, muted glow. There was a vast window above the bed, set into the sloping roof.

"When you lie on the bed," Jamie said quietly, standing just behind her, "you can see the stars."

There was only one way he could have known that. He must have slept here with Aurora. Meg didn't know why she should feel a tinge of jealousy, she was married for Christ's sake. She had no prior claim on Jamie.

Meg shivered as he placed his hands gently on her shoulders, slipping her jacket off and tossing it aside. He sank his lips into her neck and she felt his tongue on her skin, hot and wet. She arched back, leaning her head against his shoulder. His hands roamed across her body, pausing at her breasts. Meg bit her lip as one hand went lower, pulling her shirt out of her jeans and reaching in, kneading the soft roundness of her belly. Her lips parted as her breathing became uneven.

"Do you want to see the view from the bed?" Jamie whispered next to her ear. He walked her forward, then turned her around, folding her into his arms and kissing her full on the mouth. Meg felt completely drugged by him. She wanted him now, she couldn't stand the suspense any longer. She sat on the bed, pulling him down with her, before they fell back, their limbs entwining, his pelvis hard against hers. She moaned as he undid the buttons on her shirt, his lips following, leaving a trail of wet kisses. Then Meg felt his hand on her jeans, between her legs, rubbing. She was losing it. She felt herself starting to shake. This was too much, it was too real. She didn't think she could go through with it. She put her hand over his.

"Jamie . . ." her voice wavered.

He stopped, gazing down at her. "It's okay, Meg. Look up at the stars."

She lifted her eyes and gazed out the window. It was a clear night, and the stars were endless, luminous, they were beautiful. She thought of the ceiling in Harrison's room. The stick-on stars Ally had put there. Meg swallowed. What was she doing?

Jamie leaned down to kiss her. He kissed her so hard, she almost couldn't breathe. She felt his hand at the button of her jeans, and she started to tremble again. He pushed his knee between her legs, parting them, as he tugged gently at the zipper.

"No, Jamie," she breathed. "I don't think . . ."

"Shh," he whispered softly, his mouth covering hers again. He slid the zipper all the way down and she felt his hand slip through the opening, his fingers probing down into the warmth, suddenly thrusting inside her. Meg gasped. Jamie buried his head in her neck, breathing heavily. Meg looked up at the stars and felt tears rising in her throat.

"No, Jamie," she reached for his hand, grabbing his wrist. "Stop, please. I can't."

He lifted his head to look at her. He pulled his hand away, wrapping both arms around her. "It's okay. We'll go slower. We've got all night," he said in a low voice.

She looked at him tearfully, shaking her head. "I can't. I can't do it, Jamie."

He sighed deeply. "Meg, you're just nervous." He kissed her, trying to persuade her with his lips. But Meg was past it. She felt ashamed. She'd crossed the line.

She pushed him off. "I said no, Jamie." She sat up and started adjusting her clothes.

"What the fuck?"

Meg swung around to look at him lying back on the bed.

"What kind of a fucking game are you playing, Meg?"

"It's not a game, that's the thing. I should never have come, Jamie. I'm sorry." She turned around and resumed buttoning her shirt.

She heard him sigh. "Come on Meg," his voice had softened. He reached for her arm. "We've come this far . . ."

"And it's far enough," she said determinedly, shrugging off his hand.

"Fuck!" he exclaimed, punching the mattress. Meg jumped, standing up to cross the room. She watched him sit up, dragging his hands through his hair. He looked up at her with an expression she had never seen in his eyes before. She was a little frightened.

"This is fucked, Meg. You've led me around by the dick for the last few weeks, and now you decide you don't feel like it?"

"I'm sorry, I thought I could . . . I thought it was what I wanted."

"Spoilt fucking bitch," he snarled, standing up. He looked ominous. He took a step toward her. His pale eyes were flinty now, glaring at her. Meg felt her knees trembling. If he decided to have his way, there wasn't a thing she could do about it. No one here would care.

"I'm sorry," she whispered, her voice barely making it out of her throat. "I didn't realize I'd feel this way, I wouldn't have led you on. It's just . . ."

"What?" He stared at her, his hands clenching and unclenching, his jaw set firmly.

"I can't do it. Betray my marriage . . . my husband."

"What do you think you've been doing all this time?" He strode to the door, grabbing roughly at the handle and jerking it open. He looked back at her, glaring. "Well fuck you, Mrs. Lynch."

He walked out, slamming the door behind him. It shuddered on its hinges.

Meg lurched back to the bed, shaking. She sank down, tears filling her eyes and streaming down her face. A sob rose up in her chest, releasing with a force she didn't expect. She wailed like a child, hugging herself, trying to soothe the ache inside. She wanted to go home, she wanted to hold her son. She wanted to feel Chris lying behind her, his big arms closed around her. She wanted to feel safe again.

The next morning

Meg blinked as sun streamed in through the window, flooding the bed with light. She rolled over, unravelling the quilt from around her. She looked at the clear blue sky above her as the memory of last night slowly resurfaced, reviving the ache in her heart.

She sat up. Her body felt stiff and sore, and her head was thumping from all the crying. She got up and went to look in the mirror above the dresser. Her eyes were puffy, ringed with dark gray smudges. She looked down at her crumpled clothes. All she wanted was to get changed and clean up and go home. But she would have to face Jamie first.

Meg opened the door gingerly. The house seemed quiet. She walked silently down the stairs and along the hall. There were sleeping bodies draped across lounges and chairs in the rooms she passed, but she didn't see Jamie among them. She could hear soft music coming from the back of the house. Meg walked on down the hall till she came to the kitchen.

A woman was at the sink, filling a kettle. She had long jet-black hair to her waist. She swung around, sensing someone watching her.

"Oh hello," she said kindly. "We haven't met."

She walked toward Meg with her hand outstretched. They were probably about the same age, Meg realized as they shook hands. She was an attractive woman, with unusually pale eyes for her dark coloring.

"I'm Aurora," she was saying.

Meg smiled. "Finally. We were looking for you half the night. I'm Meg Lynch."

"Yes, I thought you must be." What did that mean? "Would you like a coffee?"

"Is it real?" Meg asked, surveying the bunches of dried herbs hanging in front of the windows, and shelves lined with jars of suspiciously organic-looking contents.

Aurora laughed. "You mean real caffeine? God yes!"

"I'd love a cup, thanks."

"Take a seat," said Aurora, spooning coffee into a plunger. "About last night, sorry we didn't meet up. But I didn't get here till about eleven."

"Don't you live here?"

She nodded. "I've been away for a few days."

"And people just take over your house and have parties when you're gone?"

Aurora shrugged, reaching for a pack of cigarettes. "I knew about it." She offered a cigarette to Meg, who shook her head. "I just couldn't get back any earlier."

Meg frowned. "Sorry, I think I stole your bed last night."

"I've got plenty of beds I can sleep in. Besides," she added. "I didn't get all that much sleep anyway."

Meg felt an unexpected twinge. Had Jamie found her when he left the room last night? Did they spend the night together?

Well, what did it matter to her? It was just as well. It stopped him from seeking her out again.

Aurora lit her cigarette and drew back deeply, leaning against the kitchen cupboards. "So what are you doing here, Meg?"

"Um, I came with Jamie, Jamie Carroll."

"I know that. But what are you doing here?"

Meg wasn't sure what she was getting at.

"You don't belong here, do you?"

Meg felt embarrassed. "I'm sorry."

"No, I don't mean you're not welcome, Meg. Don't take it the wrong way. But you don't belong here. You've got a family somewhere, haven't you?"

Meg stared at her. "You talked to Jamie?"

Aurora nodded.

Meg didn't want to discuss this with her. She was mortified that Jamie had told Aurora all about her. "Where is he, do you know? I have to get going."

"He's gone," Aurora said simply, turning to switch off the kettle.

Meg felt like someone had just kicked her. "What do you mean 'gone?'"

Aurora turned around. "He left last night. Well, more like early this morning." She watched the expression on Meg's face. "I'll get you that coffee."

Meg sat dazed until a mug was placed in front of her.

"Milk?" Aurora was asking.

Meg nodded. "Thanks."

She poured some milk into the cup. Meg picked it up and gulped down a couple of mouthfuls. Aurora sat down opposite her.

"Um," Meg started vaguely, "I had a bag . . . in the car."

"He left it here for you. It's in the hall."

Meg breathed out. She didn't feel like talking to this woman about any of this. She felt like crying.

"You know you're not the first."

Meg glanced across at her. "Do I look that naïve?"

Aurora smiled. Meg noticed that she had a kind expression in her eyes, eyes that were somehow familiar.

"Jamie's had a lot of women. Some of them have been young wide-eyed things that follow him across the world, only to find he's tired of them. Or, if they grow up along the way, they tire of him," she added wryly. "Others have been like you."

There had been others like her?

"Married, unhappy, bored. Whatever. He likes the challenge."

Meg felt humiliated. This was too much to take in.

"Don't get me wrong," Aurora continued gently. "He really believes he's doing a service, giving you experiences you would never have had without him. Educating you."

Meg listened intently, sipping her coffee.

"Did he take you to visit John and Libby?"

She nodded. She remembered the look they gave her when she'd mentioned she was married. They were probably thinking "not again."

"To be honest, I think he feels he's freeing you from your shackles. But don't think for a minute that he'd hang around to clean up the mess."

Meg sighed heavily. "What am I supposed to do now?"

"Go home to your family. Put it behind you." Aurora paused, considering her. "He told me what happened last night. That took a lot of courage. Not many women can resist Jamie's charms."

"You seem to know an awful lot about him?"

"I've known him forever."

That's what Jamie had said about her.

"I'm his sister."

Meg's eyes widened. "He didn't say . . ."

"He likes to keep an aura of mystery about himself," Aurora smiled. Now Meg realized. She had Jamie's eyes.

"We have the same mother but different fathers. Jamie never knew his father, he was a young surfer who didn't hang around long enough to know he'd even made my mother pregnant."

"So what happened?"

"Oh, Mum stuck by us. She was a great mum, if a little unconventional. We never stayed in one place for long, which is why neither of us can now." Aurora gazed across the room, out the window. "It was harder on Jamie, though."

"Why?"

"He's part of the fatherless generation. He's never learned how to be a man, because he didn't have anyone to show him. I don't know that he'll ever grow up."

Meg sat quietly. "Thanks, you didn't have to tell me all that."

"You're entitled to know."

"I feel like an idiot."

Aurora shook her head. "Why should you? He's gorgeous, and I love him to death. But I wouldn't wish him upon my worst enemy."

An hour later Meg sat on Katoomba Station waiting for the train to Sydney. She'd cleaned up and changed her clothes, and Aurora had kindly offered to drive her to the station.

It occurred to her that she hadn't checked her messages since yesterday, so she reached into her bag for her mobile. She rooted around for a while until she remembered. Shit! She'd left it in Jamie's car, or Thommo's, whoever it belonged to. God, what if Chris rang and Jamie answered it? Surely he wouldn't? He didn't like mobiles, he'd probably just ignore it. What would she say to Chris? That she'd lost it?

She wondered if Ally had tried to ring her. Meg glanced around the station for a public phone, but the train was already pulling in. She told herself to stop stressing. Nothing would have happened. It never did any other time. She'd ring Ally once she got to Sydney.

It was nearly three hours before the train pulled into Central Station. Meg was exhausted. Apparently there was track work, so the passengers were herded off the train at Wentworth Falls and bussed down to Glenbrook. By the time she got another train to Central, Meg felt like she'd been traveling all day. She walked wearily out to a waiting taxi. It wasn't until they had driven off that she realized she still hadn't phoned Ally. She was too tired to care anymore, she just wanted to get home.

Meg paid the fare and got out of the cab. She put her key into the door, and pushed it open, peering down the hall. The house was dark, and eerily quiet. She expected Chris to appear at the end of the hallway, but there was only silence. She was about to call out, but maybe they were both napping, though it was a bit late in the afternoon.

She closed the door and tiptoed down the hall. She glanced into the lounge room. Chris was just sitting there in the half-light. The blinds were drawn. The television was off, and the stereo. Meg started to feel uneasy.

"Hi," she said quietly.

He cleared his throat. "Hello."

She walked into the room, and set her bag down. "What's going on. Where's Harrison?"

"He's sleeping."

"It's late for him to still be asleep."

"We've been in casualty all night."

"What?"

"The doctors suspected meningitis. But he's been cleared."

Meg was visibly shocked. She felt like the wind had been knocked out of her. "Did you say meningitis?" She turned toward the doorway. "My God! I have to see him—"

"No," Chris said firmly. "He's sleeping, leave him be. He's had a rough night."

"But he should be in the hospital—"

"He was!" he almost barked. "Stop and listen to me, Meg!"

She turned around slowly.

"I said he's been cleared. He has a secondary infection in the chest, and he's on antibiotics. He needs to rest."

Meg felt like her head couldn't contain all of this. "You said he was fine yesterday."

"He was. But when he woke from his nap he had a raging fever. It wouldn't come down no matter what I did, and he wouldn't stop crying."

"You should have called me . . ." As soon as the words came out of her mouth, Meg realized what was going on. Chris sitting here in the dark, the anger in his voice.

"I did call you."

She held her breath. She had no idea what he knew at this point. Maybe nothing. She'd say she lost the phone soon after talking to him yesterday . . .

"You weren't answering your phone, so I called Ally."

Meg swallowed, watching him.

"She said you were asleep." He paused. "I told her that I believed you'd want to be woken if your son was sick."

Chris just sat, not moving. His eyes were accusing, disbelieving, hurting. She couldn't bear it.

"Where have you been, Meg? I think I deserve to know."

She crumpled down into a chair. There was a long silence while she composed her thoughts.

"Where were you?" he repeated grimly.

Meg was trembling. "Um, yesterday, I went to Wonderland." God, she felt so stupid.

"What?" Chris frowned. "For the whole night?"

She tried to steady her breathing. "No, I stayed in a house up in the mountains last night."

"Who were you with?"

Meg froze. But she couldn't lie anymore. What was the point now anyway?

"He was just someone I met at a shoot. But I swear nothing happened," she blurted. "I mean, something started but I stopped it. I didn't want to. Nothing happened . . ." Her voice trailed away.

"Yes it did."

Meg watched Chris stand up and cross the room. He picked up an overnight bag. She hadn't noticed it till now. "Where are you going?"

"It doesn't matter. You can reach me on my mobile."

"Will you be at your mother's?"

"No, I don't want to involve her and Dad yet."

That gave Meg the tiniest glimmer of hope.

"I've written down all the dosages and times for Harrison's medication. It's all out on the kitchen bench."

He walked to the door. "One more thing. If Harrison asks for me, with so much as a hint of distress, I want you to call me. I don't care what time it is. My phone will be turned on."

She nodded.

"I had to listen to him scream for his mother last night. I won't put him through that again."

Tears sprang to her eyes. Somehow Meg found the strength to stand up. She turned to face him. "I can't tell you how sorry I am, Chris. I never meant for this to happen."

He turned and walked through the doorway without saying another word. She heard the front door open, and close again quietly, his footsteps on the front path, and the squeaking of the gate.

Meg stood there, rooted to the spot. Her whole world was collapsing around her and she couldn't do anything to stop it. She walked out to the kitchen and reached for the phone on the wall. Her hand shook as she dialed Ally's number.

"Hello?"

"Ally—"

"Meg, my God! Where have you been? I've been trying to call you."

"I'm sorry, Ally," she said weakly. "I'm home now."

"How is Harrison?"

"He's okay."

"Chris was talking about meningitis last night . . ."

"Apparently he was cleared. He's okay."

"Thank God." Ally paused. "Meg, what happened to you? Why weren't you answering your phone?"

Meg sighed. "After I spoke to Chris in the afternoon, I stuck it in the glove box of the car. I forgot about it."

"I didn't know what to say to him when he rang," Ally explained. "First I told him you were in the shower and I'd get you to ring back. I tried to reach you on your mobile, but you weren't answering. He called back after a while, I said you were asleep, which was just so lame. He said, 'Don't you think she'd want to be woken?' He knew, Meg. It was awful."

"I'm so sorry, Ally. I didn't mean to put you through that."

"It's okay," she dismissed. "What did Chris say when you got home?"

"Not a lot."

"Where is he now?"

"He's gone."

"Gone? Gone where?"

"I don't know," Meg felt tears welling. "He's left me."

Ally didn't know what to say. "Oh Meg."

"The stupid thing is, nothing happened in the end. I couldn't go through with it." She heard a weak cry from Harrison's room. "Harrison's waking, I have to go."

"Are you going to be alright?"

"Sure," she sniffed.

Ally hesitated. "I'll come up and see you this week."

"No, don't worry—"

"Just give me a few days to work it out."

"You don't have to do that, Ally."

"I want to."

"Thanks."

"I'll talk to you later."

Meg hung up the phone and walked up the hall to Harrison's room. She opened the door. He was standing in his cot. He was pale and glassy-eyed, but he managed a weak little smile when he saw her.

He reached his arms out to her. "Mama."

Meg gathered him up and held him close to her. She sat down in the rocking chair and started to sob. Harrison lay listlessly against her as tears streamed down her cheeks.

He looked up into her eyes and reached his hand up to touch her face. "No cry Mama."

Tuesday

"Ally! Ally!"

Ally turned around. Frances Callen was rushing toward her. She was in the middle of Bowral shopping center, walking along in a daze, having forgotten what she came here for. She couldn't stop thinking about Meg, she had never heard her sound so hopeless. Ally was planning to get up to Sydney as soon as she could, but she felt torn because there was still so much to do for the wedding.

"Hi, Frances," Ally said as she caught up to her. "How are you?"

"I'm fine, thanks," she replied, breathing heavily. "I've been calling you all the way down the street."

"Sorry, I didn't hear you."

"Are you okay?" Frances asked, frowning at her.

"Sure," Ally mustered a smile. She certainly didn't know Frances well enough to involve her in her problems.

"I was going to phone you at home. I have some good news," Frances continued.

"Oh?" Ally could do with some good news.

"I have a friend coming down next weekend, he's a photographer with *Habitat*." She paused for effect. "He's interested in doing a shoot at the restaurant. He wants to feature you."

Ally burst through the doors to the kitchen of the restaurant. Rob and Matt were sitting having a beer.

"Where's Nic?" she blurted, out of breath.

"She had to go and pick up something from the post office. What's up?" asked Rob. "You look like you've just won the lottery or something."

"Oh, I should wait for Nic before I tell you," she started. "But I can't! They want to feature us in *Habitat* magazine!"

"Who's 'they'?" asked Rob, disinterestedly.

"Whoever decides these things!" Ally exclaimed. "I bumped into Frances Callen just now, up the road, and she has a friend who's a photographer for *Habitat*, and she told him all about this place, and he thinks it would make a great feature!"

Ally wanted to feel happy about something, just for a little while. She looked at them, waiting for a response. Matt took a sip of his beer. Rob seemed thoughtful.

"What is wrong with you two?" Ally cried. "I should have waited for Nic, she'd realize what a good break this is. Think of the exposure!"

"*Habitat*," Rob mused. "But it's a house magazine, isn't it?"

"So what? All sorts of people read it, people who come for weekends away down here."

He shrugged. "Might be alright, I guess."

Ally slumped on a stool, opposite them. "What about you, Matt?"

"What's it got to do with me?"

"Well, she said they'd give me a mention. I'm sure they'd do the same for you."

He looked at her. "I'd rather they didn't."

"Why?" she frowned.

"I don't need the, what did you call it, 'exposure'? I've got a bloody waiting list as long as my arm already."

"Around here, you mean," Ally reminded him.

"That's right."

"But this is a *national* magazine."

"So?"

"Well," Ally was getting flustered, "you could work wherever you chose."

"I chose here, a long time ago."

"Philistine," she muttered.

"*Ally!!!*" Nic's voice screeched from the front hall. There was more than a hint of hysteria to it. Maybe she had bumped into Frances as well?

"Ally!" she screeched again as she burst through the kitchen doors. "It's a fucking disaster!"

Ally looked at her face. She was carrying a large flat box. Oh no. The bridesmaid dress.

"I said *peach*, didn't I? I mean, you heard me, on the phone? You heard me too, Rob?"

He shrugged, frowning.

"I even sent a swatch. You saw it, didn't you Ally?"

"What's happened?" Ally said calmly, handing her Rob's beer. She took a swig.

"Look in the box. Just look at what they sent!"

She was almost afraid to, but Ally knew that whatever she saw, she had to claim that it was beautiful, and even better than Nic's original idea.

She lifted the lid and moved back the layers of tissue paper.

"It's orange!" Nic wailed.

"No, it's not!" Ally lied.

Nic pulled the dress out of the box and held it up, staring at Rob. "Is this peach?"

"I'm a chef, love. Peach is a fruit."

"Matt?"

He shrugged. "Looks orange to me."

Ally dug him sharply in the ribs.

"Ow."

"What am I going to do? This is awful."

"Nic," said Ally evenly. "It's quite attractive, if you'd just calm down and look at it. Okay, it's not exactly what you had in mind, but it's not as though it's *bright* orange. It's more like . . . sherbet."

Nic looked at it. "Maybe . . ."

"And I know a way to really fix it."

"Shoot my sisters, so we only have to buy you a new dress?"

Ally ignored her. "We could use something like georgette, or even tulle, something sheer, and make an overlay."

"What do you mean?"

"Well, you put a sheer fabric over one color and you'll get a completely different effect. Like, a very pale pink over this could make it look more like peach. But another shade may look even better."

"But how will we be able to find something like that down here? In two weeks? And then get the alterations done?" Her voice rose hysterically with each new thought.

"Nic, have another drink," Ally said, picking up the bottle of beer and handing it back to her. "We already have the dressmaker booked for me. I'll take this around and show her what we have in mind. She can work out how many meters we'll need for three dresses." Ally took a breath and continued. "I'm going up to Sydney at the end of the week, so I can look for the fabric."

"Why are you going up to Sydney? We have so much to do!" Nic cried, alarmed.

"I'll only be gone overnight."

"But why now?"

"I promised Meg. She needs me."

"Well so do I!"

Ally didn't want to debate who had the greatest need at this point. She remembered she hadn't told Nic about the photo shoot. That would change the subject. "Nic, we've had some fabulous news. I forgot to tell you."

"What is it?"

"They want to do a feature on the restaurant in *Habitat* magazine!"

Nic stared at her wide-eyed. "Classic! How did that happen?"

"A friend of Frances Callen's is the photographer. He's coming down next weekend!"

"Oh my God! My family's arriving Thursday, so they'll be here for it. That should impress my parents! And it will get right up Deidre's nose." She sniggered with that last thought.

Ally sighed with relief. That seemed to have taken Nic's mind off the dress debacle, at least for the meantime.

"There could be a problem with the date," Rob said suddenly.

"What date?" Nic frowned.

"The date of the wedding."

Oh for crying out loud, why was he bringing it up now?

"Apparently the last weekend of September is all the footie grand finals. My brothers nearly hit the roof when the invitations arrived in the mail."

"Didn't you mention the date to them before now?"

"Probably. I doubt they would have taken much notice."

"Well bad luck, it's only a football game."

"Nic, they're from Melbourne, remember."

"So?"

"It's a religion down there," Matt explained.

"It's a big deal to them, Nic," added Rob.

"So is my wedding!" she cried. "What do you expect me to do? The invitations have all been sent, my family's virtually on their way from England. Get real, Rob! It's only a bloody football game!"

"We could promise them we'll arrange to have it taped," Ally broke in. "And they can all sit down that night, after the reception, and watch it."

Matt shook his head. "I don't think they'll . . . Ow, Ally! Will you stop elbowing me?"

"If you'd stop opening your big mouth!" she said under her breath.

Nic took a few gulps from the bottle. "Ally's right, we'll tape it. That will have to do."

Wednesday

Meg had finally stopped crying. When she phoned Simon to tell him she wouldn't be coming in on Monday, she started to cry as soon as she heard the concern in his voice. She cried every time she looked at Harrison. And each evening when Chris rang to check on his son, she dissolved into uncontrollable sobbing after he hung up. She couldn't stand the distance in his voice. He was her best friend. Or he used to be. Meg had created the distance. Not just last weekend, but for months now she had been walking away from him.

This morning she had only cried on waking. But after she washed her face and pulled herself together to go into Harrison, she didn't cry again. He was standing as usual, his arms stretched over the top of the cot, reaching for her. But today his cheeks were pink and his eyes bright.

"Mama!" he squealed delightedly.

Meg scooped him up in her arms. He held her face and gave her a sloppy kiss. "Kiss for Mama!" he exclaimed.

"Are you feeling better today, Harrison?"

Meg noticed a twinkle in his eye as he nodded eagerly.

"Choc lol-lol for Harry?"

Now she knew he was all better. She smiled for the first time in three days.

Meg sat on the back step in the midmorning sun watching Harrison play happily in the garden. He hadn't been outside for a week, and he was relishing it. Chris's mother was coming around for a couple of hours later on, giving Meg a chance to go into work, see if there was anything needing her attention. Mostly she just wanted to talk to Simon. She hadn't told him anything the other day on the phone, it was too hard. He thought she was upset over Harrison, and Meg had let him believe that for the meantime. Today she would fill in the rest. And there was something else she had to do.

She picked up the handset she'd brought outside and dialed her mobile number. Eventually a male voice answered, but it didn't sound like Jamie's.

"Hello, is that Jamie?" Meg said uncertainly.

"No, this is Brett."

Who the hell was Brett? "Oh, look I'm sorry to bother you. You don't know me, and this is probably going to sound odd, but you're speaking on my phone."

"Oh, then you must be Meg!"

She was taken aback. "Yes, that's right."

"I've been telling Jamie he ought to get in touch with you. You keep getting calls and he never answers them, reckons he doesn't know how. Bloody halfwit."

"Well, I would like to get the phone back . . ."

"Sure! Got a pen? I'll give you the address, I'm at Bondi."

"You're Taylor's brother?"

"I am. How'd you know that?"

"I've met Taylor a couple of times."

"Then we're like old mates. Listen, tell me when you're likely to come around, and I'll make sure someone's going to be here."

"Well, actually, I'll probably have a chance later today."

. . .

Meg found Brett's place easily enough. It was one of the shabby, nondescript blocks back from the beach. She walked up a flight of stairs to the first floor and knocked at number six. There was music playing inside, and she wasn't sure she'd been heard. She was about to knock again when the door suddenly opened. Jamie stood on the other side. They stared at each other, not moving. Meg couldn't think of anything to say; besides nothing would come out. She didn't seem to have a voice.

Jamie broke the silence. "You've come for the phone?"

She nodded.

"Brett said you called. Come in, I'll get it for you."

He turned and Meg followed him down a narrow hallway into a small living room. There was a backpack opened in the middle of the floor, half packed.

"It was here somewhere," Jamie was saying, moving around papers spread out over the table. Meg noticed a passport, and a Thai Airlines ticket folder.

"You're going away?" she asked, finding her voice finally.

He nodded. "Here it is," he said, scooping the phone out from under a newspaper. He handed it to Meg.

"I thought you didn't have the money to get away at the moment?"

"I worked something out."

They stood there, not saying anything. Jamie thrust his hands in his pockets. Meg was beginning to feel awkward. Maybe she should go. But she felt like something needed to be said.

She cleared her throat. "Jamie . . ."

He looked at her, waiting.

"I, um." She didn't know what to say.

"Look Meg, I'm not really into meaningful goodbyes. Let's just say, 'no regrets' and leave it at that."

He may as well have slapped her in the face.

"I'm not sure that I don't have any regrets."

Jamie shook his head and gave a rueful half-laugh. "Fine Meg, I'll be the big regret of your life if you want."

"I don't regret meeting you, Jamie," she said slowly, her thoughts forming as she gave voice to them. "But I do regret what I did to my husband. I thought I could do whatever I wanted and not hurt anyone. It doesn't work like that." She paused. "But I don't regret knowing you, Jamie," she repeated.

He turned to her with a strange look in his eyes.

"See, I thought I was missing something in my life," Meg continued. "You gave me the chance to see things from another perspective. At first it all seemed adventurous and exciting. But now I realize that you're not really experiencing life, Jamie. You're running away from it. You travel all over the world, jump off cliffs and barrel down mountains, to get away from really living."

Jamie raked his fingers through his hair and paced restlessly in the corner of the room, like he was caged. Meg had never seen him look so uncomfortable.

"So, now you've been enlightened, I suppose you think that wiping snotty noses and sleeping next to the same person all your life is really living?"

She thought about it. "Yes, as a matter of fact, I do."

He stopped and stared at her. "Well, good luck to you, Meg."

"And the same to you, Jamie."

Meg turned and walked down the hallway to the front door. She left without looking back.

Thursday

"Thank you, thank you, thank you," Nic gushed, when she dropped Ally at Meg's. They'd spent the morning shopping in Sydney, having left Bowral at the crack of dawn. They had a list of fabric outlets the dressmaker had recommended, and they found a beautiful organza, in a soft cream that Nic was certain was the same shade as her own dress. It had a gorgeous effect over the orange, and Nic was thrilled. Ally was just relieved.

"Should I come in and say hello to Meg?"

Ally looked at her watch. "You'll be late. Isn't their plane due to land soon?"

Nic pulled a face. "Yeah, I suppose."

"They're your family. You must be a little excited about seeing them?"

"Why do you think I moved out to Australia? It wasn't just for the climate, you know!"

Ally smiled at her. "At least you've got family. And they've traveled all this way to be here with you."

"Sorry, I forgot."

"Don't worry about it," Ally dismissed. "Now, I will look forward to seeing you all tomorrow evening, by which time everyone will be settled in and getting on like a house on fire."

She realized this was probably overly optimistic. Nic had planned a special dinner at the restaurant, and Ally and Matt had been enlisted for support. Rob was cooking, the coward.

Nic looked at her dubiously. "Maybe not a house on fire, but something just as disastrous," she grimaced.

Ally was alarmed to see Meg's ashen face, her bloodshot eyes. She'd never seen her looking so broken. Meg told her everything. She went right back to the first time she met Jamie, until their brief meeting yesterday.

For Meg, it was a relief to have it all out into the open. She had told too many lies and had had too many secrets over the past few months.

"What's going to happen?" Ally asked.

Meg shrugged. "I don't know," she said in a small voice. "Chris is terribly hurt."

Ally looked at her. "Did you get a chance to explain . . ."

Meg shook her head. "We haven't talked at all."

"It's just that if he hears your side, I think he'll understand." Chris was the most understanding person Ally had ever known. And he adored Meg. Surely he would come back to her?

"Ally, I don't expect anything from anyone. I've betrayed you all."

"Don't say that."

"But it's true. I asked people to lie for me, and I lied to my husband, so that I could go off for a weekend with another man, leaving a sick baby." She took a breath. "How did I become this person?"

"Don't be so hard on yourself," Ally insisted. Meg was never this desolate. She always had a funny crack, something to lighten the mood. "Everyone makes mistakes sometimes."

"And I saved mine up and made the biggest one I possibly could."

Ally frowned at her. "I'm worried about you, Meg. I think I should come back and stay with you, till you get things sorted."

"What are you talking about, Ally?" Meg frowned. "What about the wedding?"

"I'll come after the wedding."

"And then there's that job you're doing, for that woman."

Ally looked at her.

"You probably thought I wasn't paying much attention, but I remember something." Meg paused. "Ally, you have your own life. Don't you dare leave all you've got to come and hold my hand."

"Meg, the wedding will be all over in a couple of weeks, and then I have one client. That's hardly a full life."

"What about Matt?"

Ally swallowed. "Okay, so I have a friend, a few friends actually. I can keep in touch with them."

Meg shook her head wearily. "Ally, why don't you just go out with the man? See where it leads? What are you so afraid of?"

"I'm not afraid of anything."

Meg looked at her dubiously. "All that stuff about him leaving his wife is just an excuse," she continued, almost to herself. "You know, it doesn't have to be like it was with your mother, Ally."

Ally felt a sudden, unexpected lurch in her stomach, like she was in an elevator that had stalled. "Look, to be honest, this is not the best time, and you're not the best person, to be trying to talk me into a relationship."

"Why?" Meg felt affronted.

"You had the strongest marriage I've ever known," Ally tried to explain. "And now look at it."

Meg sighed, thinking. "Still, I wouldn't give up what I've had with Chris for all these years to save myself the pain I'm feeling now."

Ally looked at her sideways. "Well, you're a stronger person than I am, Meg."

She shook her head. "Don't you understand, Ally? Chris has seen me at my worst. Having a baby, sick with the flu, too many 'mornings after.' He's put up with me screaming at him like a banshee, being completely unreasonable at times. He knew everything there was to know about me, and he still loved me. I don't think you can ask for more than that."

Ally knew you couldn't, but still it wasn't enough. "And the first sign of something wrong, he just walked out on you. Without even hearing your side."

"He's hurting at the moment."

"Bloody men and their bloody football-field-sized egos."

"Chris had every reason for walking out on me. I cheated on him . . ."

"No you didn't."

"I did."

"But you said nothing happened in the end."

"If adultery is some imaginary line in the sand, well I stood on it, and then stepped back. But I shouldn't have been on the beach in the first place."

Ally looked at her.

"I have to take the responsibility for what happened. It's not his fault. I've caused him a lot of pain, and I have to give him time to get over it."

"Do you think he will?"

"Oh, I hope so Ally. With all my heart, I do."

Friday evening

"What I'm trying to say," Alistair Longford paused for effect, "is simply that this country has no cultural heritage. It's not a criticism, Nicola, merely an observation."

Ally thought that the top of Nic's head was going to explode right off.

"How can you say that?" she exclaimed. "You really know nothing about Australia, Father, or you wouldn't make such patently indefensible assertions."

Something had happened to Nic's vocabulary since her family arrived. And there was a little plum in her mouth as well.

Nic's father was the kind of person who made it easy to understand why the Scots and the Irish hated the English. He spoke about the Thatcher years fondly, and he kept referring to Australia as "the colony."

Her mother looked permanently dazed, and just said, "Yes dear, quite so," a lot.

"Is your mother on drugs?" Ally whispered to Nic, when they moved from the lounge into the private dining room for dinner.

"No, she's always been like that."

There was one son, the youngest child, and the heir apparent to his father's arrogance. At twenty years of age, Crispin Longford had a sneer permanently fixed on his lip, and an expression that suggested he could smell something bad, all the time.

Deidre was all that Nic had described. The first words she uttered to Ally were, "But you're huge, how will we all look together?" Deidre and Sally were as tiny as Nic, and Ally did feel tall standing near them. But at five foot six, she felt the word "huge" was an overstatement.

Sally was relatively harmless, though the most intelligent comment she'd made all evening was to declare her discovery that "Ally and Sally rhyme!" followed by an excited giggle.

Matt caught Ally's eye and smiled. He looked particularly handsome tonight, wearing a dark jacket over a crisp white shirt. She'd never seen him so dressed up. But it wasn't just that. Ally had felt a sense of relief when Matt had arrived earlier. It was comforting to know he would be there through the evening. She had got used to having him around, she realized. And she just realized she was staring at him.

What was the matter with her? She sipped her wine, looking around the table self-consciously to see if anyone was watching. Nic was insisting that Australia was not a colony just because the people had voted against becoming a republic, but her father wouldn't have it.

"I said as much to your mother, didn't I, Primrose?"

"Yes dear, quite so."

Ally glanced furtively again at Matt. This whole drama with Meg had left her emotionally raw. She'd started to think about him again, replaying that damned episode at Circle's End over and over in her mind. Wondering where they'd be now if she hadn't stopped him.

"What do you think, Ally?"

Nic was staring at her, appealing for support, and Ally didn't have a clue what they were talking about. Was it still the republic?

"I think," she said, glancing quickly around the table, "that we seem to be out of wine!" She jumped up. "I'll go and round up a couple more bottles, shall I?"

"Champion idea, I won't argue with that!" Alistair chortled. "One thing you colonists have learned is how to make a jolly good wine."

"Let me help," said Matt, standing up.

Once they were safely behind the bar, they both breathed a sigh of relief.

"I think I'd rather be having teeth pulled," said Matt.

Ally smiled. "I don't know, I'm finding it all a bit amusing."

"You seemed a million miles away in there just then," Matt said quietly. "Maybe a little sad?"

She looked at him sideways, but he wasn't teasing her.

"It's just my friend Meg," Ally explained, opening the fridge and scanning the labels on the wine bottles. "Her husband left her."

"Oh?" Matt reached up to the wine rack for a bottle of red.

"She was seeing someone, but she put an end to it. He left her anyway."

He pushed a corkscrew into the bottle, saying nothing.

"It's hard to believe their marriage is falling apart. I thought they'd be together forever. They had everything going for them."

Matt pulled the cork out of the bottle, and Ally handed him the white she had chosen from the fridge. She watched him, folding her arms. "Why did you leave your wife?"

The bottle slipped sideways as Matt went to insert the corkscrew. "What?"

"I asked you why you left your wife?"

He looked uncomfortable. "I told you, we weren't getting on—"

"I don't buy it," said Ally bluntly.

Matt stared at her, obviously stunned. Ally took the bottle from him and started twisting the corkscrew.

"You're not the kind of person who'd just take off like that, without a very good reason."

Now he looked embarrassed. God, maybe he was that kind of person.

"I'm sorry, it's none of my business—"

"There was someone else," he said abruptly.

"You had an affair?" Ally's voice was faint.

"No, it was Sharyn." He sighed, leaning back against the bar. He didn't make eye contact with her. "I found her, um, I found them together one day."

"Oh, sorry." The cork popped quietly as she removed it from the bottle. That would be devastating, surely, to actually see your wife with someone else?

"You know, Meg's husband would be feeling pretty shithouse at the moment. Excuse the expression."

There was hurt in his eyes even now, Ally realized. "I'm sorry, I shouldn't have brought it up."

He shrugged. "It doesn't matter, it was a long time ago."

"I've just been in a strange place lately," she tried to explain. "Between one marriage that's falling apart, and another that's just beginning . . . it's hard to know what to believe in."

They looked at each other for a moment. Ally realized she hadn't taken a breath. She wasn't sure what to say next.

"Don't worry about Rob and Nic." Matt smiled, breaking the silence. "He's still prepared to marry her, despite the in-laws."

Ally returned the smile. The subject was dropped, the awkward moment over. "Listen, I don't know that his family's much better. His brothers called this afternoon. You won't believe what they're bringing with them."

"What?"

"A television set."

"*What?*"

"It's true. They wanted to make sure there was somewhere they could set it up in the restaurant. They're not about to miss that football game."

"You're not serious?"

Ally nodded. "Rob found an aerial connection in the private dining room."

"What did Nic have to say about that?"

"She doesn't know about it."

"You're kidding?"

"It's better that way. Poor Rob, I don't know who intimidates him more—Nic or his brothers. So it will be our little secret, along with Johnno, Blue and 'Muncher.' "

"Muncher? How did he get that name?"

"I don't know, and I don't want to know. He's my partner for the wedding."

They broke into laughter. Ally handed him the bottle and picked up the other from the counter. They turned and walked around the bar.

"Save me a dance?" said Matt.

"Pardon?"

"Save me a dance, at the wedding."

She turned to face him. They were just outside the door to the private dining room.

"Sure, I'll be the 'huge' one in the orange dress!"

Matt smiled as the door burst open.

"Oh!" It was Nic. "Come on, you two, people are dying of thirst in here. And," she added in a whisper, "I'm just dying!"

Watsons Bay

Meg walked up the hall to answer the door. She knew it would be Chris, and it tore at her heart that he was knocking on his own door. She fixed a smile on her face and opened it.

"Hello," she said pleasantly. It was really hard to know how to behave. She didn't want to act happy, because she wasn't. But it didn't seem appropriate to pile her sadness onto him either.

"Hi Meg." Chris smiled faintly, but the pain in his eyes was evident. Meg hadn't seen him since last Sunday when he walked out. She realized they had not been apart for that long since the day they met.

"He's all ready," said Meg. "I packed his bag."

"You didn't have to, I could have done that."

She shrugged. "It was no trouble." They were still standing in the doorway. "Come in. Harrison will be so excited when he sees you."

Chris stepped into the hall as Meg called out to Harry. "Daddy's here!"

They heard the squeal from the family room, and a moment later Harrison appeared at the end of the hallway, his eyes shining.

"Dadda!" he cried happily, running into his father's outstretched arms. Chris scooped him up, hugging him close.

"Dadda make cubby?"

Chris glanced at Meg. "Not today. What if we go and see the animals, at the zoo?"

Harrison squealed delightedly and launched into his repertoire of animal noises. Meg felt empty. They had talked about taking him to the zoo again soon, now that he was bigger. It should have been a family outing. Not that she had any right to complain.

"I'll have him back by five," Chris said to her.

"It's okay, whenever it suits you." Meg didn't want it to sound like an arrangement. He was Harrison's father, he could take him for as long as he liked. He didn't have to check with her. That would make them sound too . . . separated.

The phone started to ring.

"I'll let you get that," Chris said, and all of a sudden they were gone. Too quickly. Meg hesitated for a moment before she dashed down the hall to the kitchen and picked up the handset.

"I thought you must have been out."

"Neil?"

"How you going, Meggie?"

She didn't want to answer that. "Neil, where are you?"

"I'm here in Sydney. I just flew in."

"What happened?"

"Long story. I'll tell you when I get there."

"No!" Meg blurted.

"What?"

"You can't stay here, Neil. Not this time." She didn't have the energy.

"Meggie, come on, just for a night or two."

"No, Neil."

"Have you talked to Glen?"

Meg sighed. "No, I haven't talked to Glen." She dreaded to think what that was about. "Look, Chris isn't here . . ."

"Then, I'll keep you company."

"You don't understand. Chris left."

"Left?"

Meg swallowed. "Left me."

"Shit Meg, what happened?" Neil sounded genuinely shocked.

"Long story."

"Meggie, let me come round. I won't stay. I just want to make sure you're alright."

Neil worrying about her? That was a switch. Not that she'd ever given him cause for worry before.

"Or at least meet me somewhere? Just to talk," he urged.

Meg gazed around the house. It was so quiet she could hear the clock ticking.

"Okay, I'll come to the airport. I'll be there in about half an hour."

Neil sat staring at her, a look of disbelief in his eyes. They were sitting in the cafeteria, their coffees long finished and pushed aside. Meg had recounted the whole story and Neil was clearly dumbfounded.

"What have you done, Meg?"

"Screwed up, basically Neil."

He sighed heavily. "Do you think Chris will forgive you?"

She shrugged. "He's very hurt."

They were quiet for a moment. Meg looked up at Neil eventually, feeling his eyes on her.

"You'll have to forgive yourself first, Meggie."

Since when did Neil get all insightful?

He leaned forward across the table. "You're so hard on yourself, Meg. Such a perfectionist. You were setting yourself up for a fall, and when people like you fall, they fall hard."

She smiled faintly. "Whereas people like you just stumble along all their way through life?"

Neil laughed. "It makes it easier when you don't have such huge expectations of yourself."

Meg paused, watching him. "What happened, over there in WA, with you and Glen?"

"Nothing. I had a great time."

She looked at him suspiciously. "Then what are you doing back already?"

"Meg, it's been over six months. Besides, I've got a job back in Queensland. It's all set."

"Really?"

He nodded. "My supervisor put in a good word for me."

"Your supervisor? Not Glen?"

"Glen didn't need to."

Meg studied him. "Have you had some sort of road to Damascus experience over there? Been hit by a lightning bolt or something?"

Neil laughed. "Nothing that dramatic. But it was an eye-opener being with Glen again. You should see the respect he commands over there. I mean, he's still the same Glen, our nice, unassuming brother. But he's in charge of huge projects worth millions of dollars."

"He's just been lucky, hasn't he?" Meg said wryly.

"I said that, didn't I?" Neil smiled, shaking his head. "He's got it all, Meg. His wife's lovely, his kids are terrific. It's pretty confronting to have your twin living this ideal life. It was like being in one of those movies where the hero gets to see what might have been, if only he'd made different choices."

Choices, Meg sighed. There was that word again.

"So you're choosing Queensland?"

"I've got three beautiful kids, Meg. It's about time I started being a father to them."

"Good for you, Neil," Meg smiled at him.

They sat quietly for a while, absorbed in their own thoughts.

Neil cleared his throat eventually. "You ought to call Mum and Dad, tell them what's happened."

Meg shook her head. "Why would they care?"

"Of course they care," Neil insisted. "In their own way."

She rolled her eyes doubtfully.

"This is what I was trying to say before," he explained. "Your standards are too high, Meg. Not just for yourself, but for everyone around you as well. I know they weren't the greatest parents on the planet—"

"That's an understatement."

"But think about it from their perspective," he continued, undaunted. "All of a sudden, they had three kids, a house, bills. Dad was twenty years old. What did he have to look forward to?"

Meg's stomach lurched. She was nearly twice that age, and she'd had the same motivation. She'd risked everything for a fleeting thrill, a moment of excitement. Maybe it was genetic.

"He made some bad choices too," said Neil. "They both did. You can't hold it against them forever, Meg."

Perhaps he was right. Who was she to stand on her high horse after what she'd done? Meg was over being perfect. And she could use all the support she could get at the moment.

She glanced at her watch. "I have to go soon, Chris will be bringing Harrison home."

He nodded.

Meg looked at him, thinking. "Why don't you come with me? You probably wouldn't get a flight now anyway."

Neil smiled slowly. "Are you sure?"

She nodded. "I think I'd like to spend some time with my new, improved brother."

"Okay, as long as you let me cook."

Meg feigned shock. "Wonders never cease."

"It's about time you let go and let someone else take over for a change, Meg."

She looked at him. "Maybe it is."

Mr. & Mrs. Alistair Longford

of Great Britain

take pleasure in inviting you

to celebrate the marriage of their daughter

Nicola Jane

To

Robert Michael Grady

youngest son of

Kevin and Trish Grady

of Wangaratta

at One o'clock

on Saturday 28th September

Saturday

At seventeen minutes past one, fashionably late, Nic walked up the aisle carrying a gorgeous bouquet of white tulips and smiling as though she was about to burst.

She had chosen the perfect dress for her petite build. It was made of ivory delustred satin, cut in a simple princess line. Ally did feel a little overgrown alongside the diminutive Longford sisters, but what could she do about it? Besides, she noticed Matt cast an appreciative eye over her as she passed him along the aisle. For once she didn't blush. She just felt this delicious surge of electricity run through her. Today he was in the full dark suit and tie. Good enough to eat.

Listening to the minister performing the ceremony, Ally realized it was a long time since she had attended a service for a happy occasion. But despite that, she still felt like crying.

Weddings always made her cry. It just seemed that it was the purest moment between two people. After all the hassle of the preparations, they stood there in front of their families and friends, both looking gorgeous, like they were a big wrapped present for each other. And then they vowed to love each other forever. Of course, most people didn't live up to their vows, Ally was all too aware. But at that precise moment, they loved each other enough to believe that they would.

Ally couldn't help feeling that she would like to experience a moment like that, just once in her life.

"Where have they all gone this time?" Nic said to Ally, glancing down the empty bridal table as the fourth course was served. "Who has to go to the loo this often?"

"Haven't you noticed how much beer they've been drinking?" Ally quipped, getting up from her seat. "I'll go and find them."

"Thanks, it'll be time for the speeches soon."

The Grady boys were giving Ally a headache. They had started off more discreetly, only ducking out one at a time to watch a few moments of the game, and coming back to report the score. But gradually, the more beer they consumed, the longer they stayed away. Then the next one would go and check on his brother, and so on. Word had slowly filtered around the place, among the rest of Rob's extended family, and now half the guests had disappeared from their tables.

Ally opened the door and squeezed into the room.

"Excuse me, Muncher, are you there?"

"Shh!!" someone hissed.

"That you, Al?" It was Muncher's voice, but she couldn't see him. "Won't be a minute, darl. It's nearly three-quarter time."

"But—"

"Shh!!"

Ally had had enough. She walked back out into the hallway. Nic was engrossed in a conversation with a cousin from England. Ally crossed the main room and pushed through the doors into the kitchen. She weaved her way around the small army of chefs Rob had contracted for the day, until she found what she needed. She made her way back again, skirting around the edge of the room, hoping she wouldn't be noticed.

"Hello, where are you off to?"

"Matt! You gave me a fright."

"What have you got there?"

"Nothing, never mind," she said, keeping her hands behind her back. "I have to go and deal with Groucho, Harpo and Yobbo."

"The football crowd? Need a hand?"

"No, I think I've got it under control."

Ally made it to the hall and slipped inside the room. She pushed her way through the crush until she reached the television.

"Hey, get out of the way!" someone complained.

Ally took a deep breath. In one swift movement she pulled the plug out of the electrical socket and turned around to face the crowd, looping the cord across the blade of the biggest chef's knife she could lay her hands on.

There was a collective gasp in the room.

"Hey, what do you think you're doing?"

"I think I should be the one asking that question!" Ally said in her best teacher's voice. "You should all be ashamed of yourselves! This is a *wedding*. Hopefully the only one that Rob and Nic will ever have. And you're in here, fixated on a stupid football game!"

"Hey, steady on!" someone sang out, as the rest grumbled in agreement.

"Don't interrupt me," Ally boomed, holding the knife and cord up higher. "I'm not afraid to use this!"

They fell silent.

"Now, unless you all get out, and stay out, until the speeches are over, I will slice the plug clean off the end of this cord and you won't get to see the end of the game."

Everyone started jeering.

"Go ahead," said Ally, moving the blade tantalizingly along the cord. "Make my day!"

The room started to empty. Muncher looked at her warily.

"You wouldn't really do it, would you?"

"Try me," said Ally squarely.

He shook his head and wandered thoughtfully out into the hall. Ally placed the cord down on the table next to the television set and walked out, closing the door behind her. As she paused at the entrance into the main room, Matt came up behind her.

"What's going on? You look a little flushed."

"It must be adrenalin."

"From what?"

"I think it might be power!" Ally winked. She handed him the knife. "Could you do something with this? I'm needed at the bridal table."

It would have helped Ally's cause if Nic's father had hurried his speech up a little. But being a judge, he was used to ruminating out loud, in front of a captive audience. Rob kept his speech mercifully short, and Muncher, as best man, positively galloped through his, carefully avoiding eye contact with Ally the whole time.

"Now, if you could remain upstanding while the bridal party walks through to the marquee," the MC announced. "We will follow, for the cutting of the cake and the bridal waltz."

The marquee was a concession to Nic's dream of an outdoor wedding. The budget could not stretch to pay for the grounds to be put into order, that was a much longer-term project. So Nic's florist friend had supplied large tubs of white flowering azaleas and impatiens, and the whole marquee was strung with fairy lights. It was the first real spring day this year in the Highlands, and the end wall had been rolled up, the view of the distant hills providing a stunning backdrop.

"Where did everybody go?" Nic frowned.

There was only her family and a small group of the English guests milling around. Rob's mother was helping his grandmother to a seat, and Matt was chatting casually to a handful of women, Rob's sisters-in-law among them, who kept glancing nervously toward the entrance.

"I've had enough of this," said Nic. "I want to know what's going on!"

She marched out of the marquee and back through the main entrance of the restaurant. Rob looked helplessly at Ally as they both skittered out to catch up with her.

In the hall, people had spilled out of the private dining room, craning past each other to see inside. The volume was turned up and the call of the game could be plainly heard.

Nic swung around, glaring at Rob as he came into the hall.

"What's going on? It's not that bloody football game?"

Rob nodded weakly.

"That's a television set in there! How could you let them do this?" she said, her voice breaking. "It's our wedding day, and they're ruining everything!"

Ally slunk back. This was on Rob's head, he could get himself out of this one.

"It doesn't matter," he said.

Was that the best he could come up with?

"Oh, if that's the best you can come up with, Robert Grady, that's just . . . pathetic." Nic was disgusted.

"But it doesn't matter what they do," he insisted. "They could fall through a hole in the ground for all I care. The only person that matters to me today is you, Nic."

She just stared at him.

"I married *you* today, *you're* the one I'm going to spend the rest of my life with. These other people will come and go, but you're the only one who matters to me."

For once, words escaped Nic.

"So, if it's okay with you, I'm going to take this chance to dance with my beautiful wife, before I have to share her around with anyone else."

He held out his hand, and Nic took a step toward him, placing her hand in his. As they walked past her, Ally noticed Nic's eyes were filled with tears. She sighed, and wandered out behind them. Rob was saying something to the vocalist, and a moment later he took Nic in his arms as the band started to play.

Ally leaned against a column at the entrance to the marquee, conscious of the bittersweet sting she felt as she watched them.

"Crisis over?" Matt asked, coming to lean on the column opposite.

Ally nodded, swallowing down the lump that had risen in her throat. "Have you ever felt cherished, Matt?"

"What do you mean?"

"You know, like in the wedding vows. *To love and to cherish*. It's such a beautiful word." She sighed. "I don't think I've ever felt cherished."

"I thought you realized now that your grandfather loved you?"

She shrugged. "But I didn't feel it at the time. It doesn't count if you don't *feel* cherished, does it?"

"Does it make a noise if a tree falls in the forest and no one is there to hear it?"

Ally smiled wistfully.

He put out his hand toward her. "Dance with me?"

She breathed in deeply as Matt led her onto the dance floor and held her in the circle of his arms, not too close, but close enough. She was intensely conscious of where their bodies touched. His hand on the small of her back, the other holding her hand, gently but firmly, her arm draped across the breadth of his shoulder. And sometimes, as they moved, his chin brushed against her cheek. Ally thought of the last time he'd held her . . .

"You know, Ally," he said, moving back slightly so that he could see her eyes. "Until you believe you're worth cherishing, you won't ever feel it, or even know that someone does."

He gazed at her, unblinking. Ally couldn't look away, she couldn't see anyone else around them, she forgot there was anyone else there. They were at the far end of the marquee now, where the wall opened to the view. Ally felt a soft breeze brush past. A lock of her hair fluttered loose.

Matt smoothed it back behind her ear. "You're a hard nut to crack," he said huskily, his face close to hers.

Suddenly they heard a roar from the house, and the footie crowd burst through the entrance of the marquee.

"Aussie! Aussie! Aussie! Oi! Oi! Oi!"

Ally moved a step away from Matt, turning to face the crowd, but she could still feel his hand protectively on her back. A waiter walked past with a tray of champagne, and she grabbed a glass, nearly downing it in one go.

The MC stepped to the microphone. "As you're all in the mood for cheering, let's see if we can't persuade the bride and groom to cut the cake."

For the next hour Ally didn't let a waiter pass her by without taking another glass. Right through dancing with Muncher, Blue and whoever, assorted cousins, Mr. Grady and Mr. Longford, and finally Rob, who said all sorts of nice things to her, which she couldn't remember anymore.

The MC announced that the bride and groom were about to leave. Ally picked up another glass from a passing tray and walked unsteadily to the circle forming around Rob and Nic. She hoped this was not going to take too long, she was not sure how much longer she'd be able to stand up.

Then she felt somebody behind her, gently supporting her.

"You were swaying," Matt said quietly, right near her ear. His breath tingled down her neck.

"It's the music," Ally insisted, glancing over her shoulder at him. She saw something in his eyes that made her gulp down the remainder of her glass.

Nic and Rob made their way around the circle, saying goodbye like there was no tomorrow. Everyone was lubricated with enough alcohol to be totally without inhibition. Family members who usually didn't speak to each other expressed undying love and devotion, tears fell, men kissed each other on the mouth. Nic and Ally were woeful.

"I love you! You're the best friend I've ever had in my whole life!"

"No, you are," Ally slurred. "I don't deserve a friend like you."

"No, I don't deserve you . . ."

And so it went on, till somebody prized them apart, and Rob swept Nic out of the marquee and into a waiting taxi.

Ally turned around and buried her tear-streaked face into Matt's chest, before she realized what she was doing. Oh well, he didn't seem to mind.

"Are you okay?" he said eventually, handing her a handkerchief.

She nodded, taking it from him, and wiping her cheeks.

"Tears aren't a bad thing, you know."

"I know."

"They're so . . . *appropriate*, don't you think?" she said looking up at him. "You know, you feel bad, and your heart starts hurting, a lump rises in your throat, and then big salty tears spill over your eyelashes." She sighed heavily, leaning on his chest again. "They're just perfect. I mean, imagine if you laughed when you felt sad, or got the hiccups or something. It wouldn't be the same."

She lifted her head to look at him. "They're kind of like your own private rain."

"Mm?"

"You know, happy tears are like summer rain, and sad tears are like," she paused, considering. "They're like the rain that falls on a bleak, wintry day."

He smiled at her indulgently.

"I'm crapping on, aren't I?" she said.

"Just a little."

"I'd better have another drink."

"Or," Matt sidestepped her back onto the dance floor, "we could finish our last dance. Remember, we were interrupted?"

"Okay," she said. "But I'm a little bit drunk . . ."

"Are you?"

She nodded as he drew her into his arms. She leaned her head heavily on his shoulder and brought her arms up around his neck.

"In fact, I might have trouble standing up if you let go of me."

"I'm not planning on letting go of you any time soon."

They swayed to the music for a while. Ally relaxed into it, though her brain occasionally felt like it was swishing around independently of her skull.

"Did you know," she said eventually, "I've been a bridesmaid three times now? You know what that means?"

"I didn't think you'd be superstitious."

"Still, it's pretty pathetic at thirty-five years old, to still be a *bridesmaid*. Lucky I look okay in fucking pastels. Whoops," Ally covered her hand with her mouth. "Sorry, I always start swearing when I'm pissed. And," she whispered, close to his ear, "I think I might be a little pissed."

"You don't say?"

"So there you go, three times a bridesmaid. But you know what's worse?" she said lifting her head.

He looked at her expectantly.

"You know what they call you if you have a baby after you're thirty-five?"

"Mum?"

Ally frowned. "It's not a joke! This is really true. It's a medical term." She paused, thinking. "They call you an elderly primavera!"

"Isn't that a pasta sauce?"

"Matt!" she admonished. "It's something like that, there might be a 'g' in it. Primagravity, maybe. Anyway, that's not the point. The point is, the 'elderly' bit. Fucking, *elderly* primagravy is what they call you!"

Matt laughed, and Ally nudged him. "It's alright for you to laugh. Blokes can have babies at any age and they don't get called elderly."

She leaned her head against his shoulder again.

"Do my arms look flabby in this?" she said suddenly.

"No," he said, smoothing his hand along her upper arm. "You've got beautiful arms."

"Then why don't you like me anymore?"

"Why do you think I don't like you?"

"You don't ask me out anymore."

"Because you always turn me down."

"Mm, but you think I'm a pain in the arse."

He lifted her chin so that he could look at her. "Not all the time," he smiled.

"Well, maybe you should ask me again sometime."

"Maybe I will."

The morning after

"Ally, Ally . . ."

She covered her head with a pillow. "What's all the shouting about?" she wailed.

"I'm not shouting."

That was Matt's voice. If she was in bed, where was he? Ally took the pillow off her head anxiously, squinting up at him. He was leaning above her, fully dressed, she was relieved to note.

"How are you feeling?"

"Ugh, don't ask."

"Here, take this." He was holding a glass full of fizzing vermilion liquid.

"Oh, I don't think so . . ."

"Come on, it's only Berocca."

Ally grimaced. "Why couldn't they have made it a quieter color, they knew that people with hangovers would be drinking the stuff."

"Maybe it's someone's idea of a sick joke. Come on, you'll have to sit up."

Ally dragged herself upright. "Oh God." She felt a sweat break out across her face. "This is awful."

"Do you think you're going to be sick?"

"Oh," Ally covered her face. "I don't want to be having this conversation."

"It's alright, it doesn't bother me."

"Well, it bothers me!" She flinched. "My head hurts."

"You'd better take these as well," said Matt, popping two pills out of a blister pack.

He gave her the headache tablets, and she swallowed them down with half the contents of the glass.

"How did you get in?" she said, peering through the veil her hair had formed across her face.

"Ah, with the secret key. I know all your little secrets now."

"How did I get home last night?"

"Safely."

Ally frowned at him. She glanced down at the T-shirt she was wearing, and then at her bridesmaid dress hanging neatly on a hanger over the curtain rail. "How did I get undressed?"

"Well, Cinderella, after midnight your coach turned into a pumpkin, and everything went back to normal."

She pulled a face. "Did you look?"

"Ally, your dress was strapless, remember? I just helped you get the T-shirt over your head, which took some doing, I might add. You weren't very cooperative."

"Sorry," she said grumpily.

"Then I unzipped you, and the dress dropped to the floor. I didn't see a thing."

"I suppose I'll have to take your word for it."

"Ally, you were completely tanked. There are rules about that kind of thing."

She sighed. "Thank you for being such a gentleman." She rubbed her forehead. "I just can't remember anything! Oh, except dancing with you."

"Mm, it was either that or fall over."

"I have to lie down again now."

She buried herself back down under the covers. "Was I really embarrassing? Did I do anything terrible?"

"You'll have to apologize to Mr. Longford, but apart from that . . ."

She pulled the covers down and stared at Matt, wide-eyed. He burst out laughing.

"Oh, that's just unkind," she whimpered, turning away.

"I'm sorry. Nothing happened. Don't you remember seeing Rob and Nic off? Their parents left straight after."

Ally recalled dimly. "So I didn't embarrass myself?"

"You just got very philosophical and shed a few tears."

"Oh, great. I must look awful!" she cried. She knew she wouldn't have cleaned off her make-up. "Do I look like a panda?"

"No," he insisted. "Panda's are big and lumbering, and black and white. You're more like a cute little raccoon."

"Oh!" She pulled the blankets back up over her head. "You shouldn't mock someone in this condition. I'm fragile enough as it is."

"Well, it's only one more big sleep until you feel normal again."

"Okay, I'll start now."

"Uh-uh," he shook his head, easing the covers down. "You really should get something into your stomach, as long as you think you can keep it down."

Ally looked up at him. "I never throw up. My body likes to hold onto all the toxins so that I get the full poisonous impact."

"All the more reason to fill your stomach," he suggested. "Come on, my shout."

"Couldn't I stay here a little bit longer?" she moaned.

"Well," he checked his watch. "There's a café I know that serves breakfast until two."

"So, we've got plenty of time."

"It's after one now."

"What?" She sat up again. "I have to get up."

Matt shifted to give her room. She eased herself off the bed and tottered gingerly toward the bathroom.

"Oh my God!" she squealed.

Matt appeared behind her. "Are you alright? Are you going to throw up?"

"No, but I'm surprised you didn't. Look at me!"

As she suspected, her make-up was smudged and smeared down her cheeks, and her hair looked like a rat's nest. Not that she'd ever seen a rat's nest, but that's what Nan used to say.

"I look like Alice Cooper!"

Matt chuckled, his hand on her back, gently propelling her farther into the bathroom. "Have a shower, you'll feel better," he said, closing the door behind her.

Matt took a sip of his coffee. "And then I threw up all over the principal's shoes."

"You didn't!" Ally said, wide-eyed. They were sitting in a café on the main road in Bowral, at a table by the window. They had been comparing hangover stories.

He nodded. "Not only was I suspended for three days, we had to buy him a new pair of shoes."

Ally laughed. "You win."

She had polished off a plate of bacon, eggs and grilled tomato, with toast and orange juice, and she was on to her second cup of coffee.

"How are you feeling now?" Matt asked.

"Almost human," she smiled. "I don't know why a big fatty fry-up is good for a hangover, but it always seems to do the trick."

"My theory is that your liver sees all this animal fat coming and it has to work through the alcohol toxins extra fast to be ready for it."

"My poor liver!"

"You can be kinder to it tomorrow."

"Oh, I think it'll take more than one day to make up for whatever I drank last night," Ally said dubiously. "But it was a good wedding, wasn't it, overall?"

"Nic and Rob seemed to enjoy themselves. At least it was memorable."

"Memorable's good."

"In fact, the knife incident was the talk of the evening."

Ally stared at him. "Knife incident?" she said weakly, hoping it wasn't what she was thinking.

"Come on, you weren't even drunk then."

She closed her eyes. "I'd almost forgotten about it."

"You're a legend now. The Grady boys were quite impressed." He paused. "I thought you were very brave."

She smiled shyly. Ally didn't tend to think of herself as brave. "At least it's a story for them to take back home."

"Mm, 'knife-wielding bridesmaid controls unruly guests,' " Matt suggested. "Have you ever done that before?"

"Sorry?"

"When you've been a bridesmaid? You said it was your third time last night."

Ally hated hearing back things she'd said when she had no recollection of them at all. What had made her tell him she'd been a bridesmaid three times?

"Well, no, I can't say I've been pushed to threatening the guests with a kitchen knife before," she joked. "That was definitely a first."

"So, you were Meg's bridesmaid, I presume?"

She nodded. "That was a perfect wedding, because it was Meg's, and that's how she does things. But I was also bridesmaid for this girl in college . . . well, not really bridesmaid. We wore jeans and cheesecloth tops and they were married by a female Buddhist priest on a clifftop overlooking the beach. I don't know if it was even legally binding," she grinned. "What's the strangest wedding you've ever been to?"

"My own!" He laughed. "It was probably quite normal, but I didn't know what the hell was going on."

"What about the best wedding?"

"I'm still waiting for that."

Ally willed herself not to blush, but the way he was looking at her . . .

She took a deep breath. "Best holiday?"

"Actually, that would have to be my honeymoon," he admitted. "We went to Daydream Island. Twenty years old, full of lust, with a license that said we could have sex all day if we wanted."

Ally considered him for a moment. "She must have hurt you very much."

The smile slipped from his face, and he stared down at his cup.

"I mean," she tried to explain, "leaving for so long. Leaving Beck. You must have been very hurt." It had played on Ally ever since Matt had told her what had happened. She knew from Meg's experience that perhaps Matt had been justified in leaving. But Ally wanted to understand why he had abandoned his little girl.

He shrugged. "It was a long time ago. It feels like another lifetime," he murmured, staring out the window.

Ally felt that she'd spoilt the moment. They had been having such a good time, she didn't want to lose the easiness that had developed between them. She twiddled her spoon in her coffee cup, absently. "What's your best moment?"

He looked back up at her, meeting her gaze again. "Mm?"

"What if you had to define your best moment? What would that be?"

She noticed a smile playing at the corners of his mouth. "That's easy. The second they put Beck into my arms."

Ally watched the expression on his face.

"She was all slippery and covered in gunk, but she was the most beautiful thing I'd ever seen."

But you left her.

"What about you?" he said eventually.

"Hm?"

"Your best moment?"

She blinked back a tear and cleared her throat. "Still waiting."

· · ·

Matt pulled up outside Ally's place, as the dashboard clock registered five-thirty. They both stepped out of the truck. Matt came around to the passenger side, leaning back against the hood.

"Thank you for breakfast," Ally said. "And for watching out for me last night."

He shrugged. "My pleasure."

Ally lingered. She didn't want him to get back in the truck and drive away.

"You're a nice guy, Matt Serrano."

"That's what I've been trying to tell you all this time, Ally Tasker," he joked, but he was looking straight into her eyes.

Ally could feel her heart racing. She stared back at him. "Do you want to come inside?" she said quietly.

He paused, sighing audibly. "If I don't go now, I might never get away," he said in a low voice.

Ally swallowed. "So?"

He held her gaze. Ally wondered if he could hear her heart beating from where he stood.

"I've got to get up early," he said eventually. "I have to be on the road at four tomorrow morning."

Ally was jolted back to reality. "Where are you going?"

"It's the school holidays. I'm taking Beck home to Mum and Dad's, then we're doing the Great Ocean Road. I'm sure I mentioned it."

She nodded slowly, frowning.

"You've been a bit preoccupied."

"I guess."

"So, I'll see you when I get back?"

Why did she feel like crying? God she hated this, hated feeling something, only to be disappointed.

"Have a safe trip."

"Bye."

October

Meg was in the process of repacking the pantry shelves when she heard a knock at the front door. She had spent the best part of the day cleaning out the entire pantry, washing down shelves and discarding anything that hadn't seen the light of day this century. She dusted off her clothes and smoothed back her hair as she went to open the front door.

"Simon!" she declared happily. He stood on the front step dressed in jeans and a dazzling white T-shirt. "Look at you, wearing mufti! You're so cute."

He pulled a face. "Meg, I don't normally wear a suit and tie on the weekends."

"Whatever, you still look gorgeous. Give me a hug."

It was good to feel Simon's arms around her. Sometimes Meg missed that feeling more than anything. There was nothing like the strong embrace of a man, even if it was completely platonic.

She pulled back to look at him. "To what do I owe the pleasure?"

He smiled. "I miss you. I wanted to see how you were."

"Oh," she cooed. "I miss you too, Simon. Come on in."

He followed her down the hallway. "Wow, what's been going on here?" he said when he saw the contents of the pantry spread around the kitchen.

"Cleaning. The pantry today. I'm onto the linen cupboard tomorrow."

Simon looked at her warily. "Didn't you go a bit crazy like this when you were off work the last time?"

Meg shrugged. "I have to do something. Harrison is with Chris for the weekend."

She looked down, not making eye contact with Simon. She thought she might cry if she did. He always had such a poignant expression of concern in his eyes.

He sighed audibly. "How's things, Meg?"

She still didn't look at him. "The same." She turned around to the fridge. "Can I get you something to drink?"

"I don't really feel like a drink. But I wouldn't mind a coffee, thanks."

"Sure," said Meg, picking up the kettle and crossing to the sink. "I've given up anyway."

"What?"

"Alcohol. I was having a little too much of it, I think."

"Oh?"

"Don't get me wrong, I'm not an alcoholic or anything, or else I couldn't have given it up so easily." She filled the kettle and plugged it in. "But I was drinking when I was unhappy, to dull the pain. If I kept that up under the present circumstances, I'd be drunk all the time."

"Meg . . ."

She looked up at him. "I'm okay, Simon, I'm a survivor, if nothing else." Meg took two mugs out of the cupboard. "Now let me remember how you like it," she chirped, trying to lift the mood. "Black, strong and just a little sweet, like your men?"

Simon watched her make the coffee. "So, do you think you'll come back to work?"

"Yes," she insisted. "Why would you ask that?"

"Well, it's been six weeks now."

Meg had tried to return to work the week after Harrison had recovered, but she couldn't concentrate. If she had been having trouble focusing before, now it was nearly impossible. Simon suggested she take some leave, use the time to sort things out.

"I'm officially on holidays at the moment, remember? That was booked months ago."

"What happened about that. Weren't you going away?"

Meg nodded. "Chris canceled it. We lost our deposit, but that's the least of our worries." She handed Simon his coffee. "Come and we'll sit down in the comfy chairs."

He followed her into the lounge room and they sat down. Simon set his cup carefully on the coffee table. "There's something I have to tell you."

Meg looked at him expectantly.

"Jamie Carroll rang the office through the week."

"What on earth did he want?"

"To speak to you. But he only had the one phone call, so he asked to be put through to me when you weren't there."

"What are you talking about?"

Simon paused. "He was picked up carrying drugs into Sydney airport."

Meg's eyes widened. So that was how he got the money to travel this time.

"It was only cannabis, but it was a 'quantity exceeding reasonable personal use.' So they have to charge him under trafficking. He was hoping you could help him out, suggest a good lawyer, pay his bond."

"What did you say?"

"I told him it looked like he'd wasted his only phone call."

Meg grinned, but at the same time she felt tears welling in her eyes. "I've been such a complete fool," she sniffed.

Simon moved closer to her and put his arm around her. "You're not a *complete* fool."

"Oh?"

"You did some foolish things, but you're really a very nice person."

"I don't think I'm a nice person at all," she said, her eyes now brimming over with tears.

"Yes, you are. You're a very nice person, who was unhappy and confused, and you made a mistake." He drew her head onto his shoulder, while she sobbed quietly. "You're allowed to make mistakes, Meg. The world won't stop revolving."

They sat quietly, Simon stroking her hair until her tears abated. She looked up at him and smiled faintly.

"Why didn't I marry you?"

He laughed. "Because I never asked you."

"Would you have married me if I asked you?"

"No."

"Why not?"

"Don't be offended, Meg. Aren't you forgetting that I bat for the other side?"

"We could have been happy, I reckon."

He laughed again, shaking his head. "I still remember you coming into the office in raptures one day. 'I've met the man I'm going to marry,' you said."

"I'd forgotten that," Meg said wistfully.

"I've never forgotten it. I thought it was the corniest thing I'd ever heard."

She elbowed him.

"But I was glad, at least it stopped you chasing after me."

Meg smiled.

"That's better," Simon said, touching her cheek gently. "Hey, what are you doing tonight?"

She frowned at him. "Do you mean before or after I've repacked the pantry?"

"Why don't we get a video and a pizza?" he suggested brightly.

"Haven't you got something better to do on a Saturday night than sit and hold my hand?"

"Sadly, no."

Meg considered him. "Why hasn't someone snapped you up yet, Simon?"

"Well, you know the joke about men being like parking spaces, they're either all taken or they're handicapped."

"I don't know about that. The prevailing theory among the girls at the office is that all the good men in Sydney are either married or gay."

Simon shook his head. "I wish. That is such a myth."

"Is it?"

"Why else would I be having pizza with you on a Saturday night?"

"Thanks."

"Come on, I insist on anchovies on the pizza, but you can choose the video."

Bowral

The knock on the door was loud and insistent. Ally stuck her head out of the bathroom door.

"Just a minute!"

She wrapped a towel around herself and tiptoed, dripping, through the bedroom and into the living room.

"Who is it?"

"It's me!"

Ally opened the door. "Why didn't you say?"

"I just did." Nic looked her up and down. "Did I get you out of the shower?"

"No, I was just doing laps in the indoor pool."

"Oh, I get it, that's irony, isn't it? Or is it sarcasm, I always get them confused," Nic said drolly. "You should give me a key. Then I can let myself in."

Ally was dubious about inviting Nic to take even more liberties than she already did.

"So have you seen this?" she said, following Ally back into the bedroom.

"What?" she said, glancing over her shoulder. "Oh my God, is that it?"

"It is." Nic was holding the latest copy of *Habitat*. Ally snatched it out of her hands.

"So are we in it? How did it turn out?" Ally said, flicking through the pages in a flurry.

Nic took it off her, and calmly opened to the right page. She passed it back.

Ally scanned it excitedly. The largest picture was of the main room, then there were a couple of smaller pictures of the adjoining rooms, and the private dining room, as well as insets of an artichoke, and two wine glasses close up. Why they wasted space on that was beyond Ally. There was a column of text, with the title *New Partnership Brings Color to the Southern Highlands*, next to a small photo of Rob and Ally.

Ally looked warily at Nic. "What's this?"

Nic was pulling a face. She took the magazine out of Ally's hands, and started to read.

" 'Chef Rob Grady and painted effects specialist Ally Tasker have teamed up to provide the winning ingredients for a new restaurant in Bowral. "Sensational food in sensational surroundings" was the couple's motto . . .' "

"I never even said that!" Ally declared. She looked at Nic's face. "Oh, I'm sorry, Nic."

"It's not your fault," Nic sighed, plonking herself down on the bed. "What a pair of dickheads they were. They were there for hours. How could they get it wrong?"

Ally sat on the bed next to her. "What did Rob say?"

"He said not to worry about it, and he's right. At least they got the name of the restaurant right, that's all that matters."

Ally looked at her uncertainly.

"Really!" Nic grinned. "Besides, you look pretty cute."

Ally shrugged, glancing back at the photo.

"Matt liked your overalls."

"Matt?" she frowned. "When did Matt see this?"

"He was over last night."

"He's back?"

The same annoying tinny tune started to play from Ally's mobile. She didn't know how to change it.

"That'll be the phone," said Nic.

Ally picked it up off the dresser. "Hello, Ally Tasker."

"I'm sitting here, looking at this gorgeous woman in overalls . . ."

"Who is this?"

"Ally! Don't be coy!"

Now she recognized the voice. "Bryce, sorry, I wasn't expecting you."

Nic made a face. Ally turned her back to her.

"Of course you weren't! You know how long it's been since we spoke?"

She didn't have a clue. She wasn't keeping track.

"Seven months almost to the day, babe. I remember, it was just after I sold the Tamarama waterfront."

That'd be right.

"So you've come a long way in a short time."

"Oh, we just had a lucky break."

"You and . . ." he paused, obviously checking the name. "Rob Grady?"

"We're not partners or anything. He just got married, his wife was at the shoot."

"Well, she must have a head like a potato, Ally, I can see why they preferred you. All kitted up in your overalls and singlet, like a real tradeswoman!"

"I am a—"

"And have you been working out? Look at the definition in your upper arms, very sexy."

Ally inspected her arms in the mirror. Really?

"Now, it's time to get you out of the sticks and back up to the real world again."

"Mm?"

Nic had tapped her on the shoulder. She mouthed something like "I have to go" and pointed at her watch.

Bryce was still talking. Ally held up her hand, mouthing "Wait!" emphatically. Nic frowned. Ally pleaded with her eyes.

"Bryce, I have to go," she said abruptly, it was the only way to get a salesman off the phone.

"I'll be in touch soon then, after I've put the feelers out. You don't want this opportunity to pass you by, Ally."

"Sure Bryce." She didn't have a clue what he was talking about. "Thanks for the call."

She switched off the phone.

"What did he want?" asked Nic.

"Who knows?" Ally dismissed.

"Is he after you again?"

"Oh, I doubt it." She didn't want to talk about Bryce.

"Then what did he want?"

Ally sighed impatiently. "He probably thinks I'm a celebrity now. He wants to share my fifteen minutes of fame, I guess. I don't really care. What I want to know is, when did Matt get back?"

Nic looked at her vaguely. "Oh, I'm not sure, he came round last night."

"You said that before."

"Um, he got back . . . maybe Friday? Yeah, well he phoned Friday anyway."

"He phoned you on Friday?" Ally said, trying to keep her voice level.

"Well, he hadn't seen us since the wedding."

Rob and Nic had only managed to get away for a couple of days for their honeymoon, but Matt had left on his holiday by the time they got back.

Nic looked at Ally curiously. "What's your problem?"

"Nothing," she insisted. "Um, only, I've got a job I need him to do and it's holding me up, you know, and he knew that. I think. Well, I'm pretty sure . . ."

"So call him," Nic said, rolling her eyes. She started for the front door, shaking her head. "I don't know what it is with you two."

"I'll call him, not a problem," Ally sang after her.

"You do that," said Nic, with a note of sarcasm. "See you later."

Ally looked back at herself in the mirror. Okay, that was easy, she would just ring him. But not wearing a towel.

She started to dress automatically. Why hadn't he called her? He'd been home at least four days. Ally bit her lip, wondering if she'd read all the signals wrong. She tried to recall their exact words that last night, when he dropped her home.

When she asked him in, didn't he say he might never get away? And when she said, granted quite brazenly, "So?" . . . what did he say then? He just explained he was going on holidays. Maybe she had pushed it.

Ally pulled on her overalls and fastened the clips over her shoulders. She had spent time with the contrary Callen sisters and had eventually come up with something that made everyone happy. Ally had started work, practicing on one wall until she had perfected the opalescent effect she was aiming for. Frances was thrilled, and she was getting excited about what Ally might be able to do with the rest of the place. But she couldn't even finish the girls' room until Matt repaired the window. So, she had a bona fide reason to call him. A business reason. Maybe they should just stick to business.

She sat on the sofa and picked up the phone, checking her watch. He'd be at work by now, so she dialed his mobile.

"Matt Serrano."

"Hi Matt, it's Ally."

"Hello Ally, how are you?"

He was acting so casual, like she had just talked to him yesterday.

"I didn't realize you were back. How was your trip?"

"Fantastic. The Great Ocean Road was amazing, and Mum and Dad were thrilled to see Beck."

"Is she still with you?"

"No, I had to drop her back last Friday."

He had been home since Friday. Ally tried not to feel disappointed. This was a business call, after all.

"Anyway, I was calling about the windows that need repairing at Frances Callen's place. I mentioned it before?"

"Mm, how soon do you want it done?"

"Well, as soon as you can manage, at least the window in the room I'm working on. I can't go much further until it's fixed."

"Okay, give me the address, I'll call round there later today and take a look."

"I could meet you there," Ally blurted.

"No, that's alright," he said. "I can check it from the outside, I don't need to disturb anybody."

Ally's heart sank as she dictated Frances's address to him, describing the position of the window.

"Thanks," she said, resignedly.

"Anything else?"

"No, that's it."

"Righto then, I'll see you."

Ally hesitated, waiting to hear him hang up.

"Oh Ally, are you still there?"

"Yes?"

"I was actually going to call you."

"You were?"

"Are you doing anything this weekend?"

Ally was struck dumb. Was she doing anything? Only her shift at the restaurant as usual, but she could get Michelle to cover.

"Why, what did you have in mind?" Oh, that sounded too forward. He probably just wanted her to feed the dogs.

"I'm going up to Sydney around lunchtime Saturday, Beck's in the Rock Eisteddfod."

Ally sighed. "I can feed your dogs if you like."

"I don't need you to feed the dogs." He sounded amused. "Would you like to come?"

"Up to Sydney?"

"Well, I thought you might want to visit Meg. I can drop you there and pick you up on the way back Sunday."

Ally thought about it. It was hardly the most romantic proposition.

"I could use the company on the trip," he added.

That was better. She took a breath, in for a penny . . .

"I tell you what, I'll come if you can get me a ticket to Beck's concert."

"You want to see the Rock Eisteddfod?"

"If Beck's in it. Maybe you could drop me at Meg's afterward?"

"Okay. It's a date."

Was it? Ally wondered as she hung up the phone.

Friday

"Chris Lynch."

"Hi Chris, it's me, Meg."

She could picture him sitting at his desk, his demeanor shifting, the sadness in his eyes.

"Hello Meg."

She missed how he used to call her "honey." She missed the warmth in his voice when he did.

"I just wanted to check about tomorrow."

"Sure. I'll pick Harrison up at ten as usual."

"And you're having him overnight?"

"If that's okay?"

"Of course it's okay," she said quickly. Chris had Harrison for at least part of every weekend. Meg thought that was only fair, seeing as she was with him all week. She wasn't going to start any stupid "every second weekend" rule. She didn't even want to have any rules. She didn't want this to be happening at all. But here they were, two months on, still estranged.

Harrison seemed to be coping alright. He was too young to understand the significance of what had happened, thank God. He was always excited to see his father, and devastated when he had to go. But he soon settled down once Chris was out of sight.

"You know, Debbie's down for the weekend, for Mum's birthday," Chris was saying. Debbie was Chris's sister, who lived up the coast. She was married with two girls who adored Harrison and followed him around like mother hens the whole time. Harrison lapped it up. "We're all staying at Mum's together."

It had broken Meg's heart when Chris had decided to tell his parents about what had happened. But it had been getting more difficult to hide, and neither of them had wanted to lie outright. There'd been enough of that. At least he'd had the courtesy not to give them any details about Meg's "indiscretion." Not that he knew any of the details. They hadn't spoken about it this whole time. All his parents knew was that they needed a break, that they were going through a rough time. And that was the truth.

"Well, you should have a wonderful time," Meg said, trying to be generous. "Make sure you wish your mother a happy birthday, and say hello to Deb from me."

"Um, you know," Chris started, hesitating, "they'd love to see you, if you wanted to come, or at least drop in."

Meg knew his mother must have prompted Chris to invite her. She could tell he was half-hearted.

"I'll be fine, Ally is coming to stay Saturday night."

"Good then," he breathed out. Meg could hear the relief in his voice. "I'll make sure I have Harry back on Sunday to see her."

"Thanks, she'd like that."

There was a long pause. Meg knew she should just say goodbye and hang up, but she hated this polite awkwardness that had developed between them. She used to be able to tell him anything.

"Chris?"

"Mm?"

"Did you ever think this would happen to us? That we'd be having a phone call like this?"

He didn't say anything for a moment. "No, I didn't."

They were silent. She could hear him breathing.

"Meg, I'm sorry, there's a call on the other line, I have to take it."

"Of course," she swallowed. "See you tomorrow."

"Bye."

Saturday

Ally had been ready for more than an hour when Matt arrived. She was glad he couldn't see her fussing around, changing her mind about what to pack a hundred times. She'd had a sick feeling in the pit of her stomach all morning, like butterflies, only worse. In fact, she'd been like that all week. On edge, not eating much, not sleeping particularly well.

Against her better judgment, Ally had spent more time than was warranted during the week shopping for a new dress to wear to the concert. She didn't want to look like a try-hard, too dressy. But she didn't want to look too casual either. Or too provocative, though she didn't want to discourage the idea altogether. Ally had exhausted herself in the end, trying to fulfil all the criteria. She wished her brain would just switch off for a while before she went crazy.

She probably should have said no to this weekend. Or just accepted the lift to Meg's. But no, she had to muscle in and invite herself to the concert as well. Matt didn't really have a say in the matter. God, what if he was meeting Sharyn there? That would be embarrassing. Surely he would have said, Ally hoped.

Her reverie was broken by three solid knocks on the door. Oh shit! This was it.

"Hi," said Matt, as she opened the door.

"Hi." Was it her, or had he got better looking in the last three weeks? His skin had deepened in color, making his eyes seem bluer. Now the weather had warmed up, he was probably taking his shirt off when he was working in the middle of the day. Her mind drifted, forming a mental picture . . .

"Are you ready?"

"Sure, of course. I'll just get my things."

He was still standing near the door when she came back out of her room with a small bag and her dress on a hanger.

"Is that it?"

She nodded, resisting the urge to run back inside and grab everything she had tried on in the last few hours. "There's only tonight, and I'll wear this again tomorrow for the drive home," she said, looking down at herself.

"I'm not complaining," he assured her. "I just didn't expect it. Sharyn would have had a bag at least that size just for her make-up."

Ally started to relax during the drive to Sydney. Matt chatted amiably about the trip along the Great Ocean Road, and about his family. He was worried about his father's health.

"How old is he?" Ally asked.

"He was seventy last year. He's almost ten years older than Mum, and I think he tries to keep up with her," Matt explained. "I wish I wasn't so far away from them."

"Do you think you'd ever go back?" she swallowed.

He shook his head. "It's too far away from Beck. They'll be alright, Dave and Cath live right by."

"Dave's your brother, isn't he?" Ally remembered. "Is Cath his wife?"

"No, Dave's married to Julie, Cath's my sister."

"I didn't know you had a sister."

He glanced at her. "Mm, she's married with four kids. And Dave's got three boys."

"Wow," Ally murmured.

"That's not the half of it. Dad was one of four, and Mum had six brothers and sisters . . ."

"Six?" she examined.

"They were Catholic."

Ally nodded, knowingly. "So, lots of cousins, big family get-togethers?"

"That's putting it mildly."

She sighed, gazing out the window. "Must be nice . . ."

They had a good run into the city, arriving at Darling Harbor around three. Matt had booked himself into a compact serviced apartment overlooking Cockle Bay.

The concert was due to start at five, so he suggested they change first and then take a walk around Darling Harbor, maybe have a drink.

"You look . . . great," Matt remarked as Ally came out of the bathroom. Her dress was safety issue black, but it was splashed with sprigs of green and white flowers. It was cut on the bias, so it clung to the curve of her hips, spilling down to swish around her calves. The neckline was a bit lower than she remembered, though she hadn't tried it on with this bra. She hoped it wasn't too much, or too little.

Matt was wearing khaki pants and a white linen shirt. His tan looked even deeper, his blue eyes piercing. Ally felt charged, like there was a spring on a catch inside her, straining to be released. She decided just to savor it. They were a long way from home. They didn't have to explain themselves to anyone. It was a brilliant, blue Sydney afternoon. Anything was possible. Where had she heard that before?

After two glasses of wine sitting out in the warm sunshine, Ally was feeling a little tipsy. They made their way across Tumbalong Park to the Entertainment Center, and she excused herself in the foyer to find the ladies. She caught sight of herself in the mirror and sighed. Bugger, her face was all red and blotchy from the sun, or the alcohol, or both. Ally touched up her make-up, leaning forward to get closer to the mirror. She noticed her cleavage as the neckline of her dress gaped open. Crikey. There was flirting, and there was bloody open invitation. Ally straightened up, pulling the drawstring around the neckline in firmly and retieing it. She looked at the overall effect, tousling her hair a little. She would have to do.

The Rock Eisteddfod was fabulous. Ally had been before, as a high school teacher, and it never ceased to amaze her how talented the kids were. Matt was suitably impressed.

"I thought it was going to be like a typical school concert, just on a larger scale," he remarked as they waited at the stage exit for Beck.

"Well, it's definitely on a larger scale."

"Hi Mr. Serrano!" said one of the young girls filing out through the door.

"Hello . . ." he hesitated for a second. "Lisa! How are you, Lisa?"

"Good thanks. Beck's coming, she's just getting her things."

It wasn't long before Rebecca appeared, walking slowly through the exit. She was holding hands with a gangly, slightly pimply young man of about the same age, and they were gazing dreamily at each other. She dropped his hand quickly when she caught sight of her father. Ally watched the expression on Matt's face.

"Hi Dad!" Beck said brightly.

"Hello sweetheart," he returned. He moved to kiss her, but she only offered her cheek, keeping a slight distance between them. The boy hovered in the background.

"Hi Ally," Beck smiled. "Did you like the show?"

"Loved it," Ally enthused.

"Your item was the standout, naturally," Matt added.

She grinned. "Naturally."

Ally hoped Matt noticed that although Beck didn't want to be demonstrative in front of her friend, her eyes shone when her father spoke.

"So, what's happening?" Matt asked.

"Umm, well Dad, you know how it's the last night . . . ?"

"Mm."

"Well, I know we were going to have supper tonight, but everyone's invited back to Alex's—"

"Alex?"

"Alexandra Porter, Dad. We've been going to school together since kindergarten!" Beck frowned.

"Oh, right."

"The teachers are going and everything, Dad, it's all above board. Mum said you can ring her if you want to check."

Matt was frowning. He looked a little forbidding, but Ally could tell he was just taking it all in.

"Here, I'll get my mobile phone," Beck said, digging around in her bag.

"You've got a mobile phone?"

"Sure."

"Since when?"

"I've had it for ages," she dismissed, retrieving it finally. "I never bring it to your place because I can't get reception down there." She held it out to him.

"I don't need to ring your mother," Matt assured her, putting his arm around her shoulders. "Are you going to introduce me to your friend?"

Beck looked a little flustered. "This is Daniel, Dad."

Matt put his hand out to the boy, who seemed a bit uncertain at first, but then he shook it.

"Mr. Serrano," he mumbled.

"Nice to meet you, Daniel. So how are you two getting to the party?"

"On the school bus, which is leaving soon," she said, checking her watch.

"Well, you'd better get a move on."

"It's okay?"

"Sure. Are we still on for tomorrow?"

"Absolutely!" she grinned. She reached up and kissed him quickly on the cheek. "Thanks Dad. Bye Ally."

"Bye," Ally returned as Beck grabbed the hapless Daniel's hand and sprinted off before her father could change his mind.

"Bye Dad!" she called, waving.

They watched the two of them until they disappeared around the building. Ally stole a glance at Matt. He looked at her, and she smiled.

He sighed. He leaned back against the pole of a streetlight, holding both hands to his heart, feigning pain.

"I've been superseded Dumped for a fifteen year old who doesn't even shave yet."

Ally grinned.

"I thought she'd love me forever."

"She will," Ally assured him.

"But I thought she'd love me the best."

"Then you were dreaming!" She walked over to him and held out her hand. "Come on, I'll buy you a drink."

"You know, I think I'm taking this very well."

"Do you?" Ally lifted an eyebrow. "Delusional as well as obsessive."

He frowned at her. They were sitting in an Irish pub at the Rocks, in a booth toward the back, a bottle of wine on the table between them. There was a band playing lively Irish music, and a few couples milled around on the dance floor.

"Did you notice he had an earring?"

"I only would have noticed if he didn't."

"But it was one of those ridiculous ones, hanging off the top of his earlobe."

"Mm, then he must be really, really evil," Ally said, nodding sagely.

"You're not very sympathetic," he frowned.

She laughed. "You had to know that this was going to happen one day."

"Mm." He seemed to wince. "Just not yet."

"How old were you and Sharyn when you started dating?"

"Oh, and that's supposed to make me feel better? I know what we were getting up to at their age."

Ally grinned, leaning forward. "Then you best be having a little talk with your daughter."

He groaned, dropping his head on the table. Ally patted his hair. "You're verging on pathetic now."

He straightened up and tossed back the rest of his glass, refilled it and then topped up Ally's.

"What about you, Ms. Compassion? When did you start dating?"

"Oh, not until I was much older."

"Hah!"

"My grandfather wouldn't let me do anything!" she protested.

"Sorry," said Matt. "So who was your first love?"

She shrugged, thinking. "There were boys in college, but I don't know that any of them qualify as a first *love*, exactly."

"So it was that guy you mentioned, Bryce?"

"God no," Ally said without hesitation. She took a sip of wine. When she looked up, Matt was studying her closely. "What?"

"So, have you ever been in love, or are you avoiding the question?"

Ally looked down at her glass, away from his scrutinising gaze. "I don't know if I've ever really believed in the idea."

"The idea of love?" he said, frowning.

"No. I mean, of *falling in love*. I think it's more to do with infatuation, and lust, and hormones . . ."

"What's wrong with any of that?"

Ally met his gaze. She could see something in his eyes that made her feel excited and nervous at the same time.

"Nothing," she stammered. "It's just that it's a physiological thing, you know, stimulus—response." God, keep digging that hole, girl. She breathed in deeply. "For example, they've done research on kissing, and there's a lot of nerve endings around the mouth, and so, when they're stimulated . . ."

Ally was distracted by the way he was looking at her. She forgot her train of thought. She stared at her wine glass.

"Well, anyway, the body releases all sorts of hormones, adrenalin, testosterone, dopamine—you know, that's the 'feel good' hormone—"

"So," Matt interrupted, "they've done research and worked out that kissing makes you feel good? I could have told them that. Though I guess it depends on who you're kissing."

She could feel his eyes on her but Ally couldn't look at him. Her throat went dry and she gulped down some of her wine.

The band had just finished a rowdy number, and the strains of the violin took over, quieter, haunting. Ally watched the violinist, though he was probably more correctly called a fiddle player. What was it about the violin, that heart-wrenching, yearning timber, almost like a cry? The vocalist started to sing, with his gentle, lilting Irish accent. Something about love. It was always about love.

"Do you want to dance?" Matt asked in a low voice.

Ally slowly looked around at him. The message in his eyes was unmistakable. She glanced at the dance floor. Couples were entwined, slow dancing. There was no one around to stop them, they wouldn't be interrupted this time. If she said yes, she was saying yes to more than just a dance.

She met his eyes directly. "Yes."

Everything felt as though it started to move in slow motion, but Ally didn't mind, she wanted to savor every delicious moment. Matt took her into his arms on the dance floor and pulled her in close against him. There was no awkwardness, no pretense, they both knew what they were doing. Ally looped her arms around his neck and felt his hands slide slowly, so slowly, down her back and around the curve of her hips. They swayed together, deferent to the music. He brought one hand up under her hair, lingering at the nape of her neck, his fingertips teasing. Their faces were close, his lips brushed against her cheek, and she could feel his breath on her skin. She closed her eyes. She wanted him so badly it ached.

Matt took one of her hands from around his neck and held it to his mouth, kissing the hollow in the palm of her hand. Then he pulled her harder against him. She closed her eyes as his lips brushed hers lightly, pausing, then drew back, teasing her. Their lips touched again, and she felt his tongue slide across her bottom lip, then move away again. Ally was quivering, she couldn't stand it anymore. She knew they were almost making love in the middle of a dance floor, but she didn't care. She tightened her arms around his neck, pulling his mouth down hard onto hers. She didn't know if the music was still playing, or if anyone was watching them. The only thing she was conscious of was the taste of him, his lips, his tongue. Her body was screaming with desire for him. Somehow they had to get out of here and back to his room.

"How long will it take to walk back to the hotel?" she breathed in his ear.

"We'll get a taxi."

Ally felt as though her feet didn't touch the floor as they swept out onto the street and hailed a passing taxi. In the back seat they necked like teenagers, oblivious of the driver, unable or unwilling to keep their hands or their mouths off each other. When they pulled up at the apartments, Matt threw a crumpled note at the driver and turned on his heel, taking the steps to the entrance two at a time, almost lifting Ally with him. They stood, breathing heavily, waiting for the elevator, their hands clasped, fingers entwined. People wandered around the foyer, but no one came by the lift. When the doors closed on them, they clung to each other again, their mouths locked together, hungry, exploring. Matt held her so tight Ally thought she would be absorbed into him.

The lift door opened and they charged up the hall. He fumbled with the key and then they were inside, alone finally. No barriers. For one split second they looked at each other, standing apart, breathing hard, and then he caught her in his arms, pressing her against the wall, kissing her mouth like he wanted to devour her.

His lips slid down her throat while his hands moved to cup her breasts. Ally had been yearning to feel his hands on her ever since that day down at Circle's End. And she wanted to touch him. She reached for the buttons of his shirt, fumbling, until his chest was bare. She pressed herself against him, tasting the skin on his neck and then his shoulder, as she peeled the shirt slowly down his back.

He was trembling. "Oh Ally," he breathed.

She felt his hands at her sides, gathering her dress up until her thighs were exposed. She hooked one leg around him, pressing her pelvis hard against his. Ally was almost dizzy with wanting him. Matt groaned, pulling her dress up over her head, tossing it aside. Then he tugged impatiently at the catch on her bra, pulling the straps over her shoulders and letting it drop to the floor. He paused for a moment, staring at her. Then he reached for her breast, gingerly. Ally drew her breath in sharply as he touched her. He looked into her eyes and then bent to kiss her, drawing her hard against him again. They clasped each other close, revelling in the sublime sensation of flesh against flesh.

Suddenly he lifted her off the floor and swung her around to the bed. They fell together, writhing, struggling free of the last of their clothes, until he was inside her, surging through her, filling her up. Ally cried out, an exquisite, almost unendurable spasm engulfing her whole body until she could hardly breathe.

And then it was over. Matt slumped against her, their bodies limp, glistening with perspiration. Ally lay sated, catching her breath. Matt's face was buried into her neck. She stroked his hair gently, looking down at their limbs all entangled, wrapped around each other. No one had ever made her feel like that. Ever. Maybe it was because she'd been so frustrated, she didn't know. She didn't want to analyze it, but it scared her a little.

Matt shifted his weight off her, leaving one leg across her. He lifted his head to look down at her, his eyes dewy. He stroked her hair away from her face. Then they smiled at each other.

"You've done that before," Ally murmured.

"Not for a while. Was it too fast?"

"Don't worry, I was way ahead of you," she grinned. "It was building up all night, after all."

His expression became serious. "It's been building up all year."

Ally stared up at him as he lowered his head to kiss her. Not so frantic this time, the urgency had passed. His lips were tender, lingering against hers. After a while he laid his head on the pillow next to her, his eyes searching hers.

"Ally," he said softly.

She shifted onto her side, facing him, expectant.

"I love you."

Ally felt a shiver run through her. "You don't have to say that."

He frowned faintly. "I know." He brought his hand up to touch her cheek. "That's not the response I expected."

She sighed, turning onto her back. "How do you know?"

"Know what?"

Ally looked at him. "That you love me?"

"I just do."

She pulled a face.

Matt propped himself on one elbow. "What, don't you believe me?"

"It's not that, I just don't understand," Ally sighed. "I told you, I'm not even sure about the idea of being in love. How do you know when you love someone?"

"Nothing's simple with you, is it?" he said, but his tone was gentle. He reached for her hand, lacing his fingers through hers. He kissed them, then held her hand against his chest.

"I must be in love with you because you drive me crazy and I still want to be around you all the time."

"That's big of you," she smirked.

"And you've got a smart answer for everything, haven't you?"

Ally's eyes widened, looking up at him.

"It's true. You're so strong-willed, you don't want to let anyone do anything for you. And you think you're always right."

"Stop, please, I don't think I can take all this flattery." She stared up at the ceiling. So much for romance.

"But you see, then you smile and your whole face lights up, and I go weak at the knees."

Ally glanced sideways at him.

"You're funny, and you're smart. And I love every minute I'm with you, and when I'm not, I can't wait to see you again. All the conversations in my head are with you."

Ally didn't know what to say. She didn't have a smart answer for that.

"I think I remember when I fell in love with you," Matt went on. "You came running out the back door at Birchgrove with that gorgeous hair flying behind you, and your big green eyes shining, ready to start work."

Ally was amazed. She always thought she was ordinary, but he didn't make her sound ordinary at all.

"That's when you fell in love with me?" she said in a small voice.

"Well, it was when the fantasies started, at least," he grinned. "Especially once you picked up that belt-sander."

Ally smiled shyly. "So why didn't you do something sooner?"

"Oh Ally, are you kidding?" he grinned broadly.

"Okay, I know you asked me out in the first place—"

"Repeatedly," he reminded her.

"Yeah, yeah. But, I mean after the wedding. I thought something was happening, and then you seemed to back off. You didn't even call me when you came back from your holiday," she said forlornly.

He kissed her hand again. "Ally, every time we were getting somewhere, you ran away like a frightened rabbit. I thought something shifted that day, too. But I wanted to be sure. If I'd made a move and then left for two weeks, you could have changed your mind by the time I got back."

"So you played hard to get?"

He grinned. "It worked, didn't it?" He leaned forward and kissed her on the lips. "Besides, I realized something while I was away."

"Oh?"

Matt took a deep breath. "I've always felt there was, I don't know, something missing, even when Sharyn and I were still together, when things were okay. I still felt alone, deep down." He paused, considering her. "I don't feel that when I'm with you. Only when I'm away from you."

Ally tried to swallow down the lump in her throat, but tears filled her eyes. He stroked her cheek.

"What's the matter, why are you crying?" he said gently.

She shrugged. "I used to feel that too."

"What about now?"

She cuddled in close to his chest. "Just give me some time to get used to all this," she murmured. "I've never been in love before."

He lifted her chin so he could see her eyes. "Neither have I."

Sunday morning

Ally woke slowly, taking in her surroundings, blinking at the sunshine streaming into the room. She could hear the shower running, and she looked at Matt's pillow, the puckering in the sheets where his body had been. She rolled over onto her back, stretching lazily.

What a night. They had made love again, and again, it seemed to go on forever. Ally had never felt so aroused. Oh, she'd had orgasms before. Bryce had always been very methodical about that. He knew exactly what to do, and Ally had always known exactly what to expect.

Sex had been purely physical till now, she realized. But this time it felt like Matt had reached inside her, touching that place deep within, a place that had shut down a long time ago. Maybe she'd never let anyone this close before. Ally felt like she'd opened herself up to him, and now she was exposed. She felt vulnerable, and a little afraid.

She heard the shower stop, and a moment later Matt came through the door, a towel draped around his hips.

"Hello sleeping beauty." He smiled indulgently at her.

Ally remembered last night, remembered falling asleep in his arms. She wanted to hold him again.

"Don't I get a good morning kiss?"

He looked around at her, contemplating. "I've got to meet Beck in half an hour. I don't think it's safe to come over there, I might never get away."

"Chicken!"

He grinned and walked over to the bed, sitting down and leaning over her. "Hi."

"Hi," she returned quietly. His hair was still damp, and there were droplets of water on his skin. Ally reached up and pushed a lock of hair away from his forehead. She wished he didn't have to go and meet Beck. She had a feeling that things wouldn't be the same after they left this room.

He leaned down to kiss her and she held onto him tightly. She didn't want to feel afraid, she wasn't frightened of Matt.

After a while he pulled back, staring into her eyes. "I didn't know whether to wake you, you were sleeping so soundly."

"That's okay."

"But I probably won't have time to drive you over to Meg's now," he continued. "I could ring Beck . . ."

"No, it's a bus ride from here! I'll take my time. Wander around a bit."

"You're sure?"

"Of course!" Ally insisted. "You go and have a nice time with Beck."

He kissed her on the forehead. "She's going to be thrilled, you know."

"About what?"

"You and me," he explained. "She's been hoping this would happen, ever since she met you."

Ally felt her stomach churning.

"You're going to tell her?"

Matt looked down at her, frowning. "Is that a problem?"

"No," Ally hesitated. "It's just, like I said last night, I'm still adjusting to this."

"So you want to keep it secret?"

Ally could see the look of confusion, maybe even hurt in his eyes.

"You're making it sound so dramatic!" she chided. "I just need some time. Okay?"

She looped an arm around his neck, drawing him down to kiss her. She didn't want to hurt him.

"I have to get dressed," Matt said reluctantly, getting up. He tossed a notepad and pen onto the bed. "I'll need Meg's address if I'm going to pick you up."

"Oh sure." Ally rolled over onto her stomach, propping herself on her elbows. When he was dressed, Matt came over and sat down on the bed. She felt his hand on her bare back, then scooping her hair out of the way, massaging the base of her neck.

"I'll give you her phone number too, just in case," said Ally, trying to concentrate on writing it down. She felt his lips on her shoulder, as his hand traveled down her spine, lingering on the small of her back, before sliding under the sheet.

"Matt . . ." Ally warned softly. "You'll be late."

He groaned, resting his head on her shoulder. "It'd help if you put some clothes on."

She smiled, rolling over and pulling the sheet up under her chin. "What time will I expect you?"

"Probably around four, okay?"

She nodded. "What time do I have to be out of here?"

Matt looked at his watch. "Not till eleven, it's only just after nine-thirty. You can take your time."

He bent down to kiss her. "Love you," he said softly, close to her cheek.

"See you later," said Ally.

She watched him leave the room, smiling back at her before he closed the door quietly behind him. She picked up the phone on the bedside table and dialed Meg's number.

"Hello."

"Hi, it's Ally."

"So, where did you get to last night?" Meg cooed. "As if I don't already know!"

Ally sighed. "It's not what you're thinking."

"Oh?"

"Yes, I stayed here in the apartment with Matt, but it has two bedrooms." Lie number one.

"Oh, come off it, Ally! Why would you stay at all if there was nothing going on?"

"We took Beck out for supper." Lie number two. "And Matt had a few drinks." Technically the truth. "He couldn't drive and there were no taxis about." They'd managed to find one. "It was easier if I just stayed here, in the second room." Liar, liar.

"Didn't he try anything?"

"He fell asleep snoring." Whopper.

"Don't tell me he's gay or something?" Meg said, disappointed.

"He's not gay!" Ally chided. "Anyway, I just rang to say I've got a few things I want to do while I'm in the city, so I'll be there later, probably three or so."

"Are you avoiding me?"

She hated that—Meg could read her like a book, and that was exactly why Ally was avoiding her today.

"Of course I'm not avoiding you!" she insisted. Lie number . . . she'd lost count. "Look, how often do I get up to Sydney? And it's getting close to Christmas, I just wanted to start on a little shopping."

"Okay," Meg sighed dramatically. "I guess we'll see you when we see you then?"

Ally hung up. Great, now she'd lied to her best friend. The day was going downhill rapidly.

Ally didn't set foot in one shop. She didn't even notice if the Christmas decorations were out yet in Martin Place. The city felt alien to her, gray and intimidating, too rushed. She drifted in a daze down to the Quay and along the promenade to the Opera House. There was a market set up in the forecourt. Tourist fodder. Ally remembered a Japanese word she'd heard once for this stuff. *Chindagu.* It meant "useless things."

She walked past the stalls, not seeing anything, irritated by the people who dawdled in front of her. She usually loved the Opera House, she could sit and gaze at it for ages. Today she sat on a bench with her back to its imposing sails, staring at the water.

She hated this feeling. She had made love all night to a wonderful man. A man who said he loved her. So why did she feel like running away? Why was she so terrified?

Ally walked through the Botanical Gardens and up past St. Mary's Cathedral, then across Hyde Park. She was heading toward Taylor Square when a bus pulled up at a stop just in front of her. She realized that it was heading east, so she jumped on.

She loved the beach, and living at Bondi had been her happiest time with Bryce. When the bus swung around into Campbell Parade, the street was clogged, the carpark full, the beach covered in bodies. Ally slipped off her shoes and picked her way between the people stretched out on their towels, baking in the sun. Hadn't they heard of skin cancer? Or the hole in the ozone layer? Premature aging? Their brains were obviously as fried as their bodies.

The water was still cold at this time of the year, Ally realized as it lapped around her feet. She wandered along the shoreline until she joined the esplanade. It would take her farther south, and she really should have started heading north, toward Meg's. But as she walked around the rocky outcrops Ally started to breathe easier. There were still a lot of people around, and they all seemed to be in a hurry: power walkers, couples pushing three-wheeled jogging strollers, skateboarders, people of all ages whizzing by on those odd little collapsible scooters. But at least here she could look out at the expanse of the ocean, smell the fresh salty air. She didn't feel so hemmed in.

Between Bronte and Clovelly, Ally found a relatively quiet spot where she could sit for a while. She glanced at her watch. One o'clock, only a couple more hours to fill in.

What was she doing? She should be at Meg's, playing with Harrison, spending time with the friend she hardly got to see anymore. But she was already confused enough. Meg's sadness was just a reminder that nothing lasts forever. People hurt each other, they leave, they destroy the ones they're supposed to love.

It was easier to be alone. Lonely, but safe.

Ally knocked on Meg's door after three o'clock. She was exhausted. She realized she'd been walking for hours, roaming the city like some lost soul. Ally seriously wondered if she wasn't a little crazy sometimes.

"I was starting to give up on you!" said Meg as she opened the door.

"Sorry."

"And just look at the armfuls of shopping!"

"What?" Ally frowned

"I thought you had Christmas shopping to do?"

"I do! I did!" Ally lied. She wasn't going to start counting again. "I'm having it all home delivered."

"To the Southern Highlands?"

"Yes," she insisted. "David Jones delivers anywhere."

"But why would you do that?"

"Because I didn't want to have to lug it around with me all day." If only Meg didn't keep asking so many questions, Ally wouldn't have to keep lying. "Can I come in, please?"

"Oh sure," Meg stood back and Ally walked through the door.

"Where's Harrison?"

"He's with Chris this weekend." Ally could hear the sadness in Meg's voice. "They should be here soon, Chris knew you were coming."

They walked out to the kitchen.

"Do you want a drink? Something cold, or a coffee?"

"I'd love a coffee."

Meg plugged in the kettle and leaned back against the bench. "So how's things?"

"Fine, everything's fine," Ally nodded. "Busy, you know, but fine. Good, even. Why do you ask?"

Meg frowned at her. "It's not an inquisition, Al, just a friendly conversation opener."

Ally nodded. "Oh."

There was an awkward pause.

"So what's going on with you?" Meg asked eventually.

"Ah, now the inquisition?"

"Okay, if you don't want to tell me . . ."

"There's nothing to tell," Ally shrugged. "Listen though, before Chris gets here, how are you?"

Meg sighed. "The same."

"The same as what?"

"The same as the day he walked out." She paused. "Only worse."

"Why worse, what's happened?"

She groaned. "Nothing, that's just it. Two months have passed, and we're no closer to a resolution. We're not even anywhere *near* a resolution."

"What, he doesn't want to come back?"

"I don't know what he wants. He doesn't tell me anything."

"Well, have you asked him?"

Meg shrugged. "I can't."

"Why can't you?"

"Because I was the one in the wrong. I can't go making demands."

"Who said anything about making demands? Just talk to him."

Meg looked at her uncertainly. "He doesn't seem to want to."

Ally didn't know what to say.

"You're taking all the blame for this, Meg," she said after a while. "And fine, you did something wrong. But surely it's not *unforgivable*. I mean, there's a lot of his ego tied up in this."

Meg just looked at her.

"To leave his wife and child . . ."

"He hasn't left Harrison. Chris would never leave him."

Ally felt a chill in her heart. No, he wouldn't, would he?

They heard noises on the back deck, and then Chris and Harrison appeared at the door to the family room.

"Harrison! Hello sweetheart!" Meg walked through to greet her son. She picked him up and turned around to Ally. "Look who's here? Give Ally a kiss, Harry."

He leaned toward her to receive her kiss, then turned back to his mother. "Ice bok, Mama?"

Ally glanced across at Chris as Meg took Harrison into the kitchen.

"How are you, Chris?" she asked, reaching up to kiss him on the cheek.

"Fine, thanks." He looked awkward in his own house. It made Ally feel sad.

"I was thinking about collecting the rest of my boxes today, Matt's brought the truck."

"So, finally," said Meg, "the move becomes permanent."

"No," Ally denied. "It's not that. I'd just like to have all my things in the one place."

Meg looked at her.

"I could still be back for the start of the next school year."

As soon as she said the words out loud, Ally knew that was never going to happen. She couldn't imagine herself back in front of a class. So at least that was one option she could strike off the list she hadn't written yet.

"You're not serious?" Meg frowned. "And leave your business?"

"It's not really a business. I have one job, that's it. It could all dry up after that."

"But I bet you'll get a lot of work from that magazine article."

Ally nodded. "Well, if that happens, it's just as likely to be here in Sydney."

"Why would you want to come back?" asked Chris. "People dream of living away from it all, if they just had a way to support themselves. I think you've got it made down there."

Meg looked at him curiously. "Do you?"

He glanced at her and shrugged. "Sure."

"It's not everything it's cracked up to be," Ally remarked.

The doorbell rang. She looked at her watch. "Oh, that's probably Matt. I'll get it!"

She dashed up the hall, opened the door and stepped around it, so they couldn't be seen from inside the house.

"Hi," said Matt, leaning forward to kiss her. She offered him her cheek.

"Listen, I haven't said anything to Meg, so, you know," she shrugged. "Let's keep it low-key."

"You didn't even tell Meg?" he said, disbelief in his voice.

"Think about it, Matt, it's not exactly the best time for her."

"Are we going to keep this up when we get back home?"

"Can we not go into this now?" Ally pleaded. "Come inside, they'll be wondering what's happened to us."

He followed her down the hall to the kitchen.

"Hi Matt!" Meg said expansively, kissing him like they were old friends. "You haven't met my, um, my husband, Chris."

"How are you, Chris," said Matt, offering his hand.

"Can I get you a coffee?" Meg asked.

"No, I haven't long finished one. Thanks anyway."

Ally was relieved. No cozy little chats around the table.

"So, Ally was saying you were out with your daughter today?"

Matt nodded. "Shopping. I promised her I'd buy her some clothes for summer."

"What a nice dad."

"Mm." Matt smiled ruefully. "A nice dad, with a clapped-out Visa card."

Harrison toddled in from the family room with the remains of his ice-block.

"Hello, who's this?" Matt asked, crouching down.

"I Harry!" he said brightly.

"I've heard a lot about you, Harry!"

Chris stepped between them with a wet cloth. "And you don't want to get any closer until I clean him up!"

"Matt, I was hoping to take a few boxes back with me today. Is that okay?"

"Sure," he said standing up. "The truck must be a mile away though, I couldn't park any closer."

Chris picked up his keys. "Well, if you want to go and get it, I'll open the garage and you can pull into the driveway. It'll be easier to load the boxes that way."

"Matt's got a truck, Harrison!" said Meg.

"Tchuck!" Harrison exclaimed.

"Do you want to come and see my truck, Harry?" said Matt.

"Harry see tchuck, Mama!"

"Can I give him a ride back here?" he said to Meg.

"Sure! Harry, you want to go for a ride in the truck?"

Harrison squealed, clapping his hands. Matt held his arms out and Harrison walked straight to him. He picked him up and followed Chris up the hall.

"We won't be long."

Meg handed Ally a mug of coffee.

"So, let me see. Handsome, charming," she started counting off on her fingers, "great with kids . . ."

Ally rolled her eyes. "Give it a rest, Meg."

"I just don't understand you, Ally!"

"I'm going out to help."

Half an hour later Meg and Chris stood apart at the front of the house, waving Ally and Matt off as the truck disappeared up the street and around the corner. Harrison wrested out of Chris's arms, and he set him down on the footpath.

"Come on, Dadda," Harrison insisted, pulling on his hand. "Make a cubby!"

"No Harry, not now," Chris explained gently. "Daddy has to go."

Harrison's face fell. "No Daddy go!"

Meg watched as Chris crouched down to his son's level. "We'll make cubbies next time," he assured him. "Give Daddy a kiss goodbye."

Harrison pouted furiously. "No Daddy go!" he cried, lurching at Chris and burying his head into his chest. He started to pound at him with his little fists clenched.

"Harry, don't hurt Daddy."

"Come in for a while," Meg broke in. "It's not fair on him. He doesn't understand."

Chris looked up at her briefly, and then put his arms around Harrison and stood up. "Okay, calm down, Harry," he soothed, rubbing his back. "We'll build a cubby now, but only if you stop crying."

Harrison lifted his head to look at his father. Chris got a handkerchief out of his pocket and wiped his nose and cheeks. Harrison twisted around to look at Meg.

"Daddy build a cubby, Mama!" he said happily.

They went inside the house, and Chris carried Harrison out to the family room. Meg stood in the kitchen, listening to them play, wondering if she should try to join in. She had no idea what Chris wanted, he didn't seem inclined to talk to her, but he looked so sad all the time. She wished she knew how to reach him.

After a while Chris came out to the kitchen. Meg was preparing Harrison's dinner.

"He seems alright now," he told her.

Meg nodded. "Would you like to stay for dinner?" she asked tentatively.

He looked embarrassed. "Um, no, I don't think so."

"Can I get you a drink? Coffee, a beer . . . ?"

"No, I'm fine."

She stared down at the chopping board, pretending to concentrate on slicing a carrot.

"I should go," he said quietly.

"Chris—"

"Mm?"

Meg took a breath. "Um, before, when Ally was here, you said that you thought she had it made, living away from the city . . ."

He watched her, waiting.

"Did you really mean that?"

"Sure, of course."

"Is that something you'd like to do?"

Chris shrugged. "I suppose so, in the right circumstances."

And these were hardly the right circumstances, Meg realized, her heart sinking.

"What do you want, Chris?"

He was clearly taken aback by her directness, and he stared down at the floor, avoiding eye contact. Meg hated the awkwardness, but she'd said it now, she couldn't take it back.

Chris cleared his throat and looked up. "I'd like to turn the clock back a few months."

"We can't do that."

His eyes were filled with sadness. "No, I guess we can't," he sighed.

They stood there, locked inside their own pain, unable to connect.

"I have to go," she heard him say. She wanted to explain that they couldn't go backward, they had to move forward if they were going to survive. But he was gone before Meg could gather her thoughts.

Ally must have drifted off to sleep eventually, weary from her hike around Sydney. The next thing she knew, they were climbing the steep road up Mt. Gibraltar.

"Hi," Matt said quietly. "You were passed out."

Ally just smiled lamely at him and stretched her arms out in front of her, yawning. They pulled up outside the cottage and Matt switched off the engine.

"Come on, I'll help you with the boxes."

She unlocked the door and went through into the bedroom to make space.

"Where do you want me to put these?" Matt had two boxes balanced on top of each other.

Ally moved a chair out of the way. "If we just stack them here against the wall, that's probably the best place."

She followed him out to the truck, and picked up a box, carrying it back into the flat.

"There's only a couple more after these," Matt said, behind her. "I'll get them."

Ally noticed the light on her answering machine flashing, and flicked it on.

"Hello Ally. Bryce here. Call me ASAP."

Matt walked in with a couple more boxes, setting them down.

"That's it."

"Bryce again, Ally. Did you get my last message? Call me, I have some news."

"What's that about?" said Matt.

Ally shrugged. "Who knows?"

"Ally, don't you ever turn on your mobile? Call me as soon as you hear this!"

"Do you want a drink?" said Ally, noticing Matt wiping his forehead with the back of his arm.

"Just water thanks."

"Hi Ally, it's Nic. I'm ringing to see if you're home yet? Oh, so I guess you're not. Well, now I feel stupid, I'm actually talking to no one. Or am I? You're sure you're not there? Well, you would be now, if you're listening to this, but it's not like now, as I'm saying it, it's like the now that it is when you're playing it back. Well anyway, call me."

Matt grinned as Ally handed him a glass of water.

"Mad as a cut snake, that girl."

"Ally, Bryce again. So you don't leave your mobile on, or answer your messages? You're going to have to smarten up if you want to have a successful business. Which, by the way, you will have, thanks to me."

Ally wondered what he was talking about. She leaned back against the kitchen bench, listening.

"I've dropped your name to a developer, he's just acquired an Art Deco block in Manly. Well, several actually. But I'll explain all that later. He wants to meet

you! I said I'd find you something in Sydney, didn't I? This is a great opportunity, Ally, it'll get you out of the backwaters once and for all. Now, will you finally call me!"

There was a long beep and the machine cut out. It was the last message. Ally looked across at Matt. He was staring at her, the confusion obvious in his eyes. The silence was excruciating.

"It's not the way it sounds," she said in a small voice.

"Why? How does it sound to you?" he said, leaning against a doorjamb.

"I don't even know what he's talking about."

Matt sighed audibly. "You've obviously had contact recently."

"Bryce rang when he saw me in the magazine." Ally strained, trying to remember what he had said to her. "That's all it's about. He just wants to bathe in a bit of borrowed glory."

"Well, whatever," Matt shrugged. "This is exactly what you were hoping for—more exposure, the chance to work wherever you wanted."

Ally looked at him. His jaw was clenched.

"I didn't know he was going to arrange anything like this."

"What?" he said curtly. "When he said he'd get you 'out of the backwaters,' didn't that give you a hint?"

"That's just the way Bryce talks."

Matt put his glass down on the table and turned toward the front door. Then he swung around again. "I just wish you'd said something . . . before . . ."

"What?" Ally urged.

"Before last night."

"Why? I didn't know what Bryce was up to."

He looked at her darkly. "This explains what was going on today. Why you didn't want to tell anyone. Leaving your options open."

"That's not fair."

"Yeah, well neither is this," he barked.

Ally sighed. What did he expect from her? "Look, I don't even know what the issue is here. So what if I take a job in Sydney?"

He glared at her. "Are you for real?"

"I've never said I wanted to live down here forever. I've been honest."

"So that was honest last night?"

She thought for a moment. "Yes."

"Well, then it meant a hell of a lot more to me than it did to you."

"I didn't promise anything last night, Matt," Ally said calmly. "I told you I don't even know if I believe in love."

"That's bullshit."

"No it's not!" Ally returned shrilly. Now she was getting angry. "It's alright for you, Matt. You grew up surrounded by people who loved you. You never had to wonder every night when you went to sleep if there would be anyone there the next morning."

"James would never have left you."

"But I didn't know that."

"Come off it, Ally."

"I was only a child."

"Well then, when are you going to grow up?" he cried.

Ally looked at him, startled. "What?"

"I said grow up, Ally!" he repeated angrily. "Yes, your mother abandoned you, and that was tough, and you didn't deserve it. But you had grandparents who loved you and looked after you. Why are you still harping about it? It was bloody more than thirty years ago. Let it go."

She wrapped her cardigan tightly across her body, folding her arms. "Well, thanks for understanding, Matt." Her mouth had gone dry, and her voice sounded strangled.

"Ally, I've watched you get eaten away over this." His tone softened. "You're making your whole life miserable. You don't get close to people, you don't trust anyone. You're becoming exactly what you feared."

She looked at him, waiting for what he was going to say next.

"Maybe you are turning into your mother after all. You keep running away from the people who care about you the most."

Ally felt like she'd just been thumped in the chest.

"You should talk!" she spat, her voice wavering.

He frowned at her. "What?"

"Lecturing me on running away! After what you did to Sharyn?"

"I told you why I left her."

"But why did you leave Beck? She hadn't done anything to you, she was only a baby."

He dragged his hand through his hair. "You don't understand."

"Oh yes I do," Ally sneered. "Do you think you're the only man whose wife ever had an affair? That you're something special? There had to be something pretty wrong with your relationship for her to turn to someone else."

"Maybe you need to be in the same position before you judge."

"Well, I was in the same position, Matt," Ally's voice rose hysterically. "My mother left me not just once, but twice. Do you know what that does to you? It rips your heart out and leaves a great big gaping hole inside. You don't feel anything. And after a while you can't feel anything. Even if you want to."

He breathed out heavily. "This isn't about me anymore."

"It is! You did the same thing to your own daughter," Ally cried. "I would never leave a child of mine. No matter what!"

"There was more to it." Matt turned away, looking out the window, his back to her.

"Oh really?" she taunted. "More than your fucking fragile male ego?"

He swung around. "Yes!" He was almost shouting. "I found her with a woman, okay?"

Ally caught her breath. "What?"

"The someone else was another woman."

Ally just stood there. Matt turned his back to her. She watched his shoulders heaving as he caught his breath.

He turned halfway around to look at her. "You see, Ally, you're not the only one who's ever been rejected and felt worthless. I haven't been able to trust another woman since then. Until now." He took a few steps toward the door. "But you don't want to be loved. You want to push everyone away while you keep licking your wounds and feeling sorry for yourself."

He walked out, slamming the door behind him. A moment later she heard his truck start up and drive off.

Ally stood there, conscious of every breath she took, because every breath hurt her chest. She didn't push everyone away. Did she?

She walked dazed into the bedroom. She got down on her knees and pulled a box out from under the bed. It was the one she had brought from Circle's End. She opened it and sifted through, picking out photographs.

Ally sat on the bed and stared at the pictures. She looked at the laughing little girl on her grandfather's shoulders. Then at the teenager. Such a hard expression for such a young girl. Ally thought of Beck, the way she beamed at Matt. She scanned the photo of her mother, defiantly staring back at the camera. There was a harshness in her green eyes, just like Ally's. She looked up and saw herself in the mirror. But the image blurred as tears filled her eyes. Ally sobbed, feeling more tears welling in her throat. She turned around and lay on the bed, curling her legs up and clutching the photographs to her chest.

Monday morning

The phone was ringing incessantly. Why wasn't the machine picking it up? Ally staggered out to the living room and reached for the receiver.

"Hello?" she croaked.

"Are you only just getting out of bed?" It was Bryce. "I'm seriously starting to wonder if you can handle the pressures of a business, Ally."

"Bryce, I've been away all weekend, that's why I didn't return your calls."

"Okay then. Can you make lunch on Wednesday?"

Ally sat down on the couch. Lunch. Wednesday. She didn't even know what day it was today.

"Give me a minute," she said, clearing her throat.

"Paul Silvestri is very keen to meet you, I wouldn't want to put him off."

"Paul who?"

"Silvestri. Didn't I mention his name on the phone? Well, he's the developer. This is the big time, Ally. He's bought up just about every Art Deco block of apartments with water views in Manly for the last two years. He wants to give them a signature style and release them on the market all at the same time. He's hoping to lure people from the inner city and the eastern suburbs across the harbor."

Ally's brain finally caught up with the conversation. "It sounds like an awfully big job, Bryce. I don't know if I could handle it."

"Ally!" he admonished. "Remember what I always used to say? 'If it's to be, it's up to me.' "

She groaned inwardly.

"If you're prepared to face the music, Ally, one day you might lead the band."

Spare me. It was too early in the morning for this.

"Now, we're meeting for lunch at the Harborside. Come on, I know you love the water. One o'clock Wednesday. What do you say?"

Ally paused, thinking.

"I don't know why you're hesitating," Bryce continued. "You couldn't seriously be considering staying down there? You always hated it!"

"That's true. But . . ."

"But what, Ally?" he said impatiently.

She wanted to say she had her reasons. But she didn't know what they were anymore.

"Be like the turtle," said Bryce.

"What?"

"He never got anywhere until he stuck his neck out."

Oh good grief. She had to get him off the phone. "Okay. I'll see you Wednesday."

"That's one sharp, Ally! Don't be late. This is Sydney, remember, not Green Acres. Time is precious. And for God's sake, bring your mobile phone with you. And turn it *on!*"

Ally hung up the phone as a knock sounded at the door. She got up to open it.

"Ally! Bloody hell, you look awful!"

"Thanks, Nic."

"Did you sleep in those clothes?"

Ally looked down at herself. "Apparently."

"Are you alright?"

She looked at Nic's worried face. "Why, do I look sick?"

"I've just spoken to Matt."

"Oh? What did he have to say?" Ally crossed to the kitchen and filled up the kettle.

"Not a lot. But he looked nearly as bad as you do. And when I asked him how your weekend was, he said I should ask you."

Ally plugged the kettle in and turned around to face Nic, folding her arms. She might as well just say it.

"We slept together, and then we had a huge fight, which is just as well really, it would never have worked out. So now I'm going to Sydney for a job."

Nic's jaw almost dropped to the floor. "What?"

"Which part didn't you get?"

Nic pulled out a chair and sat down. "None of it. Say it again, slowly."

"We slept together—"

"Okay, stop right there," Nic said, holding up her hand. "How did that happen?"

Ally sighed. "It just did. How does it ever happen?"

She looked thoughtful. "God, I thought you two were well and truly past it, that you were friends and that was it."

"If we were smart, we would have left it at that."

"So you think it was a mistake? Like a lapse or something?"

Ally thought about the other night, on the dance floor, and later, entwined in his arms. She didn't like to think of it as a mistake. She shrugged.

"Because if that's all it is, then you don't need to be packing up and running off to Sydney!"

Ally looked at the hopeful expression on Nic's face. The kettle started to whistle.

"Do you want tea?"

She nodded, and Ally took two cups from the cupboard, then reached for the tea canister. "I hope a bag will do?"

She made the tea and placed a cup down on the table in front of Nic. Ally sat opposite, fiddling with the tea bag, avoiding Nic's gaze.

"Ally?"

"Mm?"

"Why are you going to Sydney?"

Ally sighed. "Look, nothing's definite. There's the offer of some work, that's all."

"But you've got work here."

"A little. This is something much bigger. It would be solid work for a year or so, I reckon. And it could lead to a lot more."

Nic sighed heavily. "You never really wanted to stay down here, did you?"

Ally considered her for a moment and shook her head. "I never intended to stay this long. And then one thing led to another, and here I am, still. Drifting along. It's about time I started making some decisions about what I really want to do with my life."

"And Matt's not part of that?"

Ally felt a twinge. "I think maybe we want different things."

"Do you love him?"

She realized she couldn't say no outright. "I don't know."

"Because," Nic said tentatively, "if you love someone, you make decisions together, you compromise. Like me and Rob."

"Well then, maybe I don't love him, because I don't think I can do that."

Tuesday, 7 a.m.

Ally stopped the car in front of the gates to Matt's property. She hesitated. She had allowed plenty of time to catch him before he went to work, but now she was half hoping he'd already left. Coward.

She got out to open the gate. As she drove the car through, she wondered if she needed to close the gates again. She wouldn't be here long.

But then she remembered the dogs. For some ridiculous reason that brought a lump to her throat. God, how was she going to get through this?

She closed the gates and got back in the car, driving slowly along the dusty track. There hadn't been much rain lately, there was no sign of water as the car dipped across the path of the stream.

Ally looked ahead and her heart leaped into her mouth. Matt's truck had just come into view, rounding the small grove of wattles. They both stopped. She couldn't see his face clearly, they were still too far apart.

She realized the truck was inching forward, so she did the same. It felt like an hour passed before they pulled up, almost nose to nose. She could see Matt's face now, but she couldn't work out his expression.

He was getting out of the truck. Ally fumbled with the door handle and stepped out. He leaned against the hood, watching her. She closed the door of her car and walked slowly toward him.

"Hi." He was the first one to speak.

She swallowed. "Hi."

They stood there for a while, looking at each other and looking away. Ally couldn't remember all the things she wanted to say, that she had rehearsed so carefully. It had all flown out of her head.

"I, um, wanted to catch you before you left. I wasn't sure where you'd be today."

"I'll be all over the place."

Ally nodded.

"Where are you off to?" he said eventually.

"Sorry?"

"Well, you're not dressed for work."

Ally glanced down at herself. "Um, no." Words seemed to stick in her throat.

"You're going to Sydney?"

She nodded. "Just for a couple of nights. I'm staying up at Meg's."

He was watching her, waiting for her to say more. She really needed to say more.

"I'm meeting with the developer," she blurted.

"I gathered that."

Ally stood, wringing her hands together.

"If that's all you came to tell me," he said carefully, "I really should get going. I need to tie up some loose ends today. I want to get on to the Callen house tomorrow."

"Oh, the window?"

He nodded.

This was just getting harder. "Thanks for that." She took a deep breath. "I just didn't want to leave things, you know, the way they were."

There, she'd said it.

"How was that?"

God, couldn't he throw her a line?

"Um, you know." She shrugged. Then she met his gaze directly. "Matt, I don't want to fight with you."

He sighed audibly. "Me either."

They stood for a while, not speaking.

"Can I ask you something?" Ally said eventually, looking up at him.

Matt nodded.

"Do you really think I'm like my mother?"

"Ally, I didn't even know your mother."

"Neither did I." She looked plaintively at him. "You said I push people away. Do you think I pushed my grandfather away?"

"I had no right to say those things to you, Ally. It's none of my business."

Ally stared down at the ground. "Maybe someone needed to say them." She thought for a moment. "I never wanted to hurt people like my mother did."

"It's not that, Ally. I . . ."

She looked up at him, expectant.

Matt breathed out heavily. "Sometimes I can see so much suspicion in your eyes, like you're just waiting for somebody to let you down."

She swallowed, clasping her arms around herself.

"It's pretty hard to get past. It might have been hard for your grandfather."

She brushed a tear away from the corner of her eye, nodding. "Fair enough," she said quietly.

"I know how you feel," his voice was gentle. "At first I thought it made me less of a man because of what Sharyn did. But it wasn't about me at all." He paused. "Same with your mother, Ally. You were only a child. It didn't mean that you didn't deserve to be loved, just because she didn't know how to be your mother."

Now tears filled her eyes. Matt reached into his pocket and pulled out a handkerchief. He passed it to her and she wiped them away.

"How did you get so wise?" Ally asked after a while.

"I don't know about wise, I was a mess for ages." Matt shrugged, smiling faintly. "In a pathetic attempt to prove my manhood, I worked as a laborer, a rigger, anything blokey. And I slept with any woman who so much as looked sideways at me." He shook his head, remembering. "I did a lot of drinking, a lot of spitting."

They smiled at each other.

"What I realized eventually was that the only thing that would make me a man was to come back and be a father to Rebecca." He paused. "You have to work out what's going to make you whole, Ally."

They stood for a while in silence, wrapped in their own thoughts.

"I have to go," Ally said eventually.

He nodded. "I know."

She paused. "It's just, they're expecting me."

"I know you have to do this," Matt said quietly, taking a step toward her. "And I want you to be happy."

She couldn't look at him. She glanced at the car. "Do you want me to get out of the way?"

He shook his head. "No, you go. I'll wait here."

He brought his hand up to her face and leaned forward to kiss her on the cheek. He lingered for a moment, his face close to hers.

"I hope you find what you're looking for."

Ally drove along the road toward Bowral, trembling. Tears filled her eyes, making the road ahead hazy. She blinked until they were streaming down her cheeks.

After she had been driving for about ten minutes, she pulled up at the gates to Bowral Cemetery. She hadn't been back since Lillian's burial. She'd never been back to her grandfather's grave. She drove slowly through the gates and pulled over, switching off the engine.

There was no one around. It was only seven-thirty, she didn't expect there would be. She found a tissue in her bag and wiped her eyes. She picked up the small sprig of flowers she had brought with her. Rosemary for remembrance, lavender for love, thyme for healing. Something like that anyway. Nan knew all about herbs and their folklore. Ally wasn't sure if she had it right, but it was close enough.

She wandered along the paths. She couldn't remember exactly where he was buried, she'd been in a bit of a daze that day. And it had been so crowded.

She spotted a new headstone, in the older section. There it was, right next to Nan's. She should have remembered that. They used to come and tend her grave at least once a month. Ally stooped to pull out a dandelion that had grown through a crack in the stone.

She looked at James's headstone. Ally remembered Lillian checking the wording with her, but she had only given it a cursory glance at the time.

Beloved husband of Margaret
Loving father of Jennifer
Devoted grandfather of Ally

Ally sat on the grass at the foot of the grave. She started to cry. Not tears of self-pity like she'd had that day, but tears of regret. They should have had so much more together. But they were both so wounded and afraid, they didn't know how to reach out to each other. He loved her the only way he knew how, Ally understood that now. He protected her and kept her safe. And he never left her.

She laid the sprig of flowers on his grave and stood up. Maybe she should arrange a plaque for her mother. Nan would have liked that.

Watsons Bay

"What kind of a bloody fool are you?"

Ally looked at Meg, startled. She'd just finished recounting the last few days to her, up to where she said goodbye to Matt this morning.

"I swear I just don't get you, Ally!" Meg stood up, strutting around in a circle before crossing to the fridge and yanking the door open. "I need a drink and I don't even drink anymore! See what you're driving me to!"

She watched Meg push the corkscrew into the bottle like she was trying to punish it. "You're my best friend, and I love you," she said, with each twist. "But you're an idiot."

"That's a bit harsh," said Ally quietly.

"Well, somebody's got to tell you!" She pulled violently on the cork till it popped out. She grabbed two wine glasses by their stems and sat back at the table.

"Here," she said, holding the glasses out to Ally, who took them both and set them down. Meg splashed wine into each glass, then picked up one in a toast.

"To blind, ignorant stupidity."

"You expect me to drink to that?"

"Why not? It comes easily enough to you."

Ally didn't say anything. She knew Meg didn't mean to hurt her, but it hurt all the same.

Meg sighed. "I'm sorry, Al. I just can't watch you do this anymore! I can't stand it!"

She frowned. "What?"

"Why is it so hard for you to let someone love you?"

Ally breathed out heavily. What had Matt said? She was too busy licking her wounds? She picked up her glass and took a mouthful of wine. "I think that when I lost Nan, and then my mother left me again, I must have decided not to get close to anyone. The pain when they're gone, it's just too hard . . ." Her voice trailed off.

Meg looked at her. "All this time, all your excuses, you were scared of what you were feeling for Matt."

Ally felt an ache in the back of her throat. Tears filled her eyes.

"Oh no, don't, you'll make me start," said Meg, moving closer to her and putting an arm around her shoulder. "You can't live like this, Ally, running away from your feelings just in case you get hurt."

"Why not?" Ally wiped the tears away from her cheeks. "Feeling nothing for years was a lot easier than this," she sniffed.

"That's because you've always associated love with pain. It doesn't have to be that way," Meg paused. "What's in your heart, Ally?"

She shrugged. "A great big hole, most of the time."

"Is that how it feels now?"

"I don't know."

Meg was thinking. "Do me a favor. Close your eyes."

"Don't be weird, Meg."

"Just humor me, okay?"

Ally frowned at her, but she closed her eyes.

"Now, picture Matt, the last time you saw him."

Ally saw him in the rear-vision mirror, watching her drive away. She felt like crying.

"Ally?"

She changed the image. She saw him working at Birchgrove, his shirt off, wiping his brow. She saw him leaning over her frowning, when she was sick. She saw him holding her in his arms on the dance floor.

"What are you feeling?"

"Sick in the stomach," she said, opening her eyes.

A smile formed slowly on Meg's lips. "Oh Al, you're in love!"

"This couldn't be love, it's awful."

"I know, isn't it great!" she enthused.

Ally looked at her dubiously.

"It settles down eventually," Meg assured her, before smiling wistfully. "And then you miss it when it's gone. Look what happened to me and Chris. Or me, at least."

Ally watched her twiddling with the stem of her glass. She hadn't touched her wine.

"What are you going to do, Meg?"

She looked at Ally. "Wait."

"For how long?"

"For as long as it takes." Meg stared at nothing across the room. "You know, after he left, on one of the nights I couldn't sleep, I went into the bathroom and looked at the tiles. You know what they are? Plain white standard tiles. I remember I chose them because they were safe. They would never date, they looked good with anything, and I'd never get sick of them."

"But you said you were sick of Chris."

"No, I was sick of myself, and I blamed it on Chris," she said sadly. "I love those tiles. They're so perfect and simple and true. I want him back, Ally, he's a good man, and he has a good heart. I don't want to be with anyone else."

Ally folded her arms. "Why are you telling me this?"

Meg looked at her.

"You have to tell Chris."

Eight p.m.

Ally had not let it alone for the past hour. She could mind Harrison. There was nothing to stop Meg from going to see Chris tonight, she insisted.

But there was. What if this was too much for him to forgive? What if there was no hope? Living in limbo was easier than facing that.

Ally had finally picked up the phone and dialed Chris's mobile, thrusting it into Meg's hands when it started to ring. He agreed to see her. And now here she was, standing outside the door to his apartment. She couldn't remember ever feeling so nervous. Meg took a very deep breath and knocked.

The door opened and Chris stood, wearing that faint sad smile she was so used to seeing on his face lately.

"Hi Meg. Come in."

He stepped back, and Meg walked passed him inside. He'd rented a small serviced apartment on the edge of the CBD. It was little more than a bedroom and sitting room, with a bank of cupboards across one wall comprising the kitchen. A huge picture window faced away from the city, looking out to the east.

"Can I get you something to drink, a coffee?"

Meg hesitated. It would fill in time, occupy them for a moment. But it was only delaying the inevitable.

"No thanks."

They stood for a moment in silence. Eventually Chris cleared his throat. "Please, sit down, Meg."

"Okay." She perched uneasily on the edge of the sofa. Chris sat in the armchair opposite. He leaned forward, resting his elbows on his knees and clasping his hands together.

"What did you want to see me about?" he said quietly.

Meg swallowed. Why was she so nervous? This was the man who had always loved her unconditionally. She had to remember that.

"I want to talk about this whole awful mess," she began.

He didn't say anything. Meg watched him staring at the carpet.

"It feels like you don't want to," she said after a while.

Chris sighed heavily. "It's just hard, Meg. I never expected this. I mean, I knew there was something up . . . but I never expected this."

She could see the pain in his eyes.

"Neither did I."

"But you were the one—"

"That went off and had an affair," she finished. It had to be said, they had to stop skirting around it.

"Why, Meg?"

She paused, thinking. It was important to get the words right. "I was restless, and bored—"

"You were bored with me?"

"No!" she insisted. "It wasn't you. I didn't know what it was, but I felt like I was missing out on something. He came along, offering me a bit of excitement, pushing me out of my safety zone. But it was a shallow, empty kind of excitement."

Chris got up and walked over to the window. He stood looking out, his back to her. "Ever since we met all I've done is try and make you happy. I've been whatever you wanted me to be. You used me to wipe your feet, then you decided you didn't want a doormat."

"Is that what you think?" Meg said, standing up. "That's not how I see you at all."

He swung around to glare at her. Chris hardly ever got angry, but there was anger brewing in his eyes now. "Do you think I haven't felt bored sometimes? And suffocated? By your relentless need to control every little detail of our lives."

She was shaking. She couldn't believe what she was hearing. "Why didn't you say something?"

"Christ Meg, when's the last time you asked?"

Meg was shattered. Had she been so self-absorbed that she hadn't even noticed Chris was miserable?

"I didn't realize you were so unhappy."

He sighed heavily. "I wasn't unhappy, Meg. That's just the thing."

"I don't understand."

"I loved you, Meg." She hated that he was using the past tense. "So I stayed in a job I was sick to death of, because you wanted a house in the eastern suburbs and that's the only way we could afford it. And I let you make all the decisions, because it was important to you. I held my tongue, because it didn't matter to me as long as you were happy."

Meg just stared at him.

"So explain it to me, please Meg, explain to me when having things exactly the way you wanted them stopped being good enough?"

The bitterness in his voice rang in the air between them.

"I understand why you're so angry—"

"Well, what do you expect? You run off to 'find yourself,' bugger the consequences. And then come back and say you want everything the same?"

"I don't want everything the same," she said plainly.

Chris watched her, frowning.

"That's what I was trying to say the other day. We can't turn back the clock, pretend this never happened."

"No kidding?"

She took a deep breath. "And I'm glad it happened."

"What?" he stared incredulously.

"I don't mean I'm glad I hurt you. I never wanted to hurt you, Chris, you have to believe me," she insisted. "But it made me realize what's important to me, what I want."

"Well, what's new, Meg? It's always been about what you want."

She didn't know if he was deliberately trying to hurt her, but his words stung.

"It wasn't about getting my own way," Meg implored. "It was about stopping everything from falling apart!" She took a breath. "Do you know how scary it is for a ten year old to realize she's the most responsible person in the household? That if she doesn't remember everything, there'll be no dinner on the table, no electricity, that maybe someone might even decide you're better off somewhere else, or they'll take away the little brothers who were the only thing that kept you going?" Her voice broke. Meg paused, catching her breath.

"I never knew any other way to be, Chris. And then one day I just got tired. I couldn't do it anymore. I wanted to be free for a while. That's all it was."

They stood in silence, the hum of the refrigerator filling the room.

"Is it over?" Chris said eventually.

"It was over before you even found out about it," Meg assured him. "I shouldn't have gone off with him that weekend. But I promise you, Chris, when . . ." Meg hesitated. She didn't want to give him a mental picture of her and Jamie together. "I couldn't go through with it," she sighed. "I didn't want to be with another man."

He sighed heavily, thrusting his hands into his pockets.

"I did the wrong thing, Chris. I'm starting to understand that people genuinely make mistakes. They make stupid decisions and bad choices. But they don't necessarily plan to hurt people. I didn't think anyone would get hurt."

"Well, that was a pretty major error of judgment."

"I know that now. I made a terrible mistake." She paused. "But I'm not a bad person, Chris. I just made a mistake."

"I know you're not a bad person, Meg."

"Then why can't you forgive me?" she said, biting her lip, holding back the tears.

He sighed. "I can forgive you. It's trusting you again that's going to be hard."

A huge sob finally escaped from her throat. Meg covered her face with her hands as tears poured from her eyes. Then she felt Chris's arms around her, pulling her close.

"I said it would be hard, not impossible."

She looked up at him, her face crumpled from crying. "I wish you would believe how sorry I am that I've ruined everything."

He stroked her hair away from her face. "Well, if everything is ruined, we'll just have to start all over again."

Wednesday

Ally blinked at the numbers on the bedside clock. 7:43. Surely Harrison must be awake by now? As she came out of her room she could hear his giggles, but walking up the hall she realized they were coming from Meg's room.

"What are you doing here?" said Ally from the doorway, watching Meg playing with Harrison on the bed.

"I live here, remember?"

Ally shuffled over and climbed onto the bed next to her. She patted Meg's arm. "Didn't it work out last night?"

Meg looked up at her. "Why do you say that?"

"Well, you're here and Chris isn't."

"We have to take it slowly, Ally," said Meg. "At least I know that he still loves me. And the rest of it, we'll work out as we go along."

Ally looked at her. "You're okay?"

Meg nodded, her eyes shining. "I'm kind of, excited. We're starting over. And we're going to be completely honest with each other now, about what we want, what makes us happy. Things are going to be better, Ally."

"I'm glad." She leaned back against the bedhead, yawning. "Don't you have to go to work today?" she said eventually.

Meg shook her head. "Didn't I tell you? I don't have a job anymore."

"What?" That woke her up.

"I quit," Meg said simply.

"Why?"

"Because I'd had enough." Every time she tried to go back, she found an excuse to put it off for another day. Finally last week she dressed in her best power suit, dropped Harrison at his grandmother's, and drove determinedly into work. She went straight to Simon's office, handed him her resignation, and then took him to lunch for the rest of the day.

"But you've got a mortgage, and a child."

"Ally, I'd appreciate a bit of support," she frowned. "I feel like I'm leaping off into the great unknown without a safety net."

Which was not entirely true. Simon assured her there would always be contract work with them. Plenty of it. But she warned him not to ring her for at least a month.

"Sorry, it's just so unlike you."

"Well, it's time for a new me."

"You're not getting another haircut are you?" Ally eyed her suspiciously.

Meg laughed. "Well, thanks a lot. I take it the last one was not to your liking?"

Ally smiled at her. "What will you do?"

"I don't know. I've been toying with some ideas," she said vaguely.

"Such as?"

Meg shrugged her shoulders. "You'll probably think I'm being silly, or romantic."

"No I won't!" Ally insisted, intrigued. "As long as you're not running off with anyone called Junior?"

"Ally!" Meg frowned.

"Well, come on, out with it."

"I've had this secret little dream about owning my own gallery," she started.

"Really?"

Meg nodded, her eyes lighting up. "I know it can be a hard slog running your own business, and we'd have to move out of the city because it would be too expensive otherwise, and it probably wouldn't make much money." She took a breath. "But I've always loved art, that's why I went to college. And then the pragmatist in me took over and I went commercial. I never followed my heart, I've always taken the sensible route."

Ally smiled at her. "What does Chris think about all this?"

"I never knew, Ally—he's been sick of his job for years. But you know Chris, he'd never complain."

"And he likes the idea of moving out of Sydney, running a gallery?"

"Well, he's open to it. But he wants to take a break first."

"A holiday?"

"At least. Maybe an extended holiday. We talked about traveling across Europe, just for a few months."

"So you two really are okay?"

Meg smiled. "We will be." Harrison climbed on top of her, straddling her stomach. "I won't pretend he's not still a little shell-shocked. It's going to take time. But we'll get there."

Ally was quiet, reflecting. Chris and Meg were going to pull through after all. They'd survived. She wondered how much you had to love someone to get past so much pain.

"So what about you, Ally, what are your plans?" asked Meg.

"I've got a meeting . . ."

Meg groaned. "Aunty Ally's a silly-billy," she chanted to Harrison.

"Silly-billy!" he repeated.

"I have to go, Meg. I'm expected."

"That's not much of a reason."

"Come on! It's an incredible opportunity."

Meg frowned at her.

"It's the one thing I know I can do, and do well. I don't know how to be in a relationship. I'd stuff it up most likely."

"That's not true, Ally." Meg's voice softened. "Matt would be a lucky man to have you."

Ally sighed. "You know, he's been through a lot of pain too. It wouldn't be fair on him, if I wasn't sure."

"Still worrying about everyone but yourself? You deserve this, Ally. You deserve to be happy, to be loved. Don't you believe that yet?"

She shrugged. "Maybe I'm just not ready. If I come back to Sydney for a while, I could get a little perspective. I need to make a decision about what I'm doing with the rest of my life, not just fall into the next thing that comes along."

"You think Matt is just the next thing that came along?"

Ally shrugged. "There's only one way to find out for sure."

Ally parked her car in a station at the Rocks and strolled the short distance down Hickson Road. She walked through glass doors into the restaurant but the place appeared to be deserted up on this level. She decided to check down by the water. Ally took the stairs around the side of the building to the front, where enormous canvas sails shaded the outdoor tables. She stood near the reception desk.

"Ally!" Bryce must have been looking out for her. He was already weaving his way through the tables toward her.

"Hello Bryce."

"Well, look at you!" he said, clasping her hands and kissing both cheeks. He stood back again, holding her arms out. "Look at you!"

"You already said that!" she quipped.

"You look like a million dollars. Even better than the photo in the magazine!"

Ally knew the tone in Bryce's voice, the look in his eye. He was working her. This would be entertaining.

"And you look . . ." she hesitated. "As trim and terrific as you always do."

"Is that a veiled way of saying I haven't changed?" He lifted an eyebrow. "Because I work very hard at that. Consistency is important in my profession, Ally. Whereas, in yours, it's change, reinventing yourself. And you've done that, might I say, admirably."

She smiled. Enough with the sucking up.

"Come and meet Paul."

He led her back through the tables to where a low sandstone wall divided the diners from the passersby. The location was superb. The Harbor Bridge Pylons towered above them to their left, the bridge itself spanning north in its impressive arch. A replica eighteenth century sailing ship sat anchored in the cove just in front of them, and beyond to the east the sun illuminated the sails of the Opera House. Ally was determined to enjoy it all today.

"Ms. Tasker." Paul Silvestri stood up from the table and offered his hand to Ally. He was probably in his fifties, short and rotund, though impeccably groomed, in an immaculate suit and tie.

"Please, call me Ally," she returned, shaking his hand.

"If you call me Paul."

"Ally," Bryce continued, "I'd also like you to meet Lynda Bowden."

Ally turned to the woman at the table. She had noticed her as they approached, presuming she was Silvestri's assistant.

"Lynda is a publicist," Bryce explained.

"Oh?" said Ally, taking the hand she offered. Lynda looked like she had just stepped out of a makeover session. Blond hair swept into a perfect French roll, flawless make-up, designer power suit that fitted her like a glove.

"I'm very excited to meet you."

Was she? Didn't this woman have a life?

"I think we're going to have a fabulous relationship."

Well, that was very forward on the first date, Ally thought, suppressing the urge to laugh. What on earth were they up to? A *publicist*? She was a painter and decorator, not a celebrity. Still, she was here now, she would enjoy the show.

"I ordered champagne," Paul said as they took their seats. "I thought it was appropriate, under the circumstances."

The waiter appeared at Ally's elbow, brandishing a bottle of Piper-Heidsieck.

"Just half a glass," she said to him. "I'm driving," she explained to the rest.

"Why don't we order now, so we can get straight on to business?"

"Excellent idea, Paul," Bryce enthused.

If he wasn't careful, his head was going to get stuck up someone's bum one day.

Ally looked over the menu. There was really only one choice. She was going to milk this for all it was worth.

"Lobster sounds good," she announced.

"The live lobster, madam?"

"Why not!"

"Sashimi, or grilled with Cognac butter?"

Ally wasn't about to have live raw lobster. She had visions of chasing it across the table with her fork.

"Grilled, thank you."

"Would madam like to make a selection from the tank?"

Ally handed him the menu, winking up at him. "It's okay, I trust you."

The men ordered grilled fish, Paul on doctor's advice and Bryce because Paul did. Lynda ordered a garden salad, no dressing. Typical, thought Ally. She weighed as much as a photograph of herself, and this would probably be her biggest meal of the day.

Paul held his glass up to Ally. "To a successful venture."

"Perhaps," she replied, sipping her champagne.

"Okay, you're going to make us work for this."

Ally just smiled. They were certainly making a fuss about very little.

"Bryce showed me the magazine spread, and I have to say, I was impressed."

"Thank you."

"Of course, there were no 'before' photos," Bryce interjected. "I've seen the kind of transformation Ally achieves. I bet the place was a dump before you took over?"

"It was pretty bad," she agreed.

"I realize you're fairly new to all this," said Paul. "But I think you've got the right stuff, from what Bryce tells me, and he's never let me down yet."

Bryce was positively beaming, and speechless, momentarily.

"Has he explained the proposal to you?"

"A little."

Paul opened a briefcase and took out a folder, handing it across the table to Ally. She started to flick through. This must have been put together for investors originally. It covered the various properties, projected earnings and so on.

"A lot of that won't be of any interest to you, but you can see the style of the buildings. We want to preserve their inherent character, but bring them up to date, to appeal to the kinds of buyers we're hoping to attract."

"The twenty-five to thirty-nine years demographic is the fastest growing in the area," Bryce added.

"We like what you did in the restaurant. It's quite obviously an old building, and you worked with that, not against it."

Ally was listening thoughtfully, scanning the photographs of the apartment blocks. They were all Art Deco style, two or three stories high, typically symmetrical, with recessed verandahs. Some had curved walls, round windows, some were rendered, while others featured highly detailed brickwork.

"What are you planning to do with the exteriors?"

"If you turn toward the back, you'll find the architect's concept," said Paul. "Nothing has been finalized yet, I'm sure they'll want to meet with you to tie everything together."

Meet with her? Ally looked at the logo above the computer-generated perspective drawings. *Coulter + Pollard*. Even she had heard of them, they were a very high-profile architectural firm.

"Of course, they're working with a color consultant as well. I daresay you'll all have a lot to do with each other."

Two waiters arrived at the table with their meals. Ally's was enormous compared to everybody else's. Oh well, tough. She didn't care if she didn't finish it all, she wasn't paying for it.

She picked up her fork and tasted a chunk of lobster. Sweet and succulent. So they had architects and color consultants. She imagined they would have an interior designer, they couldn't be suggesting Ally fill that role. She started to wonder what she was doing here.

"Have you employed an interior designer?" she asked.

"In the process," said Lynda crisply, pushing lettuce leaves around on her plate. "We have our eye on a couple, but we're taking our time. It's very important that we get the right people."

"So why do you need me?"

"Modesty has no place in business, Ally!" Bryce censured, glancing nervously toward Paul.

"I'm not being modest. I just don't understand why you need me."

"Lynda, why don't you explain it to Ally?"

Lynda put down her fork. She must be stuffed.

"Ally, we'll be promoting you as part of the design team. We want our buyers and investors to feel they have got the very best for their money."

"But what will I actually do?"

"Your role will be to consult with the painters, oversee their work, liaise between them and the rest of the design team."

"Will there be any painting involved?"

"Pardon?"

"Will I be painting at all? That is what I do, after all."

"If we could clone you, Ally, that would be the way to go," Lynda smiled, glancing at the others. "Why, we'd have you painting every single room in every apartment. Imagine, a team of little Allys running around, painting furiously."

They all laughed. Ally thought they were stupid. She bit into another chunk of lobster.

"Of course it's not possible, so what we want is to have your signature, so to speak."

"Isn't that a relief?" Bryce quipped. "No more paint under your fingernails, Ally!"

"But I'm very hands-on, I do everything," Ally explained.

"We realize you're very serious about your work, that's why we chose you."

"I just don't get it."

Lynda looked as though she just might be losing her patience with Ally, but she didn't let the veneer slip.

"Ally," she said condescendingly, "in this business, perceptions are everything. When potential buyers are given the sales brochure, they'll see that we used the top architects, designers and specialists, like yourself. It won't matter that you didn't actually paint the walls in their apartment, because they'll tell their friends that you did."

It did matter to Ally that she wouldn't actually be painting the walls. "Why would their friends care? I'm not anybody."

"Not yet. But you could be," said Paul. "To really grab attention, and consequently sales, you have to use big names. Our architects are big name, established, well known, no risk. But they're expensive. Our budget won't allow us to use the top people across the board."

"The alternative is to promote the next 'big thing,' " Lynda took over. "You've been featured in a very reputable magazine. That's put you on the map. It gives us something to build on."

"How?"

"Well, I can get you into every house magazine on the market with that project alone, but are you working on anything else?"

Ally shrugged. "I have one job at the moment."

"Anything interesting, is there an angle we can hook into?"

"Well, the client is Frances Callen . . ."

"What did you say?" Lynda seemed to have lost her composure momentarily.

"I'm doing Frances Callen's country house."

"Frances Callen from the ABC?"

Ally nodded.

"Oh, this is fabulous. Of course, someone from commercial television would be preferable," she remarked to Paul. "But this is an excellent start."

She pulled out a dictaphone and turned slightly away from the table. "Note to self: ASAP, phone Frances Callen's people, arrange a meeting."

Frances had *people*?

"Good one, Ally!" Bryce's grin was almost manic.

"This is all coming together very nicely," said Paul, pushing his plate away. "I have a good feeling about this."

Ally stared out at the water. Lynda said it was all about perceptions? No it wasn't, she wanted to tell them. It was about making something beautiful. With her own hands. What did she care if she got paint under her fingernails if she was doing what she loved?

The waiter came to refill their glasses, but Ally covered hers with her hand. "None for me, thanks."

These people knew nothing about her, they were basing everything on a few photos and an inaccurate story in a glossy magazine. This was so typical of Bryce. Ally didn't want to live her life on the surface, the cardboard cutout she used to be when she was with him. She deserved more than that.

Matt said she had to find out what would make her whole. And he said he loved her. He said he loved her despite the fact that she drove him crazy. Ally smiled faintly, remembering. Matt had seen under the surface. He'd seen her dressed up, but dressed down more often than not, covered in dust, without make-up, in clothes that were ready for the ragbag. He'd taken care of her when she was sick, drunk, hungover. He'd felt her anger, shared her happiness, and dried her tears. And he said he loved her. How could she ask for more than that?

Matt loved her. Ally could feel it sitting here, a hundred miles away from him.

So what was she doing sitting here, a hundred miles away from him?

"Well," said Ally, laying her napkin down on the table. "This has been very interesting, and thanks for lunch, but I'm afraid I'm going to have to turn you down."

Paul's grin evaporated from his face. "What?"

"I didn't realize the scale of this project. I just can't do it."

"Ally." Bryce grabbed her elbow, a little too firmly for her liking. "Success comes in cans, not can'ts!"

Somehow Ally stopped herself from laughing in his face. His slogans were just tiresome. She shrugged off his grip and stood up.

"I have a partner to consider."

Bryce stood up. "You said he wasn't your partner."

Ally frowned. "Oh, you mean Rob, in the magazine? No, not him, someone else." She checked her watch. "Oh, and look at the time. I've got to run. It's quite a drive home from here."

"Home?" Bryce narrowed his eyes. "Where's home?"

Ally looked at him. He only seemed to understand clichés. "I think it's where the heart is, isn't that what they say?"

She turned on her heel and almost skipped out of the place. She could feel their eyes on her back, watching her leave. But she didn't care. Ally had somewhere else she had to be.

"You did what?"

Ally thought she'd better phone Meg so that she wouldn't be expecting her. She had made it through the city quite easily, at this time of the day, and she was already on the freeway heading south.

"You should have seen their faces!" Ally laughed. "Sitting there with their mouths gaping open, like stunned mullets."

"Well, I didn't think you had it in you!"

"Me either," said Ally. "Anyway, I just wanted to let you know I'm on my way home."

"Okay, I'll see you soon. We'll celebrate."

"No, I'm going home," Ally took a breath. "To Matt."

"Woohoo!" Meg shrieked.

"I love him, Meg. I'm so sure of it now."

"God, I'm going to cry! What convinced you?"

Ally thought for a moment. "I realized I don't mind getting paint under my fingernails."

"What?"

They were interrupted by call waiting beeps coming onto the line.

"Is that you?" said Ally.

"I don't care," said Meg breezily. "I'm not interested in what's out there anymore. Besides, I think it might be your call waiting. Can you handle it?"

Ally grinned. "I'm not quite as insecure as I used to be."

"Thank God for that! Call me later. No, better make that tomorrow, I think I'll invite Chris over for beano night tonight."

"Isn't that usually Friday night?"

"Not anymore." She rang off.

Ally smiled, waiting for the other call to connect.

"Ally?"

She groaned inwardly. "Yes, Bryce."

"What on earth was all that about?"

"What do you mean? You were there, I thought I made myself perfectly clear."

"Yes, it was perfectly clear that you were throwing away the biggest opportunity of your life."

"That depends on your perspective, Bryce."

"You made me look like a fool. I promised Paul I'd deliver you."

"Well, you shouldn't have done that, I'm not a package."

"Don't be smart, Ally. It's quite unbecoming. As was your little performance at the restaurant today."

She was not in the mood for a lecture.

"Bryce, have you got a point? Because I wish you'd get to it sometime soon."

"Ally, when you think about what you've given up here, I'm sure you'll reconsider. But you only have a narrow window of opportunity. I was able to calm Paul down, and he might consider seeing you again. If you were to contact him . . ."

But Ally had lost interest. She glanced at the dashboard clock, calculating the time she would be back. Would Matt still be at the Callens? Was there time to stop in at home and change first? He liked her in overalls.

"Are you listening to me, Ally?"

She sighed, "Yes, Bryce."

"Okay, let me go through this one more time."

I don't think so. Ally took the phone from her ear and held it in front of her. She glanced out the window. She was on the open freeway now and the atmosphere was quiet, almost surreal. Midafternoon on a weekday and she couldn't see another car in her field of vision. She looked back at the phone. Her lips curved into a satisfied smile.

She wound down the window. She was approaching a bridge that spanned a deep ravine, and she slowed the car down to a crawl. Ally considered the phone for another moment. She could still hear Bryce's voice rabbiting on as she stuck her arm out the window and hurled the phone across the railing, watching as it sailed down and disappeared out of view.

Ally pulled into the driveway of the Callens' house, behind Matt's truck. She was counting on him still being here, but now she felt sick in the stomach again. She'd just have to take Meg's word for it that this was part of being in love. She only hoped it would settle down soon.

She walked past the truck and around to the back of the house. Matt was standing in the middle of the yard, supporting the frame of the window, sliding the sash up and down. He hadn't noticed her yet.

Ally took a deep breath and walked toward him. He looked up, and the surprise registered on his face, faintly, just for a moment.

"Hi," she said from the other side of the window.

"Hi," Matt returned quietly.

"Do you want me to hold this for you?" she offered, lifting her arms to support the window.

"Um, sure," he said vaguely. "Just lean into it—"

"—it's not heavy that way," she finished. "I remember."

He looked at her for a moment, and then crouched down and started adjusting the counterweights.

"How was your meeting?"

"It was okay. We had lunch at the Harborside, you know, down near the bridge? I had lobster."

"Oh?" he said, not looking up. "So when are you leaving?"

"Who said anything about leaving?"

Matt looked up, frowning. She held his gaze.

"Honestly, they were from another planet. They had some bizarre idea I could be a consultant leading a team of painters. They didn't want me to pick up a paintbrush, except for the publicity shots."

Matt didn't say anything.

"So I told them I had a partner to consider," she added, her heart in her mouth.

"A business partner?"

"I didn't specify."

Matt stood up slowly, staring at her through the pane of glass.

"Here hold this," Ally said, leaning the window toward him. He held the frame while she slid the top sash down. Before he knew what she was doing, she had looped her arms around his neck and pulled him closer, planting a long, hard kiss on his lips. He didn't resist.

"Ally, I'm going to drop this!" he said eventually.

"So, put it down."

She noticed the smile in his eyes as he stepped back from her, lowering the window frame until it lay flat on the ground. He straightened up, looking at her, resting his hands on his hips.

"You know, Ally Tasker, you're bloody hard work."

"I didn't think you'd be afraid of a bit of hard work, Matt Serrano?"

He grinned, shaking his head. They stood considering each other, the window on the ground between them. Ally couldn't take it anymore.

"Why are you standing all the way over there?"

He folded his arms. "Because I reckon if I come after you, you might run away again."

Ally smiled sheepishly. "I'm not going to run away anymore."

"How do I know that?"

"Because I love you."

He breathed out heavily. "How do you know?"

"Fair question," said Ally, taking a step to one side of the window frame. "Well, to begin with, you make me sick in the stomach."

"What?"

"According to Meg, that's a sign."

"Oh," he nodded. "Anything else?"

"Well, I love you despite the fact you're always teasing me. And I think that maybe you're the one who has to be right all the time."

"You think?"

"And you're argumentative."

"I am not!"

"Ah! See what I mean?"

He grinned. Ally took a couple of steps slowly toward him.

"What else?" she continued. "Oh, you look pretty good without a shirt on."

"Ally!"

She was standing in front of him now. She looked up directly into his eyes.

"And all my life I've been too afraid to let anyone love me. To believe that anyone did. Until now." She paused. "I used to feel something was missing, but I don't feel that anymore, not when I'm with you, only when I'm away from you. That's how I know I love you, Matt Serrano."

"Well, it's about time, Ally Tasker."

As his arms closed around her, she realized for the first time that she didn't feel afraid.

EPILOGUE

SERRANO
(Tasker) To Ally and Matt,
on their second anniversary,
a beautiful baby boy, James.
A brother for Rebecca.
Everybody happy.

GALLERY TO RE-OPEN UNDER
NEW MANAGEMENT

Readers may have noticed the activity going on lately at the old premises of the Highland Gallery. Former Sydneysiders Chris and Meg Lynch have taken over the lease of the heritage building, commissioning local team Ally and Matt Serrano for the refurbishment.

The grand opening of "Lynchpin" is planned to coincide with Bowral's famous Tulip Festival. Meg Lynch explained that the new business is the culmination of years of dreaming and planning. Previously in the finance and advertising sectors, the couple were looking for a change of pace.

"We've traveled extensively over the last couple of years, sourcing artworks from all over Europe and Asia. But our son starts school next year, so we wanted to settle somewhere. We have friends in the area, it seemed the natural place."

The gallery will showcase an impressive collection of objets d'art gathered during their travels, as well as the work of local artists. Incorporating a café, the couple hope Lynchpin will become a relaxed meeting place for residents and visitors alike.